"I usually don't spend the night with a man I just met. You were the first and the last."

"I'm honored that you picked me. I enjoyed our time together."

Her warm eyes flashed that Lana had, too. She had a mouth made for loving. Plump, soft lips that were naturally pink. They parted a fraction, just as they had seconds before he'd kissed her the other night.

Sly definitely wanted to see more of her and explore that heat, unleash her fiery passion and enjoy a repeat of their memorable night together. He moved closer and tucked her hair behind her ears with hands that shook.

He wanted her that much. Too much.

The strength of his need scared him. If he was smart, he'd turn around and leave. But his legs refused to budge.

HOME ON THE RANCH:
MONTANA BEGINNINGS

ANN ROTH

Previously published as *A Rancher's Honor* and
A Rancher's Redemption

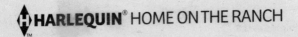

HARLEQUIN® HOME ON THE RANCH

ISBN-13: 978-1-335-00784-1

Home on the Ranch: Montana Beginnings

Copyright © 2020 by Harlequin Books S.A.

A Rancher's Honor
First published in 2014. This edition published in 2020.
Copyright © 2014 by Ann Schuessler

A Rancher's Redemption
First published in 2014. This edition published in 2020.
Copyright © 2014 by Ann Schuessler

Recycling programs for this product may not exist in your area.

Printed in U.S.A.

HARLEQUIN®
www.Harlequin.com

CONTENTS

Ann Roth lives in the greater Seattle area with her husband. After earning an MBA, she worked as a banker and corporate trainer. She gave up the corporate life to write, and if they awarded PhDs in writing happily-ever-after stories, she'd surely have one.

Ann loves to hear from readers. You can email her at ann@annroth.net.

Books by Ann Roth

Harlequin American Romance

Prosperity, Montana

A Rancher's Honor
A Rancher's Redemption

Saddlers Prairie

Rancher Daddy
Montana Doctor
Her Rancher Hero
The Rancher She Loved
A Rancher's Christmas

Visit the Author Profile page at Harlequin.com for more titles.

A RANCHER'S HONOR

To my wonderful readers. You're the best!

Chapter 1

Lana Carpenter woke up with the worst headache ever. With a groan, she cracked one eye open to glance at the clock on the bedside table. But there was no clock, and the dark wood table was nothing like her oak furniture.

She wasn't in her queen-size bed at her town house—she was in a king-size bed in a hotel room, and judging by the monogram on the sheets, it was the Prosperity Inn, one of Prosperity, Montana's, four-star hotels.

Both eyes were open now. After stealing a peek at the other side of the bed—it was empty, but a dented pillow lay close to hers—she sat up quickly, grimacing at the sudden thundering in her temples.

The clock on that side of the bed said it was just after ten. She never slept this late—even if it was Saturday!

She pulled the dented pillow to her face and the lingering scent of a man's spicy aftershave tickled her nostrils. One whiff and everything flooded back.

Kate picking her up and commiserating with her over the fact that Brent and Julia had had their baby. Driving to the Bitter & Sweet Bar and Grill for dinner and dancing to a live country-and-western band. Consuming too little dinner and too many cocktails in an effort to forget her ex's betrayal. The handsome cowboy at the table across the way, and the strong attraction that had flared between them from the first moment of eye contact.

On the way to the bar, Lana hadn't even thought about meeting a man. She was still recovering from the divorce and had only wanted to forget that Brent's new wife had given him the one thing Lana couldn't—a baby.

Then the sexy cowboy had asked her to dance, and they'd kept on dancing, with short stops for drinks and casual chitchat in between. After a while Kate had grown bored and left. Lana had stayed, with the intention of finding a cab later to take her home. But she'd soon forgotten all about the cab when dancing progressed to long, passionate kisses and the haste to rent a room within walking distance so that she and the cowboy could...

"Oh, dear God, I didn't!" she muttered, shattering the quiet.

Her clothes lay in a telltale trail that started just inside the door and ended near the bed.

She definitely had.

Which was so unlike her. Another groan escaped from her. Normally, she wasn't much of a drinker. Oh, sure, she enjoyed an occasional glass of wine with dinner, but that was pretty much it. She'd never picked up a stranger, either.

Sly, that was his name, had assured her that he was clean—Lana recalled that. She'd stated that she was clean and healthy, too. Shortly after Brent had left her for Julia some eighteen months ago, she'd had herself tested. She hadn't been with a man since.

Until last night.

She and Sly had more than made up for her year and a half of celibacy. Boy, had they.

Her cheeks warmed. Then she remembered that sometime during the night, as they lay tangled together after making love, he'd explained he'd have to leave for work early in the morning. Lana was glad he'd let her sleep instead of waking her to say goodbye, because facing him this morning would have been, at best, uncomfortable.

Mother Nature called. Clutching her head, Lana made her way to the bathroom. There on the counter she found a bottle of aspirin and an unopened half liter of water. Under the water, a note.

Last night was great. This should help with the hangover.

Bless the man for his thoughtfulness. After swallowing several pain tablets with a healthy quantity of water, she studied herself in the mirror. Despite her headache, she looked radiant, as if she was still basking in the afterglow of a night of unbridled passion. Sly was right—last night had been great.

A long shower helped revive her, and by the time she dried off, fixed her hair and dressed in last night's clothes—clean clothes would have been nice, but Lana didn't have any with her—she felt almost normal.

She was shrugging into her coat to leave when her cell phone chirped "It's Raining Men." Kate's favorite song. Lana picked up right away. "Hey there."

"You were supposed to call this morning with the scoop. Tell me that handsome cowboy you were dancing with gave you a ride home."

Lana glanced at the unmade bed, winced and plopped onto a chair. "Not exactly."

"You're saying you turned him down and took a cab instead? That's a crying shame, Lana, because for the first time in forever, you were actually having fun with a really hot guy."

Kate was right about the hot part. Tall, lean and muscled, with startling silvery-blue eyes and a killer smile, Sly was every woman's cowboy fantasy. Lana caught herself in a dreamy sigh and frowned. "He never offered me a ride."

"Well, shoot. And he seemed so into you. How much longer did you dance before you parted company?"

"Um…actually, we didn't part company. I'm at the Prosperity Inn." Which was only a few short blocks from the Bitter & Sweet.

"What are you doing at a hotel?" Kate asked, then answered her own question with a singsong "Oh." Her voice softened to an excited whisper. "You should have said something sooner. Call me later."

"It's okay—he's not here."

"You mean he's in the shower?"

"No, I mean he had to leave early this morning to go to work. I slept in."

"It's not like you to spend the night with a guy you just met."

"Tell me about it." As a rule, Lana waited for that level of intimacy until she was in a relationship. "I can't believe I did this."

"Hey, it happens. Did you at least enjoy yourself?"

Lana didn't have to think long about that. Now that her headache was all but gone, other things bubbled into her mind. Good memories that made her whole body hum. "It was pretty special."

"Ooh. Gonna share some details?"

"No!"

"At least give me his name? Maybe what he does for a living?"

"His name is Sly and I assume he's a rancher. He must be, right? Who else has to get up at the crack of dawn to go to work on a Saturday? I don't know his last name or anything else about him, except that he's never been married. I said I was divorced."

In the heat of the moment, she'd also mentioned that she couldn't have kids. "We agreed that this was a night to forget our troubles and keep things fun and light." They'd accomplished both goals, in spades. "I don't think we'll ever see each other again."

"That's so unlike you."

"So you said." As unforgettable as last night had been, Lana regretted what she'd done. She massaged the space between her eyes. "Remind me to never drink again."

"Don't be so hard on yourself. Look on the positive side—you're back in the saddle, and a darned handsome cowboy put you there." Kate hooted at her joke. "Besides, you needed to be wild for one night. Once you adopt a baby, you won't be able to overdo the alcohol or stay out all night on a whim."

"I never do either of those things."

"You did last night. Listen, I have to leave for my mani-pedi, but if you need a ride, I can come pick you up in an hour or so."

Lana supposed she could order breakfast downstairs and wait, but she wanted to change into fresh clothes. She also had a jillion things to do today—clean her house, grocery shop, do laundry, et cetera. "I'll take a cab, thanks. Send me a picture of your nails."

"Will do. Talk to you later."

Early April in western Montana usually brought mornings cold enough to see your own breath. Yet this morning, Sly Pettit was sweating like a son of a dog. He also felt like crap. At thirty-five he was no longer able to shake off a hangover with a couple of aspirin as easily as he'd done at thirty.

"Sly? I said, if you're feelin' poorly, Ollie, Bean and I can handle the rest of the branding."

Ace, Sly's longtime foreman, was staring at him oddly, and Bean, a grizzled cowhand, wore a frown. Ollie, a rangy twenty-year-old kid Sly had hired for the spring and summer, shot him a curious glance.

Sly realized he was grimacing and smoothed his expression. When he'd met his attorney at the Bitter & Sweet Bar and Grill for dinner last night, he'd planned on staying about an hour, then heading home. Instead, he'd arrived home just shy of dawn. "I'm okay," he said.

"Well, you look like you've been run over by a tractor and left for dead." Ace blew on his hands to warm them and then shook his head. "It's that trouble with Tim Carpenter, isn't it?"

Bean said nothing, but now he appeared intrigued. Ollie, too.

Sly and his lawyer, Dave Swain, had met to discuss whether Sly should sue Carpenter. The whole idea left a bad taste in Sly's mouth. Dave didn't enjoy it either, and thought Sly should try to work things out with his neighbor, who owned the Lazy C Ranch, which was adjacent to Pettit Ranch. But Carpenter's refusal to sit down and talk had left Sly without much choice.

"I'm not happy about it," Sly said. "But that's not why I look like hell. I'm hungover."

The crew members chuckled.

"Been there more than a few times myself," Ace said. "The way you're sweatin' out that alcohol, you're sure to feel better in no time."

Sly lifted the gate of the holding pen and Ace slapped the rump of one of the January calves they'd culled from the herd earlier.

As the calf loped from the pen and Sly herded her toward the calf table, he thought about the mess with his neighbor. Tim Carpenter had a chip on his shoulder a mile wide, mainly because Pettit Ranch was profitable. Not enough to replenish Sly's all-but-empty savings, but enough to pay the bills. It wasn't his fault the Lazy C continually struggled to stay solvent.

He and Carpenter had never been friends. Now they were enemies. All because a few months back, someone had poisoned Sly's cattle. Two of his heifers had miscarried and had lost any chance of future pregnancies, and three others had died. As a grown man, Sly rarely felt powerless, but he had then. He hated his inability to help his animals as they sickened, as he'd watched them die and feared that others could, too.

Autopsies and tests had proved that his animals had been poisoned with arsenic. Neither Sly nor his crew had any idea who'd do something so heinous. Then by chance, Ace had spotted a small pile of white powder just inside the northernmost pasture fence off the private service road that ran between Pettit Ranch and the Lazy C. He'd tested the powder and determined it to be arsenic. Both ranches shared the road, and no one else had access. Who else but Carpenter could have set the arsenic there?

Still, Sly had given his neighbor the benefit of the doubt. He'd driven to Carpenter's and attempted to question him. The first time Carpenter had ordered him off his land. On Sly's next try, he'd pulled out a rifle and aimed it at Sly's chest.

Which sure made it seem as if the man had something to hide. That was when Sly had quit trying to straighten things out himself and hired a lawyer. Not with the intention of suing, but to get Carpenter to cough up information that could shed light on what had happened. That plan had also failed, and now he really was on the verge of suing.

"Sly?" Ace was waiting for Sly to say something.

"I need to get to the bottom of this poisoning."

Ace rubbed his chin with his thumb and forefinger. "You're suing, then?"

Ollie and Bean looked down, as if the subject made them uncomfortable.

Join the crowd, Sly thought. "You all know how much those vet bills, tests and autopsies cost, and the cows we lost…" Sly shook his head. He wanted to be reimbursed for his losses.

The money he'd spent on all those things had been earmarked for a badly needed new drainage system. The existing one, installed some thirty years ago, functioned on a wing and a prayer. The next big rain could result in heavy flooding and wreak havoc on valuable low-lying pastureland. Sly and his men could do some of the grunt work, but they needed to bring in an expert. He'd considered taking out a loan to cover the costs, but as it was, the monthly payment on his mortgage was a strain. Any more debt and he'd be in over his head. He wasn't about to jeopardize everything he'd worked for by borrowing more.

"The way things stand," he said, "I don't see any other options."

"He's a tough nut to crack, all right." Ace pulled off his baseball cap and scratched one of his sideburns. "The Bitter & Sweet always brings in a live band on Friday and Saturday nights. I hope you spent some of the evening dancing off your troubles with a pretty girl."

Lana was no girl. She was all woman. "I danced a time or two," Sly admitted.

His foreman, who'd been married umpteen years, nodded approvingly. "Now and then a man's got to cut loose and have some fun."

Ollie, who knew his way around branding and, according to him, around women, too, grinned. "Me and my girlfriend, Tiff? We sure put the *f-u-n* in our Friday night." He made a lewd gesture with his hands. "But we're doin' that almost every night."

Fun didn't come close to describing Sly's night with Lana, but he wasn't about to talk about that. "Let's get this job done so Ace can take the rest of the weekend off," he said. When time and weather allowed, Sly and his foreman alternated weekends off. This was Ace's weekend, and he and his wife had planned a trip to Billings to visit their college-age son at Montana State.

"Ready with that iron?" Sly asked Ollie.

"Ready, boss."

The four of them spent the next few hours herding the calves one by one to the calf table so that the cows could be marked with the Pettit Ranch brand and then vaccinated. It wasn't exactly rocket science, allowing Sly's mind to replay the previous evening.

Over dinner, Dave had reluctantly agreed to prepare and file the lawsuit, but he was tying up loose ends for several other clients and needed ten days to put the suit together and file the papers. Shortly after the lawyer had finished his coffee and dessert, he'd left to get home to his wife and kids.

Sly didn't have a wife or kids, or anyone to hurry home to. His life was uncomplicated, which was exactly how he liked it. He spent his days working hard to keep his ranch profitable and successful, and enjoyed spending his evenings either going out or relaxing alone in his quiet house. But the whole lawsuit business was unsettling, and last night he'd wanted to take his mind off his troubles. So he'd hung around the Bitter & Sweet, waiting for the band to play.

As soon as the cute blonde and her friend had sat down at a table across the way, Sly had forgotten all about his problems. He'd always enjoyed an attractive woman, and when the blonde had looked at him and smiled, something had sizzled between them. He had to meet her.

From the start, they'd hit it off. Lana was fun and easy to talk to, and her eyes had telegraphed that she was attracted to him. Best of all, she'd only wanted a good time. They'd agreed not to share their last names and had steered away from deep conversation.

A dozen dances and several drinks later, Sly had kissed her. Her warmth and enthusiasm had just about blown his socks off. Neither of them had wanted to stop, and before Sly knew it, he was walking her to the Prosperity Inn and paying for a hotel room.

Under regular circumstances he wouldn't have acted so rashly. He rarely picked up a woman he'd never met before and taken her to bed. But his decision had turned out to be a damn fine one.

The sex had been phenomenal.

His only regret was that he hadn't gotten her number. He'd thought about waking her and asking her for it before he left at the crack of dawn. But neither of them had gotten much rest, and she'd been sleeping so peacefully that he hadn't had the heart to disturb her.

Just then, Sly's daydream was interrupted when on the way to the calf table, one of the calves turned renegade and tried to run off. "Come back here, you," Sly called as he and Ace cut her off.

When they caught her and steered her back, Ace took up the conversation where they'd left off. "The gal you danced with—you gonna see her again?"

"Probably not."

The more important reason Sly hadn't asked for her number was that getting involved with her would be a bad idea. His last girlfriend had accused him of avoiding intimacy, and then dumped him. Not because she'd taken up with some other guy, but because she was fed up with his so-called emotional distance.

She wasn't the first woman to accuse him of that, but Sly had always been confused as to what "emotional distance" meant. In bed, he demonstrated plenty of emotion.

Maybe it had something do with the fact that he rarely brought the women he dated to his place. All his former girlfriends had complained about that, but hell, his home was his sanctuary and his bedroom was his private space, off-limits to all but his housekeeper, who cleaned it.

After his last breakup and a few months of self-imposed celibacy, Sly had finally figured out what women meant by emotional distance. He admitted to himself that outside the physical stuff, he'd never had a truly intimate relationship with a woman. Sure, he enjoyed giving and receiving pleasure, but he wasn't about to put his heart on the line. With good reason.

People he cared deeply about tended not to stick around. First his parents, then his brother, then the girl he'd wanted to marry.

Why take the risk of getting too close? Sly wasn't about to set himself up for that kind of heartache again.

"Now that you sweated that hangover out of your system, you're lookin' a sight better," Ace commented some hours later, when they'd finished the branding.

"I suppose I'll live," Sly replied. "Go on now and have a nice weekend—all three of you."

He headed for the house. Mrs. Rutland, his part-time housekeeper—with just him to feed and clean up after, he didn't need her full-time—left at noon on Thursdays and Fridays, but cooked enough meals to last until

Monday. After showering and changing, Sly filled his belly and then headed outside again to tackle the late-afternoon chores. He fed and watered the horses, giving Bee, his bay, her usual carrot. He checked on the stock and noted additional chores that needed doing the following day.

Then he flopped on the sofa with the remote. Nothing on the tube interested him, and his mind kept wandering to last night. As worn-out as he was, he felt oddly restless—too restless to hang around at home. He considered grabbing a beer someplace, but after last night he needed a rest from alcohol.

He called his sister to ask if she wanted to catch a movie. Dani didn't answer, which wasn't surprising on a Saturday night. She was probably out with her boyfriend of the month or her friends.

Sly hung up without leaving a message. He almost wished he had Lana's number...until he reminded himself that it was better he didn't.

Moments later he grabbed his keys from the hook by the door and left through the mudroom. He wasn't sure where he was headed, but anyplace was better than sitting around here, thinking about a woman he didn't plan on ever seeing again.

It was late Sunday when Lana parked in front of the house where she'd grown up. It was a beautiful afternoon; the sun was slowly sinking toward the horizon, casting the distant, snow-covered Cascade Mountains in rosy hues. Spring was her favorite time of year, when the air smelled fresh and sweet, and life seemed to bud and surge everywhere.

Usually she looked forward to the noisy Sunday night

dinners with her parents and her younger sister and family. But tonight, Lana was dreading it.

All because last Sunday, she'd finally told her parents about her decision to adopt a baby. She'd waited until two months after the social worker had cleared her as a prospective parent, and six weeks after she'd begun to actively search for a pregnant woman wanting to give up her baby for adoption. The social worker had given her the web address of a county-wide site called AdoptionOption.com, which put prospective parents in touch with pregnant teens who wanted to give up their babies. Although Lana visited the site daily, she had yet to make a contact that might work out. Discouraging, but she understood that the process would take time. Eventually she'd find someone.

Not wanting to keep such a big decision to herself, she'd told her sister first. That had been easy. Telling her parents, who tended to be old-fashioned, not so much. Lana had known they wouldn't approve. Not of adoption itself, but of her decision to adopt as a single woman.

Apprehension had ruined her appetite and she'd barely managed to eat her mother's delicious meal. She'd waited to spring her news until after dessert, when her niece and nephew had scampered off to play. She'd quickly delivered the news to her parents, then left while they were still digesting the news.

The fallout had come later, in a series of increasingly upset phone calls, one from her dad and too many to count from her mother. All of them about finding a husband and *then* adopting. With their old-fashioned values about raising kids—values Lana had supported until Brent had divorced her—they didn't understand.

"I would love to have a husband to help me raise

a child, but I'm not even dating right now," she'd explained. "Besides, I'm thirty-two years old, and I know in my heart that this is the right time for me to adopt."

No amount of reasoning had changed their minds. So Lana was cringing at the prospect of another of her mother's lectures tonight. She was banking on her parents having to behave in front of their grandkids.

Which was why, knowing Liz et al usually arrived about five, Lana was pulling up to the house a little later.

Crossing her fingers for a pleasant evening free of judgment and criticism, she crossed the brick stoop, wiped her feet on the welcome mat and walked into the house. She hung her jacket on a hook by the door.

The living room was empty, but through the window that faced the backyard she noted her brother-in-law, Eric, and her father lighting what looked to be a new barbecue grill. Connor, age six, and Emma, who had just turned four, were racing around the same pint-size log cabin Lana and Liz had once played in. There was no sign of Lana's sister or their mother. They were probably working on dinner.

Lana was about to slip back out the door and head around the house to play with the kids when her sister called out. "Is that you, Lana? Mom and I are in the kitchen."

No chance of sneaking away now. "I'll be right there," Lana replied.

Shoulders squared, she headed down the hall. Liz understood Lana's aching desire to have a child, and supported her decision. Why couldn't her parents be as accepting?

She forced herself to be cheerful, declaring, "Something smells really good," as she entered the big, homey kitchen.

Her mother was sautéing mushrooms and didn't look up. "I'm just finishing the rice dish. Why don't you toss the salad, Lana?"

Not even a hello? Lana exchanged a glance with Liz, who shrugged. "Um, hi, Mom, it's nice to see you, too?"

"Hello," she said in a cool tone.

Liz scanned Lana up and down. "You look fantastic. Doesn't she, Mom?"

At last her mother turned her attention to Lana. Bracing for whatever she might say, Lana sucked in a breath.

"You are wearing a certain glow." Her mother gave her a curious stare, as in, "Where did that come from?"

This was good, much better than another criticism about choosing single motherhood. Maybe her mother had decided to lay off the awful lectures tonight. Lana crossed her fingers. And thought about the "certain glow" that apparently was still with her.

It had been almost forty-eight hours since her night with Sly. By now any afterglow should have faded. Yet inside, Lana was still purring like a satisfied cat. Turning away from her mother's and sister's curious expressions, she washed her hands. "I caught up on my sleep last night—that must be the reason," she said over the hiss of the water. "Did Dad get a new grill?"

"Yesterday, and this one has more bells and whistles than the old model—it does everything but shine shoes," her mother answered. "He's as excited as a boy on Christmas morning. He couldn't wait to show it to Eric."

"Men and their toys." Liz shook her head, her ultrashort bangs and chin-length hair making her appear twenty instead of thirty. "If I know Eric, he'll want one exactly like it, just to keep up."

"With Eric's construction business doing so well, you can certainly afford a new grill," their mother pointed out.

The kitchen door opened and Connor and Emma rushed inside. "Aunt Lana! Aunt Lana!"

They raced straight for Lana. Her heart swelling with love, she leaned down and hugged them both. She envied Liz, with her loving husband and two adorable children. "It's been a whole week since I saw you. What's new?"

"Daddy's gonna sign me up for T-ball in June," Connor said proudly. "When is that, Aunt Lana?"

"Let's see. Today is April 6," Lana said. "After April comes…?"

Connor screwed up his face. "Summer?"

Lana laughed. "Summer isn't for a little while yet, buddy. After April comes May, then June."

Emma gave an enthusiastic nod. "When I'm five, I get to play T-ball, too."

"That'll be next summer—how exciting." Lana made a mental note to get the dates of the games so she could cheer Connor on.

"How are Daddy and Grandpa doing with the hamburgers?" Liz asked.

"Good," Emma replied. "We're 'posed to tell you that they're almost ready."

"Then you'd both better hang up your jackets and wash your hands." Liz pointed to the powder room.

The men brought in the hamburgers, greeted Lana and helped set the food on the dining room table. Dinner was the usual chaotic but fun affair, with Connor and Emma causing lots of laughter.

Lana finally relaxed. She was almost home free. With any luck she would skate through the rest of the evening with a smile on her face and then head home filled with the warmth borne out of family harmony. Or so she thought.

Chapter 2

At the end of the Sunday meal, Emma and Connor scampered into the fenced backyard to play. The adults lingered at the table, sipping coffee and chatting.

"I keep forgetting to mention, I ran into Cousin Tim at the grocery yesterday," Lana's mother said.

Lana's cousin from her father's side was nine years her senior, but he seemed much older. Always a brusque man, he'd grown even more difficult after his wife had divorced him less than a year after their wedding. Having grown up in a bustling city, his ex had decided that the ranching life wasn't for her. Or maybe the problem lay with Cousin Tim himself. Lana wasn't sure. Her cousin rarely smiled or laughed, which made being around him a chore. After eleven years, it was long past time for him to get over his ex and move on.

"We haven't heard from him since last Christmas," her father said. "How is he?"

"Not so good." Her mother looked solemn. "He told me that a few months ago, some of the cows at Pettit Ranch died suddenly. It turned out they were poisoned. Sly Pettit has accused Tim."

Two men named Sly in the same town.... What were the odds? Lana had gone to high school with yet another. Apparently the name was popular among the sixty-thousand-odd residents here in Prosperity. She imagined Cousin Tim's neighbor, who she'd never met, to be as beefy and bowlegged as her cousin.

"That's terrible—unless Cousin Tim actually did it," Liz quipped. Both parents stared at her, appalled. "Well, he isn't the nicest person."

Their father frowned. "I don't care, he's family, and—"

"Family sticks together through thick and thin," Lana, Liz and Eric replied in unison.

They meant it, too—especially when times were tough. When Brent left Lana, they'd wrapped her in so much love and warmth, they'd nearly smothered her. But now that she wanted to adopt a baby by herself... Her parents' disapproval ruled out their support.

Liz made a face. "Just because the man is family doesn't mean we have to like him. He's never exactly been fond of us, either."

"Ranching is a tough business," her father said. "Tim inherited the Lazy C from your great-uncle Horace, and it never has been a moneymaker. That kind of stress would make anyone grouchy."

"Living all alone on that big ranch..." Lana's mother shook her head. "I wouldn't like that at all."

"He has a crew and foreman to keep him company," Liz pointed out.

Under her breath she muttered, "They probably can't stand him, either." Then, in her normal voice, she said, "He could sell the ranch and find a job in the city, where he'd collect a regular paycheck," Lana suggested.

"With acreage prices at record lows, this isn't the smartest time to sell," Lana's dad said. "Besides, Cousin Tim is a rancher through and through. As bitter and rough around the edges as he is, at heart he's a decent man. He wouldn't poison anyone's cows."

Lana frowned. "Then why would Mr. Pettit accuse him of such a thing?"

"God only knows, but I'm sure Tim is eager tell me all about it. I suppose I'd better call him, since he hasn't called me." Her father's heavy breath indicated it would be a chore.

"Changing the subject…" Lana said. "Remember the reporter from the *Prosperity Daily News* who took pictures of the day care and interviewed me back in early March? He's going to highlight the story as the Small Business Profile of the Month. It'll run in the paper a week from Tuesday."

Her father beamed. "That's terrific, honey. My daughter, the businesswoman. Just like your old man."

Prosperity wasn't just a ranching town. Thanks to heavily wooded areas, the Ames and Missouri Rivers, Prosperity Falls and the Cascade Mountains beyond, during spring and summer the town attracted thousands of outdoor enthusiasts. Lana's father had cashed in on those tourists with a popular recreational-equipment business that rented and sold camping, hiking and fishing gear.

"Eric's good at business, too," Liz said.

Lana's father smiled at his son-in-law. "That goes without saying. Eric, you know I'm damn proud of you, son."

Eric grinned. "I do, sir."

"You're the best, Eric," Lana said. "I never could have opened Tender Loving Daycare without your help. I had no idea how to remodel an old dance studio into a day care."

"That profile in the paper is sure to drum up business, so you'll probably need his help again soon for a second day-care center," her father said.

"I've been thinking the same thing—when the time comes." For now, Lana's main focus was finding a baby to adopt. But she wasn't going to mention that. She didn't want to set her parents off.

"That sounds exciting." Liz gave her a pleased look. "Any ideas where you'd put it?"

"Someplace downtown." Home to insurance and title companies, two banks, a library, a hospital, museums, shops, department stores and restaurants. "Think of all the people with kids who work in or around the downtown area. Wouldn't it be convenient if they could drop off their children near where they work?"

Her father nodded approvingly. "That's a great idea."

Everyone started talking excitedly, except for Lana's mother, who frowned. "You're already so busy, Lana. If you expand, you'll only be busier. I don't know why that social worker cleared you as a suitable mother when your day care takes all of your energy."

So much for steering clear of any controversy. Lana rolled her eyes. "Don't start, Mom. I've made my decision and I'm happy with it. Because I'm focusing on finding a baby, I'm not going to expand just now."

"If I was pregnant and wanted to give up my baby, I'd choose a married couple," her mother said.

Lana was determined to prove that she would be as good as any couple. "I'd make a great mom, and I'll do whatever I can to convince people that I'm the best choice."

Her mother's lips thinned. "You have enough trouble meeting men without bringing a baby into your life."

Lana's back stiffened. Her mom just wouldn't quit. "Just because I'm not dating right now doesn't mean I can't meet men." She'd had no trouble with Sly.... But they weren't going to see each other again, so she wasn't going to think about him. "As I've explained at least a dozen times, this isn't a decision I made lightly. I've been contemplating adoption for ages."

For nearly two years now, in fact, after having spent four years trying to get pregnant, first the usual way, and then with the help of fertility drugs.

There had been nothing wrong with Brent. Lana had been the problem, the fertility doctor had explained before delivering the staggering blow that their odds of having a biological child were slim to none.

That still hurt, and always would.

Longing for a child, Lana had suggested adoption. But Brent had wanted to father his own child, and a few months after learning of Lana's inability to conceive, he'd left her for Julia.

"I've always wanted a houseful of kids," she continued. "It would be nice if I was married, but with or without a husband, I'm going to do this, and I would really appreciate your and Dad's support."

Her mother's mouth tightened. "I don't—"

To Lana's surprise, her father cut off her mother with a warning look. "Leave her alone, Michele. I'm not happy about this either, but arguing with Lana isn't going to work. She's always been single-minded about what she wants and is not afraid to go after it. It's one of the qualities that makes her a good businesswoman."

"I just want her to be happy, Chet. If she could just get over Brent…"

"I'm right here, Mom and Dad, and FYI, I'm totally over him."

To Lana's amazement, she was. Sometime in the past few days she'd stopped hurting. Come to think of it, Friday evening. Lana marveled over how she'd changed. As recklessly as she'd behaved, that night with Sly had helped her heal.

"I'm glad to hear you say that, honey," Lana's mother said. "Now that you've finally gotten Brent out of your system, why not make an effort and put yourself out there before you act on this crazy idea to adopt a baby by yourself."

As much as Lana needed her mom's support, she wasn't going to get it tonight. Unable to bear one more negative comment, she gave up—for now.

"I still have things to do tonight to get ready for tomorrow. I'm going home." Ignoring her mother's shocked expression, she stood. "Thanks for dinner."

So much for that warm, all-is-well-with-my-family feeling. She would keep moving forward with her plan and hope that in time, her parents would come around. If not, she'd go it alone.

* * *

"Will you look at that," Sly murmured as he scanned the morning paper over breakfast on a Tuesday morning in mid-April.

Mrs. Rutland, his forty-something housekeeper, stopped working on whatever she was making for dinner to peer over his shoulder. "Ah, you're reading the Small Business Profile of the Month. I read it earlier, while the coffee percolated. I've heard great things about Tender Loving Daycare, TLD for short."

"Have you," Sly said distractedly.

Because he recognized the owner of the business from the photo accompanying the article. It was Lana, the woman he couldn't seem to stop thinking about. Even now, more than a week after their night together, a mere glance at her smile caused his body to stir.

Hell, just imagining her did that.

After a week, he realized he wanted to get to know her. Nothing serious or long-term, but a chance to explore their attraction.

Now he had her full name. Lana Carpenter. Sly grimaced at that. He hoped she wasn't related to Tim Carpenter, the man he was suing. According to the attorney, Carpenter should receive the notice sometime today.

"These monthly profiles put small businesses on the Prosperity map, both for us locals and the tourists," Mrs. R said. "With hundreds of businesses to choose from, I think it's wonderful that the *Daily News* picked a day care this time. You don't have any kids yet, Sly, but someday you will. Maybe you'll send them to TLD."

Sly had already raised a kid—his brother, Seth. And look how that had turned out. The experience had soured him on having his own children. He'd have to be nuts to put himself—or some poor kid—through that again.

He went back to the article, his eyes on the photo. Lana looked happy and beautiful, as did the boys and girls gathered around her. But, hell, if she had her arms around Sly the way she did around those little ones, he'd be grinning just as widely.

"How do you know about the day care, Mrs. R?" he asked. "Your son and daughter are grown. When they were little, Lana Carpenter was probably in day care herself."

"A couple of my kids' friends take their children to TLD. They're always talking about how great Lana Carpenter is. She has a special way with children. They love her."

She also had other special ways, private things that made a man wild. Sly's body hardened. He wished he could stop thinking about her, but so far he hadn't had much luck with that.

Which was why he'd decided to see her again, casually. He'd returned to the Bitter & Sweet last Friday night in case she was there.

She wasn't. He'd danced with a couple of different women, both of them signaling that they were open to more than dancing. But neither could compare to beautiful, funny, sexy Lana, and after an hour or so, he'd left.

Hands on her ample hips, Mrs. Rutland looked worried. "Is something wrong with your omelet?"

Sly realized he was frowning. He curled his mouth into a smile. "It's real good." He glanced at his watch and was surprised to discover how late it was. "I told

Ace I'd help him and the others move part of the herd today," he said as he shoveled in big bites. "I'd best finish and get out there."

Counting labor, fencing, feed and vet care, cattle cost a bundle to raise, nearly three thousand dollars per animal per year. Growing his own summer and fall pasture grass cut down on food costs, and the nutrient-rich crop helped keep the animals strong and healthy. But in winter and spring, Sly relied on vitamin and mineral supplements for that. Supplies were running low, so late Tuesday afternoon he headed out to pick up more, as well as a roll of barbwire for the fences, which always seemed to need mending. But instead of turning east toward Drysdale's Ranching and Farm Supplies, he headed west.

Before he knew it, he was driving along River Drive, a pretty street that followed the Ames River through town and ended at Prosperity Park and the awesome Prosperity Falls. The cascading waterfall was a popular site for marriage proposals and outdoor weddings, and drew visitors from all over.

Miles before reaching the park, though, Sly turned off, onto Hawthorn Road. The colorful Tender Loving Daycare sign immediately drew his attention. So this was Lana's day care. He slowed way down to study the square clapboard building. Painted a soft green, it had purple shutters and window boxes. April was too early for flowers in the boxes, so colorful windmills stood in their stead. On one side of the building, a big fenced yard marked a kids' paradise of swings and slides and all sorts of climbing toys. On the other was a parking lot.

Sly had to find out if the attraction between them was as strong as he remembered, so he pulled in, noting that the lot was empty except for a minivan, a light green sedan and his truck. But then, it was after six. Sly was debating whether to go inside or take off, when the door opened. Amy Simmons—no, Amy Watkins now—sauntered through it holding the hand of a pint-size little girl. Lana followed behind them without a coat, as if she didn't expect to stay out long.

Amy noticed him right away. "Well, hello there," she said, approaching him with a dazzling smile. "What brings you here?"

Sly had no choice but to slide out of the truck. "Hey, Amy." He nodded at Lana. "I'm here to see her."

Lana had moved to stand beside Amy, her eyes wide with surprise. "Sly—uh, hi," she said.

Amy gave them both speculative looks. "I didn't realize you two knew each other."

They knew each other, all right, in ways that would make Amy blush if she realized.

Lana met his gaze, her green eyes warning him to say nothing about how they'd met. He gave a subtle nod, then smiled at the girl peering from behind Amy's knees. "Is that your little girl, Amy?"

"Yes, this is Courtney. She's three now." Amy scooped up her daughter and kissed her. "Say hi to Sly, sweetie."

The girl giggled. "Hi, Thly."

She was about the cutest thing Sly had ever seen. "Hey there, Courtney." He patted her head. "How's married life?" he asked Amy.

"I'm enjoying it. Jon and I are having so much fun with Courtney that we're having another baby in the fall." She touched her softly rounded abdomen. "Well, I'd better get this little one home. See you tomorrow, Lana, and thanks for keeping her a few minutes late." Amy flashed a sly smile. "You two have fun."

"How did you and Amy meet?" Lana asked as the woman buckled her daughter into her car seat.

Sly watched the minivan roll out of the parking lot. "We dated years ago." Amy had wanted to get serious, but he hadn't and they'd broken up. "Coming here now is bad timing on my part," he added. "She's a big gossip."

"Tell me about it." Lana fiddled with the cuff of her blouse, her expression both curious and openly pleased that he was there. "How did you find me, and what are you doing here?"

"I saw your business profile in the paper. Great article." He dug his copy from the hip pocket of his jeans and handed it to her. "In case you didn't get a hard copy."

"Thanks, Sly."

As she took it from him, her fingers casually brushed his. Heat shot straight to his groin, and by the sudden flush of her cheeks, she, too, felt the powerful connection between them. Yes, the pull between them was as strong as he remembered.

He cleared his throat. "I didn't get a chance to say goodbye before I left you that morning."

"I'm glad you let me sleep in. Oh, and thanks for the aspirin. It helped."

"No problem."

Silence.

In the uncomfortable moments that stretched between them, Lana glanced over her shoulder at the day-care door, as if she wanted to slip through it. "I—"

"You—" he said at the same time, then paused. "Go ahead," Sly insisted.

"I want you to know that I usually don't spend the night with a man I just met. You were the first and the last."

"I'm honored that you picked me. I enjoyed our night together."

Her warm eyes flashed that she had, too. She had a mouth made for loving. Plump, soft lips that were naturally pink. They parted a fraction, just as they had seconds before he'd kissed her on the night they'd spent together.

Sly definitely wanted to explore that heat, unleash her fiery passion and enjoy a repeat of their memorable night together. He moved closer and tucked her hair behind her ears with hands that shook.

He wanted her that much. Too much.

The strength of his need scared him. If he was smart, he'd turn around and leave. But his legs refused to budge.

Finally Lana swallowed and backed up a step. "Is there anything else you wanted?"

Besides kissing her and more? At the moment Sly couldn't think of a thing. He was debating whether to ask her out or walk away while he still could when she spoke.

"Okay, then," she said. "It's chilly out here and I left my coat inside. I also need to get ready for tomorrow. Thanks again for the article."

She left him standing in the parking lot, feeling both relieved and confused.

Clearly he'd misread her. She wasn't so happy to see him after all.

Actually, that made sense. He wasn't supposed to think about her and he sure wasn't supposed seek her out. They'd agreed on that.

Yet here he was standing in the parking lot of the business she owned, aching for her, even though getting involved with her could be dangerous.

What the hell was wrong with him?

Chapter 3

Lana made a practice of responding to TLD emails by the end of the same day she received them. She usually took care of that chore before leaving work, but thanks to Sly, today she'd been too rattled.

If that wasn't enough, her father had called to say that Cousin Tim was being sued by his neighbor. No one in the family had ever been sued, and they all were upset and banding around Cousin Tim. They offered to be character witnesses, lend him money for an attorney and whatever else he needed. Cousin Tim was too proud to accept their money, but said he'd let them know if character witnesses would help.

Still a little flummoxed, Lana stood in the kitchen, waiting for the kettle to whistle so that she could make a cup of herbal tea. For days now, she'd tried to push the night with Sly from her mind, without much success. She assured herself that she'd eventually forget the handsome cowboy who dominated her waking thoughts. She certainly hadn't expected to see him again, and had been both surprised and elated when he'd shown up at the day care.

But her feelings had quickly turned to disappointment. Sly hadn't asked for her phone number or a date. He hadn't asked her a single question or said more than a sentence or two. In fact, he hadn't seemed interested in getting to know her at all, or wanting her to know anything about him. Instead, his heavy-lidded expression had told her exactly what he wanted.

More of what they'd shared on that wild night.

Against Lana's better judgment, she'd wanted that, too. The attraction between them was more potent than anything she'd ever experienced, even during her honeymoon days with Brent. To the point that when Sly had moved close to her, her mind had all but emptied.

She frowned. How could she feel so strongly about a man she'd just met? She had no idea what his last name was or whether he really was a rancher, where he worked or anything about his family. Although she had a hunch that Amy would fill her in tomorrow when she picked up Courtney after work.

At last the kettle whistled, and Lana pushed Sly from her mind. Tonight she had better things to do than fantasize about the sexy cowboy. She carried her steaming mug to her home office, which doubled as the den.

The only positive thing about his visit this afternoon was that he'd distracted her from dwelling on the lack of interest her profile had generated at AdoptionOption.com. With input from the social worker, Lana had carefully created the online profile with her photo and other information. Although many girls had contacted her, nothing had stuck.

Lana wished she could figure out why. Was it because she was single, or something else? The lack of any serious interest was discouraging, and she wished she'd waited to share her decision with her family until she'd formed a promising relationship with an expectant mother.

Not about to give up, she decided tonight she'd check the website after she checked her email. She sat down and scrolled through her inbox. There were ten—ten!—inquiries from parents who'd read the profile in the paper and wanted to visit TLD. Her friend Kate had also emailed, whining about an upcoming blind date her mother had orchestrated. Several other friends had sent the usual jokes and gossip.

But one email stood out. "Baby," the subject line read, from Sophie@AdoptionOption.com. Hardly daring to breathe, Lana opened the email.

I got your name from the AdoptionOption website. I'm Sophie and I'm four months pregnant. I'm looking for the right person to adopt my baby. When I saw the article about you in the paper today and read your online profile at the website, I couldn't believe it. You seem to really care about kids, and I would like to meet you. Text me at 406-555-2223.

This was the chance Lana had waited, hoped and prayed for. Sucking in an excited breath, she jotted down the number with shaky hands.

Yet as badly as she longed for a baby, she had to

admit that she was also a little scared. Raising a child without a partner was going to be a huge job.

Too antsy to sit, she paced to the window and looked out. Despite the lights from the other town houses and the shade tree in her yard, she could see the crescent moon and the stars studding the sky like diamonds. Tonight they seemed especially bright. Lana took that as a good omen.

Regardless of the challenges ahead, she wanted a child with all her heart. She wasn't about to let this opportunity pass by. She grabbed her cell phone and texted the girl.

Hi, I would love to get together. How about Big Mama's—my treat. Tell me when and I'll be there. Looking forward to meeting you,
Lana

She'd chosen Big Mama's Café because everyone loved the restaurant's food. Less than a minute later, Sophie texted back. Saturday @ 10?

Gleeful, Lana replied. Sounds perfect. I'm 5'6" and have longish blond hair.

Sophie texted. I know what u look like from yr profile and the pic in the paper. CU.

A baby of her own!

"Don't get ahead of yourself," Lana cautioned out loud.

Sophie might decide she wasn't the right person to raise her child, and allowing herself to imagine otherwise would only set her up for heartache.

Still, she was too excited to worry about that now, or to read the other emails. She logged in to Adoption-

Option.com and checked Sophie's profile. The girl was sixteen and a junior at Jupiter High School on the far side of town. She had short hair, dyed white-blond with neon-pink streaks and bangs that fell into big, soulful eyes lined in thick eye pencil. Despite the alternative look, she was very pretty, and Lana guessed that the baby would be beautiful.

"She's not the mother of my child yet," she reminded herself.

Not that it calmed her down. Laughing, she danced around the room while she speed-dialed Kate. After three rings, her friend answered.

"It's happened," Lana said, skipping the usual pleasantries.

"You have a blind date, too? Ugh. You know that sewing circle my mom belongs to? That's where it happened. I cannot believe she went behind my back and fixed me up with her friend's sister's son. That sounds like a really bad joke, doesn't it? Too bad it's real. Save me, please."

The whole thing *did* sound awful. Lana's mother had her faults, but she wouldn't set up a blind date without first checking with Lana. Bonus points for her. "You never know," Lana said. "It could work out."

"With the son of the sister of some woman in my mom's sewing circle? Puh-leeze. You said *it* happened. Don't tell me Sly finally found you."

"He did, but this is about a baby. Tonight I got an email from a pregnant girl who saw the article on TLD in the paper." Lana squeezed her eyes shut and squealed. "She wants to meet me."

"Wow, that's great. But back up a minute. Did you

say that Sly found you? I knew he would! Why didn't you phone me?" Kate sounded hurt.

"Because it happened late this afternoon, and I haven't had a chance to call until now."

"I want details."

"Okay, but first let me fill you in about Sophie—the pregnant girl."

"Believe me, I want to hear all about her. After you spill on what happened with Sly."

Realizing Kate wouldn't let up until she got the information she wanted, Lana threw up her hand. "All right, but there isn't much to say. He read my business profile in the paper. That's how he learned where I work."

"That piece was terrific, by the way, and look at the results you're already seeing. A pregnant girl contacts you and Sly shows up at the day care. Why can't they run an article about *me* in the paper?"

"Start your own business and it just might happen."

"I like managing the Treasures Gift Shop at Prosperity Falls just fine, thanks. Back to Sly. What did he say, and what did you say?"

"He apologized for leaving the morning after without a goodbye." He'd seemed so sincere and contrite that Lana had almost melted. "And he brought me a copy of the newspaper article."

"What a sweetheart. When are you two going out?"

"He didn't ask me out," Lana said. "I never had a chance to find out his last name or anything else about him. He was only interested in kissing me."

"Ooh. Did you let him?"

"Of course not." But Lana had wanted to. Badly.

"Are you crazy? If you don't want to kiss Sly Whatever-his-last-name-is, send him my way."

"Ha, ha, ha. I didn't let him kiss me because he's only interested in one thing."

"I thought you liked doing that one thing with him."

Lana gritted her teeth. "You're not helping, Kate. I don't want a sex-only relationship. I want more than that." Especially now, when she just might have a chance at a baby....

She wanted a relationship based on shared mutual interests and honest conversation, things that formed a basis for something that lasted. True, those very things had failed to hold her marriage together, but that was because Brent had found her lacking.

"But he's so darned hot," Kate said. "And he seemed very into you that night...."

She was right on both counts. Sly had seemed just as into Lana today, but not in the way she wanted. "If he was that interested, he'd have at least asked for my phone number."

"You mean, he didn't?"

"Nope. Unfortunately, his attraction to me is purely sexual."

"Bummer," Kate said. "Just once, I'd like to meet a man interested in getting to know me before he tries to jump my bones. You keep saying he's out there. If he is, I sure haven't met him."

"Yeah, well, I haven't found my Mr. Right, either." Lana had thought she had with Brent, but he'd turned out to be Mr. Wrong instead. "Wouldn't it be funny if your blind date turns out to be 'the one'?"

Kate snorted. "Don't hold your breath. Now tell me about the pregnant girl."

"Her name is Sophie, and we're meeting Saturday at Big Mama's. I'm treating her to brunch."

"How exciting! I'll keep my fingers crossed for you. Good luck."

"Do you think I need luck?" Lana bit her lip.

"It's just a figure of speech. Be yourself, and Sophie will love you, like everyone else who knows you."

More than anything in the world, Lana hoped her friend was right.

"So, Lana, how long have you and Sly been dating?" Amy asked when she arrived to pick up Courtney on Wednesday afternoon.

Amy was a great mom, but as Sly had pointed out the other day, she was also a big gossip. Lana was glad that her two assistants had gone home for the day and that only she, Amy and another mom named Sheila were at the day care. "Actually, we're not dating," she said.

Amy lifted a skeptical eyebrow. "Sly sure didn't stop by yesterday to pick up a child. He doesn't have kids of his own, or any nieces or nephews that I'm aware of. He said he was here to see you."

In the act of helping her four-year-old son with his jacket, Sheila widened her eyes. "You must be talking about Sly Pettit. He was here?"

Amy grinned. "In the flesh."

Wait. Sly *Pettit*—the rancher who was suing Cousin Tim? Lana tried not to show her shock.

"What's wrong, Lana?" Sheila asked.

"I'm just surprised that you both know him."

"We certainly do," Amy said with a smirk. "We both used to date him, though not at the same time. I haven't seen him in a good four years, and he's still as gorgeous as ever," she told Sheila. "I'm guessing he's still a heartbreaker, too."

Sheila zipped her son's jacket and directed him to get his lunch box. "We dated about six years ago. By our second or third date I was head over heels for him. I was sure I'd be the one to snag him." She gave her head a sad shake. "Unfortunately he didn't feel the same way about me. I couldn't even get him to show me his ranch. After a few months, we broke up."

Amy nodded. "My story is similar. Sly showed me the ranch, but only because I asked. I'd heard that his bedroom was off-limits to the women he dated, but I always hoped I'd be the one he fell for, the one he'd invite to his bed. He never did—we always ended up at my place. I tried everything to make him love me, but no luck." She let out a sigh, followed by a shrug. "I guess I ended up lucky after all. I met and married Jon, and we're so happy."

"Sly has dated a lot of women and broken a lot of hearts," Sheila said. "Be careful, Lana."

"Thanks for the warning," Lana said, but she wasn't worried. She and Sly weren't dating, and now they never would.

Not with him suing her cousin.

Sly and his sister, Dani, were close, and as busy as they both were with their jobs, they made sure they got together a couple times a month. On Wednesday night they met at Clancy's, a bar and pool hall south of town. Clancy's was always crowded, but boasted a dozen pool tables—enough so that he and Dani were usually able to snag one.

"I met a woman," Sly told his sister over the loud country-and-western music adding to the noise. He hadn't planned on saying anything and wasn't sure why he'd made the confession. Especially when lately, he hadn't dated much and she'd been bugging him about it. Now she'd *really* bug him.

But Lana... Sly was still thinking about her, even though she'd shut him down. There was something about her, and he needed to tell somebody.

In the middle of placing the balls, Dani swiveled her head his way. "Oh?" Her eyes, the same silver-blue as Sly's and Seth's, sparked with curiosity.

Not wanting to make a big deal out of what he'd said, he tugged on her ponytail like he had when she was four. Before life had knocked them both upside the head.

"Stop that." Hiding a smile, she batted his hand away. "I'm not a little girl anymore. I'm twenty-eight years old."

Dani was seven years younger than him, and one of the few people he trusted. He flashed a grin. "You'll always be my baby sister, even when you're fifty."

"By then you'll be an old man, and probably too frail to pull my hair."

Sly scowled, but Dani thought that was real funny. "I'll take solid, you take the stripes," she said.

While she eyeballed the table, aimed her cue and broke the balls, Sly thought about how far they'd come since he was eleven and their mother had died. Two years later their father had followed her, leaving them orphans. Sly had wanted to take care of his siblings, but he'd been too young.

Their only family had been an uncle Sly and his siblings had never met, a man who lived in Iowa. Uncle George had grudgingly taken in Sly and his younger brother, Seth, who was ten at the time, but he hadn't wanted Dani.

She'd entered the foster-care system in Prosperity. Sly had worried about her constantly and vowed that someday he would reunite their little family.

But it turned out that he and Seth had gotten the raw end of that stick. Their uncle had disliked kids and had mostly ignored him and Seth, which was better than the alternative. His idea of attention had been to yell and raise his hand. Sly and his brother had quickly learned to steer clear of him.

Sly had become his brother's caretaker and parent of sorts, raising Seth as best he could. His best hadn't been so great, though. A kid with an independent streak, Seth had fought him on everything. By the time Uncle George had died just before Sly's eighteenth birthday, his relationship with his brother had deteriorated badly. Hoping that returning home and reuniting with Dani would help mend the damages, Sly had brought his brother back to Prosperity. Unfortunately, nothing had changed. After several minor scrapes with the law, Seth had dropped out of high school and left town. A few months later, Sly and Dani had received a postcard letting them know he'd settled in California. He'd failed to provide the name of the city, and the postal stamp had been impossible to decipher. Seth hadn't spoken to or contacted them since.

Dani had ended up with a much better deal. Big Mama, her foster mom, had loved her from the start and eventually had adopted her.

Dani hit the ball into a side pocket. Another ball slid into a different pocket. She did a little dance. "Dang, I'm good."

"Cocky, too," Sly teased. "Wait until it's my turn."

She missed the next shot. Sly chalked his cue. "Watch

and learn, little sister." He took aim and dropped a striped ball into the corner pocket. He put away four more, then missed.

Before Dani took aim, she angled her head at him. "I'm glad to hear you met someone, big brother. How and where did it happen?"

"Remember that dinner meeting with my lawyer a couple weeks ago at the Bitter & Sweet? She was there with a girlfriend. We ended up dancing the whole night."

"The *whole* night?"

Sly wasn't about to answer that. "Are you ever going to move that cue?"

Dani ignored him. "Her girlfriend must've been bored silly."

"Yeah. She went home." Sly nudged her aside. "I'll shoot for you."

"No way." She gave him a friendly poke in the ribs. "Does this woman have a name?"

"Lana Carpenter." The words rolled off Sly's tongue and left a sweet taste in his mouth.

"That sounds familiar. Where have I heard of Lana Carpenter?" Dani wondered, tapping the cue with her finger. "I don't think she's one of my regulars."

Dani worked at Big Mama's Café, a popular place open for breakfast and lunch that Big Mama had started some thirty years earlier. Someday when Big Mama retired, the restaurant would be Dani's.

His sister finally took her shot, pocketed one and missed the next shot. "Shoot," she grumbled. "You're up. Is Lana related to Tim Carpenter?"

Sly sure as hell hoped not. "Haven't asked her."

"She doesn't know you're thinking about suing a man who could be related to her?"

"I'm definitely suing." Sly was still unhappy about having to take legal action. He missed his shot, too. "He should have gotten the papers yesterday."

"I'm sorry it had to come to that." Dani made a face. "Have you heard anything back?"

"It's all going through my lawyer. When he hears, he'll call."

She nodded. "Where does Lana Carpenter work?"

"She owns a business called Tender Loving Daycare."

"Now I remember where I've heard her name. Her day care was profiled as small business of the month in the paper. Customers have been talking about it a lot. Her picture was in the paper. She's pretty." Dani gave him a speculative look. "So where are you taking her this weekend?"

Sly almost told her about stopping by the day care to see Lana, but he didn't want to stir up his sister's curiosity any more than it already was. "We're not dating," he said.

"Why the heck not?"

Because something told Sly that Lana was the one woman who could cut right past his defenses. He wasn't about to let anyone do that.

"Let me get this straight," his sister said when he didn't answer. "The weekend before last you danced the night away with Lana Carpenter. Now you mentioned her to me, but you haven't asked her out. You must like her a lot."

Sly snorted and shook his head, but Dani had a point. He did like Lana. No, he lusted after her. It was easy to confuse the two, but he knew the difference. "I'm getting awful hungry," he said. "Let's finish this game and then grab a couple of burgers. The winner treats."

"You're on." Dani lined up her cue and shot. The ball sailed neatly into a pocket. She missed the next one. "Why haven't you asked her out?"

Darn, his sister could be a pit bull about some things. He should have figured she wasn't through with the subject of Lana Carpenter just yet. "I don't have her number," Sly said.

"That's what phone books and the internet are for."

"Things are pretty busy at the ranch."

"Excuses, excuses."

Sly took his shot and missed. He swore softly. "I missed that because I'm half starved to death."

"As soon as I sink the eight ball, I'll let you buy me that burger." The remaining solid balls disappeared into the pockets. Dani eyeballed the table. "Eight ball, corner pocket." After lining up the cue, she executed the shot perfectly. Her fists shot into the air. "Hot damn— I won!"

"I'll beat you next time," Sly said. "I keep meaning to ask—how's that guy you're dating?"

"You mean Cal?" Her smile faded. "We broke up on Sunday."

"Can't say I'm sorry." His sister seemed to gravitate toward guys who treated her poorly. "You want me to punch him for you?" He was kidding, but if she wanted him to, he'd do it.

"Absolutely not." She made a face. "I'm a big girl, Sly. I can take care of myself. I just wish that I could meet a guy and have something that lasted more than a couple of months."

Sly hoped she found what she wanted. So far, she hadn't had much luck. "You and I are alike that way—both of us suck at relationships."

"Sad but true." She gave him a somber look. "The difference between us is that I *want* to find someone, get married and have kids. You don't."

Sly shrugged. "I'm happy the way I am."

"Well, I'm tired of going home to my apartment and cooking for one. It gets lonely."

Another voice cut in—a lowlife named Paul. "Hey, Dani. Sly."

He gave Dani a blatantly sexual look that made Sly see red. He managed a terse nod.

His sister perked up. "Down, big brother," she murmured for his ears only. "Remember, I can take care of myself. Besides, I happen to have a little crush on that cowboy." She tossed Paul a flirty smile. "Hi. What are you up to?"

"Lookin' for you. Can I buy you a beer?"

Dani glanced at Sly. "Rain check on that burger?"

"Do I have a choice?"

"Not really. Hey, why don't you come to Big Mama's for lunch on Saturday, my treat." She stood on her toes and kissed Sly's cheek.

"You won the game. I'm supposed to treat you."

"But I'm standing you up for Paul. Leave me a big tip on Saturday and we'll call it even."

"If that's how you want it." Sly resisted the urge to tug on her ponytail again. "You want me to wait around and give you a ride home?"

"I'll drive her home," Paul said, giving Dani a winning smile.

"I'd appreciate that." She took his arm and winked over her shoulder at Sly. "I'll see you Saturday."

Chapter 4

Saturday morning, Lana and Sophie sat at a booth by the window in Big Mama's Café. Locals and tourists loved the busy restaurant, which served great food and was always packed on weekends.

Big Mama's Sinfully Satisfying Frittata, a favorite of Lana's created by Big Mama herself, sat on the table in front of her, slowly growing cold. Having been up since dawn without eating a thing, she should have been famished. Instead, her stomach felt queasy. Nerves, and they showed. Usually she had no problem meeting new people and making decent conversation, but sitting here with Sophie, she couldn't come up with a single thing to say.

If only she were as calm as the girl, who was devouring her cheese-and-bacon omelet as if she hadn't eaten in days. She looked just like her profile picture,

and was on the thin side, with a lean, boyish shape…
until you saw her rounded belly. A snug black Mumford & Sons Live! T-shirt hugged her torso and emphasized her condition. At four months along, she definitely looked pregnant.

She stopped eating to shoot Lana a quizzical glance. "What are you smiling at?"

"When my sister was pregnant, she ate like you—as if she had hollow legs."

"I've always eaten a lot, only I wasn't fat before."

"You're not fat now—you're pregnant."

"Well, I feel fat." Sophie slathered a cinnamon roll with butter. "Why aren't you eating your food?"

Though Lana had never been less hungry in her life, she forced herself to take a bite of the frittata. "It's delicious."

After that, the conversation died.

"You're not at all like your photos," Sophie said after a moment.

"Is that good or bad?"

"It's just different. In the pictures you wore pants and a shirt. Now you're wearing a dress with little blue-and-white hearts all over it."

Wanting to make a positive impression, Lana had spent almost half an hour deciding what to wear. She'd chosen the dress because it was fairly new and she felt pretty in it. Now she wondered if she'd gone too formal. "A dress is bad?"

"Well, no, but why wear one when you don't have to?" Sophie wrinkled her nose, causing her tiny silver nose ring to stick out.

"Normally I wear jeans on weekends. In fact, I was wearing my favorites earlier. But I cleaned house this morning, which I do every Saturday," Lana explained, wanting Sophie to know she kept a tidy home. "Since this is our first meeting, I wanted to wear something a little nicer."

Sophie gave a slow nod and polished off the cinnamon roll. "I clean the apartment where my mom I and live on Saturdays, too. She works fifty hours a week for us, and it's only right that I do my part. That's what she says anyway."

Lana nodded. "That seems fair."

"I guess."

Lana racked her brain for something else to say. "Do you have an after-school job?"

"Not every day. I work part-time at the movie theater near the apartment. I take tickets and collect trash from under the seats. My shift is five to ten on Thursdays and Fridays, and one to ten on Saturdays. That's how I met Jason. He works in the concession area."

"I'm guessing Jason is the baby's father?" Lana asked.

Sophie nodded. "He doesn't want to be a father, just like I don't want to be a mom. We're too young. Now that I'm pregnant, he makes me go straight home after work to get my rest." She eyed Lana's frittata. "Are you going to eat the rest of that?"

"It's all yours. Jason sounds like a sweet guy."

"Sometimes. Last night he gave his two-week notice. He just got a new job at the candy store at the mall."

The girl's carefully blank face made Lana wonder. "Is everything okay with you two?"

"We sort of broke up last night," Sophie said to her empty plate.

She was obviously hurting. Lana felt bad for her. "I'm sorry," she said. "Breaking up is never fun."

Sophie picked at her nail. "I was getting tired of him anyway." She gave Lana a sideways look. "Did you and your boyfriend break up, too?"

"At the moment, I don't have a boyfriend and I'm not dating anyone, but I used to be married."

"Did he cheat on you? That's what my mom's last boyfriend did."

There was no reason to sugarcoat the truth. "As a matter of fact, he did," Lana said. "He wanted a baby, and when we found out that I couldn't give him one, he found a woman who could."

"That's really jacked up. Is that why you want to adopt—because you can't have a baby of your own?"

Lana nodded. "I love children, and I'm so ready to be a mother. I know I'll make a really great one." Another long silence. "Tell me what you want to be someday."

"I'm not sure. Maybe a cosmetologist like my mom. She makes decent money."

"That's a great career."

The waitress, a friendly woman named Dani, stopped at the table with a coffeepot. "Ready for your coffee now?"

Lana considered asking for the check instead and putting an end to the uncomfortable meeting. But she wanted a chance to end on a more upbeat note. She smiled. "That depends on Sophie. Do you want something else to drink?"

The girl cast a wistful gaze at the coffeepot. "Coffee, but now that I'm pregnant, I'm not supposed to."

"How about cocoa?" Dani asked. "We make ours homemade and it's excellent."

"Yeah, sure."

"I'll have that, too," Lana said.

"Two cocoas it is." For the first time, Dani really looked at Lana. "You're the woman in the paper. Lana Carpenter."

"That's right."

"It's very nice to meet you."

When Dani left, Sophie was grinning. "You're kind of a celebrity."

"Am I?" Lana laughed. "I never thought of myself that way."

"You are. Because of your picture with that story, people know you." Sophie fiddled with her napkin, then squinted slightly at Lana. "Can I ask you something?"

"Anything."

"Do you ever wish you had a boyfriend?"

Lana's mind flashed to Sly. Now, there was a terrible choice for a boyfriend—as Amy and Sheila had pointed out. Lana hadn't heard from him since he'd stopped by the day care several days ago. He wasn't boyfriend material. Even worse, he was suing her cousin. At the very thought, she felt cold and sick at heart. Angry, too. Cousin Tim wasn't the nicest person, but killing Sly's cattle? No way would he do that.

"Occasionally I get lonely," she admitted. "But most of the time I'm fine by myself. Between the day care and home projects, I keep pretty busy. Now I want to ask *you* something." She cupped her hands around her water glass and waited for Sophie's nod. "How do you feel about a single woman raising your baby?"

"It's no big deal." The girl shrugged. "That's how my mom raised me."

And here she was, a junior in high school and pregnant. Lana silently vowed to closely supervise her child throughout his or her teen years—provided she got the chance to be a mother.

"Do you ever see your dad?" Lana asked.

The girl shook her head. "My mom isn't even sure who he is."

Sophie seemed okay with that, but Lana was sad for her. She couldn't imagine not knowing her own father. *And what about my baby's father?* Lana was counting on her dad to help make up for that. Her parents weren't supporting her decision right now, but she wasn't going to lose hope. Once she had the baby, surely they'd rally. After all, she was family, and her baby would be, too.

"You should know that I'm planning to bring my child to work with me every day, and when he or she is old enough—let's call the baby a she for now—I'll enroll her in my day care. Then when she starts kindergarten, I'll cut back my hours so I can be with her after school."

"But if you do that, you'll make less money. My mom has always worked ten hours a day."

Lana nodded. "Money is important, but to me, being there for my child is even more important. I have savings that will allow me to work a little less."

The girl appeared thoughtful. "I would have liked for my mom to be around when I got home from school. I could tell you'd make a good mom when I read the article. It's why I picked you and Mr. and Mrs. Anderson as my top two choices."

"I'm not the only person you're considering?" Lana said, her voice squeaking.

She should have guessed as much, had cautioned herself to not make any assumptions. But she'd been so excited, so sure that today's meeting would be perfect and that Sophie would like her, that the idea of other potential parents had never entered her mind.

Dani returned with the cocoas. Unaware of the utter chaos her announcement had caused inside Lana, Sophie glugged down a great deal of her drink before replying, "My social worker said I should talk to more than one person so that I can make the best choice. I'm having lunch with the Andersons tomorrow, at Baker's."

An upscale restaurant with fancy food that cost twice what it did at Big Mama's, Baker's was sure to impress the girl. "That's um, nice," Lana said.

"I've never eaten there before, have you?"

"Once or twice, for special occasions."

"Is it okay for me to wear jeans and a T-shirt?"

"I wouldn't."

Another uncomfortable silence followed.

As Lana sipped her cocoa, she had the strangest sense that someone was staring at her. She glanced out the window. Someone *was*. Sly was standing on the sidewalk right in front of her.

Sophie followed her gaze. "Wow, he's cute—for an old guy. You said you didn't have a boyfriend."

"I don't."

"He's sure looking at you the way a boyfriend would. And he's coming into the restaurant."

Sly couldn't believe that Lana was sitting in a booth at Big Mama's Café. Not the fact that she was eating there—everyone did—but because she was here now, on the day Dani expected him for lunch.

As usual, the place was packed with the Saturday crowd. There were no empty tables, and no sign of Big

Mama. But then, she often took weekends off, handing the reins to Dani.

Naomi, the weekend hostess, smiled and tossed her head seductively. "Hey, Sly," she drawled with a sexy smile. She was a flirt, but it was all harmless fun. "Dani said you'd be coming in. I just freshened my makeup, and I sure am glad I did."

He gave her a grin. "With or without makeup, you're beautiful to me, Naomi. Add my name to the list for a table in Dani's area, will you?"

"You know it, sugar, but it could be a while."

"No problem. I'm in no hurry."

Sly greeted a couple of ranchers he was friendly with, then, hardly aware of what he was doing, wandered over to Lana's booth. She was sitting with a skinny girl with rock-band hair. Sly pegged her to be about fifteen or sixteen.

"Hey," he said.

Lana glanced up at him. In a dress sprinkled with little hearts and feminine lace on the cuffs of her short sleeves, she looked innocent and sweet. Also confused. "Hello, Sly. What are you doing here?"

"This is where my sister works. I came to see her and grab lunch."

Dani bustled right over. "Hi, big brother." She tugged him down and kissed his cheek. "We're a little short on tables right now. But hey, if Lana doesn't mind, maybe you can join her and her friend."

Lana's expression turned puzzled. "What makes you think your brother and I know each other?"

"The way you look at each other. But also because the last time I saw him, he mentioned you."

Sly was going to kill his sister.

A telltale flush crept up Lana's face. "You didn't say anything earlier, Dani."

"I wasn't sure I should. In case my brother forgot to mention it, he enjoyed his evening with you."

"You said you weren't dating anyone." The teenage girl widened her eyes dramatically at Lana. "I don't mind if he sits down with us. There's plenty of room next to Lana."

Lana gave the girl a what-are-you-up-to look before she sighed. "Okay, until a table opens up." She scooted toward the far end of the bench, leaving a good foot and a half of space for him.

"You want coffee while you're waiting for your burger, Sly? I just made a fresh pot."

"Sounds good."

"Be right back." Dani hurried off.

A frown tugged Lana's mouth.

"I only told her that you and I danced," Sly explained.

The teenage girl was staring at him. "You and Lana danced? I wish I could have seen that." She said it as if she couldn't believe people their age did that kind of thing.

"I don't believe we've met." He extended his hand. "I'm Sly."

"Cool name. I'm Sophie."

"Nice to meet you. Are you Lana's little sister?"

The girl looked at him like he was crazy. "No," she said with a smirk. "Lana and I just met today."

Interesting. "Then you must be interviewing for a job at her day care."

"Not that, either." Sophie smoothed her T-shirt over her rounded belly. "I'm pregnant and I'm thinking I might pick Lana to adopt my baby."

Lana seemed to catch her breath.

She wanted to adopt a baby? Sly realized his mouth was hanging open and quickly shut it. "Is that right."

The girl wore a speculative expression. "I changed my mind about leaving," she said. "I might stay a while longer. But I need to use the restroom. Excuse me." She slid out of the booth and hurried away.

"This is awkward," he said in the silence that fell between him and Lana.

"The part about me wanting to adopt, or about me not hearing from you since you stopped at the day care?" Her eyes flashed with anger. "Or do you mean because you're suing my cousin?"

So she and Tim Carpenter *were* related. Sly muttered a choice oath and put his head in his hands. With a look of alarm, Dani approached, quickly filled his cup and left.

"First of all, until this minute I wasn't aware you and Tim Carpenter were related," he said. "I didn't even know your last name until I read it in the paper."

"That's understandable, but you're still suing my cousin."

Her stony expression made him hurry to explain. "Trust me, it wasn't my first choice. Tim didn't leave me any other option." Wanting to get to other things before Sophie returned to the table, Sly added, "I'll tell you about that later. FYI, I wanted to ask for your number before I left you in our hotel room. But we agreed that we wouldn't contact each other again."

"Then why did you come to my day care?"

"I wanted to see you."

"For exactly one reason." Lana glanced around and

lowered her voice. "You wanted a repeat of what happened that night."

"True," Sly admitted, "but it wasn't just about sex. I'm not interested in getting serious or anything, but I would like to get to know you."

"Oh, really? Then why didn't you ask me for my number, or at least act like you were interested in *me* as a person? You never asked me a single question about myself."

Sly fiddled with his cup. "You didn't ask me any questions, either."

"I was letting you take the lead!"

People were starting to stare.

Lana lowered her voice. "Forget it."

"Uh, can I have your number now?" Talk about sounding lame.

"It's a little late for that, Sly. Besides, you haven't explained why you filed a lawsuit against my cousin."

"There's a simple—"

"I have to leave after all," Sophie said as she returned to the booth. "While I was in the bathroom, my mom called. She wants me to get home and finish my chores before I leave for work."

Lana nodded and then nudged Sly out of the booth and stood up. "I enjoyed meeting you, Sophie. I hope we'll get together again soon."

"Can I let you know?"

"Sure. I'll walk you out."

"You stay here with Sly." The girl's smile was meant for the two of them.

Sly squelched the urge to roll his eyes. "Nice meeting you." He sat down in Sophie's place so that he would be across from Lana.

"You, too, Sly. Hey, next time Lana and I get together, you should join us."

Sly glanced at Lana, but her attention stayed on the teen. It was obvious how badly she wanted things to work out between them.

"If I'm not too busy at the ranch," he said.

"I knew you were a rancher!" Sophie turned to Lana. "Thanks for brunch. It was really good."

"Anytime." Lana bit her lip. "Would you mind if I gave you a hug?"

"I guess."

Feeling like he was watching something that was none of his business, Sly stared as Lana embraced the girl.

When she pulled away, her eyes dropped to Sophie's belly. "You take care of that baby, okay?"

"I will."

Her eyes stayed on Sophie until the door closed behind her.

Chapter 5

Angry at Sly for suing her cousin and unhappy at how badly the meeting with Sophie had gone, Lana was ready to leave. "I have a lot to do today," she said, signaling Dani to bring the check. "Enjoy your lunch."

"Stay a little longer and tell me about this baby you want to adopt."

She didn't mind talking about that, but after Sophie's bombshell that she was also meeting with a couple interested in adopting her baby, Lana felt unusually emotional and vulnerable. Just now, she wasn't ready to share anything. But she wouldn't mind some answers from Sly. "I'll stay if you explain about the lawsuit," she said.

"Any minute now, my sister will bring me my burger, and I don't want to ruin my appetite talking about that. I'll give you the details later." Resting his arms on the table, he leaned toward her. "So you want to adopt a baby."

He gave her a long, searching look that made him seem genuinely interested. Lana wanted to explain. If she kept it short and simple, she wouldn't cry. "That's right," she said. "I'm unable to have children myself."

"So you said before. You didn't mention wanting to adopt, though."

"Because we agreed not to get into anything serious." Besides, they'd been too busy to talk much. "Anyway, now you know."

"If you're sure you want kids, adopting makes sense."

"I'm sure. I've always wanted to be a mom."

Sly nodded, but Lana was curious about the way he'd said *if you're sure you want kids.* "You don't want to have children?" she asked.

"Nope. Don't get me wrong, I like them, as long as they belong to someone else."

"You mean you don't want any right now," she corrected. "My best friend, Kate—you met her that night at the Bitter & Sweet—feels the same way. Kate says she'll be ready when she's thirty-five."

"That's how old I am now, and I mean never. I'd make a lousy father."

"Why do you say that?"

"Trust me, I raised my younger brother, and I know what I'm talking about. Me having a kid would be irresponsible."

"I'd call raising your brother the opposite of irresponsible." Lana was beyond curious now. "Do you mind my asking what happened?"

"It's no secret. I was eleven when my mom died. Two years later, my father also passed away. The child protection people managed to find an uncle who agreed to take in Seth and me. Let's just say our uncle didn't want us around. That's how I ended up raising Seth." Sly shrugged. "That didn't turn out so great."

"What do you mean?"

"For starters, he did a few stupid things that got attention from the law. Uncle George had a problem controlling his temper, so I stepped in. Or I tried." Sly let out a self-derisive laugh. "No matter what I said or what I did, I couldn't get Seth to straighten up or take responsibility for the trouble he caused. Not even moving back to Prosperity helped. Then he dropped out of high school."

That sounded like a tough situation. Lana bit her lip. "Where is Seth now?"

"I have no idea. When he was seventeen, he split. A few weeks later, he sent a postcard to let us know he was okay. He hasn't been in touch since." Sly glanced down at his empty coffee cup, then spread his hands in a gesture of helplessness. "Now you know what a great job I did."

Lana pictured a very young Sly struggling to raise his brother when he was so young himself. "You were under very challenging conditions, Sly. You were an orphan and a child yourself. Under those circumstances, no one would do well."

He was unconvinced. "Because of the situation, I grew up fast. At fourteen, I was more mature than most eighteen-year-olds. I should have done a better job. Instead, I screwed up my brother and also blew any chance of a tight relationship with him."

Lana thought Sly was too hard on himself, and felt terrible for him and his brother. "I'm sorry."

"It was a long time ago. I'm over it now. But I won't ever screw up a kid that way again."

"Isn't Dani your sister? She seems to have turned out well."

"No thanks to me. Our uncle didn't want any girls around, so Dani went into foster care. She was lucky enough to get Big Mama as her foster mom. A couple of years later, Big Mama adopted her. So yeah, I'm all for adoption."

Dani slid Sly's burger and a soda in front of him. "Here's your burger, Sly. Are you telling Lana about my adoption?" After waiting for his nod, Dani went on, "I'm so lucky to have Big Mama as my mom. Even if we *are* both hardheaded." She flashed a truly happy grin. "How about a piece of coconut cream pie, Lana?"

Lana was hungry now, and pie sounded good. But she didn't plan on sitting here long enough to eat it. "No, thanks. I'm leaving in a few minutes," she said. "We're talking about adoption because I'm planning to adopt."

"Is that why you were buying that pregnant teen brunch? I wondered. How exciting!"

"Cross your fingers. Sophie has a meeting with a married couple who also want her baby, and I'm worried she'll choose them."

"Because they're a couple and you're single?" When Lana nodded, Dani scoffed. "Big Mama was a single mom, and she did a super job raising me. Wish I had more time to talk, but as you can see, we're slammed. Sly will give you my number. Call me, and let's get together."

"That'd be great."

Dani smiled and left.

"I really like your sister," Lana said.

"She's good people." Sly took a bite of his burger.

His food smelled great. He caught her staring at his potato chips, which were homemade and out of this world. "Have one."

"I couldn't," Lana said. But she took one anyway. "I really should leave."

"I haven't had a chance to explain about the lawsuit. I get that you're upset about it, but I'd like a chance to give you my side."

Lana wanted to hear it, and Big Mama's chips were impossible to resist. As was Sly. And so she stayed.

Despite Lana's protests, Sly ordered more chips. He waited to discuss the lawsuit until Dani set a fresh plate on the table and left.

"I first met Tim Carpenter seven years ago, not long after the state reimbursed me for the small ranch I owned. They needed the property to put in a new freeway, and I needed a new ranch. Lucky for me, the Martinson place came on the market. It was bigger than the one I gave up, with a lot of potential. The Martinsons were about to go into foreclosure and asked a fair price, so I bought it."

"Then you've always been a rancher?"

Sly shook his head. "I never made a conscious decision to make ranching a career. When I was in college, I needed a job and found work at a ranch. Ranching is in my blood now, though, and I feel I was born to do it. After I bought the Martinson place, I learned that your cousin had figured on cutting a deal and buying the land dirt cheap. He wasn't happy that I offered the asking price."

"I remember hearing him talk about that at a Fourth of July family barbecue," Lana said.

Unable to imagine a worse man to spend a holiday with, Sly made a face. "That must've been a real fun get-together."

"Cousin Tim isn't the nicest guy, but at holiday gatherings he's usually in a pretty decent mood." Lana paused to munch a chip. She seemed to really like them. "I enjoy hanging out with family," she went on. "If I didn't, I wouldn't have dinner at my parents' house every Sunday. My sister and her husband and kids go, too. Sometimes my mom gets on my nerves—well, okay, a lot of the time—but the kids make it fun."

Sly wondered what it was like to be part of a family that got together for dinner once a week and attended big family barbecues. He had a few memories of his parents grilling, and friends and neighbors coming over for a meal. His family had lived in a pretty little house with a nice yard and a neighborhood filled with families just like theirs.

"The day I moved to Pettit Ranch, I made a point of going over to the Lazy C and meeting Tim," Sly said. "He was never what I'd call friendly, but we nodded when we saw each other. Then three months ago, I lost three cattle. Over the next few days, several more got sick, and two of my pregnant heifers miscarried. A cow will usually bear four to five calves over her lifetime, but those two will never be able to conceive again." The loss of ten calves meant a bundle of lost revenue.

"That's terrible." Lana grimaced. "My mom ran into Cousin Tim a few weeks ago and he mentioned that you'd lost some cattle, but he didn't share the details."

"It sucks, all right. My crew and I had no idea about

the poison at first. We tested for all the usual diseases, but the results were negative. The vet couldn't figure out what was wrong. He ordered autopsies. They showed that my animals had been poisoned."

Sly had entered Big Mama's a hungry man. His burger was delicious, but suddenly he couldn't eat another bite.

Lana wasn't going after the chips anymore, either. Her face had paled and she looked shocked. "I've never heard of anything like that before. It's horrific."

Sly agreed. He'd spent more than a few sleepless nights wondering what kind of person would poison an animal, and fearing that even more might sicken and die. The feeling of powerlessness had settled in his chest like a dark weight, just as it had after his father had passed, leaving him and his siblings alone.

"What makes you believe my cousin did it?" Lana asked.

"Long story short, there's a private service road along the north side of my ranch that runs between my land and Tim's. The only people with access to it are me and my crew, and Tim and his. Remember that freakish warm weather in January that melted all the snow? By sheer chance, my foreman was driving a truck of feed down that road and happened to notice a piece of a bag label and a small pile of white powder just inside the fence of one of our pastures. We weren't sure what it was and sent a sample of the powder to a lab. It turned out to be arsenic."

Every time Sly thought about it, a slow burn started in his blood. His fingers tightened into fists.

Lana stared at his hands with wide eyes. "I have no idea what to say."

With effort, he forced his fingers to relax. "Yeah, it's kind of a conversation stopper. Accidents happen, and at first I kept an open mind. You hit a bump, or drive over a pothole, and things can fall off a flatbed without the driver realizing. By some fluke, it could have landed inside the fence.

"None of my men had transported arsenic in their trucks. I decided to ask Tim about it. Hell, he might have had a legitimate reason for buying the stuff. I tried to talk to him twice, but he refused to even discuss the matter. He got downright belligerent, even aimed a gun at me. I figured bringing in someone else might *encourage* him to help clear up a few questions. So I hired an attorney."

Sly shook his head. "Fat lot of good that did. Tim was just as stubborn and closemouthed with him. He's been so ornery and nasty that I can't help but think that he deliberately put that arsenic on my land."

Lana frowned. "But why would he do that?"

Sly had given that a lot of thought. "I wish to hell I knew. To get back at me for buying the ranch? Or maybe because I'm turning a profit and he isn't."

"My cousin can be a real jerk, but I can't imagine him doing something like that."

"I'm sorry it had to be your cousin," Sly said, and he genuinely was.

Lana looked just as sorry. "My family sticks together through thick and thin. Once, when my mother's cousin Millie lost her job at a farm supply store due to cutbacks, the entire family bombarded the owner with calls and letters, asking that he reinstate her. He didn't have the resources to rehire her or any of the other people he laid off. Our family took out an ad in the paper, asking people in Prosperity to please patronize that store to increase business and help the laid-off employees get their jobs back. The ad generated a ton of new business, and eventually the owner was able to rehire cousin Millie and several other former employees."

Sly couldn't imagine having a family so tight. He envied Lana. "That's impressive."

She nodded. "What are you asking for in the lawsuit?"

"An apology and a reimbursement for what the poisoning cost me—thirty thousand dollars."

"That's a lot of money."

"Raising cattle is expensive. The feed, the vaccines and vitamins, the costs of maintaining all that fencing. Plus losing the unborn calves, as well as the future calves of the cows who died and the two who are now sterile—it adds up. The tests and autopsies alone cost me a small fortune. That money was earmarked for a new drainage system." Sly sipped his coffee, which had grown cold. "That's my story."

Lana dipped her head and smoothed her napkin so that her hair swung forward, hiding her expression. She was easy to read when Sly could see her face, and he wished she'd look up or say something more so that he'd have a clue what she was thinking.

Though he was sure it wasn't good.

He cleared his throat. "I should get back to the ranch, and you have things to do."

He left Dani a big tip, and walked out with Lana. As she moved toward her car, he touched her arm. "I haven't given you Dani's number. I'm sure she'll want yours, too."

Between the lawsuit and the baby she wanted to

adopt, exploring their attraction seemed impossible. But Sly lost himself in her beautiful eyes. "So would I," he added.

Lana hesitated, her expression regretful. "I want you to call me, Sly, but even if you do have a legitimate reason for suing my cousin, you aren't sure that he did it. I have to support my family. Goodbye."

She walked away.

Lana woke up Sunday morning thinking about Sly. After their conversation yesterday at Big Mama's, she liked him more than ever. But she was also convinced that they shouldn't see each other again.

As she sipped her morning coffee and read the Sunday paper, sleeting rain battered the windows. The weather was supposed to clear by noon, but the dark gloom suited her mood. This was a perfect day to stay home and work on the nursery. Because Sophie *had* to choose her.

If she didn't… Lana refused to let herself go down that path.

A few hours later, she stood in the nursery and admired the freshly painted walls. The soft yellow color made the formerly chocolate-brown room appear bigger and cheerier. It would look even better when she painted the children's mural next weekend.

After changing out of her paint clothes, Lana headed downstairs, flopped on the sofa and phoned Kate. "How was your blind date last night?" she asked when her friend picked up.

"As bad as I predicted. Henry had slippery hands and bad breath. He took me bowling. I have no problem with that, but on a first date? That's the last time

I let my mother set me up with anyone, ever. How was brunch with Sophie?"

"That didn't go so well, either." Lana filled her in. "Then Sly showed up."

"Oh?" Kate sounded intrigued.

"As it turns out, his sister is Big Mama's adopted daughter. Dani's great. You'd like her."

"I know Dani from when I eat there. She's a sweetheart. I even remember she had a brother, but I didn't realize he was Sly. Now, there's a guy I'd want someone fix me up with—if you hadn't snagged him first."

"Snagged him? You're funny. And now…" Lana blew out a heavy breath.

"That's some sigh. Tell me what happened."

"If you'll just be patient, I will."

"Okay, okay. Start from the beginning."

"Sophie was getting restless, but as soon as Sly sat down with us, she totally changed." One smile and she'd been as smitten as Lana. "He pretty much snowed her."

"Well, yeah. He's a gorgeous man. But get out! Sly sat at your table?"

"It was a booth, and he only joined us because all the other tables were taken."

"Really," Kate said in a tone that reminded Lana of a cooing dove. "And how did that go?"

"Pretty well. After Sophie left, we—"

"Sophie left? I thought she liked Sly."

"She did, but she had to get home."

"So she left and you and Sly stayed. In a nice, cozy booth. This is starting to head in the right direction. Go on."

Lana rolled her eyes. "We talked. I explained why I treated Sophie to breakfast. I also learned some interesting things about him." She filled in her friend about Sly's childhood and the lawsuit.

"You two sure made up for lost time in the talking department. I'll bet he finally asked for your number, huh?"

"He did, but I didn't give it to him."

"Are you nuts? Why the heck not?"

"Did you not listen to what I said? Sly is suing my cousin and I'm getting ready to adopt a baby. I can't get involved with him."

"That's just plain crazy. The adoption isn't for months yet, and you can't just stay home, twiddling your thumbs. As for your cousin, you can hardly stand him. The one time I met him, I didn't care much for him, either. If Tim did the crime, he *should* pay."

Lana sighed. "No one can be sure he poisoned those cows, Kate. Refusing to answer Sly's questions doesn't make him guilty."

"But he pointed a *gun* at Sly."

"Yes, but it doesn't prove anything. And don't forget my parents. I want to be able to bring whoever I'm dating to their house for Sunday dinner. If he happens to be suing a member of our family, it just won't work."

"I've met Sly, remember?" Kate said. "Besides being drop-dead gorgeous with a killer smile, he oozes charm. Lawsuit or not, once your parents meet him, they're bound to love him."

"If only it was that easy. Even if Sly charmed them to death, on principle alone they won't accept him."

"It'll be months before you're at the point where you want Sly to meet your parents—maybe long after the lawsuit gets settled," Kate said. "Heck, you two may never even get that far. But you owe it to yourself to find out."

That made sense. "When you put it that way… Now I wish I *had* given him my number."

Lana could picture her friend's big smile.

"Why don't you call him?" Kate suggested. "I'm sure his number's in the phone book."

"Only if he has a landline. I'm not going to do that."

"Then just show up at Big Mama's next Saturday. He'll probably be back. If that doesn't work, ask his sister for his number."

None of Kate's suggestions appealed to Lana. Besides, today she had other things on her mind. She checked her watch. "Sophie's meeting with that couple right now—the Andersons—but I refuse to let it bother me."

"That's the spirit."

"They're a married couple and I'm a single woman," Lana said, anxious despite her bravado. "Sophie said that didn't matter to her, but what if it does? What if she chooses them?"

"You'll drive yourself crazy worrying about that, Lana, so don't. It's obvious to me that you're interested in Sly. He seems interested in you, too, so why not encourage him? I'm not saying you should ask him out, but a phone call can't hurt."

"If I could say for sure that my cousin actually poisoned those cattle, I probably would call Sly. But I can't. My parents would flip out."

"I don't understand you, Lana. You're thirty-two years old. What do you care if they're upset?"

"You're not as close to your mom and dad as I am to mine," Lana explained. "When they're unhappy with me, they make my life miserable. Look at how they're responding to my wanting to adopt."

"Well, then, you'd better forget all about Sly Pettit."

"That's exactly what I'm going to do."

Chapter 6

Sly's truck was running on fumes when he pulled into the gas station Sunday afternoon. He wasn't the only driver in need of fuel, and the only available pump happened to be the one adjacent to where Tim Carpenter was about to fill his truck.

Talk about awkward. "Hey," Sly said with a terse nod.

Carpenter scowled at him. "Don't 'hey' me. You can sue me to hell and back, but it won't change the fact that I didn't do a damn thing to your cattle. I won't apologize for something I didn't do, and I'll die before you get a dime out of me. Stick *that* up your fancy lawyer's butt. Better yet, I'll let my lawyer do that."

His voice had grown steadily louder. People were staring now.

So Carpenter had hired himself an attorney. He

needed one. Sly raked his hand through his hair and strove for calmness, but he was seriously pissed. His neighbor's nastiness only made things worse. He shook his head. "Hasn't anyone ever told you that being an ass is a sure way to make your life miserable?"

"You're the ass." Carpenter's fist shot toward Sly's nose.

Sly dodged the punch and caught hold of the man's wrist. "I wouldn't try that again if I were you," he warned in a low voice.

Narrowing his eyes, Carpenter wrenched free and spat on the ground. "I'll get my gas someplace else."

He jumped into his truck and roared off.

Nearby, a man Sly didn't know shook his head. "He's got a temper on him, that one."

Gus Jones, a fellow rancher, left his Jeep at the pump and joined Sly. "Tim Carpenter has never been an easy man to deal with, but that was the worst I've ever seen him. You okay?"

Aside from his near miss with Carpenter's fist and a big adrenaline rush, Sly was fine. He nodded.

After filling the tank and paying, he left. When he got home, he was still so rattled that he jumped bare-back on Bee and gave her free rein. Before long they were flying across the ranch, with the wind at their backs and nothing to see but livestock and acres of his rolling fields. Eventually Sly calmed down.

That evening he called and updated Dave Swain. "After the rains we had last weekend, one of the lower pastures flooded," he explained. "I need the money Carpenter cost me for my new drainage system, and I need it now. I want you to add a penalty to the lawsuit, so that every day Carpenter delays the settlement, it costs him more."

"I wouldn't advise that," Dave said. "It'd be like rubbing salt into the wound, and could make things even worse."

Thinking it over, Sly had to agree. "Okay, so now what do we do?"

"Sit tight," Dave said, "and let us lawyers earn our fees."

Sly didn't enjoy playing this particular waiting game. Especially now, during the rainy season. Every day Carpenter delayed put the ranch in more jeopardy.

The rains were heavy over the next week, and Sly divided his long days between spring calving and digging new ditches. The old system worked only sporadically now. Though the ditches diverted some of the water and reduced the danger of flooding, copious amounts of mud clogged every low-lying pasture. Cattle got stuck in the stuff. Fortunately, as yet none had fallen or sustained injuries, but they had to be moved. Sly, Bean and Ollie had herded them to higher ground.

Between that and the usual ranching chores, they were all stretched thin. With so much on his plate, Sly barely had a moment to grab a decent meal, let alone think about Lana during the day. But at night when he should have been dead to the world, he lay in bed, wanting her. They were as mismatched as a flip-flop and a cowboy boot, and getting involved with her would only lead to trouble.

Regardless, his desire for her continued to grow, until he had to kiss her again or lose his mind. If he was lucky, he wouldn't enjoy the kiss half as much as he remembered. Then it would be easier to forget about her.

That Saturday he spent a wet morning checking for new calves and looking for signs of heifers in labor. Around noon, the rain stopped. Sly was about to head home and change into dry clothes when he came across a black heifer. She was in labor and lying on her side, pushing hard.

He stayed nearby, not too close, but within reach in case she needed help. Using his phone, he snapped a couple of photos. It was an easy birth, and mama cow did fine by herself. Finally, something to grin about.

"Way to go, you two," he said in a low voice that wouldn't startle them.

His first thought was that Lana would enjoy these photos. Covered in mud, he showered, changed, wolfed down a sandwich and then headed for her place.

She lived in a town-house community that was well maintained. Flower boxes underscored every window of her two-story place, just as they did at the day care.

Bushes lined both sides of her little yard, some already fat with buds on the verge of blooming. A pot of colorful tulips decorated the little stoop beside the door.

Sly pushed the doorbell. Seconds later, she answered. Wearing jeans and a ragged, paint-smeared sweatshirt, with her hair banana-clipped off her face and a smudge of paint on her cheek, she looked cute.

With that, Sly silently admitted that he was here for more than a few photos. He wanted to kiss Lana and find out if she was as sweet as he remembered.

"Sly," she said, her surprised expression almost comical. "What are you doing here?"

"I want to show you something."

"You obviously know where I live. I'm guessing you also have my number. You couldn't call and give me a heads-up that you were coming?"

He'd figured she'd tell him to stay away. "You asked me not to call," he said. "I thought I'd surprise you."

The couple next door, whom he judged to be about his age, stopped their yard work and stared openly at him.

Lana waved at them, then widened the door. "Come in."

After wiping his boots on a welcome mat that resembled a giant sunflower, Sly stepped into a house that felt warm and welcoming. More flowers filled a vase on the end table in the living room. She obviously had a thing for flowers—and bright colors. The whole place was painted in cheerful colors that couldn't help but lift the spirits.

"Nice place," he said.

"Thanks. I bought it after the divorce and have been fixing it up ever since. Do you want something to drink?"

"I'm fine." He shrugged out of his denim jacket and draped it over a nearby chair.

She angled her head slightly, her expression curious. "What did you want to show me?"

"This morning I came across a heifer giving birth and I snapped a few photos." He pulled out his phone and showed her pictures of the heifer licking her baby and nudging it to stand.

She studied each photo, her lips forming a provocative O that almost did Sly in. "Aww, so sweet."

"I figured you'd want to see them," he said, desire making his voice rough.

Oblivious of his need, she handed him back the phone. "You could have forwarded these to me and saved yourself the trip. You still should, so I can show the kids at the day care."

"I will. I didn't send them because there's another reason I stopped by." He slid the phone into his back pocket. "There's something I forgot to give you last Saturday."

She frowned. "Oh?"

Sly stepped closer and kissed her. For all of a blink she held herself stiff. Then she went up on her toes and wrapped her arms around his neck. She was fine boned and barely reached his shoulders. Yet as small and delicate as she was compared to his big frame, she fit as if she'd been made just for him.

He'd imagined he remembered how good she tasted, but he hadn't realized she tasted quite like this. Sweet and cinnamony and something indefinable. She was intoxicating, and he wanted to kiss her forever. And a lot more.

He urged her lips apart and tangled his tongue with hers. Lana made the sound he remembered from their night together, a mixture of a moan and a sigh that drove him wild.

She wriggled closer. God, he wanted her. Smart or dumb, right or wrong, he definitely wanted to keep doing this, keep seeing her. Sliding his hands down her spine, he cupped her hips, bringing her tight against the part of him that was already rigid with desire.

Suddenly she tensed and pushed her hands against his chest. "Stop, Sly."

Reluctantly, he stepped away.

"What was that for?" she asked, frowning but looking thoroughly kissed and sexy as all get-out.

"I've been wanting to do that since the afternoon at the day care." He ran his finger over her lush pink bottom lip, watching with satisfaction as her mouth opened a fraction and her eyes lost focus. "I'm glad I did."

Though she attempted to hold on to her stern expression, she didn't appear to be sorry, either.

"Dani says you two scheduled a get-together."

"That's right, in a few weeks."

Lana didn't invite him to sit down, and he guessed she was about to ask him to leave. "You probably heard what happened at the gas station last weekend," he said, wanting to talk about it before she kicked him out.

She shook her head. "No."

"Your cousin tried to punch me out."

Her eyebrows arched in surprise. "He didn't."

"Yep." Remembering, Sly scrubbed his hand over his face. "Our lawyers have been going back and forth." He hoped things got resolved and settled quickly, because he needed that money yesterday.

Not wanting to get into that, though, he sniffed the air. "I smell paint." He nodded at the smudge on her cheek. "That's a nice shade of green."

Lana touched the spot. Her cheeks reddened. "Why didn't you tell me there was paint on my face?"

"I had other things on my mind." His gaze dropped to her mouth, and damned if he didn't want to kiss her again.

Swallowing, she glanced away. "I've been working on the spare bedroom, making it into the nursery."

"Would you show it to me?" he asked.

"Sure. Follow me."

* * *

Lana sensed Sly checking her out as she led him upstairs. Her whole body hummed, but then, she'd been humming since he'd pulled her into his arms.

Oh, what a kiss. The man was an expert at kissing. He was also a skilled lover. But Lana wasn't going to think about that. At the top of the stairs, they started down the hall.

"It's bigger up here than it appears from outside," Sly said.

"That's one reason why I bought this place—there's so much space. There are two bedrooms up here and a small sunroom at the end of the hall that I use as a home office."

Sly nodded. "This must be your bedroom," he said as they passed the door.

"Yes." Amy and Sheila had commented that Sly always stayed the night at their places, never his. Was he imagining a night here with her? Her cheeks warmed, and she knew she was blushing. "This is the nursery."

Sly stepped into the room, his eyes on the ocean-themed mural she'd sketched out on the wall. "You never said you were a talented artist."

"I wouldn't exactly call myself talented," she said.

"You are, and this is pretty cool."

"Thanks." Lana admired her work, proud of the friendly sea creatures that were still only half-painted. "It's turning out really well. The other day I found some peel-off decals of whales and porpoises to put on the ceiling, over the crib."

"Cool idea. Whoever ends up here will be one lucky kid."

The words were a balm to Lana's heart. "I hope so.

I really want a child." Feeling suddenly vulnerable, she lowered her gaze to the carpet.

"What's wrong?" When she didn't reply, he tipped up her chin. "Lana?"

His eyes were filled with concern, and her anxieties poured out. "I wish I knew who Sophie was going to choose. I've been trying to get together with her again, but I haven't had any luck. We did talk once, but she prefers to text. She says she still hasn't decided between me and the Andersons."

Lana was scared to death about that. "Say a little prayer that she chooses me."

"Will do. Why don't you invite her over to show her what you're doing here? This nursery could tip the scales in your favor. Plus, she'd get a chance to check out the neighborhood and your house."

"That's not a bad idea."

"I understand how important this to you," Sly said. "Sophie said she wanted to see me again. If it helps, I'll come over when she's here."

"You'd do that for me?" Lana wanted to melt.

He actually blushed. Her heart expanded. She liked him a lot. Too much. "I'm not sure about that, Sly."

"Lana, Lana, what am I gonna do with you?"

He touched her cheek. Fighting the urge to sink against him, she ducked out of his reach. "We can't do this," she said.

"What's between you and me has nothing to do with my lawsuit."

"We both know that it does. But it's more than that. We don't want the same things." Except physically. Lana had never ached for a man the way she did for Sly.

As if he'd read her mind, he laughed softly. "Say

what you will. You can't fight chemistry like ours. Look, I'll give you my number. You call if you want me to be here when Sophie comes."

That sounded safe enough. "Okay," she said.

They headed downstairs. Sly jotted down his number and handed it to her. Then he grabbed his jacket and shrugged into it, his shoulders impossibly broad.

"I'll let myself out."

Before she had a chance to reply, he was gone.

Mondays were always hectic at the day care, but today had been crazy busy. Lana had scheduled meetings with four different sets of parents and their kids, all of whom were interested in the day care. If that wasn't enough, Brittany, the full-time employee, had called in sick, leaving Lana and Jasmine, her part-time assistant, to deal with the usual Monday chaos.

Naturally, this was the day the guinea pig escaped. Jayden, a rambunctious four-year-old, had been so intent on catching the frightened animal that he'd wet his pants. And he didn't have a change of clothes. Then Valerie, almost four, had vomited all over herself, which had upset all the kids.

Lana couldn't ever remember being this tired. All she wanted was to go home, put up her feet and relax. Unfortunately, she'd worked on the nursery over the weekend instead of picking up any groceries. It was either live on fast food, which wasn't a bad idea once or twice but not for the entire week, buy groceries or starve. That was how she ended up pushing a cart through Sterling Foods during the dinner hour.

To Lana's surprise, for once the busy grocery store was quiet. With any luck, she'd zip in and zip out, and be home in no time. Eager to get the job done, she wheeled her cart toward the produce at warp speed.

Until she rounded the corner and spotted Sly. Abruptly she stopped. He was loading a huge sack of potatoes into his cart. A clean denim shirt hugged his broad shoulders, faded jeans showcased his long, powerful legs, and those cowboy boots… He looked good. Really good.

Two days ago, he'd kissed her senseless. The sight of him now brought it all back—the feel of his strong arms around her, his solid chest against her breasts, his warm, soft mouth on hers….

Her lips tingled and every nerve in her body began to hum. She was about to move away and find a different aisle when Sly spotted her. A slow smile spread across his face. Her heart tumbled over in her chest.

"Sly…hi." Mustering a smile, she wheeled slowly toward him.

"I was just thinking about you," he said.

He was? "I didn't expect to find you here," Lana said. "I mean, it's the dinner hour, and isn't this a superbusy time of year for ranchers?"

"You wouldn't believe how busy. But my housekeeper's husband sprained his back yesterday, and she's taking a few days off to take care of him. Monday happens to be her grocery day, and a man's got to eat, so here I am." He spread his hands. "She made a list of what to buy—a long list. I didn't have a chance to shop until now."

"I'm usually here on Saturdays," Lana said. "But you know how I spent that."

"I sure do." He was close enough that she could see the silver flecks in his eyes aglow with heat.

Her whole body grew warm. She cleared her throat. "I was talking about the mural. I worked on it Saturday night and all day Sunday until I left for dinner at my parents'."

"Did you finish it?"

"There are a few little touch-ups left, but it's basically done." She was pleased with the results. "I'm going to call Sophie tonight and invite her over."

"Excellent plan. Call if you need me."

Sly tucked a lock of hair behind her ear, as if it was the most natural thing in the world. As if they were together. The humming in Lana's body increased.

She barely registered his words. She was too lost in his heated gaze, the familiar scent of his spicy aftershave, the warm caress of his fingers.

His eyelids dropped to half-mast and she thought he was going to kiss her. *Yes!*

Her body screamed for her to step into his arms. But voices warned her that a mother and a young child were approaching.

Stepping away from Sly, she snatched a head of lettuce from a nearby display. "I'll, uh, keep you posted," she said as she pivoted the cart and hurried away.

Chapter 7

"I keep running into your brother," Lana told Dani on Wednesday night. They were sitting at Coffee, Tea + Treats in the heart of downtown, sipping tea and eating pie.

She'd seen him Monday at the grocery, and again yesterday at the post office. Lana had been on her way inside to mail brochures to the parents of several prospective preschoolers. Sly had been on his way out. He'd lingered to chat and tempt her with his smoldering eyes yet again.

"That's interesting," Dani said. "I met my brother for dinner last night, and the sly dog never said a word about it."

"There isn't much to say, except that it's weird that we ran into each other twice in two days. I accused him of stalking me, and he said that he wondered if *I* was stalking *him*."

Lana laughed, but there was nothing funny about her feelings. Each time she saw Sly, the heat simmering between them seemed to grow more intense. Even talking about him made her feel restless. She shifted in her chair.

Dani frowned. "You're fidgety tonight."

"Am I?" Lana forced herself to sit still.

"Prosperity isn't a small town, but sometimes it feels that way," Dani said after pausing to eat her pie. "I run into people I know all the time. What if you and Sly have been doing that for years, but didn't realize because you hadn't met each other yet?"

"It's possible," Lana mused. But Sly was so attractive that she was sure she'd have remembered him. "Let's change the subject. Would you mind if I asked you a few questions about adoption? From the adoptee's point of view."

"Not at all. What do you want to know?"

"What was it like for you to be adopted?"

Deep in thought, Dani was silent a moment. "Losing our mom and then our father when I was so little was rough. I was the baby and the only girl, and my parents and my brothers spoiled me rotten. Then suddenly everyone I loved was gone. I hated being separated from my brothers, but as minors, none of us had a say in what happened. I was so happy when Sly and Seth returned home to find me."

"But Seth left again when he was seventeen, right?"

Suddenly somber, Dani nodded. "He dropped out of high school, jotted a goodbye note and just took off."

For a moment, she stared into space at something

only she could see. "Neither Sly nor I has heard from him in ages, but not for lack of trying. The postcard came from California, but we never knew exactly where. He could be anyplace." Her shoulders slumped and she let out a heavy sigh. "Seth has washed his hands of both of us, and I'm not even sure why."

Lana couldn't imagine having a sibling who refused to stay in touch. "That must be hard for you."

Dani nodded. "I try not to think about it." She fiddled with her fork. "Back to the adoption. I was six when I went into foster care. It was a relief to have a place to go. Big Mama was a good foster mom, but what I really wanted was a real mother. It turned out she'd always wanted a daughter, so ours was a match made in heaven. By the time I was eight, I had my 'real' mother." No traces of solemnity now. "Not that it's always been roses. Big Mama likes to do things her way, and I prefer my own way. We butt heads a lot, but I know she loves me. And I adore her."

Lana's heart ached with the need to share the same deep love with her own child. "Did Sly mention that I'm converting my guest bedroom into a nursery?" The night before, she'd put the final touches on the mural. "Now all I'm waiting for is the crib and changing table to arrive. Once I put them together, I'll be ready for a baby."

"That sounds exciting."

"It is. Thanks for not lecturing me about jumping the gun and spending all my spare time and some of my savings when I'm not even sure I'll get this baby."

"Who would put you on such a downer?" Dani asked.

"My mother. She's against what I'm doing. Not adoption per se, but adopting as a single mom. She believes running my own business takes up way too much time for me to raise a child, especially when I'm on my own."

"Hey, if Big Mama raised me and managed her restaurant successfully, I don't see why you can't do the same thing."

"Exactly. I painted a mural on the wall, and it turned out well. I'm hoping that if Sophie comes over I can impress her with it. I so want her to pick me to adopt her baby."

"Inviting her over—that's a great idea."

Lana nodded. "Credit Sly for that. After he saw the mural I was painting, he—"

"Hold on. My brother has been to your *house?*"

"Last Saturday, and he didn't stay long."

Just long enough to make her head spin.

Dani's eyebrows lifted. "It's not like him to just drop by without calling first. What's wrong with that man?"

"I asked him not to call, and I guess he listened." Lana could count on one hand the number of men who'd really listened to her in her life. Her father, the minister when she'd needed counseling after Brent had left, a single dad or two at the day care who asked for advice about their kids. And Sly.

The more time she spent with him, the luckier she counted herself. He was considerate and warm, he listened and he kissed like a dream. She was sorry the lawsuit prevented her from getting to know him better.

"That day at Big Mama's, he really impressed Sophie," she said. "When she mentioned something about wanting to see him again, he offered to come over if—no, *when*—she visits."

"Sly did that? He's superbusy at the ranch right now,

so that's pretty amazing. Have I mentioned what a great guy my brother is?"

"Oh, once or twice." Lana laughed.

But Dani wasn't smiling, she was dead serious. "Are you interested in him?"

"After my divorce, I'm still a little gun-shy. Besides, right now, I'm focusing on the adoption."

"So? Sophie isn't due for months yet and you can't just sit around, waiting. Occasionally, you have to go out and have a little fun. Sly is fun. But you danced with him, so you're already aware of that."

He was more than fun, a lot more. But Lana wasn't going to share that with his sister. "He has a bit of a reputation."

"You've heard about that, have you?" Dani wrinkled her nose. "It's true, my brother used to be quite the ladies' man. Not so much anymore."

"Did he have a bad breakup?" Lana asked. Sly hadn't brought up any past romances, but then, she'd never asked.

"Is a breakup ever good? Mine never are. Years ago, Sly had a serious girlfriend, and last year he dated someone for a while. But as always, things didn't work out." Dani shrugged. "As the queen breaker-upper and breakup-ee, I understand the process only too well. But eventually you have to move on. I mean, I always do."

She sounded just like Kate. "Sometimes healing the heart takes a while," Lana said. "It did for me."

"I'm sure Sly isn't carrying a torch for any of his exes. But he hasn't dated much since his last breakup. That's why, when he mentioned you, I got excited. Now that I know you, I'm doubly thrilled."

"I think you're great, too," Lana said. "But don't

expect anything to happen with Sly and me. Besides the adoption and his reputation, he's suing my cousin."

"There is that. But the lawsuit is tearing him up. Sly has never sued anyone before. He wouldn't be doing it now unless he had to. When I heard what happened at the gas station last week…"

"It sounded horrible." Lana closed her eyes a moment and shook her head.

Her cousin claimed that Sly had provoked him, but several bystanders corroborated Sly's version of the incident. If only the two men would settle their differences…

Glum, she rested her chin heavily on her fist. "I'm not sure what to think about any of it. I wish just they'd sit down and work things out."

Then, if she wanted to date Sly—and despite all the reasons why that wasn't a good idea, she did—she could do so without feeling as if she were betraying her family. She'd also have to somehow make sure that dating him wouldn't impact any possible adoptions. Of course, if Sophie chose her, Sly would pose no problem. But the jury was still out on that.

"They could definitely work it out if your cousin would pay up and apologize."

"But what if he isn't responsible for what happened?" Lana asked.

"Then… I have no idea." Dani tightened her ponytail. "Trust me, Sly has tried to talk with him several times. The way he's acted makes him look guilty."

"Cousin Tim can be a real jerk, all right," Lana agreed. "But he's family, and I have to support him."

Her parents ought to give her decision to adopt the

same unflagging support, she thought. Next time they gave her grief, she'd point that out to them.

"I guess so, but it makes me sad. Maybe this poisoned-cattle thing will sort itself out. I hope so, because you and Sly would make a great couple. If you give this thing between you a chance, you might even have a shot together. Promise me you won't write him off."

"I promise," Lana said, wondering at herself. For so many reasons, she and Sly were wrong for each other. Weren't they?

But her promise was enough to make Dani's face brighten. "Regardless of what happens between you and my brother, we can still be friends, right?"

Lana smiled. "Absolutely. What about you, Dani? Are you dating anyone?"

"A guy named Paul, but it's not serious. He's not exactly the man of my dreams, but he's cute and sexy. Unfortunately, he has a bad habit of not showing up when he says he will, and he's canceled dates at the last minute." Dani sighed. "But I like him, so I put up with it. Sly says I have rotten taste in men. He's right, but I can't help who I'm attracted to."

Just as Lana couldn't help being attracted to Sly. "I understand," she said. "By the way, my best friend, Kate Adams, says she knows you."

"Kate's great! She comes into Big Mama's now and again. Tell her I say hi." Dani glanced at her watch. "Whoa, it's almost nine. I'm due at Big Mama's at five tomorrow morning, so I'd best go home and get some sleep."

"Ugh, that's early."

"We open at six, and someone has to be there. Heck, I'm used to it. And don't forget, we close at four. That means I'm usually out of there by five-thirty, which frees up my whole evening."

Before they parted, they shared a warm hug.

"Let's get together again soon," Lana's new friend said. "Maybe Kate will join us."

Lana smiled. "It's a date."

After a day that had started at dawn and finished some twelve hours later, Sly sprawled gratefully on his La-Z-Boy, relieved for some R & R at last. The only things he was good for tonight were sipping a cool one and watching a basketball game. Halfway through the first quarter and his beer, his eyelids dropped shut. He was heading off to la-la land when the trill of his cell phone jerked him awake. Ace and the rest of the crew would call if anything went wrong, but right now, an emergency was the last thing Sly wanted to deal with. Grumbling, he slid the phone from his hip pocket.

Lana Carpenter, the screen said. His sister had programmed her number into his phone. Well, well. Suddenly wide-awake, he muted the TV and answered, "Hey."

"Hi." She sounded a little breathy and unsure of herself. "Am I calling too late?"

He wasn't about to explain that he'd dozed off. "Nope, I'm sitting here, relaxing." He was also alert now—every part of him. "You must have talked to Sophie," he said.

"We just hung up, and guess what? She's coming over to see the nursery on Saturday!" She made a *squee* sound.

Sly imagined the sparkle in her green eyes and the

excited flush on her cheeks. "That's great," he said with a grin.

"Isn't it? And she does want you to be there, if you wouldn't mind." She rushed on. "Coincidentally, the furniture store in the mall called this afternoon. The rocking chair, baby lamp, crib and changing table I ordered will be delivered to me tomorrow. I'll have to assemble the crib and changing table, but I can take care of that tomorrow night. When Sophie arrives, the nursery will be perfect."

"Putting furniture together can be tricky. If you need help, I'm your man."

Her man? Had he really just said that? Then again, it was just a figure of speech.

"Thanks, but I'll have the whole evening to tackle the job. It'll be fun."

Some women would jump all over his offer. Not Lana. She was every bit as independent as Dani. Sly admired that. He liked Lana, a lot. Only the more reason to stay away.

"What time should I be there on Saturday, then?" he asked, half regretting his offer to come over. Their kisses the other day had only strengthened his feelings for her. They scared him. It was safer to steer clear of her.

"Shoot, I just realized that I offered to feed Sophie lunch," she mumbled as if to herself. "I'll have to run to the grocery on my way home from work tomorrow night. You're invited to eat with us—if it's possible for you to leave the ranch in the middle of your Saturday."

Her tone had grown muted, as if she expected him to back out. This Saturday happened to be his day to work, but he wasn't about to renege. And not only because he was a man who kept his word.

Lana needed him, and he wasn't about to let her down. He would talk with Ace tomorrow. Knowing the foremen, Ace wouldn't mind if they traded Saturdays.

"I'll make time," he said. "Barring emergencies, I'll stay for as long as you need me." But he'd keep his distance from Lana, and when Sophie left, he'd go, too. That would work.

"Can you come a little before noon?"

Sly nodded, but Lana couldn't see him. "I'll be there."

Chapter 8

Sophie's text came in just after eight o'clock Friday night. Have 2 postpone 1 week. K?

Lana glanced at the parts of the crib scattered across the rug—screws and springs and things she had no idea what to do with. She'd been struggling to make sense of it all for what seemed like hours and wanted to cry. What kind of idiots had written these stupid assembly directions anyway?

Suddenly she *was* crying. Over impossible instructions and a silly one-week delay. Lately she'd been so emotional, a combination of nerves and PMS.

Sniffling, she replied to Sophie's text. Okay. See you a week from tomorrow at my house.

4 sure, Sophie responded.

Lana needed a break and a glass of wine. No, not wine. Since her big hangover the night she'd met Sly, she'd lost her taste for alcohol. Hot chocolate, then, because she wanted something warm, sweet and comforting. But hot chocolate reminded her of the day she and Sophie had each ordered a mug at Big Mama's. A day that had not gone especially well.

Great, now she was crying again.

Clutching her cell phone, Lana left the mess in the nursery and headed for her bedroom. She flopped on the bed. She wasn't in the best shape to make a call right now, but she had to talk to someone. Kate was going out with friends tonight, but it was early yet. Maybe she was still at home, getting ready. When her friend's voice mail clicked on, Lana disconnected.

Her next thought was to call Sly. He should know about the change in plans. She'd keep the call short, then hang up. His phone rang four times, and Lana guessed that he was probably out, too. Maybe on a date.

Her disappointment was almost as keen as it had been when she'd read Sophie's text. Lana didn't understand herself at all. Just because she was stuck at home didn't mean Sly should be. The man had a right to go out. She was gearing herself up to leave a cheerful-sounding voice message when he picked up.

"Hey, Lana," he said. His low, intimate tone vibrated through her.

Her heart let out a sigh of relief, and suddenly she felt much better. She sat up and propped herself up against the pillows and the headboard. "Hi. How are you?"

"Not bad. This has been a day and a half crammed into about nine hours. I spent most of it separating the yearling heifers from the rest of the herd and inoculating them with hormones to more or less synchronize their heat cycles."

"Why in the world would you do that?"

"So that we can artificially inseminate all of them at once—if they all synchronize, that is. It takes longer for some heifers to reach that point of their cycle."

"That sounds…interesting."

"Trust me, it sounds better than it is."

Hearing Sly's deep chuckle, Lana couldn't help but smile.

"Did you get the crib and stuff put together?" he asked.

Her smile faded. "No. It's a lot harder than I thought." Darn it, the tears were back, blurring her vision and clogging her throat. "Sophie postponed until next week," she said, her voice thick with disappointment.

"You're crying."

"No, I'm not," she said, an involuntary sob escaping. "I'm just so frustrated!"

"Because Sophie changed her plans or because you're having trouble with the furniture?"

"Both!"

Sly was quiet a moment. "She said she'll be over next Saturday, so what's the problem? You worry too much."

He was right. Lana blew her nose.

"In a way, this is good news," he added. "Now you have more time to put the furniture together and get ready for her visit."

"That's true. Thanks for putting a positive spin on this. I feel silly for crying."

"Dani does it, too, once in a while. It's a girl thing."

Lana snorted. "Guys cry, too."

"Nah, we go out and chop wood or run after stray cattle. You'd be surprised how chasing a cow into a glen and out again makes a man forget his problems. Especially when the unexpected happens. Just this morning, Ollie, a kid who works for me, helped me with a renegade heifer. On my way down the glen, I slipped on a fresh cow patty and landed on my as—butt. Ollie almost wet himself, he laughed so hard."

Picturing that, Lana laughed, too.

"And here I'd hoped you'd feel my pain."

That was even funnier. "Thanks, Sly."

"For what?"

"Making me laugh."

She could almost feel his warm smile through the phone.

"Hey, why don't I come over tonight and help you with the furniture?" he said.

It was pathetic how badly she wanted his company. She bit her lip. "I don't want to ruin your Friday-night plans. In case you're going out."

"I don't have any plans. I'll be over in half an hour."

While Lana waited for Sly, she washed her face, fixed her hair and makeup and exchanged her sweats for a blouse and jeans. She even brushed her teeth.

"Why am I doing this?" she asked her reflection. Of course, it didn't answer.

She was making popcorn when Sly knocked on the door. He wiped his feet and entered her house. He wore a pressed shirt and jeans. His short hair was damp, and he smelled fresh and clean, as if he'd showered before coming over.

They were both dressed as if this were a date. It wasn't. Lana couldn't date a man who didn't want kids and who was suing her cousin. Sly was here to help with the furniture, that was all.

If only she could stop the flutter of excitement in her stomach.

"Thanks for coming over," she said. "I really appreciate it."

"No problem." He sniffed the air. "Do I smell popcorn?"

She nodded. "I figured I should at least feed you something while we work. Would you like a beer to go with it?"

"How did you guess?" Sly said on the way to the kitchen.

He'd only been here once, and already he seemed comfortable in her house. Lana pulled a cold beer from the refrigerator. "My dad always says that popcorn and cold beer go together as well as shoes go with socks."

"Smart man."

"He is. You'd like him." He would probably like Sly, too, but thanks to the lawsuit, they would undoubtedly never meet.

She handed Sly the bottle opener and reached in the cabinet for a glass.

"Don't bother. I prefer it straight from the bottle." He frowned. "You're not joining me?"

Lana shook her head. "I haven't had alcohol since the night we, um, met. Just haven't wanted it. That hangover did me in. Tonight I'm a soda girl, and I prefer mine in a glass. I'll bring the popcorn and some hand wipes if you'll grab the drinks."

They headed up the stairs.

In the nursery, Sly set the drinks on the dresser, the only piece of furniture besides the rocking chair and lamp that didn't require assembly. He took in the mess on the floor. "You've been hard at it."

"Without much success, as you'll notice. The directions may as well be written in Chinese. They're impossible to understand."

"Those things usually are pretty useless." Sly's mouth quirked. "I study the picture, and then figure it out."

"I'm not mechanically minded. I never have been, and I hate that."

"You can't be good at everything. You're an artist and you sure are great with kids."

"How would you know? You've never seen me with kids."

"I just do. And I read that article."

After shoving a handful of popcorn into his mouth, he hunkered down and set to work. He rolled up his sleeves to the middle of his forearms. Lana couldn't help noting his thick wrists and hands.

The nails were short and clean, and his fingers and palms were calloused and scarred from ranch work. Strong, competent hands that could also be gentle and bring such pleasure....

She went warm all over before she firmly pushed her desire away and joined him on the floor. "What can I do?"

"For starters, hand me that small, open-ended wrench."

With Sly seeming to understand what went where and in what order, the job wasn't nearly as intimidating.

An hour later the drinks and popcorn were gone, and the crib and changing table were in their places near the mural.

"You saved me hours of bashing my head against

the wall," Lana said. "Now all that's left is sewing the curtains, hanging a few pictures and making up the crib."

"This room is welcoming and friendly. Hell, so is your whole house. If I were a kid, I'd sure want to live here."

Lana soaked up the compliment like a dry sponge in warm water. "I just hope Sophie shares your view."

"It's a sure bet she will."

"But is this enough for her to select me as the mom for her baby?" Lana couldn't even fake a cheerful smile.

"You look like you could use a hug."

Sly opened his arms. As soon as she walked into his embrace, he pulled her close, wrapping her in his warmth.

Lana couldn't imagine a place she'd rather be. Her worries melted away, and she was glad she'd promised Dani she wouldn't write off Sly. She could get used to this. He'd been so supportive of her problems with Sophie and her longing to adopt. Maybe she'd misunderstood him. Maybe he wanted kids after all.

They could talk about that later. With a sigh, she snuggled closer. "You give great hugs."

He made a sound of pure male pleasure. "You're easy to hug."

For a few delicious moments neither of them moved. Lana's heart pounded. Sly shifted closer and her whole body began to hum.

He tipped up her chin with his big, warm hand. "Hey, Lana?"

"What?"

His thumb traced her bottom lip. The silver flecks

in his eyes seemed to recede, making his eyes bluer and darker.

"This." He kissed her.

Forgetting that he'd vowed to keep his distance from Lana and half waiting for her to stop him, Sly brushed his mouth lightly against hers. She surprised him by wrapping her arms around his neck and pulling him in for a deeper kiss. One kiss became another, and another. She tasted of popcorn and soda and woman.

That was his last coherent thought. Already hard, he sank to the carpet and brought her with him onto his lap. Her soft behind pressed against his erection. She wriggled closer—heaven and hell. On the verge of losing control, he gripped her hips and forced her to be still. "Easy," he said.

She nipped his lower lip, licked it and shimmied her tongue around his mouth. His tenuous grasp on self-control frayed and snapped.

Keeping his mouth fused with hers, Sly undid the tiny buttons on her blouse, almost ripping them off in his haste.

Lana was making the impatient noises he remembered from their night together, little breathy sounds, urging him to hurry. She was driving him wild.

Finally she pushed his hands away and finished the job herself. Her blouse fell open. Her gaze locked on Sly as she slipped out of it.

With hands that trembled, he traced the pink lace edging her bra. Her nipples stiffened, and he hadn't even touched her breasts yet. She was so responsive, the most passionate woman he'd ever met. He slid his fingers inside her cups. Her skin was soft and warm and she smelled sweet and tempting, a mixture of gardenia perfume and her own woman scent. His fingers slid to her nipples.

She inhaled sharply. It wasn't an aroused sound, but a painful gasp.

Sly pulled his hands away. "I'm hurting you."

She shook her head. "My breasts are a little tender, but they get this way before my period."

"Should I stop?"

Instead of answering, she shook her head again, silently covered his hands with hers and guided them to where they'd been.

With a groan, he kissed her again and again, until he was desperate to touch her.

Mindful of her sensitivity, he slowly and lightly drew his finger across her nipples. "Is this okay?"

"Very okay." Her head lolled to the side and her eyes closed.

He unfastened the bra and removed it. Her breasts were full and heavy and her skin was flushed with arousal.

"I want you," he said, yanking at the buttons on his own shirt. He shed it and gently pushed Lana onto the rug on her back. Half lying on top of her, he ran his tongue over one nipple, then the other, until she was writhing and moaning with desire.

Eager to heighten the pleasure, he slid his hand down her smooth stomach toward the button on her jeans.

Suddenly she tensed and pulled her mouth from his. "*Now* I want you to stop."

What the…? Confused and breathing hard, he sat up. Lana joined him, modestly crossing her arms over the breasts he'd just caressed and loved with his mouth.

When seconds ago, she'd acted as if she couldn't get enough and desperately wanted more.

Giving his head a mental shake, Sly retrieved her blouse and bra and handed them to her. "What just happened here?"

Ignoring the bra, Lana put on her shirt and buttoned it. It wasn't see-through, but knowing she was braless under there wasn't helping him calm down.

"What we were doing—it isn't what I want," she said.

"Could have fooled me." He picked up his shirt and shrugged into it.

"It wasn't my intention to be a tease, Sly, but when I'm with you…" She glanced down to button her blouse. "I can't help myself."

Now he was doubly confused. "We're attracted to each other and we've already proved how great we are together. What's wrong with enjoying that?"

"As I explained before, I'm not wired for a sex-only thing, Sly. First, I need a deeper relationship."

There it was, the R word, his signal to cut and run.

"So where do we go from here?" he said, surprising himself. He sure as hell wasn't ready to get serious or make any kind of commitment to Lana.

"I'd be more comfortable talking about this in the kitchen."

"Fine by me." He could use a moment to pull himself together.

Trying to ignore the bra that lay on the floor, he set his empty bottle and Lana's glass in the popcorn bowl and followed her down the stairs.

Chapter 9

Lana's kitchen was about a third the size of Sly's, but homey. He especially liked the breakfast nook that faced the little backyard. The colorful curtains currently drawn against the night gave the space a cozy feel.

"Do you want another beer?" she asked.

"Sure. I'll help myself. How about you—can I get you a fresh soda?"

"You gave up your Friday night to help me out—I'll get you a beer. Please, sit." She gestured toward the nook. "I'm going to switch to herbal tea."

Sipping his beer, he watched her gather the tea fixings. She was facing the stove with her back to him, and he took advantage of the opportunity to look his fill.

Her hair, which hung almost to her shoulders, was every which way, as if she'd just had sex. Her blouse didn't cover her hips or the sweet curve of her behind.

When she pivoted around to fill a mug with steaming water, he noticed the points of her nipples poking the blouse.

Sly swallowed hard. *Hard* being the operative word. He wanted Lana more than he'd ever desired a woman. He fantasized about making love with her constantly, and it was killing him. It must be lust that had him sitting at her table, because he sure as hell didn't want a real relationship with her.

At last she brought her tea to the nook and sat down across from him. "Now I'm ready," she said.

Sly sucked in a breath and braced for the dreaded talk.

"I think we should get to know each other without having sex," Lana said.

She meant dating. He could do that and had, lots of times. No big. He let his breath out. "So you're okay about dating now? You said we couldn't because of the situation with your cousin."

"I don't want to discuss him right now." Eyes closed, she rubbed the space between her brows as if the subject gave her a headache.

"You don't like him much, do you?" She didn't reply, and he went on, "It's not as if we're talking anything serious, Lana. It's just dating."

"Are you kidding? If I started going out with you, even casually, my parents would freak out."

Now they were getting somewhere. "Dating isn't necessarily long-term, and it sure doesn't mean getting serious," he repeated.

"All the same, they'd freak out."

"You're scared of them," he suggested, marveling that a grown woman would feel like that.

"That's not it at all. We're a close-knit family. It's easier if we get along."

"Yeah, but that doesn't explain why you're afraid of them."

"I'm not!" Her chin tilted up defensively. "You don't understand what it's like. Let me give you an example. It's been weeks since I told them about my plans to adopt. My mom keeps pressuring me not to do it. She's driving me crazy."

"Tell her to stop."

Lana rolled her eyes. "Like that'd work."

Now he understood. "You're saying that if we're seeing each other, even casually, your mom and dad will give you grief."

"Big-time, and we both know why."

And they were back to the lawsuit. Sly took a long pull of his beer and Lana sipped her tea, the silence between them heavy. They seemed to be circling each other like wagons around a roaring fire.

Returning to a life without Lana was probably for the best, and using her family as a reason to forget each other provided a way out of what could easily become something with strings attached. Sly didn't want strings, but he wasn't ready to let go, either. She was the first woman who hadn't tried to change him, she'd only tried to understand him.

"We don't have to date to get to know one another," Lana said.

Totally confused now, he eyed her warily. "How do we do 'get to know each other' if we don't go out?"

"Hmm."

As she considered the question, the tip of her tongue

poked out of the corner of her mouth, which was both tempting and cute.

"We could get together as friends," she finally said.

"Friends," he repeated. Dani had a friend like that, a rancher named Nick Kelly she often hung out with. Nick was an okay guy. Their relationship was platonic. As far as Sly was aware, they'd never even kissed each other. He couldn't ever imagine a platonic relationship with Lana.

"There's too much heat between us to settle for friendship."

To make the point, he leaned across the table and ran the pad of his thumb across her cheek. Instantly her eyes softened and those tempting lips parted a fraction. Sly drew away and dropped his hand. "With one little touch, I just proved that."

"Back to the drawing board." Lana let out a frustrated sigh. "Above all else, I want a child. I hope and pray that Sophie chooses me to adopt her baby. Even if she doesn't…" For a moment Lana's face clouded. "If she doesn't, then I'll keep trying until I finally have the baby I long for.

"I want you to be honest with me, Sly." She pinned him with her big green eyes. "Do you want a relationship with me?"

He wasn't about to lie. "I'm not great at relationships—not the long-term kind," he said. "The truth is, I pretty much suck at them—just ask my last girlfriend."

"I heard plenty from Amy Watkins and Sheila Sommers."

"You talked to Sheila, as well?" He winced.

Lana nodded. "Her son is also enrolled at the day care."

God only knew what the two women had said about him. "Then you get how bad I am at serious relationship stuff." He shook his head. "Why can't we just explore whatever this thing is between us and let whatever happens happen?"

She looked at him funny. "That's exactly what two people do when they have a relationship."

"See, I call that 'casual dating.' The R word sounds way too serious."

"I'm not asking you to fall in love with me, Sly. I'm thinking ahead, to when I adopt."

That could be a long way off yet. By the time it happened, they might not even be interested in each other anymore. "A baby's a big deal," he said cautiously.

"Huge."

"Having a child will change a lot of things in your life."

"In ways I can't even imagine, though believe me, I dream about it constantly." Lana smiled to herself as if she couldn't wait. Then she sobered. "You and I talked about kids once before, and you said you don't want any of your own. But putting the lawsuit aside, can you picture yourself in a stable relationship with me and my child?"

As badly as Sly wanted Lana, getting tangled up with her and her adopted baby scared him. "No," he said.

"That's a deal breaker." She let out a sad sigh. "I guess we won't be seeing each other anymore."

As bad as Sly felt, he had to agree. The thing was, she really wanted the arrangement with Sophie to work, and he wanted that for her. "I'll still come over and help with Sophie next Saturday," he offered.

"I'd appreciate that. I'll make lunch for the three of us."

Sly nodded. "I'll call you next week to confirm the time."

"Okay." She stood up, signaling that the evening had come to an end.

At her door, Sly lingered on the threshold. He started to reach for her, but he'd forfeited the chance to kiss her.

Tipping an imaginary hat, he walked out.

"I can't make it to dinner tonight," Lana told her mother on the phone Sunday. It was almost noon and she was still in bed. "I have the flu."

"You poor thing. Are you throwing up?"

"Twice so far." First at dawn, when nausea had awakened her. She'd barely made it to the bathroom. It had happened again several hours later. She was still weak and nauseous.

"Have you eaten or drunk anything?"

"I'm afraid to."

"You don't want to get dehydrated. Try ginger ale or cola, something easy on the digestive system. If that stays down, nibble a soda cracker and see how that goes."

"Thanks, Mom. I will." If she could just get out of bed without heaving. "There's a flu bug going around the day care. I must've caught it from the kids."

She hoped Sly didn't get it. After those melting kisses… But Lana wasn't about to spend any time dreaming about that. Except for Sophie's upcoming visit, she and Sly weren't going to see each other again.

Which was for the best, but depressing all the same. She'd miss him.

"It isn't the first time," her mother said. Lana had to stop and remember what they were talking about. "Those children bring in all kinds of diseases."

Ah, they'd been talking about getting the flu from her day-care kids.

"Why don't I make you a batch of that chicken vegetable soup you love and bring it over?" her mother went on. "For later, when your stomach settles."

This was her mother at her best—jumping in to help a family member in need. Why couldn't she be this caring and supportive all the time?

As appreciative as Lana was of her mother's solicitude, right now she couldn't even contemplate food, let alone entertain. "That's sweet, Mom, but you really shouldn't. I'll be terrible company, and I don't want you to catch this nasty bug."

"I won't stay long. I'll just pop in, say a quick 'hi' and set the soup and a couple bottles of cola in the fridge for you. They'll keep you hydrated."

"Thanks, Mom." Lana yawned. "I'm going back to sleep now, so that I can get over this thing by tomorrow."

"It wouldn't hurt you to call in sick once in a while. You have two very capable assistants who I'm sure could run the day care just fine without you."

"Jasmine and Brittany are great, but I love going to work."

"Stubborn as always," her mother said. "I'll be over in an hour or so, honey."

Monday morning, Lana was still queasy, but not sick enough to stay home. She was standing in front of a cupboard at Tender Loving Daycare, choosing supplies for the Monday art project and handing them to her assistants to arrange on the tables, when Jasmine frowned. "No offense, Lana, but you're really pale. You don't look so good."

"You should have seen me yesterday," she said. "You know that flu bug that's going around? I caught it with a vengeance."

Jasmine, who worked mornings and spent her afternoons at the local community college, where she was majoring in early child development, made a face. "Gosh, I hope I don't get it, not with finals coming up."

"Me, either," Brittany said as she placed crayons in trays around the tables. She worked full-time. "I'm saving up for a new car and can't afford to miss work."

They were both in their early twenties and full of energy. They also loved kids. Lana counted herself lucky to have been able to hire them.

"I don't have any classes today," Jasmine said. "I was planning to start writing a paper for my child psych class, but if you need to go home, Lana, I can stay all day."

Lana shook her head. "I appreciate that, Jas, but I'll be okay. I'm a lot better than I was."

The words turned out to be true. By the end of the day, Lana felt her usual self. Tuesday was the same, with a few queasy moments that soon passed. She'd finally kicked the flu bug.

Wednesday morning, Brittany and Jasmine set out the instruments for the weekly music class, which was always fun. Lana was sitting at the desk in the corner, sipping herbal tea and leafing through several well-worn children's books for afternoon story time, when Brittany stilled and made a face. "Uh-oh."

"Please don't tell me you're coming down with the flu," Lana said.

"No, it's my period. I'm a few days early, and I don't have any supplies with me. Help!"

"I keep extras in my locker," Jasmine said. "Come with me."

The two women headed for the employee kitchen on the other side of the day care.

While they were gone, Lana contemplated her own cycle. Between meeting Sly and Sophie, so many things had happened over the past month that she'd barely thought about it. She counted back to her last period—it had finished at the end of March. She should have had another twenty-eight days later, near the end of April.

And here it was, the first week of May, and nothing.

She was never late, never. Was it stress? Maybe, but even during the divorce, which had dragged out for a few months and was exceptionally stressful, her cycle had remained as regular as clockwork.

The implications boggled her mind. Dear God, what if she was truly sick?

Lana sank onto one of the preschool chairs and sought to reassure herself. Aside from the flu, she felt decent enough—except for a queasy stomach in the mornings and at some points during the day. Her breasts were sore, and she'd been more emotional than usual. Even more than when she was PMSing.

Those were all signs of pregnancy.

She couldn't possibly be pregnant. Could she?

The doctor had stated that her chances of getting pregnant were slim to none, which was why she and Sly had skipped using condoms.

Slim to none. That meant there was a teensy bit of a chance.

"Look at you, sitting in one of those little chairs and pale as the butcher-block paper we laid out," Brittany said. "Don't you want to go home?"

Lana managed a fleeting smile. "No, but I think I'd better. Are you two sure you can handle this?"

"I've worked here for almost a year," Brittany said. "And Jas has been here since September. We have the day-care routine figured out."

Lana nodded. "Okay, but if anything happens, be sure to call."

"We will," Jasmine assured her. "Just rest up and get well."

Lana drove straight to the drugstore. Not quite ready to head inside and buy what she needed, she sat in the car and speed-dialed Kate, who was at work. "Can you talk?" she said.

"I haven't opened the doors yet, so now is good," Kate replied. "Shouldn't you be greeting the first kids of the day about now?"

"I left work."

"You're still sick with the flu. I'm sorry, sweetie. You've got a real nasty bug."

"It's not the flu," Lana said. "I— This is strictly confidential."

"Oh, God, don't tell me it's something even worse."

"Actually, it's wonderful." And scary.

"You've got me really curious. Let me guess—you're sneaking away to meet Sly. Now there's a yummy idea."

"I told you over the weekend that after Sophie comes

over this Saturday we decided not to see each other again."

"So? You can still sleep together."

"Will you please stop?" Lana said.

"You don't have to yell." Kate finally got quiet.

Even though Lana was sitting in her car with all the windows up, she lowered her voice to a whisper. "My period is late."

"I can barely hear you. It sounded like you said your period is late."

"You heard right."

"But you're always as regular as clockwork…. Wait just a hot damn minute. Are you saying what I think you are?"

Lana pictured her friend, face aglow with excitement. For the first time since she'd realized that she might be pregnant, she smiled. "I'm sitting in the drugstore parking lot, about to pick up a couple of pregnancy tests. Will you come over after work and keep me company while I take them?"

Kate didn't even pause before answering, "Definitely."

Chapter 10

It'd been a long day, but to Sly's relief, it hadn't rained. The weather experts predicted a long dry spell. Which was bad for crops, but good for Sly. No more mud for a while. Now would be perfect to install that new drainage system—if he only had the funds. He wished Carpenter would hurry up and pay him what he owed. Otherwise, he'd be forced to take out a loan. The thought weighed heavily on him, and by the time he wandered into the mudroom at sunset, he was grouchy, dirty and running on empty.

His belly rumbling, he wandered into the kitchen, where Mrs. Rutland was slipping into her jacket to go home. Sly pushed his worries away to focus on more pressing needs. "My mouth is watering. What did you make?"

"Beef stew," she said. "It's simmering, but should be

ready in about half an hour. Be sure to soak the pan. I'll wash it in the morning. Your salad and a coconut cream pie are in the fridge, and that loaf of homemade bread on the counter is still warm."

Sly licked his lips. "What would I do without you?" he asked, and he was dead serious.

"Either learn to eat your own cooking, live on fast food or get married. I'll be here bright and early tomorrow."

"Thanks, Mrs. R."

After a quick shower, Sly stepped into clean clothes. Barefoot, he took the stairs two at a time. In the kitchen he helped himself to a generous portion of stew and a thick slab of bread slathered with butter and jam.

As always, the food was delicious, but as much as Sly relished his solitude, tonight he wanted company to take his mind off his troubles. Female company, and not just any woman. Someone who would listen and understand, without making any demands on him. Lana.

He imagined packing up the meal and bringing it to her place to share with him. She'd insist that she was full, and then steal a piece of his buttered bread. She'd talk about her day and ask him about his.

Sly wasn't about to analyze his emotions. He knew what he wanted and that was that.

So what if they couldn't date or enjoy a short-term relationship? Who cared if their feelings for each other were too hot for friendship, or that they wanted different things? He could still drop by with dinner and say hello—if she was home.

He picked up his cell phone to find out.

* * *

"What if I'm pregnant?" Lana asked, propping her chin heavily on her fist. "What if I'm not?"

Several cartons of Chinese food from her favorite Chinese takeout sat between her and Kate on the breakfast-nook table. Normally she relished every bite and often had seconds. Tonight, she was too wound up to do more than pick at her meal.

"Which would you rather be—as if I didn't know?" Kate asked.

"Pregnant." Lana wanted that with her whole being. There was only one problem. "If I am, I'm going to have to tell Sly."

"Since he's the daddy-to-be, that's only fair."

"I suppose, but he won't be happy about it."

"He'll certainly be surprised, that's for sure. I'd want time to absorb a bombshell like this."

"Of course there's that. But once, when we were discussing having kids, Sly said he didn't want any. He raised his brother, and apparently that didn't turn out so well. He said that had been enough fathering for him."

"That was probably just talk." Looking thoughtful, Kate picked a crispy noodle from her plate and popped it into her mouth. "But suppose he doesn't want a child. What'll you do then?"

Lana had already decided that. "The same thing I've been planning to do for months now—raise him or her by myself. That is, *if* I'm pregnant. What if I'm not?"

"Here we go again," Kate muttered. "There's only one way to find out. Take. The. Test. You've been stalling since I walked in the door."

"Because we wanted to eat first." Because she was afraid.

Kate scoffed. "I'm the only one who ate. Let's do this."

"I guess it's time," Lana said. "After we clean up the dinner mess."

"It'll keep for a while. No more delay tactics. I want to find out if you're pregnant almost as badly as you do. So march your behind into the bathroom now, or I swear, I'll drag you in there."

Lana saluted. "Yes, ma'am."

Minutes later, Lana sat on the toilet lid, holding her breath while she waited for the results of the digital pregnancy test. Naturally, her cell phone rang. Several bars of Shenandoah's "Mama Knows" tinkled through the air.

Lana moaned. "That's my mother. She always did have impeccable timing. I'll let it go to voice mail."

In what seemed like seconds later, her cell phone rang again, this time without an identifying tune.

Kate, who was sitting cross-legged on the carpet just outside the open bathroom door, staring at the timer on her cell phone, glanced in the direction of Lana's phone. "You're popular tonight. You want me to pick that up for you?"

"Are you kidding? There's no way I can talk to anyone right now."

"At least let me check who it is." Kate grabbed the phone. Her eyes widened. "You won't believe this. It's Sly."

"I definitely can't talk to him," Lana wailed.

"Yeah, that would be really awkward." Kate set the phone down.

Feeling as if she would die if she didn't find out soon, Lana said, "How many seconds left?"

Kate checked the timer. "About seventy."

Those moments dragged on forever, but finally, the timer buzzed.

For all her impatience, Lana sat frozen in place.

"Well?" Kate asked. "Aren't you going to check the results?"

"I can't."

"Hand it over."

Kate studied the LED display with a blank expression. Uh-oh.

Lana's heart sank. She wasn't pregnant after all. "Bad news, huh?"

"Actually, it's the opposite." Kate beamed at her. "Congratulations, Lana. You're pregnant."

Certain she'd misheard, Lana shook her head. "Say that again?"

Kate held out the results for her to read. "In big, bold letters, it says *pregnant*. Congratulations, Lana. You're going to have a baby!"

Afraid to hope—she'd waited and suffered for so many years to be where she was now—Lana bit her lip. "Maybe I should take another test, just to make sure."

"The packaging and instructions claim that this test is ninety-nine-percent accurate, Lana."

"Which means there's a one-percent chance that it's wrong."

"All right, have it your way. But I'll bet my last paycheck that the next test results come out the same."

Lana had bought three different pregnancy test kits. She took all three, and every time the results were the same.

"I'm pregnant! I'm pregnant!" Laughing, she hugged Kate hard. "I never imagined this could happen to me."

"It seems all you needed was one night with a big, strong cowboy," Kate said. "And what a cowboy he is. Between your pretty face and his rugged features, you're going to have one gorgeous child."

The words sobered Lana. "Did you not hear what I said earlier? Sly doesn't want to be a father. And don't forget that only last Friday we decided not to see each other anymore. Then there's the lawsuit." She buried her face in her hands.

"Eventually the lawsuit will end," Kate said. "Maybe Sly changed his mind and wants to keep seeing you. He just called, right?"

"It was a mutual decision," Lana said.

"So what? This pregnancy changes everything."

"You're telling me. I can't even imagine what he'll do when he finds out. But it definitely won't be good."

"You can't be sure of that. When you discussed kids before, it was all hypothetical. This is real, Lana. A real baby the two of you created."

"But Sly and I don't love each other. We haven't known each other long enough to fall in love."

Kate waved her hand in the air in a dismissive gesture. "You have the next seven or so months for that. Quit being so negative."

"I'm just scared."

"I know, sweetie. I would be, too. But no matter what happens, I'm here for you."

Profoundly grateful, Lana teared up. "You're such a great friend."

"Don't cry, or I will, too," Kate said, blinking furiously. "I'd like to open a bottle of wine and toast the pregnancy, but I guess that's out."

"For quite a while." Lana nibbled her thumbnail.

"Sophie is supposed to come over on Saturday. What am I going to say to her? Sly is coming over, too, to help convince her that I'm the right person to adopt her baby. I'm not sure I can handle telling either of them about this, let alone both. Then there's Sunday dinner with my parents and Liz and Eric…." Lana groaned.

"Slow down, Lana. You don't have to reveal anything just yet. In fact, you shouldn't. Just in case, you should see a doctor and talk to him or her."

Lana nodded. She would make an appointment with her gynecologist right away. "Promise me you won't say a word, Kate."

"I swear on my grandpa's grave." Kate crossed her heart. "I'll help you clean up the dinner stuff. Then, unless you want me to stick around, I'm heading home."

"I'll be fine. And I'll clean up. You've done enough."

At the door, Lana hugged her friend. "Thanks for being here for me."

"That's what best friends are for. I'll probably be awake for a few hours yet, so if you want to talk later, call me. And thanks for letting me be the first to share in your excitement."

As soon as the door shut behind Kate, Lana laughed out loud.

A baby!

Friday afternoon, Sly took a break from his usual chores and checked his watch. Lana hadn't returned his call from the other night, and he needed to know if she still wanted him to come over the next day. At least that was what he told himself. The truth was, he hadn't talked to her in a week. He missed her.

He waited until he figured she was home from work before reaching for his cell phone.

"Sorry I haven't called you back," she said. "I've been waiting to hear from Sophie."

"And?"

"Not a peep."

She sounded different somehow, but Sly couldn't put his finger on what had changed. Her voice, maybe. He guessed their decision not to see each other anymore had something to do with it. That and stressing about Sophie.

Wary now, he asked, "Have you changed your mind about me coming over tomorrow?"

"I hate for you to drive all the way over here if you don't have to."

Sly figured she was probably fidgeting the way she did when something bothered her. Everything hinged on whether Sophie showed up. He almost asked for the girl's phone number so that he could contact her and make sure she followed through. But he figured he should let Lana handle that. Otherwise, she'd probably bust his chops.

"Don't worry about Sophie," he said. "Trust me, she'll approve of your place and the neighborhood."

Lana's heavy sigh could mean anything.

"Are you still okay with the decision we made the other night?" he asked.

"You mean about not seeing each other anymore?" A long pause. "Are you?"

She hadn't answered the question, but if she wanted him to answer first, he would. "To be honest, no. I enjoy being with you." Dog that he was, he missed kissing her and fooling around.

"Okay, then," she answered, as if she hadn't heard what he'd said. "Why don't you come tomorrow around eleven-thirty."

Wishing he could read her mind, Sly agreed and disconnected.

Women. He just didn't get them.

Chapter 11

"Hey," Sly said when Lana answered the door late Saturday morning.

"Hi." Without meeting his eyes, she stepped aside and gestured him through the door.

He took in her stiff posture, solemn expression and too-pale skin and knew something was wrong.

"You okay?" he asked.

"Still shaking off a flu bug." She waved her hand toward the living room.

"When we talked yesterday, you didn't mention the flu."

"I came down with it last Sunday and it didn't seem important." Lana took the armchair, leaving him the sofa.

"I'm lucky I didn't catch it from you," he said.

Yeah, instead she'd given him a healthy dose of lust that was impossible to shake.

She gave a distracted nod. Her face, usually an open book, was drawn and tight, as her index finger traced and retraced a wavy line on the fabric of the armchair.

"Did you have to miss work?" Sly asked.

She gave him a puzzled look. "What?"

"Because of the flu."

"I took Wednesday off. Otherwise, I've been feeling okay."

She didn't seem okay now, not with the green tinge that suddenly tinted her complexion. She appeared paler, too. More puzzling was the tension emanating from her.

Sly cleared his throat. "We've been real busy at the ranch. It seems that no matter how hard my crew and I work at it, there's always some length of fence to repair or replace. We've been digging ditches, too, because the old drainpipes aren't working anymore."

He wasn't about to mention Tim or the fact that, tired of waiting for her cousin to pay up, he'd stopped by the bank and picked up a dreaded loan application.

With an absent look, Lana attempted a smile that didn't quite make it. "I can't imagine."

Enough was enough. "Is it me being here, or is it waiting for Sophie that has you wound up so tight today?" Sly asked.

"Uh..." Her cell made the *blip* sound that meant she'd received a text message. She glanced at it and frowned. "What a surprise—Sophie won't be coming today after all."

She flicked a piece of lint from the knee of her jeans,

her hair hanging like a curtain around her face, hiding her expression.

Sly could only imagine what she must be going through. "Let me guess—she wants to postpone for another week."

"Seems that way. And you drove all the way over here."

"No worries—I could use the break." Wanting to lighten the mood, he sniffed the air and licked his lips. "Whatever you're cooking smells great."

"It's a chicken recipe I got from my mother. Sophie ate a lot that day at Big Mama's, and I made a huge amount of food. What am I going to do with it all?"

"I'll help you out with that," Sly teased.

Instead of smiling, Lana nodded somberly. "It's just about ready."

The table was set for three. Sly helped bring the food to the table, and they sat down across from each other.

Lana had definitely put a big meal together—chicken wrapped in dough, curried fruit, salad and hot rolls. Sly dug in. "This is delicious," he said, licking his lips in appreciation.

Lana toyed with her plate of untouched food. "Thanks."

Sly set down his fork. "What's the deal, Lana? Since I've been here, you refuse to meet my eyes, you don't seem to hear what I say and you sure aren't talking much. Something's off."

With a sigh, she finally met his gaze. "You're right—I'm upset."

"About Sophie?"

"Her, too."

"So it's me you're upset with," he said, mentally

smacking his forehead. *Of course.* "I tried to talk about us when I called last night, but you wouldn't. I meant what I said on the phone. I don't want you out of my life."

He hadn't planned to say that, hadn't even realized it was true until now. "If you're willing, we can work this out."

Finally she met his gaze, her expression bleak. Her hands twisted together in her lap. "Oh, Sly, I…"

She swallowed hard and with a sickening realization, it dawned on him—she'd met someone. He was a fool. "Who's the lucky guy?" he asked, keeping his tone and expression bland.

"Pardon me?"

"The man you're dating."

She looked puzzled. "I'm not dating anyone. If I were, I'd tell you."

Sly released the breath he'd been holding. "Then what's wrong?"

She jabbed her fork listlessly at her chicken before setting it down.

No appetite, pale… "You're still sick," he guessed.

Without answering , she nudged the chicken platter toward him. "Please, help yourself to seconds."

His belly was still empty, but he couldn't eat another bite. Not with the odd tension simmering in the air. "No, thanks," he said.

It was painfully obvious that she didn't want him around now that Sophie had canceled. That stung.

"Thanks for lunch." Sly pushed his chair away from the table and stood. "I should be on my way, and you should probably be in bed."

Lana searched his face, her eyes shadowed with indecision, and then sighed. "Don't go just yet, Sly. There's something I should tell you."

Ominous words. But she couldn't be dumping him—they weren't together. He sat down again. "Go ahead."

"I— Oh, jeez." She covered her mouth with her hand and bolted for the bathroom.

Lana finally let go of the toilet bowl and staggered to her feet. She washed her face and rinsed out her mouth. Although she was weak, she felt much better now. This part of pregnancy was no fun at all.

But telling Sly would be far worse.

He was sure to be shocked, unhappy and angry. Lana felt sick all over again.

Keeping the pregnancy to herself until after she met with her doctor seemed the smart thing to do, just in case the tests were wrong and she wasn't pregnant after all. Yet deep down, she was certain that she was.

As the baby's father, Sly deserved to know. Not after the doctor's appointment. Now.

Even if she was shaking clear to her toes.

Squaring her shoulders, she opened the bathroom door. Just outside, Sly was waiting for her. "How are you?"

"Better now."

He walked her to the living room and sat her down on the sofa with such care and gentleness that she wanted to weep. "Can I get you a glass of water?" he said.

"Yes, thanks."

While waiting for him to return from the kitchen, Lana steeled her courage.

He watched her closely as she drained the glass, reminding her of an anxious parent. After setting the glass aside, he sat down beside her, tucked her hair behind her ears and peered at her face. "You have more color now, but you should probably be in bed."

Oh, how she longed to do just that, burrow under the covers and forget all about sharing her news with Sly. But if she didn't say something to him now, she couldn't live with herself. "Forget about bed," she said. "I need to talk to you."

"So you said right before you threw up. Whatever it is can wait until you're better."

"No. You have to hear this now."

The somber expression on his face and the dark concern in his eyes tore at her. He may not want a relationship with her, but he cared.

"My God, you're really sick." Sly was rigid with dread.

Lana forgot her own fears. Wanting only to reassure him that she was healthy, she smoothed his furrowed forehead with a caress. "I promise you, I don't have cancer or any other disease."

"Thank God." He sagged against the sofa cushions, the relief on his face touching her deeply. "My mother died of cancer, and I don't wish that on anyone."

"You were eleven, right?" she asked.

He nodded. Lana couldn't imagine losing a parent, especially at such a tender age. Her worries at that age had centered on being popular and whether her mom would let her go to a sleepover.

Then to lose a father two years later... "That's so sad," she said.

"It was a long time ago." Sly pulled her hand to his lips and kissed her knuckles. "So it is just a bad flu."

She forced herself to meet his gaze. "It isn't the flu,

either. I threw up because…" Knowing the world was about to change forever, she paused a moment. "Because I'm suffering from morning sickness."

"I… Huh?" The confusion on Sly's face was almost comical. But there was nothing funny about their situation.

"That's right, I'm pregnant." There. Her secret was out.

"Pregnant," Sly repeated with a stunned expression. "From that night?"

Lana nodded. "You're the only man I've been with."

"But you said you couldn't get pregnant."

"That's what I believed. My ex-husband and I tried for four years, first the normal way, then using artificial insemination. We didn't have any luck. Tests showed that I was the one who couldn't conceive. That's why Brent left me."

"The jerk." Sly scrubbed his hand over his face. "If you can't conceive, how can you possibly be pregnant?"

"Because miracles happen?"

"You're happy about this baby," he said, looking anything but.

Lana nodded. "I've wanted children for as long as I can remember, since I was a child myself."

Sly glanced at her stomach, which was still relatively flat. "When did you find out about this?"

"Wednesday—the night you called and I didn't answer. When the phone rang, I was waiting for the results of the first pregnancy test. I took two more to make sure. But even without the tests, I knew. I have all the symptoms."

Although her body still looked the same as always

and she couldn't yet feel the life growing inside her, she already loved her baby.

Sly frowned. "You waited until now to tell me? What were you planning to do if Sophie had come over today? Spring it on us both together?" He barked out a laugh that totally lacked humor. "Oh, that would've been a real kick." He eyed her coolly. "It's obvious that you're keeping the baby."

She nodded.

"Do I get a say in this?"

His reaction was every bit as bad as Lana had expected. She hated the shuttered expression on his face and the cold look of betrayal in his eyes. Somehow she managed to keep her back straight and her chin high.

"If you don't want to be involved, I understand." She bit her lip. "I wasn't even going to say anything until I met with my doctor. In case...you know." She couldn't even say the words. "But I'm certain that I'm pregnant."

His expression unreadable, Sly gave a terse nod. "When is your appointment?"

"Tuesday after work." She planned to leave the day care early.

He blew out a heavy breath. "I can't believe this has happened. I always use condoms. Always. I wish to hell I'd used them that night."

Lana hadn't expected him to jump for joy, but his re-action hurt. She couldn't stop a bitter smile. "As I recall, you were in too much of a hurry to stop for protection."

"Because we're both clean and you assured me you couldn't get pregnant." Once again, he scrubbed his hands over his face. "If I'd suspected this could happen I would have taken the extra few minutes."

"And you think I wouldn't have? I didn't plan to get

pregnant that night, Sly. But I won't lie—I'm aching for this baby, and I'm beyond grateful that I have a chance to be a mom. I'm also sorry that it happened this way, with neither of us having a say in what we wanted."

"That's something, at least." He rolled his shoulders as if they were too tight. "I need time to think."

Lana nodded.

With an odd, humorless smile, Sly stood. "I guess Sophie won't be coming over next weekend after all."

Lana hadn't thought that far ahead. "Probably not. Sly, I really am sorry for springing this on you."

"At least you told me."

She started to get up, but he gestured for her to stay put. "I can let myself out. I'll be in touch."

Hugging her waist, Lana stared at the empty fireplace until the door clicked shut behind him.

Determined to push her troubles from her mind and keep the pregnancy from her family for a while, Lana pulled to a stop in front of her parents' house for Sunday dinner. Hoping to stave off any nausea, she'd gobbled a few crackers on the drive over. So far, so good.

It was a beautiful May day, the late-afternoon sun still high and warm, and she couldn't help but feel lighthearted. Not ready to endure lectures or scrutiny from her mother just yet, she headed around to the backyard.

As usual, her dad and Eric stood in front of the smoking grill. "Hey, guys," Lana said as she reached them. "Something sure smells wonderful."

Eric grinned. "Grandpa Jake's ribs always do."

The family recipe had been developed by their grandfather decades ago. "Fourth of July ribs in May?" Lana licked her lips. "What's the occasion?"

Instead of answering, Eric glanced at Lana's father to reply. Her father tapped his cheek for a kiss. "Hello, favorite oldest daughter." He winked. "You're looking especially pretty today."

Lana smiled. "Must be this new spring dress. Thanks, Dad."

Connor and Emma noticed her, shrieked and came running.

"What are you two up to today?" she asked after hugging them.

"We're playing hide-and-seek, but Emma always jumps up and shows me where she's hiding." Connor rolled his eyes. "Will you play with us, Lana?"

"Sure, but how about a little later? I want to visit with Grandpa and your dad. Then I'm pretty sure Grandma and your mom would appreciate my help with dinner."

"That reminds me," Lana's father said. "Your mother booked us a trip next weekend. We're driving over to Helena to visit Aunt Jessica. So no family dinner next week."

"Okay." Lana was secretly relieved. Keeping the pregnancy a secret wasn't going to be easy, and she could use the break.

She was chatting with Eric and her father when the kitchen door opened. To Lana's shock, Cousin Tim stepped outside.

Her jaw dropped. Of all the days for her surly cousin to visit… She was in no mood to face him. The mere sight of him made her remember the lawsuit and Sly, and right now, she didn't want to think about Sly or yesterday, or any of the secrets she was keeping from her family.

"What's he doing here?" she grumbled in a low voice.

Her father's eyebrows rose a fraction. "Come on, honey, he's family. Didn't your mother tell you? She called yesterday and invited him to dinner."

That explained the ribs.

Her father gestured her cousin over. "Glad you could make it, Tim."

Lana's cousin joined them at the grill with his usual stiff nod. "That's some fancy grill. I see you're putting it to good use, making Grandpa Jake's ribs." He almost cracked a smile, making him appear much more approachable. "I haven't eaten ribs since last year's Fourth of July picnic. Before I forget, Michele says it's too nice to eat inside. She wants to eat out here."

"Great—we'll use the picnic table," Lana's father said. "It's been a few weeks since we touched base, Tim. How are things?"

"Lousy." Cousin Tim's jaw tightened. "That damn lawsuit…" He looked as if he could spit nails. "I figured out why Pettit's picking on me. He aims to bankrupt me, ruin my reputation and drive me off my land by making me pay for something I didn't do."

Cousin Tim had it all wrong. Sly would never do that. Lana warned herself to stay out of it, but the urge to defend Sly was too strong. "That's an awful thing to say," she retorted.

Her cousin seemed taken aback. She was just as surprised at herself, but unable to stop. "It's not as if he's asking for the sun and the moon. He wants restitution for the animals he lost and an apology."

"I sure as hell won't apologize for something I didn't do, and I won't pay, either."

Cousin Tim's thinned lips and fisted hands made Lana's knees shake, but this was important. "Have you ever actually made the effort to explain to Sly that you didn't do it?" she asked.

All three men stared at her, and she realized she'd referred to Sly by his first name. As if they had some sort of connection. Which they did, but her family had no idea about that.

She continued, "You and Sly—er, Mr. Pettit—have never really discussed the poisoning, have you? When he attempted to talk with you, you pointed a rifle at him and ordered him off your land. If you would just sit down and engage in a rational dialogue, you could work this out."

Cousin Tim's eyes narrowed. "Why are you defending him?"

Lana swallowed and came close to explaining exactly why. But this wasn't the right moment to reveal that she was carrying Sly Pettit's baby.

Imagining her family's shocked reaction to *that,* her stomach flip-flopped. So much for the crackers. *Oh, please, not a bout of morning sickness now.*

No, she decided. This sick feeling had nothing to do with morning sickness and everything to do with fear. She'd done what she dreaded most—stirred up family controversy. If she wanted to make it through the evening in one piece, she'd better keep her mouth shut.

Tim was waiting for her reply. "I've heard a few things," she hedged.

"What you've heard is wrong. Pettit outright accused me of poisoning his cattle, when I never did any such thing. I hope the bast—the so-and-so rots in hell."

Lana managed to bite her tongue, but she was sure her cold expression spoke volumes.

After a lengthy and somewhat tense silence, Eric

cleared his throat. "Pretty amazing that the Grizzlies made it to the tournament this year. How do you figure they'll do next year, Tim?"

As the men launched into a lively conversation about basketball, Lana released a silent sigh of relief. As much as she enjoyed the sport, she needed to escape. "I'm going to help Mom and Liz now," she said.

After promising the kids a game of hide-and-seek after the meal, Lana headed inside. Anything her mother said was preferable to listening to her cousin and fighting with herself to keep her mouth shut. Though why she was defending a man who now probably wanted nothing to do with her or their child, she had no idea.

Chapter 12

Sly's sister had invited him over for dinner Monday night. Not in the best mood, he debated canceling. A couple of times, he picked up the phone to do just that. But he was tired of being alone with his thoughts, thoughts that only seemed to go around in circles.

Lana was having a baby. *His* baby. He couldn't get his arms around that, was still numb with shock. But she seemed happy about it. Because she'd wanted a baby. Him, on the other hand... Sly didn't want a baby, didn't want to screw up his own kid like he had Seth.

Tough crap, huh? Whether he wanted to or not, he was having a kid.

He only hoped Lana hadn't told anyone. He didn't want the news spread around town just yet. And it would spread. Amy and Sheila and everyone else in

Prosperity would make sure of that. Sly made a mental note to ask Lana not to say anything to anyone just yet.

Wanting to enjoy himself for a few hours, he arrived at Dani's place with a bottle of wine in hand.

"Hey, big brother." She hugged him. "I'm fresh out of wine and was hoping you'd bring a bottle."

Her cat, named Fluff for his white fur-ball appearance, meowed and butted Sly's calf for some attention. Sly bent down and scratched the cat just behind his head. "Hey there, big guy." Disapproving of the girlish name Dani had stuck the male cat with, he never used it.

The animal purred happily.

Sly sniffed the air. "Do I smell homemade mac and cheese?"

Dani nodded. "With ground beef."

As much as he loved the stuff, he knew what it meant. "Uh-oh—your trademark breakup dish. This can't be about Cal—you two split up weeks ago. Who's the bum this time?"

Dani filled two glasses with wine and handed him one. "I wasn't planning to go into that just yet. I'd rather talk about something else."

"May as well get it out of the way." He straddled a chair backward at her little kitchen table. The twenty-pound cat jumped onto his lap.

"All right, we'll get it out of the way." Dani plunked into the other chair and raised her glass. "But first, a toast. Here's to a fun evening together—eventually."

She had no idea how bad Sly needed fun. He saluted with his glass. "I'll drink to that."

When they set down their drinks, Dani sighed and got right to it. "Paul dumped me."

"I know he took you home that night we played pool

at Clancy's, but I didn't realize you two were seeing each other."

"We were."

"I'm glad to hear he's out of your life. He was bad news."

"I didn't think so." Dani picked at the label on the bottle. "I really liked him."

"I have no idea why. He wasn't good enough for you."

"You say that about every guy I date."

"Because it's true."

"Hey, I don't do that to you." When Sly didn't comment, she added, "At least I'm out there, trying. You aren't even dating."

His errant thoughts wandered to Lana. The baby. He wished to hell that—

"What's wrong?" Dani asked.

"Nothing." He schooled his expression into bland calmness, but his sister appeared unconvinced. He couldn't fool her.

"Nothing I'm ready to talk about. Let me top off that wine."

Dani held out her glass. "So I have to talk about my problems but you don't have to share yours? No fair."

"Too bad."

"Stubborn man. Fine. How's the lawsuit going?"

"At the moment, nothing is happening."

"Bummer," she said with sympathy. "Now what?"

Sly thought about the loan application he had yet to fill out. Dammit, he couldn't really afford the added debt, especially with Lana pregnant. Because the one thing he knew was that he wasn't going to let her pick up the tab for anything.

Carpenter *had* to pay up, period.

Sly wanted his money *now*. He didn't hide his impatience. "I wait while my attorney and his go round and round."

"It's taking forever, and you need that new drainage system."

"Yep."

"At least the weather is dry now. It could stay this way for months. Maybe you can put off spending the money for a while."

"Yep."

She gave him a worried look. "Can't you try talking to Tim Carpenter again?"

"And get shot? He's just mean enough to make good on that threat. No, thanks."

"This is how long-term feuds start. I'm thinking the Hatfields and the McCoys."

Sly shrugged. "It is what it is."

His sister examined him closely, then fixed him with her pit-bull stare. "Something else is bothering you, brother mine. Spill."

Just a little thing. Lana was pregnant with his baby. Sly slid his wineglass around. "I'm dying of starvation here. Is that mac and cheese about ready?"

"You won't talk. Message received, but only because I'm starving, too."

The next few minutes were filled with setting the table, serving up and eating.

Wanting food, Fluff jumped onto Sly's lap again and butted his hand, begging shamelessly. Sly gave the cat a hunk of ground beef, then pushed the beggar off his lap.

"Have you talked to Lana lately?" Dani asked a while later when they'd both taken the edge off.

Here we go. Sly swallowed a mouthful of food and

chased it with wine before replying, "Saw her Saturday."

His sister's expression brightened. "You went out?"

He shook his head.

"Dang, I wish that lawsuit was over so you could date. But you saw her?"

"I went over to her place because Sophie was supposed to come over. Then at the last minute, she baled. Again."

His sister made a sympathetic sound. "Lana must have been so upset. She's dying for a baby of her own. I wonder why Sophie keeps flaking out."

One thing was certain—Lana hadn't told Dani about the pregnancy yet. That was a relief. Sly wanted to be the one to give his sister the news. But first he needed more time to come to grips with the whole thing and figure out what to do about it. Right now, he didn't want to talk about Sophie or babies.

"How's work?" he asked.

"Tourist season is revving up and we're busier than ever. Which reminds me—guess who showed up for Sunday brunch with a big announcement?"

Sly didn't even try to guess and didn't have to wait long for the answer. Lit up with excitement, Dani blurted the news. "Rayna and Troy Madison. After five years of marriage, they're finally expecting!"

Sly knew the couple. They owned a local real estate company. Dani launched into the particulars and said something about a baby shower.

Pregnancy and babies. They seemed to be everywhere. "Must be in the air," Sly muttered.

"Pardon me?"

"I said, if they're happy, that's good news."

"Of course they're happy. Like Lana, Rayna's been wanting a baby for a while now. I sure hope that Lana will—"

"Could we not talk about Lana anymore?"

Dani's eyes narrowed a fraction and she gave him a canny look. "You can tell me about it, Sly. I'm a great listener, and I won't say anything to anyone."

She *was* a great listener, but Sly wasn't about to say squat about his situation. The pregnancy was new and tenuous, and he was still feeling sucker punched. Besides, as true-blue as Dani was, she never had been able to keep secrets for long. God knew who she'd spill the news to. Plus, she and Lana were friends. Whatever he said to Dani might get back to Lana.

Sly wasn't taking any chances. "I sure am hungry tonight." He refilled his plate and began to eat.

Dani looked genuinely concerned. "I don't understand why you won't talk about Lana."

Sly frowned. "Why are you so vested in the idea of Lana and me together?"

"Because she's great and you're great. You two *should* be together."

Sometimes his sister drove him crazy. "I don't need a matchmaker," he growled before returning to his meal.

"Jeez, you're touchy. All right, let's talk about the weather. It's been pretty nice lately. After the winter we had, you and all the other ranchers in Prosperity must be pretty happy. Especially with the decent rainfall and sunshine this spring. And let's see, there was an article in yesterday's paper about local tourism. This year it should be up again, for the third year in a row.

"Oh, and starting a week from Friday the mall will host a huge Memorial Day weekend sale. I'm planning to call she-who-you-do-not-want-me-to-mention and invite her and her best friend, Kate, to go shopping with me. Fascinating stuff, huh?"

"As long as you three don't talk about me." Sly kept his eyes on his rapidly emptying plate.

"I can't promise you that. Wow, you polished off your second helping fast. Going for thirds?"

He shook his head and decided to call it an early night. "Come on, I'll give you a hand cleaning up."

While he helped Dani with the dishes, his thoughts circled to Lana again. She'd mentioned a doctor's appointment tomorrow. Sly wanted to know what the doctor said, and how Lana was feeling. That morning sickness stuff seemed brutal. He decided to call her tomorrow evening and find out.

"—for ice cream," Dani was saying. "I'm in the mood for some rocky road. Let's go to Lannigan's Ice Creamery and get ourselves a couple of cones."

The ice creamery was one of Sly's favorites. As tempted as he was, he was ready for solitude. He shook his head. "I'm beat, and tomorrow's another busy day."

"I have to get to bed early, too, but it's such a warm, beautiful evening, and I have my heart set on rocky-road ice cream. I need the sugar hit, and by your long face, so do you."

"Another time." Sly handed her a bill. "Get yourself a treat on me."

Dani refused the money. "All right, I'll go by myself and enjoy my ice cream without you. But I sure hope you cheer up soon. You're a lot more fun when you're in a good mood. My gut feeling is that this has something to do with Lana."

"Yeah? Well, my gut is telling me it's full." He patted his belly.

"Ha-ha. I'm serious about this. If you'd just quit fighting yourself and accept that Lana is the right woman for you, your life would be so much better."

"Thank you, Dr. Dani."

Dani bowed from the waist. "Anytime. I hope you're listening to me. Work things out with her."

He wasn't sure that was possible. Lana was pregnant, and the baby was his.

What the hell was he supposed to do now?

A few hours after her ob-gyn appointment, Lana relaxed at home with a book on pregnancy. Her intention was to devour every word, but she was so elated, so excited, that she could barely concentrate.

What a shame she couldn't share the joy with Sly. She hadn't heard a word from him since she'd revealed that she was pregnant, and figured he was still coming to grips with the idea.

Over the past few days she'd realized that no matter where life took either of them, she wanted him to be part of their child's life. Of course, that choice was his, and she wasn't going to pressure him.

Suddenly her cell phone rang. The screen said Sly Pettit. Lana's heart bumped happily, yet in the same instant, she was worried what he might say. She answered cautiously. "Hi, Sly."

"Hey," he said in the deep voice that usually made her hum inside.

Not tonight. She was too nervous. She caught her breath and waited.

"You saw the doctor today," he said.

"Dr. Valentine. That's right."

"And?"

"She called the pregnancy a miracle. Everything appears normal." The smile Lana had worn since that moment deepened.

Sly's relieved exhale told her that he'd been wondering and maybe worrying. A hopeful sign that maybe he had some feelings for their baby.

"How's the morning sickness?" he asked.

"The same. I've been eating crackers between meals, but Dr. Valentine suggested I also keep a supply by the bed to eat before I get up in the morning. I'll try that tomorrow. She also said that by the second trimester of pregnancy, when I'm about four months along, the morning sickness should disappear. So in another five or six weeks, I'll be fine."

"That's a long time to feel nauseated."

A small price to pay for the gift of life inside her. "I'll survive. By the way, the baby's due date is January second next year."

Sly's reply was more a gruff sound than a word. Lana's heart sank. He wasn't on board about this baby after all. Not yet anyway.

She bit her lip. "I know you're not pleased about this, Sly, but I'm thrilled. And I want to reassure you that I don't expect anything from you. But if you want to be part of the baby's life..." She let the words trail off.

"I'm not sure what I want yet, except that I'm not going to abandon my own kid."

He sounded surly and overburdened. Lana closed her eyes against a wave of sadness. "Have you thought about how you want to be involved?"

"Like I said, I haven't figured that out yet."

"There's no rush. The baby isn't due for another seven and a half months, which gives you plenty of time to figure out what you want to do."

"Those months will go by fast. We need to talk more about this, a lot more."

Lana agreed. "Just tell me when and where."

"It's real busy around here right now, so it'll be a while."

"Got it." In the meantime, she would continue to fix up the nursery, read the baby books and shop for baby supplies.

"Have you told anyone?" Sly asked.

"Just my best friend, Kate. You met her at the Bitter & Sweet. She was here when I took the pregnancy test. She promised not to say anything, and I'm positive I can trust her."

"No one in your family knows?"

"Not yet," Lana said. "I'm not ready. When the time comes, I'll do it the same way I did with my decision to adopt. First I'll tell my sister and her husband, and then my parents."

She dreaded that, even more than when she'd explained her decision to adopt. "They'll be surprised. Happy that I'm able to conceive when we all were convinced that I couldn't. But they won't be pleased about the way it happened—they're kind of old-fashioned and think marriage should come before the baby."

"So I should expect your dad to come after me with a shotgun?"

"They aren't that bad. They just… It's going to take a while for them to get used to the idea."

"Tell me about it," Sly muttered. "Do *you* think two people should get married before they have a baby?"

"In a perfect world, yes."

"What about us?"

Lana wasn't about to lie. "I'm not ready for marriage."

Sly exhaled loudly, his relief clear. "Me, either. Wait till your folks find out I'm the baby's father."

"There's that, too." Imagining their reaction, Lana shuddered. A root canal would be more pleasant.

"Dani doesn't know yet, either," Sly said.

"I'm going with her and Kate to the mall in a week or so. Should I give her the news?"

"She mentioned your get-together. But no, I'll tell her. For now, let's keep it to ourselves."

Keeping the news from Dani wouldn't be easy, but if Sly wanted it that way… "Okay," Lana said. "Let's agree to keep this to ourselves for a few more weeks."

"Works for me. Just give me a heads-up when you're ready to spread the news around. I don't want my sister finding out from someone else. What about Sophie? Have you talked to her?"

"Not yet. I guess I should call her tonight."

"What are you going to say?"

Lana wasn't sure. "I'll come up with something. By the way, Sunday night I went to my parents' for dinner, expecting to see just my sister and her family. But my mother invited someone else without warning me. Care to guess who came to dinner?"

"Just say it."

"Your favorite person—Cousin Tim."

Sly swore. "Must have been one hell of a rotten evening."

Lana recalled her cousin's negative attitude and the bad things he'd said about Sly. During dinner, she'd sat as far from him as possible and had attempted to ignore him. Still, she hadn't been able to enjoy Connor or Emma, and Grandpa Jake's ribs could have been dog meat for all she'd have noticed. "It wasn't fun," she said.

"I'll bet he called me a bunch of names."

"Among other things. He claims he didn't poison your livestock, Sly."

"Which is more than he ever told me."

"That's why I suggested he sit down with you and talk about it instead of running you off his land with his shotgun."

"You said that to him?" Sly sounded incredulous.

She'd also wanted to bolt and run, but she wasn't going to admit that. "Someone had to."

"I'll bet he loved that. Now you have a taste of what I've put up with all these months."

"I wish you two would work it out," Lana said.

"You sound just like Dani."

"I'll take that as a compliment. When she finds out about the baby, do you think she'll be happy?"

"Probably. We had dinner last night and she kept mentioning you. She believes we belong together." Sly sounded as if he was rolling his eyes.

Lana wished that was true, but they wanted different things. "She mentioned you'd had dinner together when she called last night."

"What else did she say?" Sly asked.

"Nothing much, except that you weren't your usual self."

"Yeah, well, I'm still in shock. It didn't help that she kept nagging me about you."

Despite Sly's grudging words, Lana detected a teasing smile in his voice. "What did you tell her?" she asked.

"To butt out."

Picturing that, she grinned. "Hey, are you interested in coming to my next doctor's appointment?"

"Why would you need another appointment? Unless something's wrong. You said everything was fine."

For all his talk about not wanting a child, he sounded just like a worried father. Lana took heart from that. "As a pregnant woman, I'll be seeing Dr. Valentine every month for a checkup," she explained. "Then during the last month of pregnancy, I'll go every week. That's how she gauges how I'm doing, and how close to the due date I really am."

"I didn't know that," Sly said. "I only know about pregnant cows."

Lana laughed. A blink later, for the first time in what seemed forever, Sly actually chuckled.

"When is the next appointment?" he asked.

"A month from now, on a Tuesday. If you want to come, you're welcome."

"I'll get back to you on that."

Lana took heart from his words. At least he hadn't said no.

Chapter 13

As soon as Lana disconnected from Sly, she called Sophie.

The girl sounded surprised to hear from her. "I was just about to text you."

"Let me guess—you're going to cancel our get-together next Saturday."

"Um…yeah," Sophie admitted in a sheepish voice. "How did you know?"

"You've done it twice already, and I figured…" Lana wasn't about to get into a blame game. "Why don't you tell me what you were going to text."

"Can I just send the text instead? It's kind of hard to say."

"Say it anyway."

"Okay. I, um, sort of decided that the Andersons should adopt my baby."

Lana had already guessed as much.

"It's just, they're a couple," Sophie went on. "And as my social worker says it's easier for a couple to raise a child than a single parent."

"That's true, but even without a partner, I believe in my heart and soul that I'll be a terrific mother," Lana said.

"You will. But I've been thinking about this a lot. My mom did okay with me, but I kinda missed not having a dad, you know?"

Lana couldn't even imagine. "If I was in your shoes, I'm sure I would," she admitted.

After losing his own father, Sly surely realized the same thing. Lana hoped he remembered that when he decided how he wanted to be involved in their son's or daughter's life. They didn't have to live together or even have a romantic relationship—although she wanted that, if the lawsuit ever settled—in order to both participate in raising their child.

"Are you mad?" Sophie asked.

If not for her own pregnancy, Lana would have been crushed. "I think the Andersons are very lucky people to become the parents of your baby."

"You do?"

"Absolutely."

"I didn't expect you to be okay about this. You're really nice, Lana. I hope that someday you'll get a baby."

"Thanks. That means a lot." Lana was dying to tell the girl that she was pregnant, but because of the agreement with Sly, she didn't. "Take good care of yourself, Sophie. I wish you a very bright future."

"You, too."

* * *

After a grueling day spent moving six hundred head of cattle to the pastures with the greenest grasses, Sly was beat. So was Bee.

"You worked hard today, girl," he said as he brushed the horse down. Soothing work he enjoyed almost as much as Bee.

Slanting sunlight filtered through the barn windows, and the scents of leather, hay and animal filled the lofty space—some of Sly's favorite smells.

"I'll bet you're glad today is Friday," he added. "I sure am."

The horse nickered and seemed to nod. When Sly finished brushing her, he led her to her stall. On the way, she butted his backside playfully.

"Want a treat, do you?" Chuckling, he dug a carrot from his shirt pocket and offered it to her.

Bee took it straight from his palm. They had an understanding of sorts. She let him ride her hard whenever the need arose, saddled up or bareback. In return, she asked only for food, exercise, a good brushing and a daily carrot or two.

Why couldn't all women be as easy as Bee?

Sly snickered at that. Plenty of women were easy enough.

But not the one who mattered.

He hadn't spoken to Lana in over a week, not since her doctor's appointment. She was giving him the space he'd asked for, and he was grateful. At the same time, he felt like a jerk for keeping his distance.

It was his turn at bat. Trouble was, he still wasn't sure whether to bunt or hit a home run.

He was latching Bee's stall shut when Ollie entered

the barn. Stetson in hand, he trudged toward Sly without his usual cocky swagger. He'd been unusually quiet all day.

Sly frowned. "It's Friday afternoon and you're free until Monday. I was sure that by now you'd be showered, changed and on your way to pick up your girlfriend."

"We didn't make any plans."

"You sick?"

"Uh-uh." Ollie shifted his weight. "I gotta talk to you."

Curious as to what was eating the guy, Sly gestured him to a worn bench along the planking. Nearby, reins and bits and other horse tacking hung on hooks. "What's on your mind?" he asked when they were both seated.

Ollie kicked the wall with the heels of his boots. "I got a problem."

"Something you want extra time off for," Sly asked. As busy as the ranch was just now, he wasn't sure he could afford to give that to anyone.

"Not exactly." Ollie pulled a toothpick from his shirt pocket and stuck it between his teeth. For some reason, the toothpick made him appear more like a boy trying to be a man than an actual man.

Tired, hungry and wanting a shower, Sly prodded him along. "Spit it out, Ollie."

The kid tugged at the collar of his T-shirt, as if it was too tight. "Tiff—my girlfriend? Well, we just found out that she's pregnant."

He didn't look at all happy about that. Sly understood just how he felt. "I take it this isn't good news," he said.

"It sucks. Tiff wants to keep the baby and raise it. I don't."

This sounded, oh, so familiar. Sly eyed him. "What are you going to do?"

"That's what I'm here to talk to you about. I'm giving you my notice."

"Hold on, there. You signed on through September," Sly reminded him. He liked the kid and had been considering offering him a permanent job.

"I said I'd stay, but now I have to leave town."

"What does Tiff think of that?"

"Haven't told her." Ollie tossed the toothpick into the nearby trash barrel.

"Let me get this straight. Your girlfriend is pregnant with your baby, and you're going to walk out on her? I'm guessing without even a goodbye."

"That's the plan." Ollie's voice cracked.

"It's a bad plan, one you need to rethink. Instead of running away, be a man and deal with the situation."

Stern words, but Ollie needed to hear them. With a shock, Sly realized he was also talking to himself.

God knew he had his faults, but he'd always prided himself on taking responsibility for his actions. Lately, though, he'd done the opposite, just the way Seth used to.

Damn.

Sly was not his brother. He didn't run away from trouble.

Or did he? Sure as hell, he'd been trying to run from the idea of being a father. The realization made him frown.

"Don't look at me like that," Ollie said. "I'm only twenty—way too young to start a family."

"You should have thought about that when you and Tiff had unprotected sex."

"You get how it is, man. There comes a point when you're too far gone to keep your head on straight. Besides, she said it was her safe time."

"I hear you," Sly said. "No matter what a woman tells you, always use protection. I do."

Except for that one night with Lana.

"Look, this is a busy season at the ranch," he went on. "I need your help. Why don't you stick around for another week and think it over?"

"But I ain't ready to be a daddy."

"You're going to be one anyway." He let that hang in the air a few moments. "At least talk to Tiff. You owe her that much. Maybe you two can work something out."

"I guess I could do that," Ollie said with a grudging shrug. "But I'm only sticking around for another week." He left the barn.

Sly stayed. Too restless to sit, he paced around without really seeing the horse stalls or bales of hay stacked against the wall. It'd been almost a week since Lana had told him she was pregnant. Instead of thinking about her and the baby, he'd spent all of those days focused on himself and how he'd screwed up with Seth.

For years he'd assured himself that he would never saddle a kid with his poor example of a father. But life had turned on him, and Lana was pregnant with his baby and she was determined to raise it. Which made Sly no different from Ollie. Like the kid, he needed to man up and face his responsibilities.

Looking at situation that way, Sly realized what he had to do. Right there in the barn, he pulled his cell phone from his pocket and called Lana.

The phone rang four times, then went to voice mail.

He left a message. "The Memorial Day weekend is right around the corner. If you're free a week from Saturday, I'd like to take you to dinner." Knowing what'd she say to that he added, "This won't be a date. We have to talk about our situation and we both need to eat. Why not over dinner? Call me back."

Sly disconnected. Feeling lighter than he had in days, he whistled as he exited the barn.

Dani wanted new shoes, and after a quick dinner the Friday of the Memorial Day weekend holiday, Lana and Kate headed to the mall to meet her. Thanks to the mall-wide sale, the parking lot was full.

"Don't mention the pregnancy," Lana warned Kate as she searched for a place to park.

Her friend gave her a puzzled look. "You're keeping it a secret from Sly's sister?"

"Sly wants to tell her himself, but he isn't ready yet. I'm not ready to say anything to my family, either. We agreed to wait a while. Oh, and you also can't mention the dinner tomorrow night."

Kate made a face. "You're not leaving much to talk about."

"Sure I am. Guys you're dating, guys she's dating, shopping, food. What else is there?" Lana teased.

"That'll work. What do you think Sly will say when you go out tomorrow night?"

"I have no idea, and it isn't a date," Lana reminded her.

For now it was enough that he wanted to get together and talk. At last she spied a parking space. "We're meeting Dani at Altman's," she said as she maneuvered the car into the space.

Kate rubbed her hands together in anticipation. "I love that department store, and they have great shoes."

Ten minutes later, the three of them entered the women's shoe section. Dani went straight for the sandals.

"What do you think of these?" she asked, showing Lana and Kate a yellow strappy sandal with three-inch heels. "I have the cutest sundress to wear them with."

Lana loved them. "They're really sexy, but too high for me. If I tried to walk in those, I'd probably fall flat on my behind."

"No, you wouldn't," Kate said. "I want a pair, too, in red. So, Dani, is there a special guy you want to wear them for?"

Dani sighed. "I just went through a breakup."

Lana felt for her, but she was also confused. "When we met for coffee, you weren't seriously involved with anyone."

"As with most of my relationships, it didn't last long. But hey, if I wear these, some cute guy is bound to ask me out. Why don't we each try on a different color?"

Kate nodded. "I'm in. This way, Lana, you can test them out and see if you can walk in them."

A few minutes later, Lana admired herself in the mirror. "Yay, me," she said, very pleased with herself and the silver sandals. "I've walked to the wall and back and haven't stumbled or fallen over. And wow, look at my legs."

"Very sexy." Kate grinned. "If I were you, I'd wear them tomorrow night."

Dani's eyes widened. "You have a date tomorrow night! Who with?"

Lana glared at Kate. Her friend shrugged. "Hey, I didn't say anything."

"It's not an actual date," Lana explained. "Sly and I—"

"You and my brother are finally going out? Score!"

"I repeat, it isn't a date," Lana stated firmly. "We're getting together to talk—that's all."

"Sounds like a date to me." Dani looked like the cat who'd swallowed the canary. "You should definitely wear those sandals."

Lana itched to tell her about the pregnancy, but she'd given Sly her word. Things between them were precarious enough without her breaking her promise. She rolled her eyes. "Fine, I'll buy them. But it isn't a date."

Chapter 14

Wishing she could relax with a glass of wine instead of making due with sparkling water, Lana sat across the table from Sly at an Italian restaurant on the outskirts of town. The out-of-the-way eatery was packed, and diners filled every table. Carpeting and acoustic ceiling tiles muted the noise level, and dim lighting, linen tablecloths and generous spacing between the tables added an air of privacy. Sly had chosen the perfect place for them to talk over dinner.

Lana was glad she'd dressed up in a silk sheath and, yes, the new silver sandals. Sly had also dressed up. In dark pants, a pressed shirt and tie, he was movie-star handsome. But then, he also looked great in jeans and a T-shirt.

"I've never eaten here before," she said. "How did you find this place?"

"A couple years ago, I stopped here for lunch on the way home from a cattle auction. The owner's mother makes the pasta from scratch using old family recipes. I think you'll like it."

Lana was already salivating. "I'm sure I will."

"I also figured that way out here in the boonies, there's less of a chance we'll run into family."

He'd thought of everything. On the forty-minute drive here, they'd made small talk. Lana had shared that Dani had assumed they were on a date tonight, which had caused some muttering. Then she'd updated Sly on her phone call with Sophie and shared a funny story about one of the kids at the day care, a boy who'd pretended he was a dog all week, barking and crawling around.

"Does he have mental problems?" Sly asked.

Lana shook her head. "He's fine, just quirky. Some kids are."

"I once had a dog who believed he was a person," Sly commented, his lips curling into a smile. "He was quirky, too."

He told Lana about a run-in with a coyote and the family of meadowlarks that had hatched in his backyard.

It was a conversation any couple on a date might have. Except this wasn't a date. They were here to talk about the baby—or so Lana thought. Waiting for the *real* conversation was nerve-racking. But she wanted to give Sly the space he deserved.

Meanwhile, doubts ate at her. What if he wanted nothing to do with her or their child? She felt an anxiety that all but killed her appetite. But if that was the case, she doubted they'd be sitting in this nice restaurant, having a nondate.

The waiter delivered the salads.

"Remember, we're going Dutch treat," she reminded Sly as they reached for their forks.

He nodded.

"I haven't heard lately—what's happening with the lawsuit?" she asked, wanting to know.

"Not a damn thing." He snorted in frustration.

"What's taking so long?"

"Your cousin. He's stalling. My attorney is doing what he can, but I'm about out of patience."

"Cousin Tim is about as easy to budge as a boulder," Lana said.

"On that, we both agree."

A short while later, the waiter removed their salad plates and placed their dinner in front of them. "I don't want to talk about the lawsuit anymore," Sly said. "I want to enjoy this meal."

Throughout the delicious main course, Sly steered the conversation away from serious matters and kept things light and easy. Despite the amazing food, Lana's frustration level grew until she wanted to scream. Why wouldn't he get to the point?

Finally, the waiter cleared their plates. "Dessert?" he asked.

Lana shook her head, but Sly ordered coffee, tiramisu and two forks.

When the dessert arrived, Sly nudged the plate between them. "Half of this is yours."

"I'm too nervous, Sly." *And too impatient to wait one more second.* "I feel like there's an elephant in the room. You invited me to dinner to talk and I've been giving you space to bring up our situation when you're ready, and I'm frustrated."

With a somber expression, he set down his fork. "I was planning to wait until after the meal, but if you'd rather talk now, it's okay by me. I made a decision about the baby." He paused, his steady gaze revealing little.

If only Lana could read his mind. He claimed that he didn't want to abandon their child, but for all she knew, his idea of sticking around could be to offer monetary support and nothing more.

Aware of how he felt about having a child, she assumed that had to be it. Disappointed, but determined not to let on, Lana widened her eyes. "What did you decide?"

"I want to be part of his life."

She was surprised, and so relieved she sagged in her seat.

His expression confused, Sly scrutinized her. "You're not happy about that."

"Just the opposite. I'm so glad our baby will have the chance to get to know his or her daddy. What do you have in mind?"

"I'm still working on that, but for starters, I'll go with you to your next doctor's appointment. If the offer is still open."

"It is. It's going to be a very special appointment. We'll get to hear the baby's heartbeat."

Sly didn't exactly seem excited, but at least he'd agreed to be there. It was a beginning, and Lana decided she'd do whatever she could to encourage him.

"What time should I pick you up?" he said.

"Since I'll be coming straight from work, it'll be easier if we meet at the clinic."

He nodded. "Give me the details and I'll be there."

Lana gave him the information, then picked up her fork. "Now I'm ready to eat some of that tiramisu."

"We were supposed to split the bill," Lana said as Sly pulled onto the highway and headed toward her place. "You should have let me pay my share."

Despite her words, she didn't seem too upset that he'd insisted on paying. The truth was, she hadn't stopped smiling since he'd announced he wanted to be part of the baby's life.

His chest was full and warm. Maybe he didn't want a kid, but he felt good that his decision had made her happy. He wasn't about to analyze why that was so important. It just was.

Darkness had fallen, but in the faint light of the dash he caught that soft smile. Desire slammed into him. If not for the truck's bucket seats, he'd have pulled Lana close and snuggled her against his side.

But that wasn't what tonight was about, and if he was smart, he'd spend the rest of the evening pissed off at her cousin or thinking about how being a father would mess with his life. Or anything to keep his mind off sex.

Unfortunately, his body wasn't cooperating. It wanted other things—specifically, to get nice and close to Lana. Fighting the hunger wasn't easy, but Sly was damned if he'd give in.

"You pay next time," he said.

"I'm going to hold you to that."

They were both quiet, until out of the blue she turned to him. "You'll make a great father, Sly. I know it."

He wasn't at all sure of that, but since he was going

to be a father regardless, he intended to do much better with this kid than he had with Seth.

"When are you breaking the news to your family?" he asked.

The smile he so liked disappeared. "Probably after the next doctor's appointment."

It was as clear as day that she wasn't looking forward to that.

For the rest of the drive, they rode along in comfortable silence while the radio spit out a steady stream of rock 'n' roll and country-and-western songs.

When Sly stole a glance at Lana sometime later, he saw that she'd fallen asleep. He lowered the radio volume. At last, he pulled up in front of her town house and shut off the truck.

Reluctantly he woke her. "Lana, honey, we're here."

"Hmm?" She yawned and stretched, then smiled at him, her eyes unfocused and drowsy. "I guess I fell asleep. It's the pregnancy—I'm always tired." She frowned at the front of her dress. "I must have spilled something on myself."

The tender feelings that stirred in Sly's chest were new to him and difficult to understand. He gave her a goofy smile and blurted the first thing that came to mind. "That's just a little slobber. You slept with your mouth hanging open."

"I didn't. I'm so embarrassed."

"You looked cute."

For a moment he lost himself in her warm eyes, forgetting where he was and what he was doing. All that mattered was being here with Lana.

That worried him on several levels. He didn't like his

strong feelings and didn't want her to get the wrong idea and assume he was getting serious about her. He wasn't.

Sly was wondering how fast he could make an exit without being a jerk when the raw desire on her face stopped him.

Fresh hunger roared through him. No, not fresh. His desire for Lana was a constant simmer inside him. It had just flared up. He'd never wanted a woman so much.

He glanced away, grateful for the lights around the town-house complex and for the people still outside after ten at night. They had no idea how bad he needed chaperoning.

"Thanks for everything, Sly," she said. "For your decision to be a part of our baby's life and for a really great dinner."

"Sure," he said, once again all warm in his chest. "I'll walk you to your door."

"Don't bother. It's only twenty feet away, and you see all the neighbors out and about. Besides, this isn't a date, remember?"

The manners his parents had once taught him wouldn't allow that. "I don't care what it is," he said. "I'm walking you to your door."

"Stubborn cowboy." She let out a soft laugh. "All right, walk me if you must."

By the time he rounded the truck and reached the passenger side, Lana was standing beside it, waiting for him. Her dress clung to her curves and showed a good length of leg. Her skimpy little sandals made her legs seem impossibly long.

Sly itched to run his hands up her calves and thighs. All the way up…

Hardly aware of what he was doing, he slipped his

arm around her and shortened his stride so that his steps matched hers.

It was a warm night and her silk dress had tiny sleeves that barely covered her shoulders. Her skin was smooth under his hand, and the faint scent of lavender he'd come to associate with Lana filled his senses.

His whole body tightened. If not for the unsuspecting chaperones all around, he would have stopped right here, pulled her to him and kissed her until they were both out of their minds.

Stepping onto her little concrete slab of a porch, she faced him. "This was the best nondate I've ever had."

"You go on a lot of those, do you?" he said, his lips twitching.

Laughing, she placed her hand on her barely rounded stomach for a nanosecond. It was long enough to draw Sly's attention.

He sobered. "You touched your belly a lot tonight. Does it hurt?"

"Not at all. I'm hardly aware that I'm doing it. I just— It's because I'm growing a baby, and I still can't quite believe it."

The joy on her face was something to see. "May I touch?" he asked.

Her smile broadened. "Sure, but you won't feel anything yet. It's too early. We should probably go inside first. Lord knows what the neighbors might think if they notice your hand on my stomach."

Sly told himself to remain outside, where they were both safe. But when she unlocked the door, he followed her inside.

She stopped in the entry and turned to him. "Now you can touch me."

He gently placed his palm against her stomach. Her silk dress was thin, and through it he touched her navel and her warmth. Maybe he didn't feel the baby, but he felt plenty. He was lit up from the inside out. Not the same kind of heat as sexual desire. This was different.

"You're right—I don't notice anything different," he said, his voice husky from his tender emotions. "You sure don't have much of a belly yet."

"Even after all the food I ate tonight?" Lana laughed again. "Actually, I have grown a little. That's why I'm wearing a dress without a waist. Some of my skirts and pants are already too tight to button. In another month, this pregnancy will be obvious. Just wait and see."

His hand was still on her belly. He realized that he couldn't feel the elastic band of her panties. Maybe she was wearing bikini panties. Or maybe…

Sweet Jesus, was she naked under there?

"I don't want to wait for anything." Forgetting that he should keep his distance, he cupped her behind. He didn't find elastic there either, just warm, soft flesh. "Are you wearing panties tonight? Because I sure don't feel any."

"It's a thong. That way, you don't notice a panty line through the dress."

He growled softly. "Yeah?"

"Mmm-hmm." Her pupils dilated and her lips parted in the signal he'd been waiting for.

"You drive me crazy, you know that?"

She started to say something, but before she could, he pulled her hard against his body and kissed her. The spicy scent of Sly's aftershave filled Lana's senses and his shoulder muscles bunched under her hands. Her heart thudded so loudly, she was sure he and the entire neighborhood could hear it. Then he kissed her and everything else faded away.

Home. She was home.

All too soon, the kiss ended. He touched his forehead to hers. "I've missed this."

The silver flecks in his hot eyes seemed to glow with heat. After weeks of wanting him, Lana was in no mood to stop now. Eager to melt into another kiss, she tightened her arms around his neck. "Come back here, cowboy, and do that again."

Sly groaned and kissed her with a fierce need she felt clear to her toes. He slid his tongue across hers. He tasted of coffee and tiramisu and passion. Between her legs she grew damp and aching for him. She tried to hook her leg around his thigh but her dress was too tight. Stepping out of her sandals, she stood on his boots so that she could fit her body to his. With a sound of pure male satisfaction, he walked her backward toward the sofa. Thigh to thigh, hip to hip, his body hard in all the right places.

They sank onto the sofa, glued so tightly together they may as well have been one person. Only their clothing prevented them from joining fully. Several long, heated kisses later, Sly slid his hands to her breasts. Lana nearly moaned in relief.

He started to cup her through her dress, then hesitated. "Are you still sore?"

"Not so much." She pressed her palms to his hands, showing him what she wanted.

"Okay?" he asked.

She nodded. "That feels... Yes."

While his skilled fingers delivered dizzying pleasure to her breasts, he kissed her neck. Somehow her skirt got hiked up and one amazing hand traveled up the inside of her bare thigh. Lana's muscles became mush, and she was glad she was sitting down.

"You have the softest skin," he murmured as his warm hand slid toward the part of her that most wanted his attention.

Lana caught her breath until finally he breached her thong. It soon disappeared. Then, oh, dear God, he touched her most sensitive spot.

Moaning in pleasure, she lifted her hips right off the sofa.

"Your passion turns me on," Sly said before he caught her in a searing kiss while his fingers drove her toward the brink.

"Sly," she gasped against his lips. "If you keep doing that, I—I'm going to…"

"Climax? That's good, Lana."

"But I…" Whatever she was planning to say faded away. She flew apart.

When she floated back to earth, he kissed her. "That was beautiful. You're beautiful."

Lana knew better. She was probably a big mess. She smoothed the skirt of her dress down, brushed her hair out of her eyes and glanced at Sly's pants. His erection was obvious.

The corners of his mouth lifted. "I'm a guy—I'm used to it. I'd better leave now while I still can."

She barely had the chance to recover before he moved away from her. "Walk me to the door?"

He stood, clasped her hands and pulled her up.

Standing in the little entry, he touched her face and kissed her again. A sweet kiss, tender and filled with promise. "Good night, Lana."

"Good night, Sly."

After locking the door behind him, she sank against it and hugged herself.

Good or bad, right or wrong, she was falling in love with Sly Pettit.

She shouldn't, and not only because of the lawsuit and her family. Sly cared for her and wanted her, but he wasn't a relationship kind of man. She would only get hurt. Then there was the baby. For his or her sake, Lana should forget about love and focus on a long-term friendship with Sly that would last.

Those arguments made a lot of sense, but her heart didn't care.

Chapter 15

Monday morning, Memorial Day, Sly whistled as he met Ace, Bean and Ollie near the barn.

"You seem happy today," Ace said with a searching look. "Going to the celebration at Prosperity Park later?"

Every Memorial Day the town hosted an annual celebration and picnic at the park.

"Not this year," Sly said. He was giving his crew half the day off, but there was too much to do at the ranch for him to leave.

He should have been in a lousy mood for that and several other reasons. Ollie was still here—that was hopeful news—but he half expected the kid to ask for his paycheck and leave town at any moment. Also, Lana was pregnant, and Sly needed sex. Had needed it badly since Saturday night. But instead of going for what he wanted, he'd concentrated on Lana and drawn his own pleasure from hers.

He was still shaking his head over how good he felt about their whole evening together. So good that not even the prospect of being short one hand could bring him down. "I had a great weekend," he said.

The foreman's eyes lit with curiosity, but he didn't pry. Not that it'd have made a whit of difference. Sly wasn't going to talk about Lana.

"The wife and I went to some friend's house and played poker Saturday night," Ace said. "We beat the pants off them—won two whole dollars." He thwacked his thighs and chuckled.

Sly grinned. "What are you going to do with all that cash, Ace?"

"It went into our vacation jar, for that trip to Hawaii my wife wants."

Bean shared that he'd attended a country-and-western concert and was headed for a family picnic at the park later.

Ace glanced at Ollie, who had yet to say much. "How was your weekend, kid? Did you and that gal friend of yours go out dancing Saturday night?"

"Not this weekend." Not a hint of a smile crossed Ollie's face.

"Trouble in romance land?" Ace asked.

Ollie kicked at a hard patch of dirt that didn't budge. "I gotta talk to Sly."

"I ain't stopping you."

"Alone."

Ace held up both hands, palms out. "Sure, kid. You want to help me with that clogged irrigation pipe, Bean?"

"I'll meet you later," Sly said. When Ace and Bean disappeared from sight, he settled his hands low on his hips and studied his young ranch hand.

"I talked to Tiff." Ollie scratched the back of his neck.

"Good man. What did you two decide?"

"I guess I'll stick around for a while—if you haven't hired my replacement."

"I haven't."

Ollie nodded. It was obvious that he was finished talking.

Sly clapped his shoulder. "Let's get to work, then."
Sitting in the crowded waiting room of the medical clinic, Lana thumbed through a parents' magazine. There were several interesting-looking articles she wanted to read, but at the moment she was too distracted.

It was almost time for her appointment, and there was no sign of Sly. Saturday night he'd stopped by with takeout. Technically it hadn't been a date. Over dinner, Lana had reminded him about this appointment. After the meal she'd let him kiss her…and more. *Let* him? She'd made the first move. They'd stopped short of making love—she wasn't ready for that. But whenever she thought about the things she and Sly did—and she thought about them constantly—her insides went hot and soft.

Her heart was full to bursting with feelings for him. Risky, but there it was.

He didn't care as deeply for her as she did for him and probably never would, but it was obvious that he did care. And he wanted to be involved in their child's life. No matter what her own heart wanted, that was the most important thing.

Once her parents knew about the baby, she could relax. Not that telling them would change anything. Their strong belief that family loyalty stood above all else wouldn't allow them to accept Sly.

There was only one way around that obstacle. The lawsuit had to end in a way that worked for both Sly and her cousin.

As if that would ever happen.

The elevator chimed and she swung her head around. Sly exited the car. In faded jeans, cowboy boots and a chambray shirt rolled up at the cuffs, he was tall, handsome and all cowboy. As he entered the waiting room with his graceful, long-legged stride, men and women stared openly at him.

He spotted Lana, nodded and held her gaze. Her heart lifted and she forgot about her family, the lawsuit and everything else. Oh, she had it bad.

Just as he reached her, the receptionist called her name. "Lana Carpenter."

"I'll be right there," Lana replied without taking her eyes from Sly. "You made it," she said.

"Sorry to cut it so tight. I got a flat on the way here. I would have called, only I was charging my cell phone and accidentally left it at home."

They made their way to an exam room. A friendly nurse named Janet led Lana to the scale and weighed her, then jotted notes on her chart. "You gained a pound since last month. Way to go."

Sly raised his eyebrows at that.

"We like our patients to gain thirty to forty pounds over the pregnancy," Janet explained. "Two to four pounds the first trimester is ideal." She led them to an exam room, where she took Lana's pulse and blood pressure. "Everything appears normal. Dr. Valentine will be in shortly."

"How are you feeling today?" Sly asked when the nurse left.

"I was a little queasy this morning, but I'm fine now. How about you?"

"I'm doin' okay." His gaze flitted over her blouse and pants before his eyes narrowed on her legs. "What's that on your knee?"

Lana shook her head at a blob of dried paste on her leg, then wet her finger and rubbed at the spot. "We did an art project this morning. It must have—"

The knock at the door wiped the rest of her sentence from her mind. Dr. Valentine entered in her usual white lab coat and low-heeled pumps. Lana liked her doctor, who was a few years older than she was, smart and friendly.

She smiled. "Dr. Valentine, this is Sly—the baby's father."

"It's nice to meet you, Sly."

They shook hands before the ob-gyn turned to Lana. "You had your physical last month. This appointment you get to hear the fetal heartbeat."

"I can hardly wait!" Lana stole a glance at Sly. He didn't seem nearly as thrilled but he was here. That counted for something.

Dr. Valentine smiled. "This is an exciting time. Hop onto the exam table and we'll have a listen."

As soon as Lana lay down, the doctor lifted her top and positioned the sound device over her stomach. Lana heard a whooshing noise. "Is that it?"

"Not yet." Sure hands moved the device slowly over Lana's abdomen. "Right now, your baby is about the size of a tadpole, so it can be hard to find. Ah, here we are."

A rapid *thump-thump-thump* filled the room. "You're hearing your baby's heartbeat."

Overcome with emotion, Lana reached for Sly's hand.

He grasped on, a concerned expression on his face. "That sounds too fast."

"Not at all," Dr. Valentine assured him. "At this stage, one hundred and sixty beats per minute is normal for a fetus."

"Good to know." He blew out a relieved breath and squeezed Lana's hand.

For the first time ever, they were listening to their baby's heartbeat, sharing the awesome, unforgettable moment together. A look passed between them, understood only by the two of them.

"Do either of you have questions?" Dr. Valentine asked when she finished the exam.

Sly had a few that she answered before she reached for the door. "Nice meeting you, Sly. I'll see you again in a month, Lana. Be sure to stop at the front desk and schedule your appointment."

When they were alone in the little room, Sly grabbed for Lana's hand again and cleared his throat. "Now it's real."

The wonder on his face and the tender huskiness of his voice meant more than Lana could say.

Something had shifted in him, and she was now certain that he was 100 percent on board with the baby.

She realized then that she loved him.

* * *

As Sly and Lana headed into the parking garage, feelings he didn't understand crowded his chest. Feelings that scared him, but were too powerful to push away.

Time to cut and run.

He opened his mouth to say he needed to get back to work, but something else came out instead. "I'd like to show you my ranch."

Astounded at himself, he shut his mouth. His home was his private refuge, the place where he could let go and be himself. Over the years a few women he'd dated had come to the ranch—at their own invitation, not his. But this was different. Lana was carrying his child. She ought to see the ranch.

While he was reeling from the implications of his offer, Lana dazzled him with a smile that almost brought him to his knees.

"I'd love to get the tour," she said. "Just tell me when."

Sly glanced at his watch. It was just after five. Mrs. Rutland would be on her way home and his men should be finished with the afternoon chores and relaxing in their trailers for the evening. Sly didn't want anyone who worked with him catching sight of Lana and getting ideas.

"Now works," he said. He'd quickly show her around, then send her on her way. "Why don't you follow me in your car."

"Okay. But I should warn you that I haven't eaten in several hours, and this baby likes for me to stay well fed." Laughing softly, she laid her palm over her belly. "I'm going to need food pretty soon."

Her laughter was contagious, and Sly chuckled. "Not a problem. My housekeeper makes dinner before she leaves for the day. It should be ready to heat up."

What the hell? Had he really just invited her to dinner?

"You have a cook? Lucky you."

"She cleans, too, and don't I know how lucky I am. Mrs. Rutland is the best."

Lana's happy expression faded. "There is one little problem—you live next door to Cousin Tim."

Sly frowned. "Have you ever been to the Lazy C Ranch?"

"Not since I was thirteen and my cousin was a newlywed."

"Tim used to be married?"

"Not for long. About six months into the marriage, his wife filed for divorce and left him."

Sly hadn't been aware of that, but it explained a few things. Such as why his neighbor seemed mad at the world. Or maybe the guy had been born that way.

"Then you know that his spread is five hundred acres," he went on. "Mine is almost double that, and a fair amount of land separates our houses. You aren't likely to run into your cousin."

Lana still appeared worried. Sly figured she was having second thoughts about going to his place. Which should have been a relief but wasn't. Oddly disappointed, he shrugged. "Look, if you'd rather not..."

"No, Sly. I want to see it."

He nodded. "Then follow me."

Chapter 16

As Sly turned at the black-and-white Pettit Ranch sign and rolled up the long, gravel driveway, satisfaction filled him. He'd spent a decade building his ranch into what it was today. From the freshly painted barn and outbuildings to the rolling pastures dotted with grazing cattle and horses, he was proud of it all.

He glanced in the rearview mirror. Lana trailed close behind him. He wondered if she was impressed. In a few minutes he would find out.

Just beyond the barn he signaled for her benefit, pulled over and braked to a stop. Standing beside his truck, he waited for her.

It was that magical time of day when the very air seemed bathed in oranges and pinks. Moving toward him, Lana looked unbelievably beautiful, like some woman in a painting at sunset.

Desire and those feelings Sly didn't comprehend steamrollered him. He swallowed hard. And wanted Lana gone. The sooner, the better. When she left, he would find something physically demanding to mellow him out and knock sense into his Lana-crazed brain.

"This is my ranch," he said.

If she heard any brusqueness in his voice, she didn't let on. Wide-eyed, she took it all in. "It's huge, Sly, and beautiful—exactly what I imagine the perfect ranch to be."

His chest swelled. "Come on, I'll show you around before I put dinner in the oven."

Lana was full of questions. As Sly answered them and explained how he ran his operation, he relaxed.

Some twenty minutes later, her stomach growled. With a sheepish look, she placed her hand over her belly. "Oops."

Sly chuckled. "I'll heat up dinner."

He followed her up the front steps to the veranda that spanned the entire width of the house.

"What a great porch, and that love seat seems cozy," Lana said. "I want to curl up there with a good book."

Sly nodded. "It's a swing, too, and one of my favorite places to sit in the evening, after the chores are done."

Lately he'd sat out here a lot at night, working on just how he was going to fit his kid into his life without screwing up.

Lana glanced upward. "This house is huge—at least twice the size of my town house."

Too big for one person, but Sly had had nothing to do with that. "The people I bought it from had three kids. I guess they needed the room."

"What happened to them?"

"The bank was getting ready to foreclose on the property, and they wanted out."

"That's too bad."

"Ranching isn't easy, and they were relieved to trade this life for one in the city. Last I heard, they were doing okay." He opened the front door and gestured Lana inside.

As she stepped into the vestibule, Sly couldn't help but picture her and their child here, filling the house with noise and laughter.

That stopped him. No way, no how. He enjoyed living alone.

Cursing himself for inviting Lana over, he turned away from her questioning gaze. "This way," he said with a curt nod.

She fell into step beside him.

"I envy you all the space in here," she said as she entered the kitchen.

It was big, all right, with room enough for a small horde. Usually Sly and Mrs. Rutland were the only ones in here, with periodic visits from Dani and an occasional crew member.

Having Lana in here felt…different. Felt right. Frowning, Sly switched on the oven.

"What can I do to help?" she asked.

Go home, he thought, *before I do something we'll both regret.* But it was too late for that. She'd already agreed to eat with him.

She gave him one of the smiles that erased his common sense. Hell, who was he kidding? As bad an idea as bringing her to the ranch was, he definitely wanted her here. He wanted her, period.

"Sly?" Lana was shooting him a funny look. "I asked if there's something I can do to help with dinner."

"How about setting the table."

After Lana washed her hands, he showed her where to find the place mats and utensils.

As she bent down to arrange them out on the table, she kicked the ordinary task to a whole new level of hot.

He really was losing it. Tired of his one-track mind, Sly grabbed two glasses from the cabinet. "While dinner heats, I'll give you the five-cent house tour."

He showed her the main floor—living room, den, dining and powder rooms.

"All the bedrooms are upstairs?" she asked.

"That's right—all four of them."

Her sudden, telltale blush revealed that she was thinking about all the beds in those rooms, just as he was. But inviting her, or any woman, to bed at his house was off-limits.

And yet he considered breaking his rule just this once, and giving her a hands-on tour of his king-size bed.

The oven buzzed and Sly jerked his thoughts back to the here and now. His brain heaved a relieved sigh, but his body wasn't happy.

The sooner Lana left, the better.

"Time to eat," he said, and they returned to the kitchen.

Sly didn't say much as Lana sat down at his kitchen table. Without so much as a "help yourself," he silently passed her a steaming casserole that smelled amazing.

He seemed ill at ease, but so was she. For some reason, sharing the evening meal at his ranch table felt like a big step.

Too big for a man who wasn't into relationships.

Plus, whether he wanted to be or not, they were on the verge of the relationship of their lives—parenting their child. It would be a huge change they both needed time to adjust to.

Wanting to ease the tension, Lana smiled. "This is delicious. Please thank your housekeeper for me."

"Will do."

Sly didn't say another word, and for a while the only sounds were their cutlery against the plates.

She tried again. "What would you be doing if I weren't here right now?"

"Probably eating in front of the tube."

"Sometimes I do that, too, or I read the paper." Better either of those than focusing on the loneliness of eating alone. "And occasionally I work while I eat."

"Not me. I pay bills and do any paperwork *after* the meal. Less indigestion that way."

He seemed more at ease now. Lana relaxed, too. "My parents would agree with you," she said. "When my sister and I were kids, they insisted on no television or phone calls during dinner. We tried to eat together every night, but once Liz and I started high school, we both had so many after-school activities that family dinners were hard to manage."

"What kinds of activities?"

"Liz played soccer and joined the swim team, and I worked on the yearbook and the sets for our school plays."

Sly actually smiled. "With your artistic skills, I can picture you painting scenery."

"That's exactly what I did. What about you, Sly?" Lana asked. "What sorts of activities were you involved in?"

"Like your sister, I was into sports. Football, baseball. That's how I was able to attend college—on a baseball scholarship."

"No kidding." She'd never have guessed. There was so much she didn't know about Sly. "Did you ever consider going pro?"

"Sure. I figured I'd do that after high school. Then my coach took me aside and convinced me to get a college education instead. And he was right. As it turned out, I was an okay ballplayer, but not good enough for the pros."

"I used to think I wanted to go to New York and be a set designer for one of the theaters—maybe even Broadway," Lana said. "Then in college I took a couple of child psychology courses and decided I wanted a career that involved kids."

"You made the right choice," Sly said.

"Seems that we both did."

"For me it was pure luck. The scholarship covered tuition, but I still needed money for books, room and board. I told you about finding work at a ranch, and here I am."

Lana nodded. "When I was little, I begged my parents to buy a ranch so we could live there. But they saw how hard my great-uncle Horace struggled to make ends meet. They didn't want that. Cousin Tim inherited the Lazy C from Horace."

"Dealing with Mother Nature and crop prices is always a struggle," Sly said. "But the work is rewarding. I enjoy it."

His face was lit up now. Lana smiled to herself. "How did you come to own all this?"

"The rancher who hired me, a guy named Bill Hodges, respected my work ethic. When he asked me what I wanted to do with my life, I said I wanted to own a successful ranch like his. He took me under his wing and mentored me just as a father would a son."

Sly sat back and stared into space a moment, as if remembering. "With his help, I was able to purchase a small spread north of town. A couple of years later, the state bought my land for that new freeway. I netted enough to buy this place."

Lana was impressed. "Are you still in contact with Mr. Hodges?"

Glancing down, Sly shook his head. "A year after I bought this place, he passed away."

He'd lost so many people he cared about. Lana's heart ached for him. "That's a shame. He'd be so proud of you now."

"I like to think so. My turn to ask the questions. Did you have any serious boyfriends in high school and college?"

"A couple of boyfriends, but nothing that lasted. Brent was my first real relationship. We met just before we graduated from college and dated almost three years before we got married."

Then four years of marriage and another eighteen months mourning the breakup... With a shock, Lana realized she'd spent eight and a half years of her life focused on Brent. And she had nothing to show for those years, except that she was sadder, wiser and older. She counted herself lucky to be free of him.

Otherwise she wouldn't be pregnant now.

She touched her belly and smiled. "I'll bet you had lots of girlfriends."

"A few."

"Anyone serious?"

"There was one girl I was serious about in college."

His somber expression made her curious. "What happened?"

"We talked about marriage, but her parents disapproved of me. I was a kid from a broken home and not good enough for their precious daughter. I didn't even own a suit, and that was real important to them. Apparently she decided they were right—she broke up with me." He gave a dismissive shrug.

"Ouch. But a broken home? Your parents died."

"True, but it was more that I didn't have two dimes to rub together, and they didn't think I ever would."

Indignant on Sly's behalf, Lana scoffed. "There are lots of college kids who start off poor and end up doing really well. You did. Those people were total snobs."

"Hey, it was a long time ago. I got over it." Sly glanced down at his work shirt and faded jeans. His mouth quirked. "If they could only see me now."

The meal was winding down. Soon Sly could plead fatigue or evening chores and send Lana home. It was what he should have wanted. And yet he lingered at the table.

Lana slanted her head his way. "A nickel for your thoughts."

Tonight he'd revealed more about himself than most people ever knew. Not just because she'd asked, but because she cared. A lot—too much. Usually when that happened, Sly felt hemmed in by a relationship and wanted out. He wasn't about to analyze why this time felt different.

"I was considering asking you to help me clean up this mess," he teased.

Lana arched her eyebrows. "That depends, Mr. Pettit, on whether you're planning to bribe me with the brownies over there on the counter."

"Mrs. R made them, and they're killer. Help me with the dishes and you can have as many as you want."

"For brownies, I'll do just about anything."

"Anything?" he drawled, letting his gaze rove slowly over her.

In the silence, desire hung between them in the suddenly thick air.

Lana shifted restlessly in her seat, the sudden blush on her face and hunger in her eyes burning him like a heated caress.

His body throbbed to life. He had a fair idea what Lana wanted tonight, but he wasn't going there—not here. If they'd been at her place, sure. But at his ranch, in his bed? No way.

He cleared his throat and stood. "Let's get this done."

Fifteen minutes later the leftovers had been stowed in the fridge, the kitchen was clean and Sly had managed to corral his randy libido.

With a smile tugging her lips, Lana held out her hand. "I'll take that bribe now."

Sly pulled the plastic wrap from the brownie plate. "It's a nice evening," he said. "Let's have our dessert outside."

Where the air between them was bound to be cooler.

On the porch, Lana plunked down on the swing. His swing.

Sly grabbed a brownie for himself, passed the plate to her and then bypassed several porch chairs to sit on the top step, a good five feet from her. Able to breathe better now, he sucked in the fresh air.

Lana frowned. "Why are you sitting all the way over there on the hard steps when you could be sitting in a chair or sharing this nice, padded swing with me? And hey, in case you didn't realize, you can't trust me with these brownies."

Trust. A rarity in his life. She'd always been straight with him and he sensed that she always would be.

Which explained why, against his better judgment, he *was* beginning to trust her.

He hadn't wanted to do that—trusting someone only led to pain.

"I don't bite, you know," she added when he remained silent.

Oh, he knew. He was about to ask her to leave when she spoke.

"I think I'll have another brownie. They're so delicious, I just might finish them all. Then I'll get sick, and it'll be your fault for not helping me eat them."

"Those things are really rich," he said. "You'll never be able to eat the whole plate."

"I'm pregnant, remember?"

"You drive a hard bargain."

"That's what people tell me." She patted the seat beside her and smiled serenely.

Sly gave up. "All right." He ambled over and sat down, keeping the brownie plate between them.

They ate and chatted about this and that, both of them pushing the rocker back and forth in the growing darkness. It would have been really comfortable if a certain part of Sly's body wasn't primed and ready for action.

Down, boy, he ordered it. Not here and not tonight.

"Now that we've heard the baby's heartbeat, I'm ready to say something to Liz and Eric about pregnancy," Lana said. "If it's okay with you, I'm thinking I'll do it after work tomorrow."

That she was checking with him first sat well in his chest. "Sure," he said. "I'll tell Dani then, too."

There was one brownie left. Sly was eyeing it when Lana divided it and handed him half.

"What about your parents?" he asked as he polished it off. "When are you planning to give them the news?"

Lana had been about to eat her brownie. Now she bit her lip and set it down again. "Liz and Eric will be excited and happy for me. If I know my sister, it won't be easy for her to keep something this big to herself. Especially from our mom and dad. I should tell them right after I tell her." She let out a heavy sigh. "I dread that."

"If family is as important to them as you say, they'll support you no matter what."

"I'm not so sure about that." She offered a weak smile.

"Because I'm the father and I'm suing dear old Cousin Tim."

She nodded.

Sly swore. No matter how carefully he examined the situation, there was no easy way out. No out, period.

Neither of them spoke after that. The swing creaked as he pushed it with his foot. In the distance, an owl hooted.

"Know what I like about you?" he said after a while.

"My ability to consume vast quantities of sweets?"

"That, and the fact that no matter what, you're always straight with me."

"I'm not wired to hold in my thoughts."

"Except when it comes to sharing them with your parents."

"I want to get along with them."

Her beautiful eyes pleaded with him to understand, and he lost himself in them. "I'll come with you when you tell them," he offered.

She glanced away and her hands started their fidget routine, a sure sign that something was bothering her. "I don't know, Sly. That probably isn't such a great idea."

"They can hate me all they want. You're carrying my baby, and you don't want to face them alone. I want to be there with you."

"You'd do that for me? You're a good man, Sly Pettit. I'm awful glad my baby will have you for a daddy."

Her warmth and sincerity went straight to his heart. She stroked his cheek, then leaned across the plate, cupped his face in her hands and kissed him. Nothing passionate, a light brush of her lips against his. But her sweetness was there, tempting him like a siren's song.

Fighting a losing battle to control his desire, and forgetting that on his ranch he wanted to keep his distance, he caught hold of her hand and kissed the sensitive inside of her wrist.

He heard her swallow and felt her pulse bump against his mouth, pounding almost has hard as his heart.

The brownie plate clattered onto the porch planking, a loud warning that what he was about to do was a bad idea.

"Oops," Lana murmured, her voice husky with desire. "There goes the dessert plate." Her lips parted, her eyelids lowered and she wrapped her arms around his neck.

Need roared through him, crushing the last of his tenuous grip on his control. He pulled her onto his lap and gave in.

Chapter 17

Sly's mouth was hard, demanding. Weak with desire, Lana sank against him. Her mind blanked and her whole world shrank to just her and him, slowly rocking in the cooling night air. Hours later, or maybe it was only a few minutes, Sly pulled away.

His breathing was labored, as if he'd just sprinted a quarter mile. "If we don't stop now, Lana, I won't be able to."

"I don't want to stop," she whispered. She tried to kiss him again, but to her frustration, he lifted her off his lap and deposited her on her side of the swing.

"You've been saying you're not ready."

"I am now."

"It won't hurt the baby?"

Lana shook her head.

"You're sure you want to do this?"

Lana had never been more certain. Without hesitation, she nodded.

Sly's exhale sounded like pure relief. "First we have to get a few things straight."

"Let me guess what you're going to say—you're not into relationships," she ventured.

"Right. I like you, and I want to be part of your life while we raise our kid." He glanced at his erection. "It's obvious that I want to be with you sexually. But my feelings about a committed relationship haven't changed."

What he'd described sounded like a committed relationship to Lana, but just now she was too impatient to quibble over definitions. "Got it," she said. "Now, please, take me to bed."

Sly hesitated, searching her face a moment, before he grasped her hand, tugged her to her feet and pulled her inside.

Foreplay was Sly's second favorite part of lovemaking. He enjoyed taking his time, but with Lana molded to him and kissing him hotly on the way upstairs, that proved challenging. Her passion and enthusiasm scorched him and nearly sent him over the edge. Halfway up, he lifted her into his arms and carried her the rest of the way.

"Mmm, you're carrying me. Why?" she asked in a sexy voice that thrilled him.

"I want to make sure we reach the bedroom while I still can."

Moments later he set her down. Standing a few feet in front of him with her gaze locked on his, she slowly removed her top. Her skin was flushed with desire. She wore a lacy black bra she almost spilled out of, and her taut nipples were clearly visible.

"Now you," she said.

She didn't have to ask twice. Sly unbuttoned a few buttons of his shirt, then pulled the thing over his head.

They shed their pants at the same time. Then he was down to his shorts, and she… In a black bra and a matching pair of bikini panties, she looked sexy as hell. So beautiful.

His.

Sly swallowed. "As much as I like your underwear, it has to go."

With a seductive look, Lana reached behind her and unhooked the clasp. The bra dropped to the floor.

"Now I can see the changes in your body. Your breasts are bigger." He cupped her reverently in his hands. "Heavier."

Lana's eyelids drifted down.

"Your nipples are darker." Aware of her sensitivity, he lightly traced each rigid tip with his finger, pleased when she shivered.

Continuing his study of her, he placed his palm over her belly, just as he'd watched her do to herself count-less times. "Your stomach is slightly rounded."

"Y-yes," she replied, as if talking were difficult. "Does that bother you?"

Sly shook his head. "You're perfect." He let his fin-gers trail lower. "Warm, too, and smooth."

He reached the elastic band in her panties. As he dis-posed of them, Lana sucked in a breath.

"You're incredibly responsive," he said, slipping his finger inside her. "It's hot."

"It's you, Sly. What you're doing now... I don't think my legs will support me any longer."

"Don't worry, I've got you." He lifted her off the ground and gently deposited her on the bed. "Now, where were we?" He parted her folds. "This part hasn't changed at all. But maybe I should check more closely."

Lana tensed. He tasted her most sensitive place, enjoying her gasps of pleasure.

In no time, she shifted restlessly and moaned. Moments later, she let go and shattered.

After recovering she gave him a wicked smile. "Your turn, cowboy. On your back."

With her blond hair every which way and her proud breasts heaving, she straddled his thighs. His very own, very hot goddess. She wrapped her hand around his arousal. Sly saw stars. He stopped her before he lost control.

Lana frowned at him. "Hey, I was just getting started."

"I don't want to finish without you. Understand?"

Still on his back, he positioned her where he needed her. One thrust and he was deep inside her, exactly where he wanted to be.

Shuddering with desire, Lana contracted her muscles and squeezed him. Heat and pleasure roared through Sly, and he forgot about taking it slow. Gripping her hips, he thrust upward. Harder and faster and deeper, until he was mindless with need. Lana cried out and together they spiraled out of control.

When he finally came down to earth again, she lay sprawled across his chest, her head tucked under his chin. Spent and utterly sated, he held her close. "Wow," he said. "That was even better than I remembered."

She raised her head and smiled at him with lips that were swollen from the deep kisses they'd shared. "It was pretty amazing."

Keeping his arm around her, he rolled her to his side. After a while Lana's breathing evened out. Sly figured she'd fallen asleep.

Feeling tender and protective, he pulled the covers up over her shoulders. Lana mumbled and burrowed closer.

Sly felt unbelievable. Great. Complete.

Hold the fort. He didn't want these emotions, couldn't take the risk of caring too much.

She could leave him, and as with most everyone else he'd ever cared about, probably would. That scared him even more than his overpowering feelings for her.

As he started to untangle his limbs from hers, his groin accidentally brushed against her hand.

Just like that, he was hard again. He slid his palm over her bottom, then between her legs. Her breath caught in the aroused little sound he'd come to anticipate.

They began to make love again, and for a long time Sly didn't have a single coherent thought.

Much later, after enjoying the best sex of his life—twice—Sly lay on his back with one arm under his head and the other around Lana.

It was going to take a while to recover. Then she kissed his rib cage with her soft, warm lips. As spent as he was, his body stirred and he wanted her all over again.

God help him, he couldn't get enough of her, and didn't think he ever would. While he debated how to deal with that, she propped herself on her elbows.

"I never knew it could be like this," she said, staring at him as if he were something special.

"We have great chemistry."

"It's more than that. When we make love, you're so considerate and caring."

"Are you saying your previous lovers weren't—not even your ex?"

"Let's just say that Brent was more into his own satisfaction than mine."

Sly didn't understand guys like that. "He didn't deserve you. You were right to divorce him."

"*He* divorced *me*," she corrected in the straightforward way he admired. "I was hurt and it took me a while to move on. But I can't say I'm sorry about the divorce. Because if Brent and I had stayed together—" she planted a sweet kiss on Sly's chest "—I wouldn't be here now with you."

It was about as close to a declaration of love as she could get without saying the words. Sly wasn't ready for that, but she knew the score. She kissed his rib cage, then his belly. His mind blanked.

He was tasting his way down her body when her stomach growled. Loudly.

Chuckling, he gave up. "I guess it's time to feed you again."

Lana smiled and shrugged. "Apparently."

They were in the kitchen, foraging through the fridge, when the first bars of "Mama Knows" filled the air. "Is that your cell phone?" Sly asked.

Lana straightened and turned away from the fridge. She was wearing one of his clean T-shirts. It almost swallowed her up. Sly liked that.

"Yep. It's my mother—the last person I want to talk

to. It's almost ten-thirty. She's usually in bed by now."
She shot Sly a panicked look. "What if something's
happened?"

"Maybe you should answer it."

"Talk to my mom right after you and I had sex?"

"She won't know that. This might be a good time to
mention me," he suggested.

He saw right away she wasn't ready for that conversation. "Tell her some other time, then," he said. "Listen,
I haven't checked my phone since I left here before your
doctor's appointment. I'll do that while you talk to her."

Before Lana answered her cell phone, she sat down
at the kitchen table. Sly was standing at the counter, listening to his messages. Shirtless and barefoot, with the
top button of his jeans undone, he looked like a walking
ad for sex appeal—except for the stunned expression
on his face. Lana was so curious about that, she almost
ignored her chirping phone.

She answered just as Sly disconnected and joined
her at the table.

"Hi, Mom," she said, rolling her eyes at him. "You're
calling so late. Is everything okay?"

"Yes, fine."

"That's a relief." Lana let out a sigh. "I'm sort of
busy right now. Can I call you back in the morning?"

"Let me guess—you're online, visiting that adoption
site again, hoping to find a pregnant girl who wants her
baby to go to a single mother."

If that wasn't the beginning of a lecture… Lana was
relieved she'd never told her mother about Sophie, and
anxious to get her mother off the phone. "No internet

for me tonight," she said. "This is something completely different." She smiled at Sly.

His solemn expression puzzled her.

"Well, it must be important," her mother said, sounding out of sorts. "In the past hour, I've called you twice. Both times I had to leave a message. I'm glad you finally decided you could spare a moment to talk to me."

"Way to guilt-trip me, Mom. I, uh, left my phone in the kitchen, and didn't hear it ring before."

Which was true. Her phone had been in her purse, which she'd placed on the counter. "You're usually asleep by now. Whatever you have to say must be important."

"It is. Your father and I heard from Cousin Tim earlier and I have some interesting news. He's decided to countersue Mr. Pettit."

Lana's jaw dropped. "Cousin Tim is countersuing Sly…er, Mr. Pettit?" she repeated for Sly's benefit.

She saw by his grim expression that he'd already heard. He pointed at his phone. Someone must have left him a message about it.

"That's right," her mother said. "It seems a few of Cousin Tim's cows have turned up sick. One even died. He's claiming that Sly Pettit poisoned them."

Sly wouldn't do that. Or would he? Of course not, Lana assured herself. Yet she distinctly remembered what Sly had said that night at the Italian restaurant. That he was tired of waiting for the lawsuit to settle and that he wished he could do something to push it along.

Was this was his way of righting the wrongs he believed her cousin had done?

Doubts crept in, unwanted but impossible to ignore. As Lana met Sly's gaze, she suddenly felt sick.

In a blink, his eyes lost all warmth. His entire expression shuttered and closed, almost as if he'd read her mind.

Without a word, he stood and spun away from her, his shoulders set and his spine stiff. Lana realized that somehow he'd sensed her suspicion.

He opened the back door, walked out and shut it behind him with a firm click.

Her mother was saying something about Cousin Tim, but Lana couldn't focus. "I have to go," she said.

She disconnected and then headed outside to find Sly.

Chapter 18

Sly was still reeling from Dave Swain's message. Tim Carpenter's accusations and countersuit—all of it was a big load of bull crap, stuff he would deal with when he contacted the attorney in the morning.

What he couldn't handle was Lana's off-the-cuff gut reaction to the news. Her expression had clearly revealed that she suspected he'd poisoned Carpenter's cattle.

That stung and made him mad, too. Mostly at himself for breaking his own cardinal rule and trusting her. And for starting to care.

What a damn fool he was. He wanted to head for the barn, jump on Bee and gallop through the darkness until his mind emptied. But he needed his boots for that, and they were in his bedroom. Sly wasn't about to return to the house until he pulled himself together.

And so he paced the porch in his bare feet. The motion-activated lights kicked on, and he could easily see where he was going. Step around the furniture. *Thud-thud-thud.* Pivot around and don't think. *Thud-thud-thud.*

He was starting his third lap and nowhere near calm when the back door opened and Lana slipped outside. Light from the kitchen sliced right through the T-shirt he'd loaned her, silhouetting her naked body. The body he lusted after and couldn't get enough of.

Even now, smarting and angry, he wanted her. Sly called himself every name in the book—idiot, lame-brain, stupid jerk and a few four-letter epithets he wouldn't use on his worst enemy.

Lana reached out to him. "Please, can we talk?"

"What for?" He stepped away from her. "You assume I poisoned those cows."

On the slim hope that he'd misread her, he sucked in a breath and waited for her to deny it. She didn't.

His laugh sounded hollow even to his own ears. "You should leave," he said.

"Not like this."

"That's right—you're wearing my shirt. Go upstairs and get your clothes."

"That's not what I meant, Sly, and you know it. If you want me to go, I will, but not while you're angry. First we have to straighten this out."

"You should have thought about that before you assumed I poisoned your cousin's cows."

Barefoot or not, if he didn't get some space, he'd explode. He strode down the porch steps and kept going, wincing as he stepped on pebbles and God knew what else, until he heard the kitchen door close as Lana re-entered the house.

Before long she was outside again, in her own clothes, purse slung over her shoulder and keys in hand. She stopped right in front of him, just beyond the reach of the porch light. Even so, he could see the gleam of her pleading eyes.

"You wouldn't poison anyone's cattle," she said. "Neither would Cousin Tim. I just… His countersuit caught me by surprise."

Nothing she said explained the shock and horror on her face when her mother had told her what had happened. That Lana had suspected him, even for a moment, was unacceptable. Unbearable.

Sly's heart constricted painfully. He had trusted her, but she couldn't trust him. He gave a terse nod. "Good night, Lana."

Her mouth trembled, and for a minute he feared she was going to cry. God above, he hoped not. He was already treading on thin emotional ice himself, hurt to the quick and barely holding it together.

But she only raised her chin and walked past him, into the darkness and toward her car.

Sly woke up Wednesday in a bum mood, and things only got worse after he spoke with his attorney. "I didn't do it," he told Dave.

"I know that, Sly."

His attorney believed in him. Why couldn't Lana?

He was still kicking himself for letting his guard down last night. For allowing her to get too close.

"The question is, can you prove it to Tim Carpenter?" his attorney asked.

"How the hell am I supposed to prove I didn't do it?" Sly grumbled. "I assume he had an autopsy done on the animal that died."

"He used the same vet as you. His heifer had arsenic poisoning. The three that are sick have the same symptoms, but they'll probably survive."

"Sounds very similar to what happened to my cattle," Sly said. "Carpenter must think I'm retaliating for what he did. Oh, that's rich. What am I supposed to do now?"

"My suggestion is for you and Tim Carpenter to work with a mediation attorney. I can recommend one who's top-notch. I spoke with him earlier and he's willing to work with the two of you to reach some kind of resolution."

"There's nothing to resolve," Sly said. "I didn't do it."

"As you know all too well, Tim Carpenter is claiming the same thing."

Sly mumbled a few choice words and for the first time, considered a new angle. What if someone else was involved? "Let me think about the mediator and get back to you."

He spent most of the next two days alone on his horse, galloping across the ranch in search of calves that had become separated from the herd. He didn't find any. Which was a good thing, but Sly needed the distraction that herding a lost calf or two would have provided. With effort he managed to steer his mind away from Lana and their night together. That had become too painful to remember.

Instead, he focused on the new turn of events with Carpenter. Before the countersuit, he'd believed the situation was as bad as it could get. He'd been wrong. His life seemed to be spinning out of control.

The poisonings were too similar to be a coincidence, which meant someone was messing with them. But if another person was involved, how would Sly ever recoup the money he'd lost, and how could he possibly find that person?

Late Friday morning he made a decision. He couldn't go on like this, and he hoped Carpenter felt the same. He would attempt to talk to his neighbor again, so that they could straighten out this mess. Just the two of them, without a mediator or any lawyers involved.

His mind made up, he rode Bee to her favorite pasture, removed her saddle and slapped her lightly on the rump. She trotted to a big shady hawthorn and began to nibble sweet grass. Sly slid his cell phone from his pocket. He was searching for Carpenter's number when his own cell phone rang.

The screen identified the caller as Timothy Carpenter. Speak of the devil. "Carpenter," Sly said by way of greeting. "I was just about to call you."

"Were you, now. Planning on cussing me out?"

"Something like that. You and I need to sit down and talk. No lawyers—just you and me, man-to-man."

"Damn straight, we do."

That the rancher was willing to talk with Sly at all was progress of a sort. "Where and when?" Sly asked.

"My place. Now."

"As long as you don't point any guns at me or try to take a punch at me."

"I won't, if you don't accuse me of something I didn't do."

"No guns, no accusations," Sly agreed. "Just the two of us talking things through."

Fifteen minutes later he drove up Carpenter's driveway, past a barn that had seen better days. He stopped next to the house, which could use a coat or two of paint. The buildings at the Lazy C needed work, but the fields beyond were green and populated with livestock. Sly noted a tractor and a few men in the distance.

His neighbor was standing on the porch, wearing reflector sunglasses and a Stetson. As Sly crossed the yard, Carpenter folded his arms over his chest.

Matching his unwelcoming scowl, Sly climbed the stairs. Neither of them removed their hats or their sunglasses. "I didn't poison your cattle," he stated.

"Yeah? Well, I didn't poison yours, either."

Though Carpenter had five or six years on Sly, they were roughly the same height and both muscular and strong. Despite the sunglasses, Sly sensed his hostile glare.

He rested his hands low on his hips. "You gonna ask me to sit down, or are we going to do this standing up?"

His neighbor nodded at a pair of lawn chairs in the front yard, in the shade of an old black walnut. They both sat down, their weight causing the old chairs to creak.

"I'd have bet my left arm that you poisoned my cows to get back at me for dragging out the lawsuit," Carpenter said.

Sly snorted. "That's not how I work. Ask anyone in town. I prefer to solve my problems by talking them out."

The ones that weren't too personal, that was. He tended to keep those close to the chest. "I'm starting to wonder if someone else might have set us both up."

Carpenter bent down and plucked a blade of grass, the expression of doubt on his face reminding Sly of Lana.

That she believed him capable of poisoning Carpenter's cows hurt. But he didn't want to think about that. Pushing the pain inside, he waited his neighbor out.

Carpenter straightened again, stuck the blade of grass between his lips and rolled it to the corner of his mouth before he went on. "You're smarter than you look, Pettit. Something came to my attention this morning that put me of the same mind."

Sly tipped his hat back and pulled off his shades. "What are you saying?"

Carpenter, too, removed his sunglasses and met Sly's gaze. "That someone who wanted to do me serious harm set me up by poisoning your cattle and making me look guilty. When things didn't go as fast as he wanted, he upped the ante and poisoned some of mine."

Sly swore. "You must have made some nasty enemies." Given Carpenter's sour disposition, not hard to believe. "Just who is this crazy person?"

"A son of a dog by the name of Pitch Alberts."

Sly had never heard of the man. "I'm not familiar with him."

"You wouldn't be. About a year and half ago he came into town looking for a job. He worked for me until mid-November of last year. That's when I found out he was stealing hay and cattle feed from me. Of course, I sacked him. He didn't have any money. I knew he'd never pay me back for what he'd stolen, and the loss wasn't big enough for me to press charges.

"Pitch didn't appreciate losing his job just before the holidays, but that was his fault. I told him he was lucky I didn't call the sheriff."

Sly probably would have done the same thing as Carpenter.

"Pitch hadn't crossed my mind since, until Eddie, a guy on my summer crew, said he ran into Pitch last night at a bar. Pitch had had a few and was bragging that he'd fixed my wagon. From there it was a matter of putting two and two together."

Sly shook his head. "I trust you've been in touch with Sheriff Dean."

"This morning, right after Eddie told me. Sheriff Dean's been out searching for Pitch, to take him in for questioning. As yet, that's all I know, but I'd stake my ranch that he did it."

"If that's true, then I owe you an apology," Sly said.

"I'll take it. I'll owe you one, too. By the way, my lawyer advised me to keep all this to myself for now. I wouldn't want Pitch suing me for slander." The corner of Carpenter's mouth lifted, the closest he'd ever come to smiling.

"Copy that. I'll do the same, then. Keep me informed."

"After my lawyer, you'll be the first person I'll contact."

They shook hands and parted almost amicably, Sly in a much better mood than when he'd arrived. Things hadn't turned out at all as he'd expected, and he shook his head at that.

Regardless, he still needed the new drainage system, and he still didn't want to borrow money to pay for it. He'd been so focused on either getting reimbursed by Carpenter or taking out a costly loan that he hadn't considered other options. There had to be another way.

His mind spinning, he returned home. Sitting in the truck in his driveway, he phoned Dave and filled him in. "I'll keep you updated," he promised.

Then he contacted Bob Haggerty, the engineer who owned the drainage-system company, and set up a meeting for later that afternoon.

It was a relief to have the answers to all the questions he'd had for months now. Lana would want to know what had happened, and Sly itched to fill her in. But he and Carpenter had agreed to keep it quiet for now. Besides, after the other night, Sly wouldn't be telling her anything.

His high spirits nose-dived and his chest constricted. He felt as if he was suffocating. If not for a recent physical and the news that he was as fit as a kid half his age, he'd have called his doctor.

There was just time to fit in a ride on Bee before the meeting with Haggerty. Sly stalked toward the pasture and whistled for his horse. He rode her bareback, racing into the wind until finally his mind cleared and he could breathe again.

Over the past few days, Lana had tried to act as if she was fine and nothing had changed. Apparently she sucked at faking happiness. Jasmine and Brittany tiptoed around her with sympathetic expressions, and even the most rambunctious kids had behaved.

By Friday she was a basket case, in need of a friendly ear. After a quick SOS to Kate, she went directly from work to her friend's apartment for pizza and sympathy.

"The pizza should be here soon," Kate said when she let Lana in. "Sit down and tell me what's wrong."

Out of habit, Lana placed her hand over her stomach, but even the beloved child growing inside failed to bring her comfort.

Kate's eyes widened a fraction before she gave Lana a stricken look. "You're okay, right?"

"The baby is fine," Lana assured her, and counted her blessings that at least that part of her life was going well.

"That's good." Her friend blew out a big breath. "So what's the matter?"

Where to begin? "For starters, I'm in love with Sly."

"That's obvious. He wants to be part of the baby's life, right? He even showed up at your doctor's appointment the other day. You can't ask for more than that from a commitmentphobe. We haven't touched base since before the appointment. How did it go?"

"Great. Sly and I got along so well that after the doctor's appointment, he invited me to his ranch and showed me around. He fed me dinner, too. He doesn't do that with just anyone."

"No wonder we haven't talked all week. Sounds to me as if Mr. Single is getting serious. Go on."

"We had sex."

Kate gave her a funny look. "He disappointed you?"

Lana shook her head. "Sly is the best lover I've ever had."

"Lucky you," Kate said. "That sounds pretty darned perfect. So what's the problem?"

"Everything was wonderful—then my mother phoned."

"You answered her call when you were with Sly? Are you nuts?"

"I'm beginning to think I might be." Lana gnawed on her thumbnail…or what was left of it. "We were in the kitchen, grabbing a snack." They'd been happy and relaxed. "It was later than she usually calls, and I was worried."

Lana wished she could go back in time and switch off her phone, or at least ignore the call. Unfortunately, that was impossible. "It wasn't an emergency. She wanted to tell me that someone had poisoned Cousin Tim's cows. One even died. My cousin is blaming Sly and countersuing."

"No." Kate's jaw dropped. "Sly would never do anything like that!"

Lana envied her friend's instant certainty. If she'd reacted with the same outrage, Tuesday night would have ended very differently.

"That's a pretty sad face you're making," Kate commented. "Things can't be that bad."

"You haven't heard the whole story yet." Lana's head hurt. She massaged her temples. "I really screwed up, Kate. When I heard about the poisoning, I couldn't help but wonder whether Sly had done it."

"After all the great things you've said about him, you really believe he'd do something like that?"

"Not in my heart. It was sort of a gut reaction."

Kate just shook her head. "And you said this to Sly?"

"I didn't have to. He saw my face, and you know what an open book that is." Dropping her head to her hands, Lana groaned. "It was horrible of me to suspect him, even for a moment."

Wonderful friend that Kate was, she didn't comment, she just sat quietly and waited for Lana to pour out the rest of the miserable story.

Lana gave her all the awful details. "I'd do anything to change those seconds of doubt," she concluded. "I wish there was a way that I could convince Sly that I believe in him, and that I'm absolutely certain he would never do what my cousin is accusing him of."

"I think you should tell Sly what you just told me. If he's as good a man as you claim, he's bound to forgive you."

"You weren't there. The way he looked at me..." With shuttered eyes and a cool disdain, as if he were seeing her for the first time and didn't like the woman he saw.

Lana wanted to sob. "Trust doesn't come easy to him, but I'm pretty sure he was beginning to trust me. And I blew everything by not trusting *him*. I hurt him, Kate." She hung her head. "I lost my chance with him."

Now Kate became glum, too. "There must be something you can do."

For the life of her, Lana couldn't come up with anything. "Like what?"

"Well..." Kate tapped her finger to her lips and appeared pensive. "Invite him over and cook his favorite foods. Then apologize and swear you'll always believe in him."

"He's angry at me. I doubt he'd come. Besides, words and a meal wouldn't prove anything. It has to be something important." An idea popped into her mind that she needed to test on Kate. "What if I go to my parents' house right now and tell them about Sly? Then I could drive over to Cousin Tim's and convince him that Sly would never hurt his animals."

"Great idea," Kate said. "It's about time your parents knew about Sly. As for your cousin, he doesn't strike me as a man easily swayed by anyone else's opinion. How will Sly even know that you went to bat for him?"

Lana wasn't about to let that stop her. "I'll pound on Sly's door and make him listen. If I want a chance with him, I have to restore his trust in me, and prove that I trust him."

"Wow, lady, you're on fire." Kate thought a moment. "I hate to bring this up, but what if it doesn't work?"

Refusing to consider the possibility, Lana raised her chin. "It will. It has to." She reached for her purse and stood.

"Now?" Kate frowned. "But what about the pizza?"

"Eat a piece for me. This won't wait."

Chapter 19

As Lana rode the elevator down from Kate's fourth-floor apartment, "Mama Knows" sounded from her cell phone.

She picked up right away. "Hi. I'm glad you called." She could almost hear her mother's surprise at that. "I'm on my way over to the house now. I have something important to tell you and Dad. I'll be there shortly." Before her mother had a chance to question Lana, she disconnected.

She wasn't going to reveal her pregnancy to her parents just yet—one step at a time. Besides, she wanted to tell Liz and Eric first. Tonight was about Sly.

Thanks to the usual Friday rush-hour traffic, she didn't pull up to her parents' house for a good twenty minutes. Which gave her way too long to imagine their shocked reactions. As she parked in front of their house, she was a giant mess of nerves. Weeks ago, Sly had pointed out that she was afraid of them. Although Lana had denied it, she *was*.

Which was embarrassing for a thirty-two-year-old woman to admit, even to herself. She finally had to face those fears and move through them.

Not about to let that stop her, she squared her shoulders and entered the house.

Her parents were seated in the living room, obviously waiting for her. Mustering a smile she didn't feel, she greeted them. Her mother had set out cookies and lemonade. Having skipped dinner, Lana was famished. She ate a cookie, but was so focused on the task at hand that she barely tasted it.

"Let me guess why you're here," her mother said. "You've found a teenage girl with a baby to adopt."

"Actually, I've put the adoption idea on hold," she said. Now would be a perfect moment to announce that she was pregnant, but first things first.

Her mother looked relieved. "Is that what this visit is about? I'm glad you finally came to your senses. I was beginning to—"

"Could you save it, Mom? I need to tell you something important." Lana's mother shut her mouth. "I've met someone, a man I've fallen in love with."

Her parents shared a knowing glance. "I figured that sooner or later you would," her dad said. "But this seems a little sudden. I'd hate for you to get hurt again."

Thanks to her own actions, Lana was already suffering. "Actually, Dad, we've known each other several months."

"You kept something so momentous from your own

parents?" Lana's mother shook her head. "How could you—"

"Michele," her father warned, placing a warning finger against his own lips.

"I didn't want to be judged and criticized for my choice," Lana replied.

The pained expression on her mother's face revealed that she was well aware of her own behavior. "I realize that occasionally I get on your and your sister's nerves," she said. "Surely you know that I only want the best for you."

"I get that, Mom. But I'm an adult, and I have been for a while now. It's past time that you and Dad trusted me to make my own judgments about what's best for me."

Lana's father considered that for a bit, then nodded. "I agree."

After staring at her hands, her mother raised her head. "From the moment you were born, I've guided you toward where I thought you should go. Not that you listen much anymore." Her attempt at a humorous smile failed, and she gave Lana a pleading look. "You're my daughter and it's hard to let go. But you're right, you're an adult with a good head on your shoulders."

Grateful that they understood, Lana nodded. "Thank you—both of you."

"When will your mother and I get a chance to meet this mystery man of yours?" her father asked.

"How about at dinner this Sunday?" Provided she and Sly made up and he agreed to come. Lana wouldn't let herself worry about that now.

Her parents glanced at each other again and shrugged.

"That'd be nice," her father said before letting her mother take over.

"What's his name and what does he do for a living?" she asked.

Oddly calm now, and ready to test her parents' resolve to trust her, Lana sat up tall and spoke with the confidence and certainty borne out of her love for Sly. "His name is Sly Pettit. He owns Pettit Ranch."

Her mother's eyebrows jumped halfway up her forehead, and for once, she seemed at a loss for words.

Equally shocked, Lana's father opened and closed his mouth.

"Sly is a wonderful man with a good heart," Lana said. "You'll see that that when you meet him."

Her mother frowned. "I want to trust your judgment, Lana, but I'm not sure Sunday dinner is the suitable event…" At Lana's resolute expression, she broke off.

"I look forward to our weekly dinners and would hate to miss them—but if Sly isn't welcome, I won't come, either." Lana paused and bit her lip. "All I ask is that you give him a chance."

After a long, uncomfortable pause, her father cleared his throat. "If you really love him, then of course he's welcome."

Lana glanced at her mother. "Mom?"

"I won't lie to you, Lana—this upsets me." She sighed. "All right, Sly is welcome at our table. But I have no idea what your cousin will think." Her worried frown encompassed both Lana and her father.

He shook his head, then shrugged. With that, they sat back.

Lana exhaled the breath she'd been holding. "Don't worry about Cousin Tim. I'm going to drive over to his place right now and talk to him. In my heart, I'm convinced Sly didn't go near his cows."

"How can you be sure?" her mother asked.

"Because I know Sly. He'd never do that." Lana kissed both her parents. "We'll see you Sunday."

Feeling several pounds lighter, she hurried to her car.

Traffic was light now, and Lana sped through the twilight toward the Lazy C. Convincing Cousin Tim to drop his lawsuit might be impossible, but she was determined to try. Not that she had any idea what she would say, but she'd figure it out. For the sake of her peace of mind and the future of her and Sly's unborn child, she had to.

She passed the black-and-white Pettit Ranch sign and her heart lurched painfully. She couldn't help wondering whether Sly at was home or if he'd gone out. What would he think if he knew where she was headed?

Cousin Tim's ranch was a couple hundred feet ahead. Lana signaled, slowed and pulled into the driveway. It was early evening, not quite dark yet but getting there. Yet there were no house lights on. Her cousin's truck was parked near the front door, though, which meant that he was probably at home. She pulled to a stop beside the truck and slid out of the car.

Every bit as nervous as when she'd talked to her parents, she climbed the steps and knocked at the door.

A few seconds later, Cousin Tim answered with two bottles of beer in hand. "You sure got here fas— Lana." His face was a mask of surprise. "What brings you out here?"

"Sorry, I should have called first, but I took a chance that you'd have a few minutes to talk."

Her entire adult life, she'd never stopped by to visit her cousin, but he seemed to take it in stride. "Sure, but I'm expecting someone. Come in."

He left the door cracked open, maybe for his company. A girlfriend no one was aware of? Interesting idea, but just now Lana couldn't spare a moment to speculate. She had more important things on her mind.

"Uh, you want a beer?" her cousin asked, offering her one of the bottles.

Lana shook her head. "No, thanks."

The entry opened into the living room. She still hadn't decided exactly what she was going to say, but as she crossed the worn carpet, she realized that if she spoke from the heart, she couldn't miss.

Her cousin sat down so that he was facing the door, probably to watch for his mystery guest. Lana took the armchair across from him, the one that faced the backyard. The drapes were open, and she briefly noted the fenced lawn and beyond that, rolling fields extending as far as she could see.

As soon as she settled into her seat, she got straight to the point. "I'm here to talk to you about Sly Pettit."

Sly returned from the meeting with Haggerty in good spirits. The engineer had recently built a new home and needed help with the landscaping. He'd agreed to drastically reduce his fee for the drainage system if Sly would lay down sod and fence the front and backyards. Sly also promised to provide Haggerty with a free side of beef every year for the next ten years. The large quantity of meat would feed Haggerty's family for months.

In a few weeks, the engineer would start work on the new system. By then, Sly figured he'd be finished with the man's yard, and he and his crew could do some of the grunt work on the new drainage.

He was finishing dinner when Carpenter called. "Get your butt over here," he said. "I have some great news to share."

Anticipating a celebration, Sly had grabbed a couple of cold beers. Then, for the second time that day, he headed for the Lazy C. As he rolled up the driveway, he spotted Lana's light green sedan next to Tim's truck.

He braked to a stop. What was she doing here?

He'd bet the ranch Carpenter had no idea that he and Lana knew each other. As curious as Sly was about her reasons for being here, he was in no mood to face her. He almost turned around and left. But he was no coward. Besides, Carpenter was expecting him.

He was about to start up the front steps when he noted that the door was cracked open. In the still twilight air, Lana's voice carried easily.

Sly paused where he was, knowing he should announce his presence. But something made him keep quiet. He silently placed the beers on the second step and eavesdropped.

"Sly would never poison your cattle," she said.

What the hell? Sly frowned.

"You're friends with Pettit?" Tim asked, sounding puzzled.

"I met him before I heard about his lawsuit against you."

"You never said anything, not even when I came to your folks' for Sunday dinner last month."

"I was afraid of how they'd react, and even more scared of you. But I'm not anymore." Despite her brave words, Sly heard her swallow hard. "I just came from my parents' house, and I told them exactly what I'm telling you—that Sly and I have been seeing each other."

She'd talked to her parents? Sly could only imagine how difficult that must have been for her.

"You mean dating?" her cousin said.

"Something like that." Her voice seemed to grow stronger with each word. "You're my cousin and you're family, and that means a lot. But I can't sit by quietly and let you countersue Sly. He's a good man, an honest man. He values all cattle too much to harm them."

Sly was so surprised that he had to sit down. He joined the beers on the step.

"For you to vouch for him this way, you must know him pretty well," Tim said.

"I do. Besides my dad, Sly Pettit is the best man I've ever met. I would trust him with my life."

Realizing his jaw had dropped open, Sly shut his mouth.

"That's quite a statement," Tim said.

"It's the truth. I wouldn't fall for a man I couldn't trust."

"You're in love with Sly Pettit." Carpenter sounded shocked. "Is he aware of this?"

"Not yet. I know in my very bones that he would never poison an animal. Well, maybe a mouse or a rat. I'm asking you to please drop your counter lawsuit."

"You'd side with him against me?" Gruff Tim Carpenter sounded like a hurt kid.

"I'm not siding with anyone," Lana said. "I don't believe you poisoned his cows, either. Sly would realize that, too, if you would just sit down with him and talk.

Before he sued you, he tried to do that, but you wouldn't give him the time of day."

"Pettit never wanted to talk. From the get-go, he came at me with accusations."

"Then it's all the more important for the two of you to talk now. The sooner, the better. Otherwise you'll never get to the bottom of this mess."

"You're comin' at me with a damn lecture, just like Michele. Don't get me wrong, I love your mother, but her lectures give me a headache."

"I'm not my mother, and I'm not lecturing you." Lana sounded indignant. After a pause she said, "Well, darn it, maybe I am. I'll think about that later. What matters is that I'm here for a good reason. You and Sly are both hardheaded, and this lawsuit business is out of control. Someone levelheaded has to intervene. That would be me."

Him, stubborn? Sly barely stifled a loud snort.

But he had to admit that Lana was right. His head was as hard as the concrete step under him. Instead of approaching Tim Carpenter as someone who could help him find the answers he sought, Sly had accused, tried and found the man guilty.

In jumping to conclusions, he'd created a world of trouble.

Tuesday night he'd done the same thing with Lana, brushing off her suggestion that they talk. He'd been suffering mightily ever since, and guessed that she had been, too.

But even hurting, she was here, fighting for him because she loved him. She loved him.

Sly thought he might love her, too. No, he knew— he did love her.

Accepting and admitting this blew him away. He should have been scared, but wasn't. The truth was, he didn't feel half-bad—except when he realized he'd almost lost out on a lifetime with Lana.

What a damn fool he'd been.

He stood, brushed off his butt and grabbed the beers. Making no effort to be quiet, he strode up the steps. Neither Lana nor Tim was speaking, and Sly figured they'd heard his footsteps.

He knocked, then without waiting for an answer, stepped inside. The shock on Lana's face was comical, but this was no time for laughter.

"I was starting to wonder if you'd ever show up," Tim said.

"I've been here for a while now. Hold these, will you?" Sly handed him the beers, then turned to Lana. "Did you mean what you said? Do you really love me?"

"You were eavesdropping?"

Unashamed, he nodded. "I didn't expect to find you here tonight, but I spotted your car next to Tim's truck. He left the door open, and I wanted to hear what you were saying."

"You heard it all?" she asked, looking wary.

"I heard what matters—that you believe in me." Needing to touch her, Sly clasped both her hands and pulled her to her feet. "That's awesome—you're awesome."

Holding back none of his feelings, he kissed her thoroughly.

When he pulled back. Lana wore a dazed expression. "I love you, Sly."

Smiling, he gently brushed the hair out of her eyes. "Don't fall over when I say it, but I love you, too."

Tim growled. "If you two don't quit with the mushy stuff, I swear, I'll bring the hose in here and spray you down."

Sly and Lana laughed.

Not about to let go of his woman, Sly sat down in the armchair and pulled her onto his lap.

"I can't believe you're sitting in my cousin's living room," Lana said. "What are you doing here—with two beers each?"

"Sly's here because I invited him to come back," Tim said.

"Come back?" Lana echoed, confused.

Sly nodded. "I was here this afternoon, when Tim and I patched up our differences."

"Hold on a darned minute." Lana slanted her cousin a look. "You let me go through my whole spiel about how stubborn you and Sly both are without once mentioning that you'd already settled things?"

"I wanted to hear what you had to say," Tim said. "And it wasn't quite settled, but it is now."

"Will one of you please explain what's going on?" she asked.

Sly caught her up on what he knew, then turned to Tim. "I'm guessing Sheriff Dean called."

"About an hour ago. It took a while for him to find Pitch and get him to talk, but he finally confessed. It's just as I figured—he set us both up.

"I talked to my lawyer. First thing in the morning, he'll contact yours. He doubts that either of us is likely to get any restitution from Pitch. He's broke—he's always broke. But he'll probably spend a few years in jail."

"That's good enough for me," Sly said.

Carpenter nodded. "From now on, if we have issues with each other, let's talk them through."

"You have my word on that." Sly tipped up Lana's head and kissed the tip of her nose. "So do you."

"All this talk has made me thirsty." Carpenter reached for the bottle opener on the coffee table. "Have a cool one with us, Lana? There's a glass in the kitchen."

"Um, I can't." She looked at Sly. "We should tell him."

"Before your sister or your parents or Dani?"

She nodded. "After watching us get all mushy, it's the least we can do. Okay with you?" When Sly nodded, she glanced at her cousin. "Do me a favor, and don't contact the family for another forty-eight hours."

Carpenter seemed surprised by the request, but shrugged. "I guess I can do that. What's this about?"

Before making their announcement, Sly and Lana stood up. She threaded her fingers with his, and he nodded at her to do the talking.

"Sly and I… We're expecting a baby."

Her cousin almost choked on his beer. "Say what?"

Sly nodded. "It's true. The due date is early January."

"That's not long to wait," Carpenter said. "Congratulations, you two. It's a damn good thing we settled this cattle business."

He shook hands with Sly and patted Lana's shoulder. "I know how difficult your parents can be, Lana," he said. "If you want me to be there when you give them the news, I'll vouch for Sly."

"You'd do that?" Lana smiled at him. "Has anyone ever told you that you're a nice guy?" Standing on her toes, she kissed her cousin's cheek. Even his ears turned red. "Your offer means a lot, but Sly and I will do it together."

Chapter 20

"I haven't been to the falls in ages," Lana commented as Sly drove down River Drive early Saturday morning. "This will be fun—even if you did wake me up at the crack of dawn on my day to sleep in."

Remembering exactly how that had gone down, Sly gave her a heavy-lidded look. "You didn't seem to mind."

"Only because waking up to your kisses is a lot more fun than an alarm clock." Wearing the glow of a woman thoroughly loved, she smiled.

Sly grinned at her. Neither of them had slept much last night. They'd been too busy making love and talking. In the wee hours, Sly had come up with the plan for a picnic breakfast at the falls, followed by visits to Lana's sister and Dani.

He was happier than he'd been since… He couldn't

recall ever feeling this fantastic. He enjoyed having Lana in his bed and didn't think he'd ever grow tired of waking up beside her.

The very idea would have terrified him a few months ago. Today he felt like the luckiest man alive.

They headed into Prosperity Park, where woods and acres of manicured lawn surrounded the falls. "There's the gift shop where Kate works," Lana said. "Too bad it's so early. Otherwise we could stop in and visit her."

Sly wanted Lana all to himself for a couple of hours, which was why he'd suggested the early-morning picnic. "We'll catch her another time."

"Who should we tell first—my sister or yours?" Lana asked as Sly drove past walking and hiking trails, toward the falls.

"You remember how swamped Big Mama's is on Saturday mornings, especially during tourist season. Let's talk to your sister first, then drive over to the restaurant and grab Dani for a quick break. Why don't we finish up by stopping in at your parents'? I'd hate to spring the baby on them during my first Sunday dinner."

A week ago, the suggestion would have upset or worried her. Today, she looked calm and assured. "This afternoon it is." She glanced at the clock on the dash. "It's seven-thirty, and Liz is sure to be up. I'm going to call and make sure she'll be home later."

By the time Lana finished the call to her sister, Sly had parked in the large lot near the falls. Picnic basket and blanket in hand, they took the pathway that led to the falls, sauntering past beautiful flower gardens. As Sly had intended, at this early hour they had the place to themselves. Birds twittered in the trees, and playful squirrels chattered and chased each other. In the distance he heard the unmistakable sound of a waterfall.

A quarter mile later, the path curved sharply south, revealing a stunning view of the falls.

The sight of the steep rocks jutting several dozen yards up from the earth and the powerful cascade of water spilling over them in a thick curtain of spray never ceased to amaze Sly. He and Lana both stopped to take in the sight.

"This view always takes my breath away." Lana's chin tipped up and wonder filled her face. "How beautiful they are."

As Sly gazed down at her, warmth and tenderness flooded his chest, and he silently swore to do everything in his power to make Lana happy. "You're the beautiful one," he said. Then he kissed her.

Because they were in public, he kept it shorter and lighter than he would have preferred. Regardless, she was flushed and breathless when he pulled away.

His passionate woman.

The love in her eyes humbled him, and he was sure that life didn't get much better than this.

A safe distance from the reach of the water's spray, they found a flat, grassy place perfect for a picnic. Sly spread out the blanket, and Lana helped set out the food Mrs. Rutland had prepared for his weekend alone. Sly planned to introduce his woman to his housekeeper in the very near future. Mrs. R was going to like Lana. His crew, too.

Despite enjoying a snack in the middle of the night, the long night of lovemaking had made them both ravenous. For a while they forgot about conversation and chowed down. Lana's hearty appetite was one more thing Sly loved about her.

"Do you think your parents will be upset about the baby?" he asked, smiling to himself as she filched a chunk of his blueberry muffin.

"I won't lie—I want them to be happy about it. If they're not, I'll be sad," she said. "But I love you and you love me, and no matter what they think or say, that's the bottom line."

Sly couldn't have dreamed up a better reply. He felt as if he'd waited all his life for the amazing woman sharing his blanket.

So what are you waiting for? a voice whispered in his head.

In that moment, he made up his mind. He pushed the plates aside and knelt on the blanket, pulling Lana up to face him. She gave him a questioning look.

"I don't have a ring or anything, but I'd be…" Suddenly choked up, he stopped to clear his throat. "Lana, I want… Oh, hell." He was going to lose it.

"If this is a proposal, the answer is yes!"

"No kidding?"

"I've never been more serious in my life."

She wrapped her arms around his neck and he kissed her again, with all the love in his heart. When they came up for air, she rested her forehead against his and sighed. "I now have exactly what I've always dreamed of." She moved away from him and sat down again. "There's only one problem."

Unable to think what it could be, Sly gave a puzzled frown and tilted up her chin. "We solved all our problems. Tim and I dropped our lawsuits, we're about to tell your parents about the baby and we're getting married."

"I'm talking about the beautiful mural I painted in the nursery. What am I supposed to do with the town house?"

"Sell it or keep it as a rental—whatever you decide is okay by me. Heck, if you want, paint murals in all the bedrooms at my place."

"Your house is definitely big enough for a family."

"A whole houseful of kids, if I have my way." Picturing several little Lanas running around, creating pandemonium, he grinned.

"What if this is our only pregnancy?" she asked, suddenly somber.

"Then we'll adopt. Either way, I consider myself the luckiest man in the world."

The love and trust shining from Lana's eyes filled Sly with sweet certainty that no matter where life took him, Lana would be at his side.

"Come on." He rose to his feet and pulled her up beside him. "Let's go share our good news."

Two years later

"You're awfully quiet this afternoon," Sly said as he parked in front of Lana's parents' house for Sunday dinner. "Feeling okay?"

Being a rancher's wife and the mother of a toddler, not to mention setting up the second day care and finding a capable person to manage it, made for some very busy times, but Lana wouldn't have traded her life for anything. "I could use a nap, thanks to a certain little someone waking me up in the middle of the night."

She turned around to smile at their beautiful daughter, Johanna, named after Sly's mother.

The little girl beamed, her straight blond hair flying as she bounced in her seat. "'Hanna see cousins and Gammy and Gampa."

"That's right, sweetie," Lana said.

"She's already talking in full sentences, and she's barely eighteen months old," he said proudly.

"Smart like her daddy."

"And her mom."

Lana and Sly grinned at each other. She leaned toward her husband for a quick kiss. "Have I told you lately that I adore you, Mr. Pettit?"

"Not since early this morning, when you and I, uh—" He glanced at their daughter in the rearview mirror. "When we were in bed."

Lana was lost in his eyes when Johanna let out an excited shriek. "Cousins!"

Liz and Eric had just arrived, and Connor and Emma were racing toward the car.

Johanna wanted out. Sly lifted her from her car seat in time for her to cousins to greet her. Moments later, Connor and Emma raced for the backyard, Johanna squealing and toddling after them.

Eric nodded at Sly. "Come on, let's catch up to our kids."

"What you guys really want is the chance to check out Dad's new grill," Liz teased with a wry smile.

Neither man denied it.

Lana and her sister followed behind, catching each other up on the busy week they'd both had.

In the yard, Lana's parents greeted everyone with smiles and hugs. Lana's mother smiled at Sly. "Guess what I found at the specialty store? That microbrew beer you've been wanting to try."

"Thanks, Michele." Sly kissed her cheek. "You're the best."

After two years, Lana still marveled at the warm relationship her mother shared with Sly—better than she would ever have imagined.

Her dad clapped his hands on Sly's and Eric's shoulders and steered them toward the smoking grill, where steaks were sizzling. "Wait'll I show you what this baby can do."

Some fifteen minutes later, as everyone headed for the picnic table, Lana's father gave his head an admiring shake. "What a beautiful family we have."

Lana couldn't have agreed more.

* * * * *

A RANCHER'S
REDEMPTION

Dani's Instant Cocoa Mix

Makes approximately 12 servings

(Note: for smaller batches, mix 2 tbs. each of sugar and cocoa per cup of powdered milk, then add a pinch or two of salt.)

Ingredients:

3 cups instant nonfat powdered milk

6 tbs. sugar

6 tbs. dry, unsweetened cocoa powder

½ tsp. salt

Combine and mix thoroughly. Store in an airtight container in a cool, dry place.

To prepare cocoa:

Put ⅓ cup of cocoa mix in a 12-ounce mug. Stir in a little boiling water and mix until blended into a paste. Fill mug with boiling water. Stir or whip until blended. Add marshmallows if you like them.

Chapter 1

Dinner was starting to smell so good that Dani Pettit's mouth watered when Nick Kelly knocked at her door. Only a few short minutes ago, she'd buzzed him into the building.

Although they talked and texted regularly, she hadn't seen him in a while. But tonight she really needed to be with her best friend.

"He's here," she told Fluff.

The tomcat meowed and trotted daintily toward the door. Which was funny because at twenty pounds and half a ton of white fur, Fluff wasn't exactly tiny. But he'd never let Dani down, and so she stifled the urge to laugh at him. There weren't many true-blue males in her life—just the cat, Nick Kelly and Dani's oldest brother, Sly. She dearly loved all three.

To prevent Fluff from darting out, running across

the hall and shamelessly begging food from Mrs. Det-meier, Dani scooped him up before she opened the door and managed a smile. "Hi, Nick."

The handsome rancher flashed his pearly whites at Fluff, then gave Dani a gentler grin. "Hey."

In his large hands he cradled a bottle of wine and a white bag bearing the Lannigan's Ice Creamery logo, which was, bar none, the best ice creamery in Prosperity. Although the central Montana town of sixty thousand people boasted at least a half-dozen ice cream specialty shops, several much closer to her house than Lannigan's, Nick had chosen well. He sure knew how to brighten a girl's spirits.

Dani eyed the bag. "I hope that's rocky road."

"A whole gallon of the stuff."

"You sweetheart!" She rubbed her hands together.

Nick chuckled. "Nothing but the best for Dani Pettit."

He kissed her cheek, then set his things down to shrug out of his leather bomber jacket. He hung the jacket on the doorknob of the coat closet, just as he always did, his navy flannel shirt stretching across his strong, broad shoulders.

He was a beautiful man—tall and muscular without an ounce of extra fat, thanks to the physical demands of running a ranch. His long legs did wonders for the loose, faded jeans he favored.

Yet as gorgeous and sexy as he was, theirs was a strictly platonic relationship and always had been. Dani adored him—as a friend.

Nick stuck his fingers into Fluff's thick fur and scratched behind the cat's neck. "Howdy, Big Fella."

He refused to use the name "Fluff," which he considered too sissy for a tomcat.

Fluff didn't seem to mind. He was too busy purring and batting Nick's hand for more. A moment later, sated and content, he jumped out of Dani's arms and strolled off.

"I brought a couple of DVDs for later," Nick said. "Unless you'd rather catch a movie out. It is Saturday night."

Date night. Only twenty-four hours ago, Dani had assumed that she and Jeter would be out dancing tonight at the Bitter & Sweet Bar and Grill in downtown Prosperity, where the live music and great dance floor made the bar a happening place.

Now, dateless for the first time in three months—Dateless in Prosperity, she thought wryly—she shook her head.

After last night's painful breakup and an especially irritating day, she wanted only to relax and hang out with her best friend. "Would you mind if we stayed here? I'm not in the mood to go out."

"Staying in works."

Nick shot her a sympathetic look, and tears she refused to shed gathered behind her eyes. Jeter had never exactly treated her well, and over the months they'd been together, she'd done more than enough crying.

"I'll bet you could use a hug," Nick said. "I know I could."

Which reminded her that she wasn't the only one hurting. Earlier in the week he'd broken up with Mandy, a woman he'd seemed to really like—at least for a while. Nick had commitment issues. He claimed that he didn't want to settle down with anyone, ever, didn't want to marry or have kids. They weren't just words, either. He meant it.

Dani stepped into the warm, comforting embrace she'd needed since Jeter had dumped her. She smelled Nick's sandalwood shaving soap and fresh Montana air. And underneath both, his own "Nick" scent.

For a few long moments they held each other tightly. When they let go and stepped back, Dani felt better.

Nick sniffed the air, rubbing his belly and licking his lips, making her smile for real. "Man, that smells amazing. I've been dreaming of your mac and cheese all day."

"Even while you worked on the barn roof in the freezing rain? You're lucky it didn't snow."

It had been almost two years since Nick had repurchased Kelly Ranch, once owned by his family and then sold. Now he was slowly and painstakingly making improvements on the property, which, because it had been neglected, was rundown. His current project was the leaky barn roof. He could have hired a professional roofer, but he was watching his bank balance. Also, he claimed to enjoy doing the work himself.

"I'd prefer snow to the icy stuff we got. And yeah, I thought a lot about dinner while the sleet was pounding my head. I could eat a whole cow."

As if in agreement, his stomach growled loudly— just as the oven timer pinged, signaling the casserole was ready.

"If that isn't great timing," Dani teased. "Come on."

They linked arms and headed toward the kitchen of her little apartment, swapping fond looks with each other. "What's next on your agenda, Mr. Ranch Fixer Upper?" she asked.

"Mending fences so that we can move the livestock when the spring grass comes up. Now that it's March, that's just around the corner. I also have to install the new irrigation system soon."

"You're keeping busy, I'll give you that." Too busy to reflect much on his recent breakup. "Ever notice how you use physical labor to avoid thinking about certain things?"

He shrugged. "Hey, if it works…"

He did seem in a better frame of mind than he had when they'd talked the previous evening. "I wish I was as good at distracting myself as you," Dani said with envy.

He peered closely at her. "You've been crying."

She pulled herself to her full five-foot-six-inch height. "I was, but I'm finished now. I'm excited to spend the evening with my best friend—eating, sipping wine, having ice cream, watching a movie, eating more ice cream…."

She expected a laugh, and Nick didn't disappoint. "You and me both," he said.

While he uncorked the wine, Dani donned oven mitts and brought the casserole to her cottage-style kitchen table. "When did we last have a pity party together?" she asked as they sat down in their usual seats.

"You mean at the same time?" Nick's thick-lashed, mocha-colored eyes narrowed in thought. "I don't believe we ever have. It's usually either you or me hurting, never both of us at once."

"A first for us, then, and after sixteen years of friendship." They'd met in middle school at the age of fourteen, and had bolstered each other up through too many breakups to count.

"Bummer, huh?" Nick said. "If this is a first, we

should make a toast." He filled the glasses. "To no more breakups at the same time."

"I'd rather toast to no more breakups, period," Dani said. "But I know us both too well for that."

Neither of them stayed in a relationship for long.

After setting down his glass, Nick eyed the casserole. "I'm sorry about Jeter, but I gotta say, I sure enjoy your choice of comfort food."

Dani laughed. "You always cheer me up." His sense of humor was one of his many positive qualities. "And I agree, there's nothing better than mac and cheese with hamburger." She nodded at the steaming dish. "Help yourself."

"After you." Beaming the sexy smile that made women swoon, Nick nudged the casserole her way.

He was such a gentleman, which was also sexy. "Have you heard from Mandy since you broke up with her?" she asked when they'd both filled their plates.

"You want to talk about this now." He gave her a wary frown. "Are you trying to ruin my appetite?"

"Is that even possible? It's just that I remember how Jasmine stalked you with phone calls and texts when your relationship ended." Jasmine had been Nick's previous ex.

"She was unstable. Mandy isn't like that. We both knew we weren't going to make it."

"Too bad—she was great." Dani sighed. "What a shame she wasn't your Ms. Right."

Nick almost choked on his wine. "You're such a fairy-tale romantic. I've told you, there *is* no Ms. Right, not for me."

His track record so far certainly proved that. He never went too deep into the reasons why he found his previous girlfriends lacking, but it happened over and over. Dani suspected that his issues stemmed from his mother's extramarital affair and the subsequent breakup of his parents' marriage when he was a kid. That and the broken heart he'd suffered in his early twenties.

In all the years they'd been friends, she'd only seen Nick in love that once. He'd met Ashley in college. They'd dated for nearly a year before they graduated and moved in together. Within months of that, they were talking marriage. Then Ashley's mom, who lived in Missoula, had been diagnosed with Lou Gehrig's disease. Ashley had gone home to take care of her. She was only supposed to stay for a few months, but her relationship with Nick had fallen apart, and she never returned.

Nick claimed he'd been relieved. Even so, it had taken him ages to get over what had happened. Or maybe he never had, because he hadn't let a woman into his heart since.

Whereas Dani fell head over heels several times a year.

"And *I've* told *you* that all it takes is the right person," she said. "You can deny it until you're hoarse, but I believe that your true love and mine are out there."

"I'm not opposed to love, Dani—you know that. I just don't do it." With a shrug, he bent his head toward his plate.

"Sly used to say the same thing, and look at him now. He's happily married, with a little girl." Dani's brother and his wife, Lana, had an adorable two-and-a-half-year-old, the happy result of Lana's miracle pregnancy.

"If it can happen to Sly, it could happen to you," she went on. "And to me—I hope." She crossed her fingers and held them up.

Nick failed to comment.

"Out of all the women in the world, one is perfect for you," she said. "Someday when you meet her, you'll see."

"Trust me, between the available women in Prosperity and the summer tourists who come through every year, I'm a happy man."

"Except before, during and after the breakups." She bit her lip. "I did everything I could to make Jeter love me as much as I loved him. What's wrong with me?"

Nick shook his head. "That's the wrong question. You should be asking, *what's wrong with Jeter?* You've got to quit trying to please the guys you date and be yourself. You're great just as you are."

Nick had always been wonderful at boosting her self-esteem. "You're sweet," she said.

"I mean it, Dani. Now, about the guys you date. You say you want to get married and have a family, but you pick guys who don't. Guys like me." He shook his head. "Most of them are jerks, too. That's why you get hurt."

"So you and Sly keep pointing out." Dani fiddled with her napkin. "I guess I'll take a little break from dating."

"That's probably a wise idea."

Except that she hated sitting home alone on a Saturday night. "I'll make plans to go out with some of my girlfriends instead." But that posed a problem, because at the moment, most of them were either in a relationship or married. "That is, if I can find someone who's free to get together on a Saturday night."

"I'm available," Nick said. "You can hang with me."

"Until your next girlfriend comes along."

"That could be a while."

"Ha." Dani hated being single. Maybe her plan to take a break from dating had been made too hastily. She let out a heavy sigh.

Nick gave her a measured look. "You're already wishing you had another guy in the wings, aren't you? Just do me a favor. The next time you date someone, hold on to your heart until you're sure he's worthy enough to give it to."

"And just how do I do that?"

He stroked his strong chin pensively. "It might help if you try going out with a different kind of guy than your usual type. Someone who isn't a bum."

He was right, most of the males Dani dated were pretty much jerks. As she sipped her wine, she thought about why she made such poor choices. There was nothing more attractive than a good-looking man with a spark of wild in his eyes and a devil-may-care attitude. She'd certainly fallen for enough of them.

And where had that gotten her? Every new relationship started out filled with promise, making her ever hopeful that this time, this boyfriend would love her and treat her right. And although she tried everything to make him happy, from wearing clothes he liked to embracing the activities he enjoyed—even when she didn't—sooner or later things always soured.

Nick just might have a point. She sat up straight. "You're right—I should try dating someone I wouldn't normally choose. Drumroll please. When I do decide to date again, I'll pick a man I wouldn't usually look twice at."

Nick frowned. "Define a man you 'wouldn't normally choose.'"

"Well, someone hard-working, with both feet on the

ground. And he has to have a good job." That way, he wouldn't ask to borrow money from her, as Jeter had. "If he's impatient about getting physical and refuses to move slowly, he's out."

"Having a regular job doesn't make a man a decent human being," Nick said. "At first, guys tend to put their best foot forward. How can you tell the square shooters from the jerks until you get to know them?"

"Hmm." Propping her chin on her fist, Dani pondered the question. "Well, I'll do what you said, and hold my heart in check for a while. And maybe, instead of waiting for the man to ask me out, I'll do the asking. I'll start by observing him for a while when he isn't looking, and I'll pay attention to how he treats other people. That'll give me a glimmer of an idea of his character."

Nick gave an approving nod. "That's not a bad plan. It's definitely worth a try."

Dani smiled. "So glad you approve, Mr. Kelly."

After three helpings of mac and cheese, Nick's belly was satisfied. He and Dani lingered at the table, both of them relaxed. He was also too beat to move. Fixing up the ranch and making it profitable was an all-consuming job, filled with unexpected obstacles and on-going challenges. Not that he minded. He loved his land. But with another full day starting at oh-dark-thirty tomorrow, he was ready to head home and fall into a dreamless sleep. Dani appeared to be just as tired.

"Are you sure you want to watch a movie tonight?" he asked after she yawned for the second time. "You have to get up even earlier than I do, and with Big Mama riding your case...."

"Don't remind me." Dani grimaced. "Ever since the Poplar Tree restaurant opened and the *Prosperity Daily News* ran that story about them, business at the café has been slipping. How many times have I told Big Mama that we need to step things up and make some changes in order to compete? Does she listen? Heck, no."

Everyone who knew Trudy Alexander called her Big Mama. The nickname suited the five-foot-eleven, two-hundred-plus-pound female. Although she towered an intimidating five inches over Dani, Dani gave her as good as she got. They were both strong-willed women, and they often butted heads. And yet, their love for each other was obvious.

At the tender age of four Dani had lost her mother to cancer. Two years later she'd also lost her father, when a tree limb had crashed through the windshield of his car, killing him instantly. The freak accident had left Dani and her two older brothers orphans. The boys had been taken in by an uncle in Iowa. He hadn't wanted a girl, and Dani had gone into Prosperity's foster care system. Luckily for her, she'd been placed with Big Mama. A couple years later, the older woman had legally adopted Dani, with Dani keeping her original last name.

"I know our customers," Dani went on. "I should— I'm there six days a week, from five o'clock in the morning until we close at 2:00 p.m., and often for a few hours after that. I waitress, I order food and supplies, help with the hiring and firing, and I sort the mail. Most of those are responsibilities I've handled since I was in high school. The only things I don't do are the cooking and the financial stuff."

"You work hard," Nick agreed. As hard as he did, for which he respected her.

"And I do a good job—a really good job. So why doesn't Big Mama trust me to make decisions that could help our restaurant?" Dani snickered. "Heck, she doesn't even trust me to get through a Saturday or Sunday without nagging me about one thing or another."

Presumably Dani's mom, now in her late sixties, would retire someday and Dani would take over. But handing the reins over to anyone, even her daughter, wasn't proving easy for her. For now, Big Mama preferred to run the business her own way, keeping Dani on a tight leash. Nick had been hearing about it from Dani for several years now. "Of course she trusts you," he said. "She just prefers to be in control."

"If she trusted me she wouldn't *have* to be in control. You wouldn't believe the day I had, much of it courtesy of her." Dani grimaced again. "Which is a long way of answering your question. No, I don't want to call it a night just yet. I'm so ready to escape into a movie, and I want to do it with my best friend."

As bone-tired as Nick was, Dani needed him and he wasn't going to let her down. She and Big Mama were like family to him. He was a lot closer to them than to his own sister and mother. Dani was loyal to the people she cared about. Even when she was in a bad relationship, she stayed true to her boyfriend. His fickle mom, on the other hand, didn't know the meaning of loyalty.

"Today was worse than usual?" he asked.

"It was pretty bad."

"What happened?"

Dani slanted her head. "Are you sure you want to hear about this?"

If talking about her day took her mind off Jeter, Nick was all for it. "Sure."

"How long have I been running the restaurant on weekends so that Big Mama can take a few days off?" Dani grumbled. "As if she's ever really 'off.' Business has slacked a little lately, but that doesn't mean I stand around, twiddling my thumbs. She must've called ten times today, making sure I'd done this chore and that one. Have I cleaned the tables and reset them after customers finished and left? Have I checked the salt-and-pepper shakers and the sugar bowls to make sure they're filled? You'd think I was a new hire. I just wish she'd get that I know what I'm doing and let me do it."

She didn't expect a comment, so Nick just nodded.

"I've done tons of research on steps we could take to increase our business," she continued. "But no, she finds something wrong with every one of my ideas. I even suggested she watch *Restaurant: Impossible,* the Food Network show about saving restaurants from going under, so that she could see what other restaurants are trying. She claims she doesn't have time for that."

Dani's lips pursed in irritation. She was definitely in a tough situation.

"Maybe I can help," Nick offered. "Big Mama's crazy about me." She always had been. As a teenager, he'd spent more nights at her dinner table than his own mother's. "Let me talk to her."

"No, thanks. I'll handle this myself. Besides, she's so stubborn that not even your Kelly charm could budge her on this. It's enough that you're letting me whine."

Dani had always been an independent female—except when it came to men. She fell in love fast, and tried way too hard to please whoever she was with.

Nick didn't do love, period. What was the point of falling for a woman when love would ruin a man's life?

Because sooner or later, the relationship was bound to end. Women were fickle and not to be trusted—Dani excepted.

"Big Mama started her business forty years ago," he said. "Anyone would have difficulty letting go."

"And I get that, but it doesn't make my working life any easier. I want her to trust me, Nick." Dani *needed* her mother's trust. Owning and running a restaurant wasn't easy, and Big Mama wasn't getting any younger. She deserved to retire and let Dani take over. "Okay, I'm through complaining—for now." She switched gears. "Let's watch a movie so that I can forget about work and Jeter."

"Soon," Nick said. "But first, ice cream with hot fudge sauce, if you have any. Let's eat in front of the tube."

Her eyes lit up. They were an unusual silvery-blue, the same color as Sly's and those of their brother, Seth, whom Nick had met a few times when he and Dani had first become friends. But then Seth had left town, and Dani and Sly hadn't seen or heard from him in years. They had no idea where he was.

"I like the way you think, Mr. Kelly. And yes, I happen to have bought a fresh jar of hot fudge sauce on my way home today—just for you."

Nick had been to her apartment so often, he knew where she stored everything. In the pine cabinet to the right of the sink, he found the bowls. The drawer next to the stove yielded the ice cream scoop. Dani opened the jar of fudge sauce and heated it in the microwave. By the time he piled ice cream into the bowls the fudge sauce was nice and hot.

"I want first crack at that sauce," Dani said with a

teasing twinkle in her eyes. "Otherwise, you'll eat the whole thing."

Nick gave her a look of mock hurt. "I'd never do that."

"Ha. Your sweet tooth is so big that mine dims by comparison. But you never gain an ounce, you lucky man." She sighed. "I wish I could eat whatever I wanted and not put on weight. That's the one good thing about my breakup with Jeter. I won't have to diet anymore."

Jeter had ridden Dani's case about her weight but Nick thought he was nuts. "What do you care about some Neanderthal's opinion?" he said. "You're perfect the way you are."

And she was. Curvy in all the right places. With pretty eyes and a plump mouth made for kissing, she could attract any man she wanted. Plus, she was warm and friendly, with a heart as big as the Montana sky.

Nick was crazy about her, but not in a sexual sense. As attractive as Dani was, he considered her a cross between sister and best friend. That was the whole reason they'd stayed close all these years. Sex would just mess up their relationship.

Dani finished drizzling a stream of hot fudge sauce over her rocky road. "Have at it." She handed Nick the jar of sauce, but kept the chocolate-coated spoon for herself.

After slathering his ice cream with enough chocolate to satisfy his sweet tooth, he stuck his finger in the jar and scraped it clean.

Dani laughed. "Sure you got enough?"

Her smile was contagious, and Nick grinned. "For now. Let's go watch a movie."

They headed for the living room. "What DVDs did you bring?" Dani asked.

"Only the first two James Bond movies ever made— *Dr. No* and *From Russia with Love.*"

"James Bond?" She stuck out her lower lip. "Come on, Nick, my heart is broken. You know that when I'm sad my preference is for three-hanky love stories." She brightened. "I haven't watched *The Holiday* since last Christmas. I could put it on."

Nick had seen the chick flick with her so many times he'd memorized most of the lines. He made a face. "After every one of your breakups, we watch movies that make you cry. You've cried too much over Jeter."

Within weeks after they'd started dating, Jeter had hurt her by sticking her with their dinner tab at a restaurant and taking off with his friends. Nick had wanted to deck the loser and teach him some manners, but that would have infuriated Dani. Instead, he'd encouraged her to quit trying to make the bum happy when he wasn't doing a thing to make *her* happy. He'd also suggested she break off with him. But she'd already been in love and Nick's words had fallen on deaf ears. It was a relief to know that next time she'd choose a different kind of man.

"Why don't we mix it up and try a spy film. How about it?" He tugged on a lock of her pretty brown hair, which she wore straight and almost to her shoulders, then picked up the two DVDs. "Trust me, either of these classic Bond flicks will take your mind completely off your broken heart and your bad day. But hey, if you'd rather cry instead and waste another box of tissues…"

"You're right." She squared her shoulders. "Okay, I'll

give *Dr. No* a try. But if I can't get into it, we switch to *The Holiday.* Deal?"

"Fair enough."

Dessert in hand, they shoved the four colorful throw pillows—Dani was big into bright colors—to one end of the couch and then sat down.

Looking hopefully at Dani's bowl, the ridiculously named Fluff jumped up between her and Nick. "No," she said in a stern voice. "The vet put you on a diet, remember? Besides, this stuff is bad for you." She shooed the cat away.

Undaunted, he jumped onto the floor and then butted Nick's shin, his yellow eyes pleading. Nick was unmoved. "You heard the lady. This sundae is all mine."

Tail high, the offended tom stalked off.

Nick slid *Dr. No* into the DVD player, then dug into his sundae. With any luck the combination of the sugar jolt and the action would keep him awake for a few hours.

Within moments Dani was totally engrossed in the film to the point that her ice cream melted. It was obvious she wasn't thinking about Jeter or the restaurant now.

Mission accomplished. Nick smiled to himself.

He watched the film for a while, but not long after he finished his sundae, his eyelids grew too heavy to stay open. He set the bowl on the coffee table. It was the last thing he remembered.

Chapter 2

Dani opened her eyes. As entertaining and exciting as *Dr. No* was—and it was so dated that it was both—she'd fallen asleep in the middle of the action. Now she was snuggled against Nick's side, with her head on his chest. His arms were wrapped around her, holding her close.

When had that happened?

By the steady rise and fall of his rib cage, he'd also fallen asleep. Poor guy was exhausted, and yet he'd come over tonight so that they could cheer each other up. Although he'd done most of the cheerleading.

Tenderness flooded her. She loved him dearly, but cuddling with him stretched the bonds of their platonic relationship.

Doing her best not to disturb him, she gently began to untangle herself from his grasp. Not so easy, as he was holding on tight. Without meaning to, she woke him. His sleepy, sexy smile stole her breath. She was marveling at the power of that smile when he lowered his head and kissed her. On the mouth. He'd never done that before.

As startled as Dani was, she liked the solid feel of his arms anchoring her close. Liked his lips brushing warmly over hers. Dear God in heaven, he could kiss. Without knowing how it happened, she melted into his hard body and kissed him back.

He tasted of chocolate and ice cream and something subtle that she recognized as uniquely him. His big palms slid up her sides, dangerously close to her suddenly tingling breasts.

Okay, this was getting out of hand. Dani stiffened and pushed him away. "Don't, Nick."

"Jeezus." He released her as if she'd burned him. "What are we doing?"

She touched her lips with her fingers, noting that his gaze followed and settled on her mouth.

"I'm not sure," she said. "All I know is that sometime during the movie we both fell asleep. And then—"

"We were making out. Wow." Nick scrubbed his hand over his face. "Sorry about that."

Dani should be, too. Only she wasn't.

No wonder the women Nick dated went nuts over him. Not only was he sexy and funny with good manners, he also knew how to kiss. Fan-yourself-go-soft-inside kisses that emptied the mind of all common sense.

Dani sensed that he could also do a lot of other equally wonderful things with his mouth. Blushing furiously, she leaned forward and stacked their bowls.

She almost wished...

But no. Nick was exactly the kind of guy she'd just

sworn off of, a man who moved from woman to woman and kept his heart under close guard. Besides, he was her best friend. His friendship was important to her, and she wouldn't do anything to jeopardize it.

Nick lifted the dishes right out of her hands, then stood. "It's late, and tomorrow will be a long day for both of us. I should go," he said, taking the words straight from her kiss-addled brain.

Dani wanted him to leave so that she could recover from a colossal mistake. She also rose. While Nick deposited the bowls in the kitchen, she fluffed the throw pillows and repositioned them along the couch.

When he returned, he shrugged into his jacket, which only accentuated his flat belly and broad shoulders.

"I'll, uh, talk to you later." He grabbed hold of the doorknob as if he couldn't get out of her apartment fast enough.

Normally when they parted he kissed her on the cheek. Now that she was tingly and hot everywhere, even the most chaste kiss would be dangerous.

Fluff came running. Why couldn't he have fallen asleep between them and prevented what had happened? Dani scooped him up and held him to her chest like a shield, poor cat. She opened the door and stood well out of reach until Nick moved through it and strode rapidly down the hall, away from her. After shutting the door, she let Fluff down. She didn't draw in a normal breath until she heard the elevator close behind Nick.

Nick was up at the crack of dawn Monday morning, relishing the busy day ahead. After a hearty breakfast he pulled on wool socks and entered the mudroom, where he tugged on boots and donned a heavy jacket.

He stepped onto the back porch, his breath puffing from his lips like smoke. It was a cloudy March morning and chilly, but not quite cold enough to snow. Instead, heavy rain was predicted. Not the best working conditions for installing an irrigation system.

As always, the sight of the rolling fields filled him with pride and made him think of his father, a man who had died way too soon. Nick Senior had taught Nick that land was the most important thing a man could own, but his actions had jeopardized everything.

Kelly Ranch had belonged to the family for generations, until Nick's parents had fallen on hard times—thanks partly to the vagaries of Montana weather, but mostly because of his father's lavish spending habits. Nick remembered the jewelry, fancy appliances and high-end new car his father had bought his mother. He'd been so wrapped up in keeping her in luxury that he'd neglected the ranch. Neglect that had cost them all in the worst way possible.

Before long, unable to keep up with the mortgage and credit card debt, the family had been forced to sell. Nick's parents had moved with him and his older sister, Jamie, to the east side of Prosperity. The poor side of town.

Both his parents had soon found jobs that paid regularly and provided a much-needed steady income that helped stave off the bill collectors. But no one had liked living in the city. Nick's parents had fought constantly, and his mother started working late. She'd taken up with a man at work, someone else's husband. The affair had ended, but not before it destroyed both marriages and broke up two families.

Breathing in the crisp air, Nick started down the

back steps. He'd always wondered what his life would have been like if his parents had managed their debt better and had held on to the ranch. Would they have stayed together? If they had, his life would have been totally different.

But playing the what-if game was an endless circle of unanswerables. Nick didn't want to remember that time, or the bitterness that had clung to his father like a shroud afterward and until the day he'd died.

He headed across the yard toward the shed where he stored tractors and other large ranching equipment, the cold earth crunching under his boots. The only positive thing to come out of his dad's untimely death was the insurance policy he'd left Nick. Thanks to that unexpected gift, Nick had suddenly had the funds for a down payment on the family ranch, which had just happened to be on the market. It was rundown and had come dirt-cheap, and he'd been able to put down a decent amount. Using what remained of his inheritance, he was slowly making much-needed improvements.

Unfortunately, the cost of the new irrigation would eat up the last of the money. And there was so much yet to do before Kelly Ranch finally turned a profit. Several outbuildings still required repairs, and the ranch needed a new hay baler. Nick also wanted to add more cattle to his herd. While those things would have to wait, Nick was proud of the fact that the ranch should be fully restored and profitable within in the next two years—as long as he kept his eye on his goal. He wouldn't slip up like his father, who'd lost everything. All for a woman who'd ended up leaving him, anyway.

At least the land was back in the family, where it belonged.

From the direction of the trailers that housed his ranch crew, a rooster crowed as if in approval. Nick had three permanent ranch hands. Two were married, and their wives raised chickens.

With an eye to cutting costs, he'd commandeered two of the men to help with the grunt work on the irrigation system.

They were waiting for him at the shed. Nick nodded at Palmer, the foreman who'd agreed to stay on when he'd bought the ranch, and Clip, a brawny twenty-five-year-old who wasn't afraid of hard work. Jerome, the third member of the crew, was tackling the regular chores today.

"Morning," he greeted them. "Kenny Tripp, the irrigation specialist I hired to install our new system, should be here soon."

While they waited, they stood around, sipping coffee from thermoses and talking about their weekends.

"Hey, how's Dani doing?" Clip asked.

She occasionally visited the ranch, and the crew knew that Nick had gone to her place Saturday evening, to console her after her breakup.

Unsure how to best answer Clip's question, and preferring not to discuss about what had happened between him and Dani, Nick took a long pull on his coffee. He wasn't often confused by his own actions, but kissing her…

What the hell had gotten into him?

Yeah, he'd been half-asleep when it happened, but that was no excuse. Over the years they'd fallen asleep beside each other plenty of times without him ever making a move on her. She meant too much to him to wreck their relationship by getting physical.

But then, he'd never guessed that kissing her would be so mind-numbingly powerful or that she'd get under his skin the way she had. The feel of her lips under his, the sweet press of her breasts against his chest…

"She's doing okay," he said gruffly.

He drained the last of his mug, screwed the cap on the thermos and gave himself a mental kick in the butt. Dani was his best friend. Kissing her or anything beyond that was off-limits. He'd had no business pulling her as close as he could, and no business wanting to strip her naked and get even closer.

At the mere thought, his body tightened. Turning away from Palmer's narrow-eyed scrutiny, he set his empty thermos on a shelf near the door. Tonight he would call Dani and assure her he wouldn't be crossing the line with her ever again.

Clip grinned. "Now that she's single again, I just might ask her out."

The bachelor cowboy was full of himself.

Nick gave him a warning look. "I wouldn't."

"Why not? She's available."

"Because she deserves a man who'll stick around and build a life with her."

"Heck, I'll stick to her." Clip chuckled at his joke until Nick glared at him. The cowboy sobered right up. "Chill out, Nick, I'm only funnin' around."

The sound of a truck rumbling toward the shed drew Nick's attention. "That must be Tripp now. Let's go."

He opened the door and Palmer and Clip followed him out.

On Mondays, Big Mama's Café was closed. As much as Dani loved going in to work, a day off was always a welcome relief. A chance to relax, read the newspaper from cover to cover and sleep in....

Scratch sleeping in. She'd been getting up before dawn since high school, and the habit was hard to break. Plus, she had a lot on her mind, first and foremost the meeting at Big Mama's house this morning. Her mother didn't handle change well, but today, Dani was determined to persuade her that making needed alterations was critical to the restaurant's survival.

The very thought of that conversation gave her hives.

Then there was Fluff, who expected his breakfast no later than five-thirty. Sitting on her chest, all twenty pounds of him, he batted her chin with his paw and meowed. Loudly and plaintively. "Oh, all right, Mr. Alarm Clock," she muttered, moving him aside so that she could flip on the reading lamp on the beside table. Yawning and stretching, she fell back against the pillow again.

She'd spent a long, restless night, and not just because she was stressing over the upcoming conversation with Big Mama. Nick Kelly had played a big roll in the tossing and turning.

They didn't get together all that often, but they touched base frequently, either by phone, text or email. But since Saturday night, Nick hadn't called or texted her once. Dani hadn't contacted him, either. Their friendship was hugely important to her, and she hoped those unforgettable kisses hadn't made things between them all wonky.

Key word: *unforgettable.* A man didn't kiss a woman as thoroughly as Nick had kissed her without making a huge impact. And what an impact it had been. Dani wanted more of the same. A lot more.

Which was just too bad, because she wasn't about to kiss Nick like that again. Ever. The smartest thing to do was to forget the other night had ever happened.

Fluff amped up his cries to earsplitting level. "Will you stop?" she snapped in a sharp tone that caused the cat to grow quiet.

He fixed her with an accusing look that caused an instant case of the guilts. None of this was his fault.

Gentling her voice, she rubbed behind his head. He promptly forgave her and began to purr. What a pushover. "You're such a sweet boy," she crooned. "Let me stop in the bathroom on my way to the kitchen. Then I'll feed you."

By the time she threw on a robe and padded into the kitchen a few minutes later, the cat was pacing anxiously in front of his food dish. Her heart went out to him. Roughly two years ago she'd adopted him from a cat shelter, not long after he'd been found abandoned and starving. He still worried about his food, and if she didn't feed him first thing in the morning, he tended to get upset.

Dani needed coffee, but it would have to wait. "You know how I am before my morning dose of caffeine," she said. "But just this once, I'll give you breakfast before I put the coffee on." She filled his bowl. "There you go. This just proves how much I care about you."

Busy scarfing down his meal, Fluff ignored her. Wasn't that just like a male? Once you gave him what he wanted, he didn't spare you a second thought.

"Story of my life," she murmured.

Twenty minutes later she felt human again. Sipping her second cup of coffee, she read most of the *Prosper-*

ity Daily News instead of skimming it, an indulgence she had time for only on Mondays.

After a leisurely shower she dressed in jeans and a pullover sweater, then grabbed her purse and a coat, and blew the cat a kiss. "Bye, handsome. Behave yourself while I'm gone."

When she pulled out of her parking space in the apartment complex, ominous clouds filled the sky. Dani groaned. Not more rain.

Big Mama lived in the same two-story bungalow where Dani had grown up. When she arrived at the house some ten minutes later, rain was coming down hard and the wipers were working overtime.

Jewel Sellers's old Lincoln Continental was parked behind Big Mama's SUV, which was in the carport. Jewel was her mother's best friend and they often palled around. Dani hoped the woman wasn't planning on staying. She and her mom were supposed to talk about the restaurant.

She parked beside the Lincoln. At the Pattersons' house next door, Gumbo, a ten-year-old mixed chow female, dashed down the steps from the covered porch, barking a hello. The Pattersons were both at work, and Gumbo was obviously lonesome.

Dani pulled the hood on her coat over her head and stopped at the chain-link fence. Hunkering down, she stuck her fingers through to pat the wet dog, who she swore grinned at her despite the driving rain. "Hey there, Gumbo. You should stay up on the porch, where it's dry."

Ignoring her advice, the dog licked her fingers. "Aw, I love you, too," Dani said. "I wish I could stay and visit with you, but it's too wet and cold. Besides, Big Mama's expecting me. When Jewel leaves, we're having a 'meeting.'" She pantomimed sticking her thumb down her throat, then lowered her voice. "If you can figure out a way to make Big Mama accept even *some* of my ideas and trust me enough to quit micromanaging me on weekends, I'd love to hear them. There'll be a doggie treat in it for you. Gotta run now."

She raced up the steps of the covered porch. The front door was unlocked, and once she removed her wet shoes and shook the rain water from her coat, she let herself in. After the damp cold outside, the house felt snug and dry. The familiar aromas of lemon oil furniture polish and freshly baked treats that smelled out of this world flooded her nostrils. Salivating, she hung her coat in the closet.

"Hey, it's me," she called out, just as she always had.

Her mother bustled in from the kitchen, her gait a little slower than it once had been, but still brisk. Dressed in her trademark off-white blouse and dark pants, bifocals propped on her head, she greeted Dani with a warm smile.

Jewel followed, as petite and trim as Big Mama was large.

"I was hoping to see you before I left." Jewel tsked in sympathy. "I'm sorry about your breakup."

"Thanks." It was no surprise that she'd heard about that. Big Mama kept her well-informed. Still, Dani wasn't about to discuss the details. "It's nasty out there, so be careful," she said.

Her mother peered out the little window in the door. "What a storm we're having. The weather people are warning about a three-dayer. Lordy, I hope they're wrong. Be safe, Jewel. I'll see you Friday night."

The woman nodded. "Six o'clock, dinner out and cards here." She patted her large handbag. "Thanks for the cinnamon roll. It will go well with my afternoon coffee. You're in for a yummy snack, Dani."

When the door closed behind her, Dani's mother opened her arms. "How about a hug for your Big Mama?"

Dani stepped into the familiar embrace. Instantly she was enveloped in Big Mama's warmth and lilac cologne, and for a few seconds all her cares faded. For all their disagreements, Dani loved her dearly.

"What was Jewel doing here?" she asked when they let go of each other.

"You know what early birds we both are. She's going to knit me a cardigan and wanted to show me possible yarns and colors."

"That's nice," Dani said. "I hope you picked something with a little color." Not that her mother wore colors much. Everything she owned was either black, brown or navy.

"I did—a soft gray. You hungry?"

Having skipped breakfast, Dani nodded. "Those cinnamon rolls smell wonderful."

"Of course they do." Big Mama grinned. "I took a batch out of the oven just before you got here. I left the nuts out, the way you prefer them. There's a pot of hot coffee, too."

Eager to eat something, and always up for another cup of coffee, Dani rubbed her hands together. Then she frowned. "Didn't Dr. Adelson tell you to cut down on fats and sweets?"

Her mother made a face. "I don't smoke and I don't drink. Isn't that enough? Besides, what's the point of living if I can't indulge in a few of the things I love?" With a defiant gleam in her eye, she raised her chin. "A treat now and then won't hurt."

Before Dani could argue, Big Mama changed the subject. "You have circles under your eyes." She scrutinized Dani critically and pursed her lips. "You're not sleeping well. It's because of Jeter, isn't it? I didn't want to ask and bother you while you were at work this weekend, but how are you doing?"

Bother her? She'd only driven Dani crazy with her frequent calls. Dani refrained from pointing this out. She had more important things to discuss. "I stayed up late last night, but that had nothing to do with the breakup," she explained. "I'm actually doing okay."

"You're already over Jeter?"

Nick's kisses had all but wiped the other man from her mind. *Kisses I'm going to forget,* she reminded herself. "Pretty much."

"That was fast—much faster than usual. Let's get at those cinnamon rolls while they're still hot. Spending Saturday evening with Nick must've done you a world of good," Big Mama said as they sauntered toward the kitchen. "I just adore that boy."

Nick was no boy—he was all man. Fighting the urge to glance away from her mother's shrewd blue eyes, Dani shrugged. "I guess I wasn't that in love with Jeter, after all."

"I'm relieved. He wasn't the one for you. What did you and Nick do to cheer each other up?"

Although the rain had changed into pounding hail, Dani suddenly wished she was outside. Anything would be better than answering that question. "We had dinner and talked. And we ate hot fudge sundaes," she said.

All of which was true. "Then we watched an old James Bond movie called *Dr. No*."

"I remember that movie. Ursula Andress co-starred with Sean Connery."

The scarred old oak table that had been around since Dani's childhood was set for two, with a couple of jumbo cinnamon rolls on each plate. More than Dani could ever eat. The promised pot of steaming coffee and a pitcher of warm milk sat beside a stick of creamery butter and a vase of pussy willow buds. Ancient furniture and dishes that weren't all that different from those at Big Mama's Café—battle-worn, but friendly and homey. The food both here and at the restaurant was always excellent, but it was also very rich. People loved eating it, but these days they also needed other, healthier options.

Pushing that conversation aside for now, Dani sat in her customary seat, facing the window that overlooked the backyard where she'd spent many a happy spring and summer day. The curtains were open to let in the gray light. Hail bounced like white BB's against the concrete patio.

Seemingly oblivious to the spectacle, Big Mama sighed as she buttered a roll. "Sean Connery—now there's a man. He's still as handsome as ever."

For a long moment neither of them spoke, other than to exclaim over the flaky cinnamon rolls. Dani thought back to when she was six and Big Mama first took her in. At the time her then foster mother had been forty-five and widowed for almost four years.

Big Mama married late in life, and she and Winston had been madly in love. They'd been husband and wife just over a year when Big Mama had learned she was pregnant. She and Winston were ecstatic.

Then one snowy night her husband had died in a twenty-car pile-up on the freeway. A few weeks later, Big Mama miscarried. After that, she'd lost her interest in men, and had spent her days running the restaurant and raising Dani.

"I made a decision I'm sure you'll approve of," Dani said. "From now on, I'm going to date only the kind of man who has a steady job. He should also want to get married and have kids."

Big Mama nodded. "That's smart, Dani. But I want you to consider something important—you don't need a man to be happy."

Her mother had never said this before. Dani stared at her. "Hey, I happen to *like* men."

"They are wonderful, but after I lost Winston, I did all right by myself. Especially when it came to you. When you were growing up, we sure had a lot of fun." She waited for Dani's nod, then continued. "I may not have given birth to you, but I raised you as my own, and I did it totally without help. And I did a darned fine job of it, if I do say so. You became a terrific young woman. I'm so proud of you."

Dani flushed with pleasure. "Aww, thanks."

Big Mama had saved her from what could have been a childhood as awful as the one that Sly and Seth, her brothers, had endured at the hands of a distant uncle. Uncle George had taken them in but hadn't wanted Dani. At first, that had hurt, but his rejection had turned out to be the best thing for her. Because Uncle George disliked kids—even his own nephews. Poor Sly and Seth had borne the brunt of his animosity.

Whereas for Dani, from the start Big Mama had made her feel welcome and comfortable. She'd taught Dani how to cook and had let her help out in the restaurant. She'd always treated her with kindness and respect—along with a strong dose of discipline. By the age of eight, Dani had become the woman's adopted daughter, in every way possible. She'd soon inherited Big Mama's love of feeding hungry diners delicious, homemade food, along with the desire to manage a well-run establishment that brought people back again and again.

That wasn't happening so much anymore, but if Dani could just make the changes she wanted, she was sure that business would pick up. "I'm forever grateful for you and the wonderful life you've given me," she said. "But I'd still like to have a husband and a baby or two. Don't you want a grandchild to spoil?"

"Of course I would, but what I want most for you is your happiness."

With her mother in such an expansive mood, this seemed the perfect moment to get down to business. Tamping down a bad case of nerves, Dani reached for her purse and pulled out a folder. "I put together a couple of new menu ideas that will appeal to health-conscious eaters, as well as an updated look for our menu." The restaurant's interior hadn't changed since Dani had first stepped inside it some twenty-four years ago. It was now dated and not exactly welcoming. In fact, the drab decor and old lighting contradicted what Dani considered important—not only delicious food, but a bright, fun atmosphere in which to enjoy it.

She pointed to the crude sketch she'd made. "I'm no

artist, but you get the gist. This design is more contemporary and will suit the new decor perfectly."

Her mother didn't bother to put on her bifocals. "Just hold on there, missy." Her lips thinned into a stubborn line. "I haven't agreed to any new decor. And we don't need new menus or recipes, either. We have great food and friendly service, and customers like us just the way we are."

Here we go. Dani stifled a sigh. "You're right, but there's a lot of competition out there now, and we're steadily losing business, especially since the Poplar Tree opened. If we want to keep the customers we have and attract new ones, we have to make changes and update the restaurant."

An emotion that Dani swore was fear crossed her mother's face, gone so quickly that she wondered if she'd imagined it.

"Not on my watch," her mother stated firmly.

Dani suppressed a groan of frustration. The restaurant was to be her legacy, and she wanted it to survive and flourish for the rest of her life and even longer. "I'm only suggesting these things because I care about the restaurant as much as you do," she said in what she considered a reasonable tone.

Her mother stiffened and folded her meaty arms over her chest.

Okay, then. "What do you suggest we do instead?" Dani said, oh, so genially.

Big Mama *humphed*—so much for going the polite route. "We won't do anything. Big Mama's Café will remain as it always has been. We serve the best breakfasts and lunches in town. If people don't believe that, then they *should* eat someplace else."

Why couldn't her mother see that the atmosphere and menu made them look out of step compared to other restaurants? "You are so darned stubborn!" Dani fumed.

"I don't want to talk about this anymore." Her mother's jaw clamped shut.

Once again she'd failed to convince her mother to make any changes. Dani threw up her hands. Back to the drawing board.

Chapter 3

By Monday evening the hail had changed into sleet. Wondering whether it would snow, Dani sat on her living room floor with Fluff at her side, listening to a Josh Turner album and getting ready to fold the laundry she'd washed this afternoon. She loved the masculine sound of the country singer's voice.

Nick's voice was deep and sexy, too…

She frowned. She still hadn't heard from him, which was upsetting. Before Saturday night, she'd have picked up the phone and called him without a thought. But now, it just didn't feel right.

Between his silence and Big Mama's refusal to make a single change to the restaurant, Dani was frustrated enough to scream. Plucking one of the throw pillows from the couch, she covered her face to muffle the sound and let loose with a loud scream. Several of them.

When she removed the pillow from her face, she was in a better mood. Fluff had darted under the couch, but with a little patience and coaxing, he came out.

Dani went back to folding her clean things.

From the time she'd first come to live with Big Mama, her job had been to sort and fold the clean laundry. The task of transforming a rumpled basket of freshly dried clothing into smooth, neat piles had always relaxed her. Tonight she needed to relax and clear her mind.

No worrying about the restaurant, Big Mama or Nick. Just her and Josh Turner, singing together.

The basket was half empty and Dani was belting along to "Would You Go With Me" and in a much better place, when her cell phone rang. She checked the screen—Nick. Finally. Her heart bumped joyously in her chest.

She tamped down that happy feeling and focused on being annoyed. After lowering the volume of the music she picked up the call. "Hi, Nick," she said, not bothering to warm up her tone.

"Uh…" A brief pause. "Am I catching you at a bad time?"

"Not really. I'm folding laundry."

"That should make you nice and relaxed."

She had been, until now.

When she didn't comment, Nick went on. "We haven't spoken in a couple days. Are we okay?"

"Why wouldn't we be?" she said, not at all okay.

Fluff chose that moment to jump into the laundry basket. Soon his long hair would be all over her clean clothes. Dani lifted up the cat and set him on the carpet. After narrowing his eyes at her he flounced off with his tail high.

"You sure about that? You seem tense. The other night—"

"We shared a few kisses," she interrupted, proud of her nonchalant tone. "They didn't mean anything."

Only long, sleepless nights and the irritating problem of not being able to forget the feel of his lips on hers. Hot and soft…

His relieved breath was loud and clear. "That's good, because those kisses didn't mean anything to me, either. I don't want things between us to change because of them."

He had a funny way of showing it. "Me, either," Dani admitted. "Why did it take you so long to call?"

"You didn't pick up the phone and call me, either."

"I guess I needed time to process what happened."

"Ditto."

During another long beat of silence, Dani racked her brain for something else to say, something to prove that she was fine.

Before she could drum up anything, Nick spoke. "How about we forget those kisses ever happened?"

"Consider them forgotten."

Liar, liar, pants on fire. Dani touched her lips, which even now tingled a little.

"You and Big Mama had that meeting at her place today. How'd it go?"

The great—and occasionally annoying—thing about Nick was that he remembered most everything she told him. "Don't remind me," she said, frustrated with her mother all over again. "I don't know why I thought she'd listen this time. I came prepared, too, with a sketch for the new menu. I even brought recipe ideas. Big Mama gave everything a thumbs-down, so I asked for *her* ideas. She had nothing to say, except that she won't make a single change. She just keeps repeating that both our food and service are excellent just as they are."

"They *are* important."

"Of course. But the same old, same old isn't enough anymore—not if we want to stay in business. We both want the restaurant to thrive again. Why won't she try something new?"

"Maybe she's scared."

"My mother?" Dani snorted. "Of what?"

"I don't know—spending the money?"

"Since she refuses to give me access to our financial information, I have no idea. All I know is that we can't afford *not* to change."

Sharing her worries with Nick helped, and as Dani talked, her anger at him melted away. Yet now, a different kind of tension simmered between them, the kind that made her self-conscious and a little ill-at-ease.

"I'm not asking her to totally gut the place, though in my opinion, that would be the best option," she went on. "But new tables, chairs, curtains and wall decorations, better lighting, fresh paint and an updated menu? That'll cost a bit, but not that much. There has to be a way to convince her, but heck if I have a clue what it is."

"My offer still stands," he said. "I can talk to her."

"No, it's best if you stay out of this. I'll handle it myself. How was your day?"

"It's your battle—got it. My day sucked. This crappy weather delayed the irrigation project. Tripp and his team won't be back until the rain eases off."

"That's too bad. When the team finally does start, how long will the whole thing take?"

"Tripp estimates about five days."

"To irrigate the entire ranch? That's not bad."

"Nope, and during the dry days of summer, I'll be glad I did it. My mom called this afternoon."

"No kidding," Dani said. Nick and his mother weren't close, but she and Dani got along okay. "It's been ages since you heard from her. What did she want?"

"She asked me to come over after work Friday."

Dani was puzzled. "I wonder why."

"If I know my mother, she needs money."

He sounded disgusted. Despite having a job that paid decently, his mother always seemed short of cash. And she often borrowed from Nick to make up the gap.

"Are you going?" Dani asked.

"If I don't, she'll nag me until I do."

There the conversation died.

They usually chatted easily about everything under the sun, but tonight Dani couldn't think of anything else to say. Apparently neither could Nick.

The ensuing silence was uncomfortable.

Finally Nick cleared his throat. "You probably want to get back to your laundry and then to bed. I'll let you go. Sweet dreams."

His signature sign-off. Tonight, Dani wasn't sure what kinds of dreams she'd have. She hoped they didn't feature Nick doing delicious things to her… "You, too," she said. "Good luck with your mom."

They both disconnected.

Feeling oddly discombobulated, she folded the rest of the laundry and wondered how long it would take before she and Nick were at ease with each other again.

* * *

After two days of torrential rain and intermittent hail, the downpour suddenly braked to a stop just as darkness hit. During the nasty weather Nick, Palmer, Clip and Jerome had spent much of their waking hours fighting to keep the swelling river at the north end of the ranch from flooding the surrounding pastures. Meanwhile Blake and Wally, two seasonal ranch hands in need of work, had offered to herd the cattle to dry ground. The two men had impressed Nick, and he'd offered them jobs to last through September.

Now hungry, muddy and wet, he showered and put on a clean flannel shirt and jeans. After phoning in an order for a jumbo pie with the works he jumped in the truck and headed for Harper's Pizza, his favorite.

As usual, the small pizza hut was packed. Salivating over the mouth-watering aroma of the pizzas, Nick nodded at people he knew and shared flood stories with several ranchers before taking his place in the crowd waiting near the takeout window. Every few minutes the teenage kid manning the window called out some lucky Joe's name to pick up their order.

In the midst of the noise, the door opened and a redhead sauntered inside. Nick wasn't the only guy who checked her out. Flashing a pretty smile, she joined him in line.

"What a big crowd tonight," she commented. "The bad weather must've kept people home for a few days, and I guess they're making up for lost time."

Nick nodded. "It's been a heck of a few days."

"My hair and I are both relieved that it finally stopped raining." With an apologetic smile, she touched her hair. "It gets crazy wild."

"Curly looks good on you," Nick said. So did the long sweater she wore in place of a coat. A wide leather belt emphasized her small waist and rounded hips. She had long legs, too. Pretty face, nice body—just his type.

For some reason he flashed on Dani and the red-hot kisses they'd shared the other night. But Dani was off-limits. They were friends, period, and they'd both agreed to forget those kisses had ever happened. "I'm Nick Kelly," he said.

"Hello, Nick Kelly." The woman tossed her head, drawing his attention to her slender neck and a pair of long, dangly earrings. "I'm Sylvie Kitchen."

They shook hands. Sylvie's fingers were slender and warm. Attraction flared in her eyes.

Nick waited for a similar spark, but felt only mild interest. Maybe if he got to know her a little better...

During the ten minutes they waited for their pizzas he learned that she worked for the local tourism department, which after ranching, was the second biggest business in Prosperity. During the late spring and early summer months, hiking, camping and bicycling swelled the town by as much as ten thousand people.

"To kick off this year's tourist season, we're going to host a joint function with Prosperity Park," she said. The park housed Prosperity Falls, an eye-popping cascading waterfall that was a popular place for marriage proposals and outdoor weddings and drew visitors from all over. "It's going to take place in mid-April. I could get a couple of tickets for you and your girlfriend."

"I don't have a girlfriend right now," he said.

"Oh?" She flashed a pleased smile. "Maybe you'll want to bring someone."

She arched her eyebrow and angled her chin slightly, as if half expecting him to ask her out.

"Nick Kelly, your order's ready," the teenage boy called out.

Nick signaled that he'd be right there, then redirected his attention to Sylvie. "I'd like to, but spring is pretty busy at the ranch. I doubt I'll be able to make it."

She seemed genuinely disappointed. "Here's my card," she said, scribbling something on the back. "If you change your mind, give me a call."

Before slipping the card into his pocket he glanced at what she'd written. *In case you want to reach me after hours,* and a number.

Minutes later, shaking his head, he carried the pizza to his truck. A beautiful woman had just given him her number, but he didn't want to call her.

What was wrong with him?

Dani liked everything about Pettit Ranch—the vastness of her brother's holdings, the hints of new spring grass coloring in the brown winter pastures, the grazing horses and cattle everywhere you looked. Most of all, the home Sly shared with his wife, Lana, and their daughter. Tonight Sly had gone to Tim Carpenter's ranch, which was five hundred or so acres down the road, for a spur-of-the-moment Thursday poker game. Lana had invited Dani over for a girls' evening.

"I come bearing gifts," she said when Lana opened the front door. "Chinese, from Chung's." A take-out place they both loved. "And chocolate chip cookies, courtesy of Big Mama's Café."

"I so love those cookies!" Lana looked grateful, as well as tired. Between running two successful daycares and being mom to Johanna, a spunky two-and-a-half-year-old, she had her hands full.

As soon as Dani stepped through the door, the little girl squealed and threw herself at her knees.

"Hi, pumpkin!" Laughing, Dani scooped her up and swung her around.

Johanna giggled and held out her arms for more. "Again, Dani!"

She was no lightweight, but Dani couldn't resist her adorableness. She spun around twice more, each time with Johanna reaching out to her and begging, "Again!"

Finally, breathless and worn out, Dani quit. "That was fun, but I'm pooped, Johanna. Now I want to visit with Mommy."

Sometime later, she and Lana lingered over the dwindling pile of chocolate chip cookies, while Johanna marched around the kitchen, pounding on an old pan with a wooden spoon.

"She's so cute," Dani said.

"The cutest two-and-a-half year old ever, but then, I'm biased." Lana laughed. "Sly and I are getting baby-hungry again." She glanced at her daughter and lowered her voice. "Yesterday we signed up with an adoption agency. Of course, another miracle could happen. We could get pregnant again. But that's unlikely, and we want another child."

"I'll keep my fingers crossed," Dani said.

Drawn by their soft voices, Johanna stopped at the table. Her eyes lit on the cookies. "I want a cookie, Mama."

"How do you ask?" Lana said.

"Please."

"May I share some of mine with her?" Dani asked.

Lana nodded. "A small piece."

Carefully breaking off a tiny chunk of her cookie, Dani gave it to her niece.

"Thank you." The happy little girl kissed Dani's cheek, then stuffed the treat into her mouth and continued marching around the kitchen.

"She adores you," Lana pointed out. "And you're so wonderful with her. Someday you're going to make such a great mom."

"First, I need to meet a guy who actually wants to settle down and start a family."

"You will."

"With my track record?"

"You forget that I'd basically given up on love when I met Sly. And look at me now." Lana gave a dreamy smile. She and Sly had been married for two-plus years and they still acted like love-sick honeymooners. Dani envied them.

Her traitorous mind went straight to the one man she was trying *not* to think about—Nick. "Things have gotten weird with Nick," she confided.

Lana frowned. "How so?"

"Swear you won't tell Sly." Dani's oldest brother, who was seven years older than she was, tended to be on the protective side.

"I promise." All ears, Lana leaned forward.

Assured, Dani explained. "You remember that Nick came over Saturday night."

Lana nodded. "So that you could keep each other company after your breakups. I've always admired how you support each other that way."

"Right. We had our usual great time together, but when we were watching a DVD after dinner, we fell asleep together on the couch. When I woke up, we were snuggled up close." Remembering Dani hugged herself. "When Nick woke up, we kissed."

"Is that all?" Lana waved her hand dismissively. "There's nothing wrong with a kiss between friends."

"This wasn't exactly a friendly peck," Dani said. "Nick and I... We've always had an unwritten rule— we might buss each other on the cheek, but never on the lips. But those kisses..."

Talking about it was like reliving the experience. Dani's lips and entire body warmed right up. She fanned herself.

"*Those* kisses? As in more than one?" Lana's eyebrows jumped upward.

"A lot more." Dani let out a sigh. "We made out, Lana."

"You and Nick *made out?*" her sister-in-law repeated, sounding incredulous.

"Guilty as charged."

"And you enjoyed it."

Dani nodded miserably. "That would be a definite yes."

"Wow." Lana shook her head slowly and wonderingly. "I always sensed that you two were attracted to each other. How could you not be? He's gorgeous, you're gorgeous... What took you so long to figure it out?"

Dani knew she wasn't half bad. She also know she was far from gorgeous. She gaped at Lana. "What are you talking about? Before Saturday night, there *was* no physical attraction between Nick and me." Or if there had been, they'd hidden it from themselves and each other. "We don't want a physical relationship. Our friendship means too much to us."

"That shouldn't be a problem. Friendship and passion are essentials for a solid relationship. Look at Sly and me. He has my back and I have his, and I consider him to be one of my best friends. And we're definitely not platonic. At all." Lana's smile oozed sexual satisfaction.

As much as Dani loved her sister-in-law, she sometimes wanted to hate her for living the life she'd always wanted. "You know how it is with me, though," she said. "Some guy gives me a sexy smile and a few decent kisses, and I'm half in love. Once we have sex, I'm a total goner. But Nick…he doesn't do love."

Lana gave her a skeptical look. "A lot of guys say that, but then they meet the right woman and bam! They're all in."

"Not Nick. He's so against falling in love that as soon as he starts to fall for someone, he ends the relationship. Trust me, I know. Getting physical would spell disaster for our friendship. We've been best friends forever, and neither of us want to lose what we have now. That's why we can't cross over the boundaries of friendship."

"Let me get this straight—you and Nick both agree that a physical relationship could jeopardize your friendship. If you're on the same page, how is that a problem?" Lana frowned.

"You wouldn't think we'd have one, would you?" Dani said. "But since Saturday night, things have gotten a little tense between us."

"Ah. So…despite what you just said about not wanting to cross the arbitrary boundaries you two have established, you and Nick aren't quite on the same page anymore."

"But we are," Dani argued. "We both agreed to forget we ever kissed."

Lana gave a wry smile. "And how's that working out for you?"

Dani rested her head on her fist. "For me, not so well. I have no idea about Nick, except that when we last spoke on the phone, it was awkward. That was Monday. We haven't been in touch with each other since."

Three whole days—an eternity.

"I wouldn't worry too much," Lana said. "Our weather has been awful. Until last night, Sly and his guys were putting in twenty-hour days, with barely a moment to eat or sleep. That's why he's playing poker tonight—to give himself a well-deserved break from the ranch. I'll bet Nick has been just as busy."

"Probably. Still, he could've called last night, just to check in. Or at the very least, texted. That's what he's done in the past."

"And you're wondering if he's staying away because of those kisses."

"A little."

Lana bit her lip in sympathy, making Dani feel even worse. "What do you want to do?" she asked.

"I'm not going to call him," Dani said. "I'm keeping busy. Which reminds me. I don't have any plans Saturday night. If you and Sly want a date night, I'm happy to come over and babysit."

"That's sweet, but my parents have already offered. They're hosting an overnight for Johanna and her cousins. Johanna is excited. So are Sly and I. We'll get a whole night to ourselves." Lana all but salivated. "Didn't you and a couple of girlfriends sign up for a silk painting class Saturday afternoon? Why don't you hang out with them afterward? Go to dinner and out dancing, or catch a movie, or shop."

The idea appealed to Dani. "I'm pretty sure Christy and her fiancé have plans, but Becca and Janelle might be free. By the way, I have a new dating plan," she said, her own words filling her with hope. "From now on, I'm going to go out with a different kind of guy. He'll have a decent job and be looking to settle down and get married."

Once she met her Mr. Right, she'd be able to forget all about Nick's kisses. Then they could return to being just friends.

Lana opened her mouth to say something, but Johanna broke into noisy tears and barreled into her mother's arms.

"What's the matter, sweetie?" she asked, pulling the howling toddler onto her lap.

"Owie," Johanna wailed, pointing to a red place on her kneecap.

"Aww, poor Johanna. Let Mama make it better." Lana placed a tender kiss on the injury.

Instantly, the cries turned into sniffles. "C-can I have a Band-Aid?"

"It'll come right off in the bathtub, but why not? Dani, will you grab the box of Tinker Bell strips from the bathroom cabinet?"

Moments later, Lana kissed her daughter's cheek. "Is that better?"

Johanna studied her bandaged knee and nodded.

"This has been fun, but Johanna needs a bath before bed," Lana said. "Then we're both going to sleep."

"I need to get to bed myself," Dani said.

After pulling on her coat and kissing her niece and sister-in-law, she opened the door.

"Good luck with your dating plan," Lana said. "Keep me posted."

Chapter 4

"Hey, Mom," Nick said when his mother let him into her apartment late Friday afternoon.

At five feet three, she was short enough that he had to bend down to kiss her cheek.

He nodded to his sister, Jamie, who was two years older than him and sitting on the couch, idly thumbing through a magazine. "Didn't expect to see you here."

She shrugged. "When Mom says to show up, I do."

They'd both been divorced twice, and were as tight as a mother and daughter could be.

Nick narrowed his eyes at his mother. "What's this about?"

"Does there have to be a reason for me to want the company of both my son and my daughter?" she asked. "I've missed you, Nick. It's been too long."

"Since the last time you asked for money." She'd

never been shy about asking him for a loan. Since his father had left him the insurance policy, the requests had only increased.

She put on her pouting face. "That's mean."

"It's the truth."

His mother didn't deny it. "For your information, I happen to have news I want to share in person."

Magazine forgotten, Jamie sat up straight and gave her mother a canny smile. "Is this about Dave?"

Dave, the fiftysomething manager of their mother's apartment complex, had been hanging around for years. Smiling like a cat who'd just snagged a bird for dinner, his mother nodded.

"He finally popped the question." Without waiting for an answer, Jamie squealed, jumped up and hugged her mother.

Nick's mother squealed, too. When they let go of each other, she held out her hand, showing off her newest engagement ring. Dave had always seemed a frugal man, but by the sheer size of the diamond, he'd spent a hefty chunk of change.

It was even bigger than the ring Nick's dad had bought for his mom not long before they'd sold the ranch.

Dave was a nice guy—a couple rungs up from his mom's previous husband. That marriage had been doomed from the start and had failed after less than two years. Nick just hoped that if, by some miracle, this one lasted, she didn't reduce Dave to the broke and unhappy man his father had become.

"Congratulations," he said, wondering why she hadn't just called with the news. "How much do you need for the wedding?"

She actually seemed offended. "I don't want your money, Nick," she said, surprising him.

He figured that after how much the ring had probably set Dave back, the man probably didn't have anything left.

"Dave and I have decided to keep things simple and private," he mother said. "We'll get married by a justice of the peace, either in late April or early May. I want you both to come."

"The spring market is the last weekend in April," Nick reminded her. Proceeds from the sale of his stock at that market paid the ranch expenses for the rest of the year. He couldn't miss it.

"Then how about the first Friday in May?"

Nick and Jamie exchanged glances.

Nick shrugged. "Works for me."

"I'll ask for the afternoon off," Jamie said. She did hair and makeup at a swishy salon. "Should be fine. I can't wait to do your hair and nails, Mom."

They squealed again.

"Jamie, if you want to invite Hank, he's welcome." Her current boyfriend. "Nick, you should bring Dani."

"Dani," he said, wondering at that. "Why would you want her to be there?"

"Girlfriends come and go, but Dani will always a part of your life. I like her. She balances you out."

Not understanding, he frowned.

"When she's around, you're happier and more relaxed than when she isn't."

Not so much anymore.

"You two are such close friends and she and I have known each other for such a long time, that I'm sure she'll want to come," she added.

In the past, a comment about his closeness to her wouldn't have bothered him. It did now, and that rattled him more than the words themselves.

"I'll ask her," he said.

"You know I'd hang out with you tonight if I didn't have a date," Dani's friend Janelle said as they stood in the parking lot of the art studio after their silk painting class.

It was dusk, and they'd spent the past four hours painting silk scarves that they could actually wear. Dani had enjoyed herself, painting, laughing and creating along with her friends. The instructor wanted to set the colors on the scarves so that they didn't bleed, and had promised to mail the finished products to each of them the following week.

"Ditto what Janelle said," Becca said. "Let's plan to go out together some other Saturday night."

As disappointed as Dani was, she understood. Just now, she regretted that she was taking a break from dating. On the other hand, this was a good opportunity to prove to Big Mama that she could be perfectly happy without a man.

All she needed was something fun to do tonight.

"I'm available," Christy said. She'd been unusually quiet all afternoon, but had seemed to enjoy the art class as much as the rest of them.

Dani's jaw dropped. In just over five months, at the end of August, Christy was getting married to her boyfriend, Per. He'd proposed last Christmas. Now they were sharing an apartment. Saturday nights, they always lined up something fun to do together. "Are you sure? I mean, you and Per usually have plans."

"I could use a girls' night out." Christy's lower lip quivered and her eyes filled.

She tended to be a drama queen, but who could ignore a statement like that? About to go their separate ways, Janelle and Becca stopped, exchanged looks with Dani, and drew closer.

"What's wrong, Christy?" Dani asked.

"If I talk about it, I'll cry."

"Like none of us has ever cried in front of you." Dani patted her large shoulder bag. "I have tissues."

Christy glanced around the parking lot, where a few women from art class lingered. "Not here."

"There's a coffee place a few blocks away," Becca said. "Let's go there."

Christy hesitated. "Don't you have to get ready for your date?"

"We're not going out until nine."

"Don is picking me up at eight," Janelle said. "That's two hours from now."

The coffeehouse, a renovated one-story bungalow, was filled with all things cowboy—lassos, Stetsons and photos of young, handsome men, some galloping across the prairie on powerful horses, others herding cattle or roping steer. Each man was attractive, but none could compare with Nick. They probably couldn't kiss half as well, either.

Dani pushed the delicious memory of those kisses right out of her head. She wasn't going to think of Nick that way.

At just after six, the café was getting ready to close and was almost deserted. As soon as they sat down with their coffees, Christy started talking.

"I've dreamed of getting married at Prosperity Falls

since I was a little girl," she said, twisting her sparkly, half-carat engagement ring around her finger.

Didn't everyone? Couples from all over the area got engaged and married within sight of the beautiful falls.

"You couldn't book the date you wanted," Dani guessed, stifling the urge to roll her eyes. This was typical Christy drama.

"Actually, I was able to schedule exactly the time and date I wanted," her friend replied.

"Okay." Becca's puzzled expression echoed Dani's own. "So what's the problem?"

"The problem is that Per wants to elope and then host a big party for our family and friends." Christy let out an indignant huff. "Elope? Is he kidding? No way! A girl only gets married once in a lifetime—at least, I hope so—and I want everyone to witness our joy and commitment!"

Every sentence was a shriek, and the few people still in the coffeehouse were staring.

"Why would he want to elope?" Janelle asked.

"To save money so that we can buy a house sooner."

A big saver herself—Big Mama had taught her the value of putting away money for a rainy day—Dani nodded. "That's not a bad idea. It's nice and practical."

Christy gave her a *whose side are you on?* frown. "A wedding is no time for practicalities. I want a big one, and I'm going to have it. I'm the bride, and it's my right."

She seemed so unhappy that Dani had to ask. "Are you having second thoughts about marrying Per?"

"No! Yes. I don't know." Christy pushed her barely touched mug away.

Becca and Janelle seemed worried now, as worried as Dani. If Per and Christy weren't solid, who was?

Christy's phone rang. She actually jumped. Clearly she was wound as tight as a spring. "That's him now. Excuse me." She stood and hurried out of the coffee-house.

"I hope they work things out," Dani said.

"They will because they love each other." Becca stirred what was left of her cappuccino. "Of course she wants to marry Per. I've always been jealous of how much he loves her. He would do anything for her. I want a man like that."

"Me, too." Dani sighed. If only she could stop fantasizing about Nick....

"It's too bad you and Nick don't want to get together."

Since when had Becca become a mind reader? Dani gave her a wide-eyed stare. "You know exactly why." After swearing them to secrecy earlier, she'd told them what had happened.

"Because Nick's similar to the guys you usually date—out for some fun, then buh-bye." Becca shrugged.

"And because you'd rather stay friends than be lovers and lose it all later," Janelle added. "Also, you have that new dating plan."

Dani laughed. "At least you both listened."

"But he invited you to his mom's wedding," Becca said.

Last night, Nick had called for that very reason, another awkward conversation that had ended quickly. "That's not for almost two months, and a justice of the peace is marrying them," Dani reminded her.

Although the entire ceremony wouldn't take more than fifteen minutes, Dani was nervous about attend-

ing. Before those kisses she was trying so hard to forget—BK, for short—she wouldn't have thought twice
about attending his mom's third wedding. But now…
From the words the couple would exchange to the rings
they would slip on each others' fingers, it was bound
to be awkward.

"Nick doesn't even want to go," she said. "He only
invited me because his mom asked him to."

"You make it sound as if he's taking you to watch a
root canal," Janelle commented.

With things so tense between them, it felt a little
like that.

They were on their second cups of coffee when
Christy finally rejoined them.

"I can't go out with you tonight, after all," she told
Dani, her expression and body language worlds lighter
than they had been before Per's call. "I'm going home
to Per so that we can work things out."

Dani and her friends breathed collective sighs of
relief.

In the parking lot they shared a group hug and then
went their separate ways.

In no mood to go home and spend Saturday night
brooding about her problems, Dani vowed to create her
own fun. She drove to Second Time Around, a movie
theater across town that played second-run movies and
old classics.

Tonight's double header was a two-for-one Ladies'
Classic Night, featuring *Moonstruck* and *An Officer
and A Gentleman*. The romance, the funny moments,
the tears, the happy endings—Dani loved everything
about both movies. The theater was almost full, with
mostly women and older couples. After buying herself

a soft drink and a large, buttered popcorn—tonight's dinner—she found an empty seat in the last row and settled in.

She sat through both movies, nibbling popcorn and sipping soda, while alternately laughing and bawling her eyes out. First for Loretta and Ronny, and later for Paula and Zack.

When the house lights came on, the popcorn and soda were gone and Dani felt very sorry for herself. Forget creating her own fun—she wanted a love like that of the couples in the movies. Like Christy and Per's.

Refusing to attend a pity party for one, she pasted a smile on her face as she left the theater. "I'm a strong person, and I'm going to be okay," she assured herself.

Then and there, she decided to start acting on her dating plan sooner rather than later. So what if she'd been single for only a week? She was ready to climb back in the saddle.

And this time she would approach dating in a smarter way. She wouldn't let herself fall in love until she was absolutely certain that whoever she dated was a steady, solid man who wanted to settle down, get married and have kids.

She considered calling Nick and alerting him that she was going to put her dating plan into action sooner rather than later, or maybe stopping by and explaining in person. But it was after eleven on a Saturday night. She needed to get to bed, and anyway, he was probably out. Besides, the way things were between them, she couldn't just pick up the phone or stop by. She would tell him when they next talked.

On the way home, she detoured to Lannigan's to cheer herself up with a double cup of rocky road, caramel sauce and whipped cream. But scant minutes before she arrived, the ice creamery closed for the night. Shoot, she wouldn't get what she wanted, after all.

Didn't that just sum up her life lately? Pathetic.

In a blue funk despite her resolve to stay strong, she headed for home. "Tomorrow's a new day," she assured herself.

Sunday was the last day of her work week. That was something to be happy about. Soon, she would start searching for someone to date. The right man for her was out there, she just knew it.

Already she felt better.

Saturday night, Nick headed for Tommy's, a bar with beer on tap and great spicy chicken wings. When he arrived, Ted and Paul, two buds from college, already had a table and a pitcher.

Ted, an engineer, was wearing his trademark red St. Louis Cards baseball cap and grinning as if he'd just been drafted as the team's first baseman. "Hey, Nick."

Nick nodded and sat down at the table. "What's with him?" he asked Paul.

Sporting a goatee and a sour expression, Paul, who managed commercial property for a big company, snickered. "Beats me. He's been wearing that dopey grin since he got here. Odds are, it has something to do with Marcie." Ted's wife. "Guy's been married for eighteen months, and for some reason he still acts like he's on his honeymoon. Crazy fool."

Paul had been divorced almost six years and was still nursing a grudge. His failure to move on reminded Nick of his father, who hadn't let go of his anger at Nick's mother until he was on his deathbed. Nick didn't blame his old man for being pissed off—he'd been just as mad at her for breaking up the family. But holding on to that anger hadn't done his father any good, and Nick was pretty sure all that bitterness had contributed to the heart attack that had killed him. At the same time, his father's desperation to please his mother had cost him the ranch. Nick didn't ever plan on being bitter or wrapped around some woman's finger that way. Making the ranch profitable was his main focus, and he wasn't about to ever let any female get under his skin and distract him. It was best to play the field and keep his sanity intact.

He poured himself a beer. "Spill it, Ted."

Instead of speaking, the man handed out cigars.

"What's this?" Nick frowned. "We don't smoke, and we sure as hell can't light up in here."

"They're symbolic—to celebrate something really huge," Ted explained. "Marcie and I are expecting."

Grinning, Nick fist-bumped him. "Congrats, man."

Ted beamed. "We're excited."

"Hey, that's great, but did you and Marcie want kids this soon?" Paul said.

"We'd planned to wait another year or so, but it's all good. Our baby's due in October."

"Is it a boy or a girl?" Nick asked. Dani would want to know—when he told her. Over the past week, they'd only spoken twice, and both times had been a struggle.

"Can't say for sure," Ted said. "We're holding out for a girl, but we won't find out the baby's sex for a couple months yet."

"That's our waitress up at the bar." Paul stood. "I'll order the jumbo plate of chicken wings, fries and another pitcher."

"What's eating him?" Nick asked as Paul strode toward the bar.

"You remember that promotion he was up for? He got passed over."

Nick didn't comment and neither did Ted, but they both understood that Paul's bad attitude was partly to blame.

"How are things at the ranch?" Ted asked.

"We're halfway through installing an irrigation system." Nick brought his friend up to speed on his plans, before moving on. "My mom's getting married again."

"For the third time?" Ted shook his head. "Maybe this will be the charm. You happy about that?"

Nick hadn't thought much about it. He'd been too worried about bringing Dani with him to the ceremony. Given the tension between them, he wasn't sure he should, even if his mother wanted him to. He shrugged. "Dave's all right."

Paul returned to the table. "The order's in, and another pitcher is coming. Hey, Nick, there's a woman over there who reminds me of Dani." He nodded across the way.

Half hoping it *was* Dani, Nick craned his neck around, where a brown-haired woman in jeans and a T-shirt was sitting with a group of men and women.

Besides being at least a decade older than Dani, she was nowhere near as pretty. "She's nothing like Dani," he said.

"Must be the way she wears her hair," Paul said. "Speaking of Dani, how's she doing?"

Nick wasn't sure. He hoped she wasn't sitting at home tonight, with nothing on the calendar. "She's getting over a breakup, but doing okay," he said.

Paul's eyes narrowed in a probing look. "Are you?"

Wondering if his friend somehow sensed that things had shifted between him and Dani, Nick narrowed his eyes. "What's that supposed to mean?"

Unphased, Nick's buddy grinned. "I was talking about *your* breakup. So Dani's okay and you're crappy. I'm getting an interesting picture here."

Just then the waitress showed up with a fresh pitcher, saving Nick from God only knew what else Paul might say. He didn't want to think about what had happened with Dani. Or talk about it. He wasn't that kind of guy.

He filled his plate and shifted the subject to basketball and March Madness, which started in less than two weeks.

To his relief, Dani's name didn't come up again.

Chapter 5

The next week, Charlie Schorr, a customer who'd become a Friday breakfast regular since moving to town some six months earlier, greeted Dani with his usual smile and held out a white carnation. "Good morning, pretty lady. This is for you."

Built like a linebacker, single and about ten years older than she was, he wasn't bad-looking. He didn't float her boat, but he'd been flirting with her since the first morning he'd sat down in her station. Lately he'd taken to bringing her a flower every Friday, which was sweet. He tipped generously, too.

"Aw, thanks, Charlie." She placed the flower in the small vase that sat on the corner of the hostess desk, for all to enjoy.

Wearing a pleased smile, Charlie sauntered to his favorite booth.

He seemed nice and had a job as a CPA. And bonus: he was single. At first glance, he was exactly the kind of man she'd vowed to date—even if she wasn't attracted to him.

But that no longer mattered. She had a new plan and was keen to test it out. Couldn't hurt to give Charlie a chance.

Dani didn't know his thoughts on marriage and kids, though. Time to find out. "Why isn't a guy like you married?" she asked as she filled his mug with coffee.

He seemed surprised by such a personal query. "I could ask you the same thing."

"I haven't found the right man yet," Dani said. "But I'm in the market."

He nodded. "Exactly."

Well, that sounded promising.

"The usual?" she asked with a saucy smile. "Or would you rather try something different?" She lowered her lashes a sultry fraction.

His eyes about popped out of his head before he boldly checked her out. "Define 'different.'"

"You always order the same thing for breakfast," she said. "We have lots of other delicious options. What else looks good to you?"

"You do."

By the dirty-boy gleam in his eyes, he was definitely interested.

Dani wasn't sure she cared for that and half wished she hadn't flirted with him. "Um, I mean foodwise," she said.

To her relief, Charlie calmed right down. "I like what I like, so why should I try something else? Give me the usual."

Solid and settled—that was Charlie.

She nodded. "Cheese omelet, muffin of the day and bacon, it is. I'll be right back with your orange juice."

Suddenly the door opened. A group of ranchers, all men, entered the restaurant. Sly was in the party, and so was Nick. Dani recognized everyone else, too. They were members of the local Montana Cowboy Association, and they gathered at Big Mama's twice a year for an early breakfast meeting. She'd been so preoccupied with her Nick problems and Big Mama's stubbornness that she'd forgotten they were coming in today.

Their business was definitely appreciated—even if coming face-to-face with Nick was a little awkward.

"Hey, Dani." Sly kissed her cheek. "I heard you and Lana had fun at the house the other night."

"We did. We missed you."

Big Mama greeted everyone. She hugged both Sly and then Nick, but Dani's gaze stayed on Nick. She couldn't quite read him, but he'd barely cracked a smile at her before her mother had wrapped her arms around him.

"My boy," she said fondly. She always had loved him like a son.

Grinning, he embraced her with the same warmth as always, and Dani released a tense breath. He was acting normal now. Things must be okay.

"Dani?" Charlie called from his booth. "Can you come over here?"

"After I seat this party."

She had no idea whether he replied. She was too distracted, waiting for Nick to shine his golden grin on her. To her dismay, he gave her a cursory smile that didn't even reach his eyes.

Apparently he was as uncomfortable as she was. Their relationship was definitely off-kilter. Dani regretted those kisses more than ever. And yet, a part of her yearned for more—much more. It was all so confusing.

She greeted the other ranchers, men filled with the warmth and friendliness she'd always taken for granted with Nick.

While they seated themselves around a big table, she dropped off Charlie's food.

"I have a question for you," he said.

"Do you want a different kind of jam or more coffee?"

Charlie shook his head. "This isn't about food. It's something else."

Just now, Dani didn't want to stand around chit-chatting. "Can it wait?" she asked. "I have to take those ranchers' orders."

"Sure, I can wait."

She nodded, and moved away from the booth. Without understanding why, she snatched his carnation from the vase, stuck it behind her ear and secured it with a hair clip.

By the time she passed out menus and filled the men's mugs with coffee, they were ready to order.

Dani started with her brother. "Where'd you get that flower?" he asked.

"From Charlie over there." She nodded toward the booth where the CPA sat. "He's one of my Friday regulars. He brings me a different flower every week."

Nick's eyes grew hooded.

Not sure what to make of that, Dani addressed her brother. "What do you want to eat?"

Sly raised his eyebrows. "Are you okay, little sis?"

He knew her almost as well as she knew herself, and she couldn't get much past him.

No, she was not okay. With Nick seated at the other end of the table, she was confused and flustered. "Doing well," she said with as much enthusiasm as she could muster. "What do you want to order?"

"No small talk today, huh? I'll have the steak and eggs, with a side of hash browns and wheat toast. And keep the coffee coming. Johanna has an earache and neither Lana nor I slept much last night."

He did seem weary. "I'm sorry," Dani said.

Sly waved her words away. "Comes with the territory."

Dani moved to Frank Edison, a fiftysomething rancher she'd met when she'd been in the high school pep squad with two of his daughters. "Ditto on the steak and eggs," Frank said. "You look real pretty with that flower behind your ear. But then, you're a pretty girl to begin with."

He'd always been nice to her, treating her almost as well as he treated his own daughters. "Thanks," Dani said.

Every man at the table echoed Frank's complimentary words. Except Nick.

"You don't care for my flower," she guessed when she was ready to take his order.

"It's fine."

Acting as if he was jealous, he crossed his arms and set his jaw. Weird.

Weirder still, Dani kind of enjoyed that. Which made her sad.

If Nick was jealous and she was happy about it, where did that leave their friendship?

The bigger question was, were they even still friends?

Dani was no longer sure. Her heart squeezed painfully. She arched her eyebrows quizically but Nick was involved in a discussion with several of the ranchers and didn't notice.

She nodded at Bill Barker, a fortysomething rancher with a wife and four young children. "How about you, Bill?" To her own ears she sounded wooden.

"I'll have the Big Mama special. Are you sure you're okay?"

She always had been an open book. Dani forced a bright smile. "I'm doing great, thanks. The special comes with your choice of a blueberry muffin or toast."

"When it comes to Big Mama's muffins, there is no choice," Bill commented.

Several men chuckled. Dani jotted down the remaining orders without any undue attention. As she left to give them to Mike, the cook, Big Mama approached her with a worried frown.

"Your face is all pinched up," she said. "What's the matter, honey?"

"Why do people keep asking me if I'm okay?" Dani snapped, earning sharp looks from Big Mama and several diners within hearing range. "I'm fine, just fine!"

Her mother glanced at the Montana Cowboy Association table, where Nick was staring at her with a crease between his brows and his lips compressed into a thin line. "What's going on between you and Nick?"

Dani longed to share the confusion and hurt with her mother, but that would mean explaining about those kisses, which she wasn't about to do. She shook her head. "I don't want to talk about it."

"Maybe you should take a break and talk to him."

Not a bad idea, except that this morning the restaurant was bustling, and Sadie and Colleen, the other waitresses, already had enough to do.

"We're too busy," she said, and hurried to turn in the ranchers' breakfast orders and refill Charlie's mug.

With Big Mama's comment about her pinched face fresh in her mind, Dani forced a pleasant expression when she topped off his coffee. "How's your breakfast today?"

"Tasty as always. You're wearing my flower behind your ear—sweet. I wanted to ask you a question, remember?"

"That's right." Dani had completely forgotten. "It's not about food, you said."

"It's about you and me. I want to take you out. What are you doing next Saturday night?"

He would ask her out when she was upset about Nick. Dani was sorry she'd encouraged him. The way she felt right now, she didn't want to go out with Charlie or any other man.

But she was eager to take action and put *something* on her weekend calendar, if only to prove to herself that she could. Besides, she reminded herself, Charlie was exactly the kind of man she wanted to date.

"I don't have anything scheduled yet," she replied.

Out of the corner of her eye, she noticed that Nick was frowning at her. She made sure her smile was nice and bright—just to make him wonder.

Assuming it was meant for him, Charlie grinned. "Now you do."

"Great," she replied with enthusiasm she didn't feel.

New times, she reminded herself. "What did you have in mind?"

"For starters, dinner at Baker's." Which only happened to be the nicest, most expensive restaurant in all of Prosperity Falls. "After that…" Charlie winked. "We'll figure out something."

The wink bothered her. In no mood for sexual innuendo or any more flirtation, she glanced at the ranchers' table. "Uh-oh, my ranchers are waving for more coffee. Excuse me."

She headed for Nick's table.

"Who is that guy?" he asked, glancing at Charlie through narrowed eyes.

"That's Charlie, the man who gave me this." Dani touched the flower.

"So you said before. But who *is* he?"

She was about to explain when two women from another table gestured her over. Then several other customers wanted things, and she never did get a chance to answer Nick's question.

Charlie signaled that he was finished. When she delivered the bill he circled her wrist with his meaty thumb and forefinger. "How about giving me your phone number."

She didn't want him touching her, especially here in the restaurant. After extracting her hand, she stacked his dirty dishes. For the life of her, she couldn't bring herself to share her number with him. "I'm easiest to reach here at the restaurant," she hedged.

He nodded. "I'll call you next week and let you know when I'll be by to pick you up."

He left his usual generous tip and sauntered out.

* * *

What was up with Dani today? She'd had plenty of time to flirt with the bozo in the booth across the room, yet she'd barely cracked a smile Nick's way.

The strange discomfort between them bothered him. He didn't care for the tension in the air when she was near any more than he liked having the urge to reach out and touch her, as if he was staking his claim.

The way he felt right now, twitchy and tense, even a casual touch was too dangerous. As hard as he was trying to right things between them, they seemed more cockeyed than ever.

Nick needed to get home to the ranch, but not until he and Dani straightened out a few things. After the meal, he hung around, waiting for the group to break up so that he could talk with her. Before long, everyone in the Montana Cowboy Association had gone except for him and Sly. The café's entire breakfast crowd had thinned, with only a handful of diners remaining.

Dani was busy with a customer. Her brother waved goodbye, and she blew him a kiss.

As Sly made his way to the coat tree near the door, he motioned Nick to follow him. They were the same height, and Sly looked him straight in the eyes.

"What's going on between you and my sister?" he asked in a low voice only Nick could hear.

"Nothing much."

"Uh-huh. That's why you're both so unhappy."

Nick wasn't about to discuss his problems with Dani's brother. He snorted. "Have you been smoking something you shouldn't?"

"Very funny, Kelly," Sly said, but his mouth barely quirked. "I don't care to see my sister hurt."

Seriously annoyed at the accusation, Nick squinted at Dani's brother. "How long have we known each other, Sly?"

"Awhile now."

"Sixteen years—since Dani and I first met. In all those years, have I ever hurt her?" He didn't wait for a response. "No. I would never knowingly cause her pain. Never, and for you to think otherwise…" His hands balled into fists.

"Easy, man. I'm only watching out for my little sister. Make sure that you do, too." Sly grabbed his jacket, clapped on his Stetson and left.

When Nick glanced around again, Dani was nowhere in sight. Scratching his head, he wandered over to the hostess desk.

Shelby, the weekday hostess, was close to Nick's age and about four months pregnant. Absently rubbing her lower back, she smiled at him. "Hey, Nick. How was your breakfast this morning?"

"Fantastic as always. Where's Dani?"

"She and Big Mama went into the office. I'm sure they won't mind if you go on in."

Moments later, Nick pushed through swinging doors that led to the restrooms and the business office at the far end of the hall.

He knocked on the door and without waiting for an answer, opened it and stepped into the room.

Dani was sitting across the old mahogany desk from Big Mama, the same desk that had always been there. As she caught sight of Nick, surprise colored her face.

He nodded at the older woman, then directed his gaze at Dani.

"Why, Nick, how nice of you to stick around after your meeting this morning," Big Mama said, as if he and Dani weren't staring holes in each other. "I expect you're here to talk to Dani. I should check with Mike about tomorrow's specials." She pushed heavily to her feet. "We'll go over the orders later, Dani."

Moments later the door shut behind her.

Dani didn't move from the chair. She was wearing a short skirt, tights and a sweater that emphasized her breasts. Nick kept his gaze on her big, silvery-blue eyes and sweet, kissable mouth… She was torturing him.

"Your brother just warned me not to hurt you," he said.

"He and everyone else around here should mind their own business."

"There's something we both agree on."

He expected a smile, but Dani didn't give him one. "Are you going to sit down?" she said. "Because I'm getting a crick in my neck."

There was only one empty seat in the crowded little office. Nick frowned. "You want me to sit in Big Mama's chair?"

"She won't mind."

Bills and supply orders lay across the desk. Careful not to disturb them, he sat. "You took the carnation out from behind your ear."

Dani nodded. "Wearing it was a little weird."

"Then why did you put it on in the first place?"

"I wanted to." She bit her lip. "Charlie asked me out."

Nick had been afraid of that. He disliked the way the man had stared at Dani, as if she was dessert and he wanted to feast on her. He shook his head. "That break you're supposed to be taking from dating sure didn't last."

She blew out an irritated breath. "I said it probably wouldn't. What matters is that I'm taking a break from my usual type of man."

"Charlie's too old for you."

"He's forty. That's not so old."

"Well, he looks closer to fifty. What did you say when he asked you out?"

"That I'd go."

The thought of Charlie kissing her at the end of the evening was more than Nick could handle. "That's a bad idea," he said.

"Why? Charlie's a CPA. That's a steady job with good pay. And he hinted that he might want to settle down someday. He's exactly the kind of man I should be dating."

"But is he a decent guy?"

"He's been coming here every Friday for six months. From what I know of him, he seems to be."

Unable to argue with that, Nick gave a grudging nod. "When and where is he taking you?"

"A week from Saturday. We're going to Baker's for dinner."

"On a first date? Wow." Impressed in spite of himself, Nick whistled.

"It is pretty amazing," she said. "I have no idea what to wear. He's complimented my brown and teal cowboy boots, but they aren't dressy enough."

"For God's sake, Dani, don't dress to please him. Dress to please yourself. If he's not happy about it, that's his problem."

Dani gave him a startled look. "Maybe I should skip your mother's wedding."

The comment from right field surprised him. "What does my mom's wedding have to do with you dating Charlie?"

"Nothing. It's just that… I get the feeling that you're in a better mood when I'm not around."

Lately, whether she was near or far away, Nick was out of sorts, but he wasn't going to admit it. "She's not getting married for another six weeks or so. Why don't you wait and decide later?"

"Okay, but if we're this uncomfortable around each other, I'm going to stay home."

The thought of them this unhappy around each other for weeks on end bummed him out. His shoulders were uncomfortably tight. In an effort to loosen up, he rolled them a couple times, which didn't do squat.

"I wish I could figure out how to get rid of this tension," he muttered.

"It's no fun, that's for sure." Dani sighed. "Our relationship is all screwed up. We never should have kissed."

Belying her own statement, she glanced at his mouth with longing written all over her face.

Nick's body jumped to life, but he was here to fix this mess, not make it worse. He tamped down his feelings—way down so that they wouldn't bubble up. "I miss my best friend."

"Me, too," Dani admitted in a soft voice.

For a long moment they stared wordlessly at each other, two confused souls at a loss what to do.

"We need to get back to where we were," she said.

He nodded. "I have to be honest here. We agreed

to forget those kisses, and believe me, I've tried. But I can't stop thinking about that night."

"Tell me about it." Dani stared at her hands, locked in her lap, before again meeting his gaze. "But if we get physical, our friendship will be over for sure. And when the physical part ends, we'll be over. For good."

This was true. "We can't let that happen," Nick said.

Dani made a glum face. "We need a plan." After a moment she brightened. "Maybe if we both get involved with someone new, we'll be so interested in them that we'll stop wanting what we can't have and go back to being platonic friends."

It wasn't a bad idea—provided they each found a new partner. "I don't picture you with Charlie long-term," Nick said, and not only because imagining the guy with his hands on Dani made him see red. "There's something about him that bothers me. I can't put my finger on what it is. All I know is, I don't trust the guy."

"He may not be right for me, but I have to give him a try." She raised her head, as if resolved. "How about you, Nick? Is there someone you want to go out with?"

His thoughts flashed to Sylvie Kitchen, the redhead he'd met at Harper's Pizza. Only last night he'd tossed her business card. As soon as he got home he'd fish it out of the trash. "There is a woman I recently met. Maybe I'll take her out next weekend, while you're out with Charlie."

Dani gave a relieved nod. "Let's plan to touch bases the next day and share how it went." She glanced at the old school clock hanging above the door. "We've been talking for a while. I'm sure Big Mama is anxious to finish our meeting and go home. I know I would."

"On my way out, I'll let her know you're waiting for her." Nick stood.

Dani rose, too, and walked with him to the door. "I'm glad we talked, Nick."

"We really needed to."

Sensing that they'd get past this, that their friendship was as solid as ever, he tugged on a lock of her hair.

In return, she shot him a dazzling smile that transformed her whole face. She was so beautiful, his chest ached. He reached for the door with a shaky hand.

"Wait," Dani said.

Standing on her toes, she planted a chaste kiss on his cheek, the same as she always had.

But this felt different. Sweeter.

The scent of her orange blossom shampoo made him want to bury his face in her hair. Then tilt up her chin and ramp up the kiss into something a whole lot hotter.

Nick stifled a groan. It was all he could do not to act on his fierce need. But his future friendship with Dani depended on behaving himself.

Unaware of the torture she was putting him through, she almost smiled. "We're going to be okay," she said. "I know it."

Not at all convinced, Nick nodded and walked through the door.

Chapter 6

"Do Sadie and Colleen need a hand?" Dani asked when Big Mama returned to the office. Sadie had waitressed at the restaurant for over twenty years, and Colleen for five.

Dani's mother shook her head. "Right now, we're not too busy." She moved toward her desk more slowly than Dani could ever remember. "You're much happier than you were when I left. I'm guessing that whatever was bothering you and Nick has been settled," she said, her smile at odds with her lumbering movements.

She sat down cautiously, as if she were sore or in pain. Earlier, she'd gotten up the same way.

"Do your legs hurt?" Dani asked, concerned.

"At my age, everything hurts."

Big Mama chuckled, but Dani found nothing funny about the little joke. For the past few days, her vibrant mother had become noticeably less energetic. Age, Dani assumed. She hated that Big Mama was getting older. "You're in pain," she said, "and I don't like it."

"Just you wait until you're sixty-nine, missy. You'll have your share of aches and pains, too. I assume you mentioned your upcoming date with Charlie to Nick. Does he approve?"

"I'm not talking about that until you tell me what's wrong."

"At times you can be so stubborn and exasperating," her mother muttered. "There's nothing wrong. My knees bother me, but that's been going on for years now. Yes, I'm tired today, but only because I didn't sleep well last night." She widened her eyes. "Does that satisfy you, missy, or would you prefer that I go into minute detail and bore us both to death?"

"Now who's exasperating?" Dani said. They both smiled. "I can guess why you couldn't sleep. You're worried about the restaurant."

Her mother's eyes flashed. *Bingo.*

"Things have been pretty slow," she conceded. "But tourist season is just around the corner, and things are bound to pick up."

"We can hope, but we have so much competition now, and not just from the Poplar Tree. If we address our problems now, we'll have a better chance of boosting our business no matter what the season. The restaurant could use a facelift and a few new—"

Her mother cut her off with a glare. "Big Mama's Café is fine the way it is," she insisted. "If you must know, the real reason why I couldn't sleep last night is because I had a bad case of indigestion."

Not finished the restaurant discussion, Dani crossed

her arms. "You can't keep pretending that our problems here will just go away. They won't, and we have to be realistic. Sooner or later, we have to make some changes. Otherwise…"

Hoping to worry her mother into taking action, she let the ominous implications hang between them. The only indication that Big Mama heard was the slight tightening of her jaw.

Several tense seconds ticked by before Dani mentally threw up her hands and changed the subject. "Nick's mom is getting married again," she said. "She wants me to go."

"She's having *another* wedding?"

"Nothing fancy this time. They're using a justice of the peace."

Her mother nodded. "You and Nick are such close friends, it makes sense that she'd want you there."

Up until now they'd been very close, anyway. But if they didn't move past their attraction to each other, any future relationship was doomed.

Unfortunately Dani was completely fixated on Nick, and not just as a friend. That had to change. She wasn't sure why she'd kissed him on the cheek earlier. Maybe to test herself. A dangerous test she'd nearly failed. For a few minutes there, it had taken all her strength not to slant his head toward her and kiss his mouth instead.

But kissing Nick the way she longed to was out. Now and forever.

"What did you eat for dinner last night?" she asked in a desperate push to tamp down her desire for him.

"Fried chicken, biscuits and gravy."

Dani's mouth watered. Her mother made killer fried chicken and side dishes. "Eating all that rich food—no wonder you had indigestion. Dr. Adelson warned you to cut down on foods that are high in fat and cholesterol. We all should. That's one reason why I believe we should offer healthier menu options for our customers." Big Mama's lips thinned in warning—the stubborn woman wasn't going to discuss even that—and Dani returned to last night's dinner. "I don't suppose you had any vegetables or a salad with your meal?"

Her mother made a face. "No, I didn't. Now you can answer my question. What's Nick's opinion of you and Charlie?"

Dani eyed her mother. "We haven't finished talking about you and your diet."

"Yes, we have." Big Mama's mulish expression signaled that that subject was indeed closed.

A second topic shut down. Seriously annoyed, Dani lashed out. "You won't discuss the restaurant and you won't talk about your diet. And you call me stubborn. You're so hard-headed, I could scream!"

"Please don't. It might upset our lunch customers. What did Nick say about your date with Charlie?"

Dani gave up arguing with her mother—for now. "He doesn't care for Charlie. He thinks he's too old for me."

With the flick of her hand, Big Mama disposed of that opinion. "That just means he's had more time to mature and settle into his CPA career. And a fine career it is. He's a good prospect, Dani. I'm pleased that you're following through on your plan to date someone different from your usual choices."

Although Dani smiled, she couldn't summon up much enthusiasm for her upcoming date. She wanted so much to be excited, wanted to like Charlie so that she'd stop wanting Nick.

"You're frowning," Big Mama said.

"Just making a mental list of the supplies I should order for next week."

Her mother nodded. "After talking with Mike, I know just what we need. Let's make that list. Then we can both get back to work."

As Charlie had promised, on Tuesday he called Dani at the restaurant. "I remembered that you have to get up early on Sunday, so I made our dinner reservation for six-thirty," he said. "Since it's outside the city limits and will take about thirty minutes to get there, I'll pick you up at six."

"All right," Dani said, hoping she sounded more excited than she was. Pushing away her dread—this date *had* to work—she gave him her address.

When she hung up, Sadie leaned in close. "You look as thrilled as a woman about to have bunion surgery. Are you sure you want to go out with Charlie?"

Dani loved the down-to-earth woman. "Is my lack of enthusiasm that obvious? And here I figured I was so convincing."

"Not with that long face. You mentioned you're trying to date a different kind of man, but I don't understand why you picked Charlie. He doesn't seem like your type."

"That's the whole point," Dani said. "He's the complete opposite of the guys I usually go for."

"Yes, but..." Sadie shook her head. "Never mind. What do I know? I've been married and divorced three times, twice with the same man."

"That just about makes you an expert," Dani teased. "What were you going to say?"

"Charlie has never been anything but polite in here, but there's something about him that bothers me. For the life of me, I can't put my finger on what it is, though."

Nick had said something similar.

Nick. The whole reason Dani had said yes to Charlie. No, this date wasn't just about Nick. It was for her, too. She wanted a man with a real job, who respected her and treated her well. If this date worked out and they continued to see each other, who knew where it would lead? Her feelings for Charlie could change for the better.

"Maybe it's because he tries so hard to make everyone like him," Sadie went on. "If he'd just relax, he might be more appealing."

"Could be," Dani said, striving to convince herself. "He's taking me to Baker's."

"Really! I've never been lucky enough to go there."

"I've been twice. Once with my date for senior prom—" she and Nick had double-dated "—and once for my twenty-first birthday." Big Mama and Nick had treated her.

She glanced across the restaurant at her mother, who was rubbing her chest and leaning heavily on the order counter.

For almost a week now, Dani had been concerned for her. Now she was plain-out worried. She lowered her voice so that only Sadie could hear. "Does Big Mama seem okay to you?"

Sadie wrinkled her nose. "Not really. Today she seems especially blah, and I don't like it. She's pale, too, similar to my daughter when she has the flu. I wonder if she's coming down with something."

"She never gets sick," Dani said. "But if she did, she'd stay home."

While Sadie locked the restaurant door some minutes later, Dani confronted her mother. "You keep rubbing your chest," she pointed out.

"It's just a little heartburn."

"You've got to start eating right. You should see Dr. Adelson."

"What for? He'll just tell me what I already know. I don't need another of his lectures on what I should and shouldn't eat."

Dani swallowed a sigh. "Will you at least schedule a physical?"

"I'm fine."

"No, you aren't. You're pale and tired, and you keep rubbing your chest."

"For heaven's sake, quit worrying about me! I'm strong as an ox."

"Please get a physical. If not for yourself, do it for me."

"And just where would I find the time?"

"That's why you have me," Dani said. "I run the restaurant on weekends. I can certainly run it for a few more hours while you're at the doctor's."

"I already take off Saturdays and Sundays. I can't afford to take any more days off."

If she trusted Dani, she wouldn't be so reluctant.

In Dani's life, she'd had precious little of that. First she'd lost her parents and the implicit trust that they would always be there. Then she'd lost her brothers for umpteen years. Add in all the guys who'd broken her heart, and trust was in short supply.

Certainly she trusted Big Mama—why couldn't her

mother do the same? She'd done everything possible to prove she could handle the restaurant. She kept things running smoothly and efficiently and handled any emergencies as well as her mother. But this was not the moment to bring that up.

"Then schedule a Monday appointment. But please, for my own peace of mind, get yourself checked."

Her mother tightened her lips.

"If you don't call Dr. Adelson, I will," Dani threatened.

That did the trick. Big Mama expelled an irritated breath and gave in. "All right, Dani, all right! I'll make an appointment."

With early spring in full force, there was plenty to do on the ranch. For several days, Nick alternated between the never-ending task of mending the fences that had fallen into disrepair over the winter and helping inseminate heifers and cows. The spring grass was starting to come up. In another week or two it would be lush and ripe. Grazing on the nutrient-rich grass enabled his cattle to put on weight—faster and more economically than feeding them hay and artificial vitamins and minerals. The more weight they gained, the better. Fat, healthy animals fetched top dollar at the spring market.

After chores late Saturday afternoon, he showered and dressed for his date with Sylvie Kitchen. They had a dinner reservation at Baker's, the same restaurant where Charlie was taking Dani.

Dani wouldn't be pleased about that, but Nick wanted to keep an eye on the CPA.

Just after six he pulled up to Sylvie's house. She lived in a well-maintained cottage in a nice area.

She answered the door wearing a soft pink dress that clung to her curves and heels that made her legs impossibly long, putting her almost at eye-level with him.

"You look fantastic," he said.

"Thank you."

She favored him with a warm smile that should have rocked his world. It didn't.

On the drive to the restaurant they chatted easily.

"How long have you been a rancher, Nick?" she asked.

"I was born on Kelly Ranch, but when I was nine my family sold it. Then a couple years ago, I bought it back."

Sylvie nodded. "I had a distant cousin who owned a ranch, but he ended up selling it. Ranching isn't easy."

"It can be a real challenge, but it's in my blood," Nick said. "What about you, Sylvie? What's your story?"

She told him about her very normal life, which included the kind of carefree childhood Nick had always dreamed about. Her parents were still happily married, and she was close to her brother and sister, who were both married with kids.

She was poised, smart, beautiful and a decent conversationalist. Nick liked her.

But she wasn't Dani.

Wasn't that the whole point?

Chapter 7

Charlie arrived at exactly 6:00 p.m. Dani buzzed him up. When he knocked on the door a few minutes later, she pasted a smile on her face and let him in. "Hi, Charlie."

In a suit and tie, he was almost handsome. The scent of Old Spice clung heavily to him.

"I like that suit," she said.

"Thanks." His gaze darted over her. "Nice dress."

Remembering the sexual glint in his eyes that day at the restaurant, she'd chosen flats and a loose blue sheath that played down her curves. To further hide her body, she'd looped the colorful silk scarf she'd painted in art class around her shoulders. Yet by Charlie's overly warm expression she might just as well have worn a snug mini-dress and do-me heels.

Dani didn't like that, and wondered what his expectations were for later tonight. Over dinner she'd set him straight.

"Did you have any trouble finding the building?" she asked.

"None."

There the conversation ended. As the silence stretched out, Charlie stuck his hand in his pocket and jiggled his change. No signs of sexual interest now. Clearly he was nervous.

When Fluff came running to meet him, Dani heaved a sigh of relief and sent a big thanks to her cat for making an appearance at exactly the right moment. "This is my cat, Fluff," she said.

Instead of greeting or petting the tom, her date stepped back.

"You're not a cat person?" Dani asked.

"I'm allergic. They make me sneeze."

So much for Fluff. "We should go."

She opened the closet and took out her dress coat, the one she wore to weddings and other special occasions. His gentleman gene showing, Charlie helped her into it.

As the elevator descended to the lobby, Dani vowed to do everything she could to put Charlie at ease. Otherwise she was in for a long, uncomfortable evening.

His new-model sedan was neat and clean, and the radio was tuned to her favorite country station. This was good.

Steve Belong was singing "Little Red Dress." "I love the beat of this song," she said, singing along for a few bars.

Charlie gave her a look she couldn't decipher. "You don't want me to sing?" she asked.

"Not really. I can't hear the music."

Dani stopped. She asked him who his favorite singers were. To her relief, he opened up a little. They discussed music and discovered they shared a taste for blues as well as country. Charlie mentioned an upcoming concert, and Dani assumed that if the date went well, he would probably invite her to go with him.

Some thirty minutes later, a smiling hostess led them to their table. Baker's was a whole different world from Big Mama's Café, but Dani absorbed every detail to mull over later. Music floated through the air, pleasant but not intrusive. Diners filled almost every table. Soft lighting, fresh flowers in crystal vases and off-white linens gave the restaurant a romantic air.

"What do you like to do for fun?" Dani asked as she and Charlie sipped cocktails.

"I'm big into fishing." Having grown more comfortable with her—or maybe it was the alcohol—Charlie launched into stories about fishing with his buddies, fellow Elks Club members in Missoula, where he'd lived before relocating to Prosperity.

Charlie ordered another drink. Dani declined.

"Why did you move here?" she asked while he drank it.

"I got a great job offer. Also, because of the Ames and Missouri Rivers in town. After the tax season, my buddies are planning to drive over. We'll fish in both."

He talked at length about his hobby—the various lures he used, how he determined which to use, and when. Then, in copious detail, he launched into how he'd built a smoker for the trout and salmon he caught. He explained how to season the fish and how to test when they were fully smoked. And on and on, without barely a pause, until Dani's eyes nearly crossed. She half wished he were still too nervous to talk.

The first course, a squash soup, was smooth and delicious despite the company. Although Charlie hardly seemed to notice the food. Instead of commenting on the dish, he kept on talking, never pausing long enough for Dani to comment, and never asking her a single question about herself. As if a pipe had burst, with no shutoff valve.

She stopped listening and glanced frequently and obviously at her watch in hopes that he would take the hint and either shut his mouth or ask for the check—neither of which he did—when to her surprise, Nick moved into her line of sight.

On his arm, a stunning redhead. As far as she knew, he rarely brought a date here. For a moment she wondered if he'd picked this restaurant because she'd said she would be here with Charlie.

Regardless, he certainly hadn't wasted any time finding someone new. She was gorgeous, too, sleek and slender. Dani didn't have a sleek bone in her body.

A funny feeling churned in her gut. Jealousy.

As if sensing her gaze, Nick looked straight at her. He steered his date toward their table. Dani managed a smile.

"Hey, Dani," he said. "Funny running into you here. Nice scarf."

Not so funny, when he'd known she would be here, but she refrained from pointing that out. "It's the one I made at the silk painting class." She pivoted toward the redhead. "I'm Dani Pettit."

"Sylvie Kitchen." Sylvie held out her hand.

"Dani's an old friend of mine," Nick said.

"He means longtime. We're not old," Dani joked.

Polite laughter all around.

"Nick and Sylvie, meet Charlie."

Charlie nodded at Nick. "I saw you at Big Mama's last week. You came in with a bunch of guys."

Nick nodded. "We had a ranchers' meeting. We do that at Big Mama's twice a year."

"I'm a CPA. We sometimes have breakfast meetings, too." Charlie ogled Sylvie and gave her a wolfish smile.

All guys looked at women, but blatantly checking someone out and flirting with her in front of Dani and the other woman's date? Charlie's crude behavior reminded her all too well of a couple of her previous boyfriends. And cemented the doubts that had been forming since he'd picked her up. Heck, since he'd first asked her out.

He definitely wasn't for her.

The hostess came over. "Mr. Kelly and Miss Kitchen, your table is ready. Unless you'd prefer to join this table?"

Nick shook his head. "No, thanks. Good to meet you, Charlie." Moments later, he and Sylvie sat down on the opposite side of the restaurant.

"That's some redhead your friend is with," Charlie said with an admiring shake of his head. "She could be Miss America."

A little envious of the woman, Dani nodded. "Everyone Nick dates is pretty." Although Sylvie was downright stunning. No doubt he was eager to make her his new girlfriend.

The main course arrived. Neither she nor Charlie spoke for a while.

This course was also delicious, but Dani picked at her meal. Her pang of jealousy turned into full-fledged heartache. Silently she chastised herself. Wasn't this what she and Nick both wanted—to meet someone who made them forget each other? She was happy for him. She was.

Charlie looked concerned, and Dani realized she was frowning. "Hey, you're pretty, too," he said, smiling at her.

Too little, too late.

If Charlie realized she was irritated with him, he didn't let on. "You two used to be involved, huh?"

"No," Dani told him. "As we explained, we're friends."

He gave a sly smile. "The kind with benefits."

"Nope. We've always been close, but ours is a platonic friendship." At least she intended for it to be once again, just as soon as she found a man who interested her.

Nick seemed to be on the right track. With any luck, Dani would catch up soon.

Right now, though, she just wanted to go home. But Charlie was only halfway through his meal.

"So what's Nick doing at Baker's tonight?" he asked.

Dani glanced at his table, where a waiter was delivering soups. "From what I can see, he's about to have dinner with his date."

"Yeah, then why does he keep staring over here?"

Dani glanced at Nick's table and caught him doing just that. She gave him a dirty look and returned her attention to Charlie.

Within ten minutes, his plate was empty. "You ready for coffee and dessert?" he asked.

Although Dani was too full for another bite, she figured Charlie wasn't. "Sure."

Soon after Charlie finished his chocolate meringue pie—and hers—he signaled for the check.

"Let's get out of here," he said, with a heavy-lidded expression that was definitely sexual.

Was he kidding? Intending to put out that fire right now, she eyed him with cool disinterest. "Listen, I have to be up at four-thirty tomorrow. I need to get home."

"Yeah, okay."

The gleam faded from his eyes. Dismissing her misgivings, she pushed her chair away from the table.

It was a relief to know that he understood.

By the time Nick pulled up at Sylvie's, it was starting to rain. He took her arm and moved quickly to her door. "Don't want to get those pretty shoes wet," he said, his breath clouding in front of him.

"Right," she said.

"We made it," he said as they ducked under the eaves and the soft porch light. When she didn't reply, he frowned. "You've been awfully quiet since we left Baker's."

"Have I? Baker's has always been one of my favorite restaurants. I enjoyed our dinner, Nick."

"Me, too." He wasn't lying. Sylvie was easy to talk to.

The welcoming warmth in her gaze assured him that she wouldn't fight a good-night kiss. Happy to oblige, he leaned in and brushed his lips over hers.

It was a decent kiss, but nothing special. He stepped back.

"It's Dani, isn't it?" Sylvie said. "You're hung up on her."

Nick added "smart" to the list of things he liked about this woman. She was right—he definitely was hung up on Dani.

But damn it, that was going to change.

"As Dani and I said earlier, we've known each other a long time—since high school," he said. "We're friends, but that's all."

"That's not what I saw. The way you looked at her, and the warmth in her eyes when she looked at you... The old 'sparks flew' cliché comes to mind. Then, all during dinner, you kept watching her. You tried to be covert about it, but I noticed."

Busted. Damn.

Nick shifted his weight. "That was rude. I owe you an apology and an explanation. The truth is, until a few weeks ago, Dani and I *were* platonic friends. It's been that way for sixteen years. We were happy with our relationship.

"Then without either of us meaning for it to happen, things changed." Not about to get into that, he cut to the chase. "We want to be in that friends-only place again, so we're dating other people."

"We," she murmured.

"What did you say?"

"You keep saying 'we,' as if you and Dani are a couple."

In a sense, they were, but not the way Sylvie thought. "I mean 'we' as friends," Nick said.

His date brushed the words aside with a *what kind of fool do you take me for?* look. "Let's see if I understand correctly. To help you and Dani regain your friendship-only status, you asked me out, and Dani went out with Charlie."

Nick nodded. "That's it in a nutshell. But that's not the whole reason I asked you out. You're an attractive woman and I wanted to get to know you better. I'm glad I did. I like you, Sylvie."

Pensive, she frowned, her forehead slightly furrowed. "Don't you think your plan would have worked better if you'd chosen different restaurants instead of showing up at the same one, at the same time?"

Nick scrubbed the back of his neck. "That was totally my fault. Dani told me where she and Charlie were going. She had no idea that I'd show up."

"Why did you take me there, Nick?" Sylvie asked.

"It's a great place to bring a date."

"Yes, but why, really?"

"Because I don't trust Charlie."

"In other words, you wanted to keep an eye on Dani." Sylvie gave him a smile that was devoid of any humor. "You don't think she can take care of herself?"

If Dani heard that, she'd bean him. "I'm sure she can," he said. "But in case there was trouble, I wanted to be there. I didn't just take you to Baker's so that I could keep an eye on her," he added. "I meant what I said, Sylvie—I enjoyed having dinner with you. You're intelligent and beautiful—a terrific date."

She was silent a moment. "And yet, your plan to distract yourself with my company didn't work."

Put that way, he sounded like a real jerk. He pointed to his face. "If you want to slap me, go ahead. I deserve it."

"I'm considering it." Her lips twitched. "At least I got a first-rate meal out of this."

Her ability to tease him after what he'd done made him sorry that he didn't feel more for her. He touched her cheek. "You're an amazing woman, you know that?"

"As a matter of fact, I do." She gave him a genuine smile. "Explain something to me, Nick. Why don't you and Dani just give in and let your relationship go where it wants to?"

"Because mixing sex and friendship won't work for either of us. Once we cross over to the physical side of things, our friendship will become a thing of the past. We don't want to lose what we have now."

"Now I'm really confused," Sylvie said. "Can't you have sex and continue to be friends?"

"That wouldn't work for us. Dani usually falls for every guy she sleeps with. Her relationships never last, and she gets hurt a lot. I'm not great at relationships, either, and I don't fall in love. I don't want to hurt her."

Sylvie studied him. "Your saying that even if Dani wasn't in the picture, you and I wouldn't have a future."

Not about to lie, he nodded. "As much as I like you, I'm not looking for a committed relationship. I was going to explain that tonight, only I didn't get around to it."

"That's too bad. I'd hoped that maybe…" Sylvie's words trailed off. "Oh, well."

"Hey, you can do a whole lot better than me. You're special, and you deserve a guy who'll give you the moon."

"That's sweet, and very romantic. I hope you and Dani work things out."

Nick hoped so, too. He kissed Sylvie's cheek and wished her a great life. As soon as she headed inside, he left.

He intended to drive straight to the ranch, climb into bed and sleep. A gut feeling he couldn't ignore or explain stopped him.

Dani was in trouble. He sped toward her place.

Chapter 8

On the drive home after dinner, it started raining. Charlie was quiet, and the only sounds in the car were the wipers and the radio.

Dani didn't mind. After his nonstop monologue all evening, the silence was a welcome change. She didn't say a word until he pulled into the parking lot. "You don't have to park, Charlie, just let me out here, by the front door. Thanks for tonight. I'll see you at Big Mama's on Friday."

Acting as if he hadn't heard her, he angled into a slot in the Visitor Parking area.

"I'd rather you didn't walk me to the door," she said to make sure he understand that she wasn't up for a kiss.

Charlie set the brake on his car. Had he not heard her? "I have to get up at four-thirty, remember?" she said. "You're not walking me to my door and you can't come up. If you drive around to the entrance, I can dash inside without getting wet."

Her words fell on deaf ears. He killed the engine.

So much for staying dry. "Well, good night," Dani said, reaching for the door handle.

He put his hand over hers, stopping her. "Don't go yet, Dani. You haven't given me my kiss."

His voice was low and warm. Sexual. Apparently, he hadn't gotten the message that she wasn't into him. "Listen, Charlie, I think you're a nice guy, but I'm not interested in you that way," she said in an effort to let him down gently.

"Then let me be your friend with benefits, like Nick."

He would mention Nick. "As I've explained twice before, it isn't that way between him and me. I don't want to kiss you or do anything else," she stated, not so gently now.

"One kiss and you'll change your mind."

"I'm certain I won't."

"I want my kiss."

It was clear that he wouldn't let her leave until she complied. "All right, Charlie, one small kiss. No tongue."

She leaned across the gap between the seats for a quick peck, but he cupped the back of her head so that she couldn't move away. Then he forced his tongue in her mouth.

"Don't," she said, struggling to get away.

His grip on her only tightened. "Come on, Dani, give it a chance."

"What part of 'I'm not interested in you' don't you understand? Let. Go. Of. Me."

"Not yet." Now his hands were under her coat, clasping her waist. "Taking you to Baker's cost me a bundle, and you don't even invite me up? I want something in exchange for tonight and for those flowers and big tips I've been leaving you for months."

Shock rendered her speechless. In the distance, thunder growled ominously.

Charlie tried to kiss her again. She slapped him so hard, her palm stung.

Instead of reeling back, he laughed. "I like a girl with spunk."

Who'd have guessed that the mild-mannered CPA was a certifiable nutcase? "I took a self-defense class last year," she warned.

It hadn't actually been a class, just an hour-long, free introductory lesson given as a preview of the full six-week session. At the time, Dani had decided not to sign up. Now she wished she had.

"Did you?" Charlie let go of her waist and squeezed both her hands in his. "Just try fooling around with me, Dani. You might be surprised at how much you enjoy it. I have a big you-know-what, and he's ready for action. He wants you to play with him."

He pushed her hands toward his erection.

More scared that she could ever remember, Dani elbowed him in the chest. Hard.

"Oof," he said, and released her.

She grabbed for the door, but Charlie was faster. "Don't fight me, Dani. You know you want it."

"I'd rather eat a cow pie."

"You little tease." Charlie reclined his seat all the way down and attempted to pull her onto his lap.

She resisted, started to scream, but he muffled her

voice with a wet kiss. Gagging and tasting bile, Dani did the only thing she could think of. She bit his tongue.

"Ow!" He let go of her.

She was scrambling off his lap when the driver's seat door jerked open.

"Get your hands off her," a threatening voice ordered.

Nick's voice. He was here.

Relief washed over her as she shot out of the passenger side of the car. Safe now and breathing hard, she sagged against a cold steel post. Rain she barely noticed pelted her head.

Nick's gaze flitted over her open coat and rumpled dress, and something hardened in his face. "Are you hurt?" he asked, his gentle tone at odds with his fisted hands.

Other than being terrified, she was unharmed. "I'm okay."

"That's good. It means I don't have to beat the crap out of this bastard."

Nick hauled Charlie out of the car by the lapels of his suit jacket and set him down some feet away. Then he got in Charlie's face. He spoke too softly for Dani to hear his words.

Hands up and palms out, Charlie scuttled backward toward his sedan. When he bumped into the hood, Nick pushed him toward the open driver's door.

"Get out of here," he growled.

Without a word Charlie jumped into the car and slammed the door shut. The locks clicked. Seconds later, he peeled off.

As Nick moved toward Dani, a fresh clap of thunder rattled the air. "You sure you're all right?" he said.

She nodded. "How did you know to show up here?"

"Something told me that you needed me. You're shivering."

She was, Dani realized.

He shrugged out of his overcoat and placed it over hers, around her shoulders. It was warm and smelled just like Nick.

Lightning crackled in the sky, and another shower of angry rain battered the ground.

"Come on." He grasped her hand and pulled her toward the entrance of the apartment building. With a hand that trembled, Dani entered the code.

Wet and slightly winded, they entered the empty lobby. It was always too hot, but tonight Dani welcomed the warmth. She couldn't seem to stop shivering. Or let go of Nick's hand.

Using his free hand, he tucked her hair behind her ears with infinite tenderness that calmed her raw nerves.

"You're freezing," he said in a gruff voice. "Come here."

Dani stepped into his warmth and held on tight. His arms around her were exactly what she needed. Closing her eyes, she sighed.

"That's my girl." Nick kissed the top of her head and then released her. "Maybe we should call the sheriff's office."

"What would I say? That Charlie tried something? He wasn't the first."

Although he'd been the first who'd tried to force her.

"Just to get what he did on record, in case he tries the same thing on someone else. You ought to tell someone so that it doesn't happen again. I'll confirm your story."

As badly as Dani wanted to forget what had happened, she knew Nick was right. "Okay," she said. "I'll do it right now."

"Why don't you wait until you're in your apartment?"

She shook her head. "I want to get it over with."

She handed him his coat, then sat down on the lobby couch, pulled out her phone and made the call. After a brief conversation, she hung up. "According to the sheriff's office, since nothing really serious happened—" Dani shuddered at the very suggestion of Charlie doing something scarier "—I can't file a report. The officer I spoke with gave me the name and number of a place to contact if I need to talk to someone."

"It was worth a shot," Nick said. "Come on, I'll take you upstairs."

Now that she was calmer, questions flooded her mind. "How did you figure out where to find me?" she asked while they waited for the elevator.

"Easy. You have to be up early tomorrow, and I guessed you'd come home straight from dinner."

That made sense. "First you show up at the same restaurant as me. Now you're here. Are you stalking me?"

His mouth quirked. "That's me, all right. I was at Baker's for the same reason I'm here now—because I had a gut instinct about Charlie. And a lucky thing I did."

The elevator arrived. He reached for her hand and pulled her into the car. Dani held on tightly.

"Charlie won't bother you anymore," he said on the ride to the seventh floor.

She let go of his hand and hugged her waist. "How can you be sure?"

"For one thing, I had a hard time understanding a word he said because you bit the hell out of his tongue.

Smart move, by the way. Did you learn that at that self-defense demo you went to last year?"

"I have no idea where it came from," she said. "I just did it."

"You should get in touch with the woman who does those demos and explain so that she can teach others."

"I will. I think I'll sign up for that class, too."

"Smart idea."

"What did you say to Charlie in the parking lot?" she asked.

"Nothing much. Let's just say, he understands that if he so much as speaks to you again, I'll come after him. Also I might have mentioned that Sheriff Dean is a friend of mine."

"He is not."

"So I stretched the truth a little. We did talk once when he stopped me for speeding." His mouth twitched.

The elevator stopped. Nick accompanied her down the hall. He stood at her side while she found her key and unlocked the door.

Dani meant to say good-night, but completely different words came out of her mouth. "I wouldn't mind company for a while."

"I was coming in regardless."

Inside Dani's apartment, Nick tossed his own coat aside and helped her out of hers. Her fingers were ice-cold, likely more from the fear Charlie had caused than the chilly night air.

Rage filled him. He wanted to go out, find the bastard and pound him into the ground so that he'd pay for what he'd tried with Dani and would never try to force any woman to do things she didn't want to do. But beating Charlie to a pulp wouldn't solve anything. Besides, Dani didn't want to be alone.

She prided herself on her strength and independence and shied away from showing any weakness. But she needed him, and he intended to stay for as long as she wanted him here.

With a meow, Fluff came running. Tears filled Dani's eyes, tears Nick knew she didn't want him to see.

"Hey, Fluff." She picked up the cat and buried her face in his fur.

Nick wanted to pull her close again and rub her shoulders or massage her feet. Anything to help her relax and feel better. But she wouldn't appreciate it if he babied her.

"You're wet from the rain," he said. "You should take a warm shower, and I could use something hot to drink. You wouldn't by chance have any of that homemade cocoa mix?"

That cheered her up. "Cocoa sounds perfect. It just so happens that I made up a batch the other day."

"I'll fix the cocoa while you shower."

Ten minutes later, Dani entered the kitchen wearing flannel pajamas, a pink fleece robe and fuzzy pink slippers. She'd blown her hair dry, and her face had some color to it. Fluff was with her.

"All better?" Nick asked.

"I'm definitely warmer."

"That's good. The cocoa is just about ready."

While Nick finished up, Fluff settled on the mini rug Dani kept for him near the heat register.

They took their steaming mugs to the living room and sat on the couch, Dani close beside him. Exactly as they'd been the night they'd fallen asleep together and their troubles had started. Nick wouldn't think about that now. Tonight he only wanted her to feel safe.

"Mmm, this is yummy," she said, sounding more like herself. But tension still radiated from her, holding her body rigid. "I hope your date ended better than mine."

Nick shrugged. "It was okay."

"Not so great, huh? Sylvie seemed nice, Nick. She's beautiful, too."

"And smart. But she's not the woman for me."

"Not even for a little while?"

He shook his head. "She wants the kind of relationship I can't give. She knows it, too."

Dani plucked a turquoise throw pillow from beside her and hugged it. "I guess it's back to the drawing board for both of us. Tell me something. What was it about Charlie that bothered you?"

"He leered at you like a dirty old man. It bugged me. And the flower thing—he had no business doing that every week."

She eyed him. "There's nothing wrong with a man bringing me a flower. You almost sound jealous."

"Hey, if he'd been a decent guy, I would have been okay with it."

That wasn't wholly true. Sure, he wanted Dani to find someone who could make her happy. But at the same time, he couldn't stand the idea of sharing her with any man. Whatever the hell that meant. He'd never felt this way before and knew his jealousy—or whatever the hell it was—had something to do with those kisses. But he wasn't about to analyze himself.

"I'm beginning to wonder if there are any decent guys out there," Dani said. "I went out with a freak-ing CPA, and it turned into the worst date ever. Also the scariest."

A shudder passed through her. Nick set his mug on the coffee table and put his arm around her. "It's all behind you now."

She stared up at him and bit her lip. "What if he comes into Big Mama's?"

Nick's protective hackles rose all over again, along with his rage. "You tell Big Mama, Sadie, Colleen, Mike and everyone else at the restaurant what happened tonight. They'll make sure Charlie doesn't come in. But if he does, call the sheriff immediately. Then call me."

"I will. Thanks for making me feel safe, Nick."

He tightened his arm around her, and she snuggled against him. No sign of that stiffness now. Nick smiled to himself. "You finally relaxed."

"Because of you. This is going to sound weird, but if tonight hadn't turned out the way it did, I wouldn't have my best friend back." Her silvery-blue eyes were wide and trusting, just as they used to be.

Relieved, and feeling as if he'd come home again, Nick silently pledged that he would never let Dani down.

"Remember when you came to Big Mama's for your Montana Cowboy meeting a couple weeks ago?" she asked.

"How could I forget? That was the first time I laid eyes on Charlie."

Dani tensed again, and Nick wished he'd kept his mouth shut.

"Did you notice anything about Big Mama?" she asked.

"She seemed to be moving more slowly than usual, I guess. Why?"

"I'm worried about her, Nick. She isn't sleeping well. She claims indigestion is keeping her awake, but what if it's her heart?"

Alarmed, he sat up straight. "Has she seen her doctor?"

"She promised to make an appointment, but I doubt she has."

"Stubborn lady. I'll give her a call and nudge her."

"Would you? Thanks."

In comfortable silence they finished their cocoas.

Dani sighed up at him. "Our plan to meet new love interests isn't going so well, is it?"

"Not so far," he agreed. "But you and I are tight again. I missed that. Missed you."

"Me, too." She let out a contented sound and burrowed closer.

Warm and soft, with her hair smelling of orange blossoms. A few silky strands teased his chin. He brushed them away, his fingers lingering on her smooth skin.

His body stirred, ready for action it wasn't going to get. Not with Dani.

Calling himself every bad name in the book, Nick warned himself to move away, before he blew everything and kissed her. But she seemed so comfortable and content that he stayed put. Leaning his head against the wall behind the couch, he stared at the dark TV screen instead of Dani.

"What are you thinking about?" she asked.

He glanced down at her, just in time to see her tongue lick some cocoa from the corner of her lip.

Did she have any idea what she was doing to him?

Damn it, she'd been through hell tonight. What kind of jerk was he to want her now?

A big one. He was so intent on her lush mouth that he had to struggle to pull his thoughts together. If he told her what was on his mind, the things he wanted to do with her, their newly resurrected platonic friendship would be toast.

Hell, for him it already was.

Forget how comfortable and relaxed Dani was. Nick had to move. Now.

"It's getting late, and you have to be up early. I should go." He pulled his arm from around her and stood. "Unless you want me to stay over."

Had he just offered to stay here all night? He must be losing his mind. "I can sleep on the couch."

Dani's gaze connected with his, and he swore he saw yearning on her face. Real, or wishful thinking? Because if she encouraged him in any way, he wasn't sure he could resist.

To his relief, she shook her head. "I'm better now."

Nick let out the breath he'd been holding. "Okay, but if you change your mind, if you need anything at all, call me."

"I will." At the door, she managed a smile. "Thanks again, Nick, for being here when I really needed you."

"Sure. Sweet dreams."

"I love that you said that—just as you always have. Right back at ya, my best friend." Standing on her toes, she cupped his face in her soft hands and kissed his cheek. The same as she had the other day, after their talk in Big Mama's office.

He'd had trouble resisting her then, and it was worse now.

The warmth in her eyes and the sweetness of that chaste kiss burned and rippled through him, and it was all he could do to suffer through it without hauling her up nice and close and giving in to his desires.

"I'll check on you tomorrow," he said in a voice that sounded ragged to his own ears. Then he made a quick exit.

Chapter 9

After spending a restless night tossing and turning, Nick woke to clear skies Sunday morning. At some point during the night the rain had stopped. This morning the winter chill was absent. The weather had definitely changed—a welcome change for him and all the ranchers in Prosperity. It was almost time to move his cattle into the grazing pastures, which meant he should get a move on and finish mending the fences that were supposed to contain them.

Nick relished the idea of hard work, which was sure to get his mind off everything that had happened last night. He still wanted to deck Charlie and hoped that Dani had banished the bastard from her mind and slept peacefully.

Had she made it in to work this morning? Knowing

Dani, she probably had. He picked up the phone to find out. She answered right away. "Hi."

"Mornin'. How are you today?"

"Sleepy, but I made it to work. Hey, thanks again for last night. You're the best friend ever."

She assumed they were back to being friends and nothing but. If she only knew that Nick wanted her more than ever. He cleared his throat. "I'm awful glad you're okay."

"You and me both. I told Big Mama what happened."

"You called her at this hour?"

"She's an early riser, so it was a safe bet that she'd be up. Besides, I had to, before she heard from someone else. You know how news spreads around here."

"I sure do. How did she take it?"

"She was upset, but grateful that you showed up. She's going to ban Charlie from the restaurant. Will you call her later, just to make sure she's okay?"

"I was planning on stopping by her place, anyway, to convince her to make an appointment with her doctor."

"I'll keep my fingers crossed. Well, I should go and get things ready."

"If you want anything, call."

As soon as Nick disconnected he blew out a big breath. That had gone well enough. Next, he phoned Big Mama.

"Good morning, my sweet, sweet Nick," she cooed. "Thank you for what you did last night."

Her praise warmed him and also made him uncomfortable. Dani deserved most of the credit for her own efforts at protecting herself. "Dani was amazing. She bit the heck out of Charlie's tongue. I expect he'll be hurting for a while. You'd have been proud of her."

"I am, but I'm just as proud of you. I just wish I hadn't encouraged her to go out with Charlie. He seemed such a decent man. Say, have you eaten yet?"

"Not yet, but I'm getting ready to."

"Come over and let me make you breakfast, as my way of thanking you."

Just the mention of one of Big Mama's breakfasts made his mouth water. During the meal he would talk to her about that doctor's appointment. "Okay. When should I be there?"

"Give me thirty minutes."

The sun hadn't come up yet when he sat down at Big Mama's kitchen table and helped himself to mouth-watering muffins, cheesy scrambled eggs and sausage. Not exactly health food.

Nick eyed Big Mama and had to admit that Dani was right—her skin was pasty, and there was no sign of her usual hearty appetite. Nick was worried. He answered her questions about the night before, then got down to business.

"This is delicious," he said. "But aren't you supposed to cut down on this kind of food?"

The scowl she gave him could have frozen the sun. "You sound like Dani. I'll bet she asked you to talk to me about my health." Before he could answer, she waved her hand dismissively. "I'll tell you what I told her. It's indigestion."

"So why are you eating foods that will make it worse?"

"Because I want to." She raised her chin defiantly, reminding him of Dani. "I want you and Dani to quit worrying about me." She reached in her sweater pocket for a bottle of prescription antacids. "A couple of these will take care of the problem."

Nick didn't believe that. "Humor me, anyway— Call tomorrow and make an appointment with Dr. Adelson."

"Oh, all right. Then will you both stop nagging me?"

Reassured, he smiled. "You have my word on that."

"You look like your regular self," Sly said to Dani when he and Lana entered her apartment late Sunday afternoon.

Dani handed Fluff to her sister-in-law, who cooed and cuddled him like a baby.

"I told you when you called that I'm fine. Instead of dropping Johanna at Lana's parents' for Sunday dinner, you both should have gone, too."

"We wanted to be with you. We'll see them next week." Lana set the cat down. "How was work today?"

"Different." News had traveled even faster than Dani had imagined. Everyone had heard what Charlie had pulled. "Follow me into the kitchen and I'll pour the wine."

"People say that Charlie Schorr's tongue will never be the same," Sly said as they headed down the hall. He squeezed her shoulder with brotherly affection. "You sure know how to take care of yourself."

"You're kind of a celebrity," Lana added. "Every-one's talking about your strong bite."

Dani laughed at that. She was proud that she'd re-fused to be a victim. She poured them each a glass of wine, and they sat down at the kitchen table. "Custom-ers kept coming up to me and offering sympathy." She made a face. "Do I act like I need people to feel sorry for me?"

"They're just showing that they care," Lana said. "Isn't it wonderful to be loved?"

Dani ran her finger around the stem of her glass. "It is nice that people care, but I'm not used to all the attention."

"What did Big Mama say?" Lana asked.

"She was upset, of course. She's banned Charlie permanently from Big Mama's Café."

"I should hope so. How's she doing? You've been worried about her health."

"She's still dragging herself around and still suffering what she claims is heartburn. She's been saying she'll make a doctor's appointment, but she keeps putting it off. Then this morning Nick went over to her house and talked to her about it. He did what I couldn't—convinced her to call the doctor's office tomorrow morning." Dani was so relieved.

"Nick's good people," Sly said. "After last night, I like him even better than I did before. That reminds me, the March Madness games start Wednesday night. We're having our usual party. This year will be extra fun because the Montana Grizzlies made it to the playoffs. You'll be at our place to watch the game, right?"

"Me, miss the best March Madness party in town?" Dani smiled. "Never. But what does Nick have to do with March Madness?"

Sly grinned. "Because this year, he'll be joining us. Hey, maybe he can swing by and give you a ride."

After last night, Dani's distinctly non-platonic feelings for Nick had upped several notches on the heat scale. Seeing him, and worse, being alone with him in a car, probably wasn't the best idea.

"Um, I don't know," she said carefully.

Sly frowned. "I thought you two were tight."

"We are. It's just… You've never invited him before, and you caught me by surprise. Besides, he lives closer to you than me, and driving all the way over here, then to your place again seems like a total waste of time and gas."

"True." Dani's brother slanted her a look. "Why am I getting the sense you don't want him to come?"

Because I have the hots for him wasn't going to work. While Dani struggled unsuccessfully for a plausible-sounding answer to her brother's question, Lana cut in.

"I'm hungry. How does Thai food sound?"

To Dani's relief, talk of food distracted her brother. As soon as Lana phoned in the order, he grabbed his keys.

"Be back soon." He kissed his wife, grinned at Dani, and left.

"Now, then," Lana said, scrutinizing her curiously. "What exactly did you and Nick do last night?"

Dani explained that Nick had brought his date to Baker's while she and Charlie were there. "He said he didn't trust Charlie and wanted to keep an eye on me," she went on. "Can you believe that? I don't need a protector. I'm pretty good at taking care of myself."

"You certainly are," Lana said. "You proved that last night. But back to Nick."

"He said that some sixth sense warned him to come over. And I have to admit that when he showed up just after I bit Charlie, I was awful glad."

"I would've been, too. That man cares a lot about you."

Dani knew that. "He was so great about everything.

He stayed with me until I calmed down. We had hot cocoa and talked." She smiled at the memory.

She'd also cuddled with him on the couch. Desire had washed over her, but for once, she'd been able to hide her longing from him and preserve their relationship.

"Now our friendship is on track again," she said. "It's a big relief."

"Funny, you don't look or sound at all relieved."

"Actually, I'm pretty confused," Dani admitted. "On the one hand, I'm super glad we're friends again, but on the other hand…" Wondering how to explain, she paused a moment and gathered her thoughts. "Since we kissed a couple weeks ago, I can't help but want an encore. And not just kisses, either. I want a whole lot more."

Lana almost smiled. "You've heard my opinion on that."

"And you know mine—mixing passion with friendship will never work for Nick and me."

Dani valued that friendship more than just about anything. And yet, if Nick had made even one small move to kiss her last night, she would have welcomed him. Which would've undone their friendship all over again. Her seesawing feelings were driving her crazy.

"He believes we're back to being platonic, and when he called early this morning to check on me and relay his success with Big Mama, I played my part. He has no idea how badly I lust for him." She buried her hands in her face and moaned. "I guess I'm saying that I shouldn't see him again until I get him out of my system. That's why I'm hesitant about this March Madness thing."

"Avoiding him won't help your friendship any, especially if he has no idea why. Don't you think you should talk to him?"

"Maybe. The trouble is, whenever I get close to him, all I want to do is kiss him again." It was a wonder he hadn't guessed. "I hoped that dating would help me forget the feelings I have for him. That's why I went out with Charlie, even though I didn't want to. That sure backfired." At the mere mention of the man, Dani grew cold. She pushed Charlie and the awful evening from her mind. "What should I do?"

"I can't answer that, but I will share an observation." Lana gave her a steadfast gaze. "I'm guessing your feelings for Nick are deeper than you realize."

"You're saying I'm falling for him?" No way, none at all. She was not letting herself do that.

"Not falling for him," Lana said. "You've already fallen."

"I haven't! Don't say that! Loving Nick that way would be a complete disaster."

"Hey, I'm just calling it as I see it." Lana spread out both hands. "Are you going to come to our party?"

After the conversation she'd just had with Lana, Dani was more certain than ever that she should steer clear of Nick. She sighed. "Unless I want Sly breathing down my neck, wondering why I'm staying away, I don't think I have a choice. But it'll be hard."

She wasn't sure how she would stay away from Nick, but somehow she had to.

"I can't say what's right for you," Lana said. "Only you can decide that. Just understand that whatever you do, you have my support."

"You're the best sister-in-law ever. I'm tired of talking about my problems. What's new with you?"

Lana got excited. "You remember that Sly and I have been looking into adopting."

"Something's happened already!" Dani guessed.

Her sister-in-law nodded. "We heard from our attorney last Thursday. There's a fifteen-year-old teenage girl in another state who's four months pregnant. She's a top student and she and her boyfriend aren't ready to take on the challenges of parenting. She picked Sly and me as well two other couples, and asked for a letter explaining why we think we're the best choice to be the parents of her baby. We're working on that now."

"How exciting! If you need a reference, I'm your woman."

"We're not supposed to use letters from family, but our housekeeper—Mrs. Rutland—and several employees and parents from the daycare have offered to write letters for us."

Dani jumped up and hugged her sister-in-law. "I'm so happy for you!"

"It's early days yet, and Sly and I don't want to get our hopes up… We probably won't hear from the girl for a few months."

"Well, you may not want to get too excited, but I have a good feeling about this."

Dani's landline phone rang. "There's Sly with our food." She buzzed him up. "We haven't even set the table yet. You let him in, and I'll pull out plates and silverware. And please, don't say a word to him about Nick."

"I would never betray your confidence." Lana pantomimed locking her lips.

* * *

Nick and his crew spent the next few days busting their chops on the fence repairs. By Wednesday night he was ready for some March Madness craziness at Sly and Lana's.

He was looking forward to seeing Dani there and actually talking to her. They hadn't spoken since he'd called to let her know that Big Mama had agreed to make a doctor's appointment, but they'd texted a few brief messages. They were both extra busy.

Dani seemed to have really bought into the back-to-being-friends thing. Nick wasn't there by a long shot, but he'd never let her know that.

Thanks to a minor disaster involving a calf moose stuck in one of the barbwire fences he and his crew had recently mended, he arrived at Sly and Lana's after the game had started.

By the number of vehicles parked in the driveway, he figured there were quite a few people inside. He spotted Dani's sedan. Great, she was here.

Nick rang the doorbell and waited, but no one answered. No doubt, everyone was too wrapped up in the game. The door was unlocked, so he let himself in. In the large entry he removed his denim jacket, then found a hanger in the closet. He noted that the great room across the way was crowded with men and women, most of whom he recognized.

All eyes were on the action on the big screen TV. Nick searched the room for Dani. She was seated on one of the smaller couches beside Lana and Sly. In jeans and a V-neck sweater that clung to her curves, she looked fantastic.

Everyone seemed to notice him at the same time. People called out greetings, and Nick returned them.

"Sorry I'm late," he said. "Had a run-in with a calf moose stuck in a barbwire fence. Her mama didn't appreciate me being there, but eventually I got the baby out."

"You missed a couple of great plays," someone said.

"I listened to some of the game on the drive here. The Grizzlies are pounding their opponents."

"Go, go, go!" a group on the sectional shouted.

Lana gestured him over. "I'm glad you made it." She stood and offered him her seat on the plush leather.

Nick shook his head. "Stay put. I'll grab a chair."

"Don't bother—I want to check on some appetizers in the oven and make sure Johanna didn't kick off her covers. Besides, I've been saving this place for you."

He didn't miss the *are you kidding me* face Dani gave her sister-in-law. Wary now, he sat down beside her. "Hey," he said, keeping his voice low so as not to disturb the others.

"Hi." Dani quickly redirected her attention to the basketball action.

Nick checked the screen. The Grizzlies had called a time-out. "How're you doing?" he asked.

"I'm good."

Avoiding eye contact and holding herself straight so as not to touch him? Sure she was. Maybe she wasn't as comfortable with him as she said. "Has Big Mama met with the doctor yet?" he asked.

Dani finally met his gaze. "She's taking a few hours off tomorrow morning to see him. I'm relieved, but also a little scared."

"Yeah, me, too." Nick put his hand over hers and gave a reassuring squeeze. The way a friend would.

Whether it was the touch or the words he wasn't sure, but she quickly pulled out of his grasp. "I'll let you know how it goes."

The game heated up, and they both trained their attention on that. During halftime, Dani busied herself helping Lana and Sly with the food, and Nick chatted with some of the other guests. When the game restarted, they returned to their seats. The last two quarters were close and wildly exciting. Once or twice Dani started to reach for his hand, but she always stopped herself.

Nick enjoyed the game, but not as much as he should have. He was too confused. What the hell was Dani's problem?

When the Grizzlies won, he knuckle-bumped Sly. Under normal circumstances he would have pulled Dani into a quick hug, but tonight he settled for a high-five.

He waited to talk her until it was time to leave. After thanking Sly and Lana, he grabbed his jacket and followed her outside.

Head down, she hurried off, as if he had the plague and she feared catching it from him. "Wait up, Dani," he called out.

She pivoted toward him. In the harsh light of the motion detector lights, her face was shadowed.

"You're in such a rush that you can't even say goodnight to me?" He frowned. "What the hell is wrong?"

"Nothing, Nick." She dug the toe of her boot into the damp earth. "It's late, and you know how early I have to get up tomorrow. I'm anxious to get home."

Not until they talked. "This won't take long." He tipped up her chin so that he could meet her eyes.

"When I left your place Saturday night, I assumed we were okay again. Things seemed all right on the phone and when we texted. But tonight you're sure upset with me."

Dani shook her head. "I'm not, Nick. You're imagining things."

"The hell I am. I know you too well. You barely looked at me tonight. Then you run out the door without a word... Used to be that you'd tell me when something upset you."

She bit her lip, a sure sign he'd hit the mark, and shot a longing glance at her car. "I... I just can't."

A sick feeling settled in Nick's gut. "Is this about Charlie? Has he been bothering you?"

If so, Nick would go after him right now. His hands curled into fists.

"No! Charlie has nothing to do with it, Nick. Can we please save this conversation for later? I really have to get some sleep."

As badly as Nick wanted answers, he couldn't force her to explain. "Whatever." He gave a short, terse nod. "Night."

In a lousy mood, he drove toward the ranch. Things between him and Dani were worse than ever. The hell of it was, this time he was clueless what the problem was, and so had no idea how to fix it.

He was halfway home when his cell rang. Wondering what new ranch emergency had hit, he pulled over to the side of the road and answered without checking the screen. "Kelly here."

"It's me," Dani said.

Wary, Nick closed his eyes. "What's up?"

"I feel terrible about the way we parted."

"Yeah, what was that about?" he asked.

"I don't want to talk about it on the phone. I wasn't going to say anything ever, in fact, just work things out by myself, but that isn't fair to you. Will you come over?"

What did she mean, *fair?* "When?"

"How about now?"

"See you in a few." Nick disconnected, executed a U-turn and headed toward Dani's.

Chapter 10

As nervous as a kid on his first date, Nick knocked on Dani's door. But this was no date. Once he understood what her issues were, he could straighten them out.

As long as he didn't bungle this up.

Holding Fluff in her arms, she let him in. "That was fast. How about something to drink?"

Nick shook his head.

"Let's talk in the kitchen," she said, and started forward.

Sitting at the table was probably a good idea. That way they could look straight at each other.

As soon as they were seated Dani cut straight to the chase. "The past few days, I've been doing a lot of soul searching." She paused and fiddled with the cuff of her sweater. "I don't think we should be around each other for a while."

The unexpected words hit like a fist to the gut. Nick winced and blurted, "If you just give me time, I swear, I'll conquer this physical thing I have for you."

She looked surprised. "You were so sweet the other night and tonight, I assumed you already had."

He let out a self-deprecating laugh. "That so called 'sweetness' nearly killed me. For the sake of our friendship I forced myself to behave. Besides, the other night, you were in no shape for what I wanted."

"But I wanted the same thing," she said softly.

The stark desire on her face almost undid him.

"As much as I want us to go back to our purely friendship place, it's impossible," she went on. "Maybe if I could forget those kisses... Unfortunately, I'm not having much luck with that." She glanced away for a moment. "The truth is, my physical, um, feelings for you have only grown stronger."

She lowered her voice to a near whisper, as if confessing something secret and private. "Lately I've been heaving dreams about us. Erotic dreams."

She had no idea what her lowered eyelids and flushed cheeks did to him. The blood in Nick's brain migrated southward, and he was grateful that the table hid his need.

How he itched to pull her close and make those dreams a sizzling reality. But he wasn't that far gone. No matter how bad he wanted Dani, he would hold back. Too much was at stake.

Oblivious of his tortured thoughts, she brushed her hair out of her eyes and went on. "That's why we have to avoid each other for a while, Nick. So that we can both get a grip. It's the only way we'll ever be friends again."

She had a point, but not one Nick wanted to live with. "There is another way," he said.

"I can't imagine what it could be."

"The other night, Sylvie made an interesting comment about our problem."

"What does she have to do with this?" Dani frowned, then looked shocked. "You told her about us. Does she know everything?"

"You mean, the reason I asked her out?" He nodded. "At Baker's, she noticed there was something between you and me. I wasn't going to lie to her. I didn't say much, only that we were trying to stay friends."

"I'll bet she was insulted that you asked her out to forget me," Dani said. "I would be."

"Actually, she was pretty decent about it. Her take was different than ours. She suggested that instead of fighting our attraction to each other, we should explore it and find out where it leads us."

"We both know exactly where it will lead." Dani's eyes were filled with longing and pain. "Having sex will effectively put an end to our friendship. Without that, what are we left with? Sure, we might have great sex, but eventually we'll part ways and stop being friends. I couldn't bear that, Nick."

He was in full agreement. And yet… "Trying to forget we ever kissed hasn't worked," he said. "And going out with someone new was a bust. We could try dating other people again, but right now, I'm just not interested."

"Me, either. After Charlie, I don't even want to date again—not for a while."

For a long moment, neither of them said a word, both lost in their own gloomy thoughts.

Nick finally broke the silence. "You know, Sylvie could be onto something."

Dani opened her mouth, probably to argue, but he held up his hands and she remained silent. "I'm starting to think that getting physical is the only way to get each other out of our systems. Why don't we give in to what we both want?"

"Because I want love and you don't believe you're capable of giving it to me."

"There is that risk." Nick raked his hand through his hair. "As bad as I want you, and lately, making love with you is pretty much all I think about, I sure as hell don't want to lose you."

"This is like being stuck between a rock and a hard place—pure torture." Dani rubbed absently at a water stain on the table. Suddenly she sat up straight. "But… Hold on a sec. If we go into this thing with our eyes open… Yes. Then your plan just might work."

Nick frowned. "You lost me."

"Look at my track record. I expected every one of my boyfriends to love me, so of course, I let myself love them, too. Then when things didn't work out, my heart got broken."

"True."

"But with you, I know the score upfront. You'll never love me. And because I know that, I'll hold on to my heart and—"

"You won't get hurt."

Dani nodded.

"Okay, but how can you be sure you won't fall in love with me?" he asked.

"I just won't."

Nick had his doubts. Not because he was cocky but

because they'd been friends for too long. No matter what she said, it could still happen. "What if you do?"

"I won't."

She leaned forward and stared him straight in the eye. That and her firm tone almost convinced him.

"I think we should test out your plan," she said. "At the very least we should kiss again, just to find out if what we felt the last time was a fluke. Are you in?"

Her eager, hungry gaze went straight to his groin, and God help him, he was *all* in.

He laughed, a strangled sound. "You're impossible."

"Maybe I am, but you, Mr. Kelly, are driving me crazy. Now for that test."

She rose and came around to him. With her hip, she shoved the table aside so that she could step between his thighs.

Nick swallowed hard. He pulled her onto his lap and rested his forehead against hers. She was so close, he could see the tiny silvery flecks in her fathomless eyes.

"You sure?" he asked, his voice ragged with need.

Dani twined her arms around his neck, bringing her soft breasts flush against his chest. "Does this answer your question?"

She closed her eyes and pursed her lips just a little, an offering to him.

With a groan, he took.

Nick was kissing her. At last.

There was no gentleness in his kiss, only raw hunger, as if he were starving and she was food.

Breathing hard, he pulled away. "It definitely wasn't a fluke."

She had to struggle to understand his words. "What?"

"The chemistry that we felt between us before. It's just as strong now."

"I'm not sure," she said. "Maybe we should do another test."

Needing to get closer, she moved so that she was straddling his lap.

"I was mistaken," he murmured several passionate kisses later. "This thing between us—it's even more powerful than it was before."

"I'd have to agree." Dani shifted closer, so that the most sensitive part of her body pressed against the hardest part of his. Dampness flooded her panties, and for a long while, she lost herself in the smell and taste of Nick. When he finally cupped her tingling breasts through her pullover, she melted into a puddle of longing. Soon, touching her through her sweater wasn't enough.

As if reading her mind, he tore his mouth from hers, grasped the hem and pulled the sweater over her head.

Dani wished she'd worn something sexier than a plain beige bra, but Nick didn't seem to mind. With eyes as dark as rich chocolate, he traced her nipple through the fabric. It beaded into a hard point. Dani moaned with pleasure, and he traced the other nipple.

Craving the feel of his hands on her bare skin, she reached behind her, unfastened her bra and let it slip from her body. Cool air whispered over her feverish breasts.

For a few moments, Nick studied her through heavy-lidded eyes. "You're everything I imagined and more," he said. He cupped her in his hot hands and squeezed gently. "Soft and warm, and beautiful."

No other man had ever sounded so awed. For some reason, Dani's eyes filled.

Instantly, Nick let her go. "I hurt you."

"Not at all." She guided him back to her aching breasts.

"Then why the tears?"

"Because..." Dani struggled to put her emotions into words. "Because you think I'm beautiful."

He froze. "Surely I'm not the first man to tell you that."

If she admitted he was, would he find her less attractive? In the end, she gave him the truth. "You're the first."

"Those other guys were blind, then."

Nick unbuttoned his twill shirt and shrugged out of it, exposing broad shoulders and a solid chest honed and defined from years of hard, physical labor. Dani traced the scar on his left shoulder, still red from an incident with barbwire several months ago. "Does it hurt?" she asked.

"Not when you touch it. Let's move to a more comfortable place."

Cupping her bottom in his big hands, he stood and brought her with him. She wasn't exactly little, but he lifted her as if she weighed nothing. She circled his hips with her thighs and pushed her breasts against the smattering of hair on his chest.

Skin to skin. Heaven.

She was almost panting now.

Nick's mouth fused with hers. He took her someplace. Dani was too aroused to know or care where. Then she was lying on her back on the couch, with Nick on top, supporting his weight on his arms. Kissing her with a passion that matched her own.

Leaving her lips, he nibbled the sensitive place below her ear. Kissed the crook of her shoulder. Planted fevered kisses along her collarbone. Then he captured her mouth in another searing kiss.

It wasn't enough. "Touch me, Nick," she whispered, placing his hands on her sensitized breasts.

"This way?"

He thumbed her nipples. Pleasure shot through her, and she let out a moan. "Yes, like that."

Soon his tongue took over. "And this?"

"Dear God, yes."

Groaning, he moved between her thighs and thrust against her. Her already smoldering body went up in flames. If only they were both completely naked. But even wearing panties and jeans, Dani was on the verge of climaxing. She whimpered with need.

Immediately Nick stilled. "You okay?"

"No. I want you, Nick."

His low laugh sent a rush of heated breath over her breasts. "Patience, Dani."

He was tugging at the zipper of her jeans, when abruptly he swore and pulled away. "That's your phone."

She hadn't even heard the ring. "I don't care." She pulled him down for another mind-numbing kiss, but he sat up.

"It's after eleven," he said. "It could be important."

Dazed, she sat up, too. Suddenly shy, she covered her breasts with her arm and headed for the kitchen to retrieve her pullover. Ignoring the bra, she tugged the sweater over her head before answering the phone.

"Hello?"

"Dani? I hope I didn't wake you. It's Jewel."

Dani hadn't spoken with Big Mama's closest friend since she'd last seen her at Big Mama's house weeks ago. Why would she call, and so late?

Warning bells sounded in Dani's head. "No, I'm awake. What's up?"

Nick had followed her and also donned his shirt. For his benefit, she switched her cell phone to speaker mode.

"Your mother came over to my house for dinner and cards tonight. Just as she was getting ready to go home…" Jewel's voice broke. "She was suddenly in a lot of pain, and we feared she was having a heart attack."

"A heart attack?" Oh, dear God. Dani sank onto a kitchen chair. "Hang up and call 9-1-1!"

"I did, honey, right away. We're at the hospital now."

"And you're just getting around to calling me?" Suddenly cold, Dani shivered. "Is she okay?"

"Yes and no."

Impatient, Nick took over. "This is Nick. What's going on, Jewel?"

"Hi, Nick. What are you doing with Dani so late, when she has to get up at four-thirty in the morning?"

No telling what the woman was thinking, but Dani wasn't going to worry about that now. She exchanged a look with Nick.

"Answer the question, Jewel," he said.

"All right. The good news is, Trudy didn't have a heart attack," she replied. "The bad news is, they're keeping her here overnight so that they can watch her. She's going to have surgery tomorrow."

"Surgery," Dani repeated, frowning. "What for?"

"She has a partially blocked artery, and the doctors want to clear it."

Jewel tried to explain further, but Dani couldn't focus. "I'll be right there," she said.

As soon as she disconnected, panic took over. Her eyes filled. "She can't die. Oh, please don't let her die."

"Don't let yourself go there, Dani."

Nick put his arm around her and pulled her comfortingly close. The heat from his body helped warm her very cold insides. Moments later, she hurried to the living room and grabbed her purse.

"My keys… Where are my keys?"

"Check the side pocket of your purse, where you usually keep them. But you won't need them. I'm driving. Let's go."

Before Nick braked the truck to a complete stop in the hospital parking garage, Dani was out the passenger door, hurrying toward the hospital entrance. Just before she reached it, he caught up and snagged her arm. "Slow down, Dani."

"I have to get to Big Mama right away," she said, sounding terrified.

"Another few minutes won't change anything." Fearing she might hyperventilate, Nick massaged her wrists and forced himself to use a relaxed tone at odds with his own tension. "For her sake and yours, calm down."

She gave a jerky nod. "I'll try."

After she pulled in and blew out a few deep breaths, Nick opened the door and they entered the lobby.

Hard to believe that thirty minutes earlier they'd been enjoying the hottest foreplay of his life. Now he wanted only to shield Dani from the pain and worry shadowing her eyes.

With her mother in such bad shape, that was impossible.

In the lobby, he pressed the elevator button for the floor where Jewel had said Big Mama was staying. On the ride up, Dani sucked in several more deep breaths.

"That's much better," he said.

"It doesn't really help. I'm scared, Nick."

As was he. He put his arm around her and kept her close.

God, he hated hospitals, this one in particular. He'd last been here roughly two years earlier, arriving shortly after his father had suffered a heart attack. His father had lingered for a few hours, hanging onto life long enough for Nick and Jamie, and even their mother, to say goodbye.

It wasn't until then, on his deathbed, that he'd finally forgiven Nick's mother for cheating on him. His forgiveness had enabled her to make peace with herself and let go of the guilt that had filled her for years.

"I wish my dad had been as lucky as Big Mama," he said. "If he'd been admitted here before his heart attack, he might still be alive."

"I can't even imagine." Dani bit her lip. "Big Mama could… The same thing could have happened to her. It still could." She swallowed hard.

"Hey, she's in the cardiac wing, where she'll be carefully monitored," he assured her. "Tomorrow, the surgeon will fix her up as good as new."

"Please let that be true." Dani closed her eyes, her lips moving as if in prayer.

As soon as the elevator door opened, Dani headed out. A few feet away, Jewel stood waiting for them.

As her gaze darted between them with interest, Nick barely suppressed an eye roll. Jewel had never been one to keep things to herself. God only knew what she'd say about him and Dani.

After they greeted each other, Jewel said, "I'm not family so they won't let me visit your mother. But they'll let you in, Dani. Now that you're here, I'm going home to get some sleep. I'll be back in time for her surgery in the morning."

"You saved her life." Dani grasped the older woman's hands in hers. "I don't know how I'll ever be able to thank you."

"No thanks needed, honey."

They embraced, and Jewel left.

At the nurses' station, a kindly nurse filled in Dani and Nick about the next morning's surgery. "It's called balloon angioplasty, and it's scheduled for seven tomorrow morning," she said. "Dr. Cruise will insert a balloon-tipped catheter in the narrowed section of your mother's artery. Then he'll gently inflate the balloon and position a stent that will expand and keep the artery open."

"Is it dangerous?" Dani asked, reaching for Nick's hand.

"Not with Dr. Cruise doing the procedure. He does one to two of these per month. Your mother will be in expert hands."

"That's a relief. Can I see her?"

The nurse nodded. "Of course, but don't stay long. She's very tired. She needs to rest and stay calm."

Dani tugged on Nick's hand. "Come on."

"Are you a family member?" the nurse asked.

"He's practically family," Dani said. "He's my..." She hesitated a moment, as if she wasn't sure what Nick was to her after those kisses and caresses. "My best friend."

Relieved that after what they'd shared earlier, she still considered him a friend and only a friend, Nick let out the breath he'd been holding.

The nurse glanced at him. "Sir, I'm afraid you'll have to stay in the waiting room."

"Not a problem." Nick let go of Dani's hand. "When you're finished, come find me out here."

She nodded, then pivoted toward her mother's room.

Chapter 11

When Dani entered the hospital room, Big Mama was asleep. Not wanting to disturb her, Dani tiptoed toward the bed. The wires attached to her chest and wrists made the normally robust woman look frail.

Dani was already worried, but seeing her mother like this only brought home the danger Big Mama was in.

She felt so powerless. If only Nick was here with her, holding her hand in silent comfort and support. She wished he would offer a lot more than that, but this wasn't the time or place to examine her deepening feelings for him.

Although she didn't intend to stay long, she was too shaken to remain standing. After quietly pulling a chair to the side of the mattress, she sat down. Behind the bed, a machine beeped quietly, an electric sentry keeping watch. She found that oddly comforting. Nick was right—here in the hospital, her mother would be watched over and cared for with the kind of attention only medical experts could give.

The nurse knocked softly on the open door and entered to take her mother's vitals. Dani stood and moved out of the way. She picked up the chair and carefully returned it to its place at the side of the little room.

As soon as the nurse lifted Big Mama's hand to check her pulse, she awoke. She gave Dani a tired smile. "Jewel must've given you a call. Come here and give your Big Mama a hug."

"As soon as the nurse finishes."

Moments later, the nurse smiled. "Pulse, temperature and numbers are within normal range, Mrs. Alexander. I'll check on you in a few hours." She slipped out.

Dani bent over the hospital bed, gently hugging her mother and furiously blinking back tears. When she pulled away, she forced a smile. "I hear you're having surgery in the morning."

Her mother grimaced. "Like it or not."

"It's a necessity. And I'm guessing that when it's over, you'll feel a lot better."

"I'll find out, won't I? You'll come visit after work tomorrow."

"I wouldn't think of going to the restaurant," Dani said. "I'm going to be right here at the hospital."

"There's no need for that, missy. You ought to be at the restaurant. Otherwise, who'll take care of business?"

"On the drive here, I called Sadie and Mike and put them in charge. I also contacted Colleen and Melanie, and asked them both to fill in." Melanie was a retired waitress who worked on an as-needed basis.

Sick as her mother was, she chided Dani. "You shouldn't use the phone while you drive."

"I wasn't driving—Nick was."

"Oh? Where is he?"

"In the waiting room. The nurse wouldn't let him come in because he isn't family."

"He's *like* family. Give him a hug for me. Now about Big Mama's Café. Sadie and Mike don't know how to run a restaurant."

"They've all worked for you for years," Dani said. "They're experienced enough."

Big Mama closed her eyes. "I'm too tired to care. Thursdays are pretty slow these days, so I guess they'll manage all right. Go on home now and get some sleep."

"Are you sure you want me to leave? I could ask for a cot and stay with you all night."

"That would just keep me awake. Go."

"All right." Dani kissed her mother's gray-tinged cheek. "I'll be back in a few hours. If you need me for anything before then, have the nurse call."

In no time, Dani was in Nick's truck again, listening to country Western music while he drove through the darkness toward her apartment building.

Over the last few hours the temperatures had dropped to below freezing, and Nick had cranked the heat up nice and high.

Warm and exhausted, Dani finally let down. "I hate that she has to have surgery in the morning, but you were right—it's a relief that she's spending the night in the hospital."

"A big load off your shoulders, huh."

She nodded. "Now I understand a little of what you

went through." She had no idea how she would even cope if Big Mama had died.

"I wouldn't wish that on my worst enemy." Nick yawned. "What did your mom say when you walked into her room?"

"That I should go to work tomorrow and come to the hospital after the restaurant closed." Dani snorted.

"That's Big Mama for you."

"Have you spoken with your mom lately?" she asked, wanting to talk about something else. "Is she getting excited about the wedding?"

"I guess. She wanted me to remind you that it's set for the first Friday in May, at three o'clock."

"Let her know that it's already on my calendar."

They chatted a few more minutes before slipping into comfortable silence.

Dani's eyes drifted shut. When she opened them again, Nick was pulling into the apartment complex.

"Did you have a nice nap?" he teased.

"Actually, I did." Groggy, she stretched. "Thanks for being there tonight, Nick."

"I wouldn't choose to be anywhere else." He pulled up to the front door and let the engine idle. "The surgery's at seven tomorrow morning. I'll pick you up at six."

She shook her head. "This is a busy season for you, and you have a lot to do. Let's meet at the hospital instead. Then you can leave if you have to."

He didn't argue. "Sweet dreams." He touched her cheek, but made no move to kiss her, even on the cheek.

The delicious kisses and caresses they'd shared only hours ago seemed unreal, from another lifetime. But Dani's feelings for Nick were totally here and now.

They went deeper than friendship. A whole lot deeper. And they would never be returned.

The second she let herself into her apartment, Fluff came running.

"It's been a rough few hours," she said as he followed her to the bedroom. "But Big Mama's going to be okay, and that's what really matters."

She readied herself for bed and climbed in gratefully. Yet as tired as she was, she didn't fall asleep right away. Fluff snuggled against her, and she curled her fingers in his thick fur. Soon his loud purrs filled the silence.

"I may have really screwed up tonight," she admitted in the dark. "No matter what I told Nick, I think I'm falling for him."

She should put the brakes on and stop things before they went any further and she got hurt. But she wanted Nick more than she'd ever wanted a man. And they'd agreed earlier that there was only one way to put out that fire—to make love. All she had to do was keep her heart out of it and she'd be okay.

Oh, *that* would be easy. She groaned. "No matter what, we can't let him know. Then our friendship will go south, fast. Got that?"

The cat didn't seem to care. He was too busy purring and batting her hand for more attention.

After all of four hours' sleep, Nick returned to the hospital. Now he was seated with Dani and Jewel in the waiting room outside the cardiac surgery area. At 6:00 a.m., they were among a handful of people who had family members facing early morning surgery.

Nick had bought both women coffees from the cafeteria. Jewel had quickly drained her cup. Dani, who claimed she couldn't function without the stuff, left hers untouched on the end table next to her chair. For once, her expression was difficult to read, but the way she curled and uncurled a scrap of paper around her index finger spoke volumes.

She'd already lost both her birth parents. She couldn't lose Big Mama, too. An ache filled Nick's chest. He put his arm around her shoulders and kept it there, ignoring the speculative purse of Jewel's lips. Let her talk.

Pretending a calm he didn't feel, he stretched out his legs, tipped his head back against the wall and closed his eyes. According to the nurse, Big Mama's surgery was supposed to be a piece of cake, but he wasn't at all sure she'd pull through. He wasn't a praying man, but he prayed now for the life of the woman who'd taken Dani in as her own, and who meant so much to him.

"A few years ago, a cousin of mine had balloon angioplasty," Jewel said. "She breezed right through it. I'm sure Trudy will do the same."

Dani crossed the fingers of both hands and held them up before again toying with the paper scrap. "Big Mama has felt lousy for weeks. She was scheduled to see Dr. Adelson this morning. I just wish… She almost had a heart attack last night! Why didn't she make her appointment sooner? If it wasn't for you, Nick, she would have continued to put it off. I should have pushed her harder to go in right away."

Nick remembered a similar guilty feeling—that if only he'd done something to make his father seek medical advice, he might not have suffered his heart attack.

"As if either of you could budge her," Jewel said. "We all know that no one can push Trudy Alexander to do anything she doesn't want to do."

The same thing had applied to Nick, Senior, which had been pointed out to Nick numerous times. He'd never quite believed it, though. For two long years he'd blamed himself.

Now, watching Dani suffering through the same thing, reality sank in. It wasn't his fault that his father had died.

A weight he hadn't realized he'd carried fell from his shoulders.

"Jewel is right," he said. "No one can force another person to do what they don't want to do."

"I guess not," Dani conceded. "But I wish I understood why she put off scheduling the appointment."

"Because she assumed she was suffering a bad case of indigestion." Jewel tsked.

"Or maybe she was scared," Nick guessed.

The door labeled Medical Staff Only opened and Dr. Cruise, a tall, fiftysomething male in scrubs and a cap, strode through. He'd introduced himself before the surgery. As he headed toward them, they all stood up.

"The surgery went well and the stent is in place," he said.

"Oh, thank God." Dani sagged against Nick. Equally relieved, he tightened his arm around her.

"What happens next?" she asked.

"We'll be keeping her in the hospital for a few days. When she goes home, she'll need to take it easy for several weeks, until she heals."

"When can I see her?" Dani asked.

"She's weak and groggy right now, but you can visit for a few minutes."

"I don't suppose Nick and I can go in with Dani?" Jewel asked.

"Not today, but probably tomorrow. Call first to make sure."

"All right." Jewel sighed. "I may as well go home, then. Let her know I love her."

"You go ahead, too, Nick," Dani said.

Needing to get back to the ranch, he nodded. "I'll check in with you later. Let your mom know that I'll stop by and see her tomorrow."

After a long day at the hospital, Dani returned again Friday morning. Jewel showed up, too. People called Dani's cell nonstop, wanting information about Big Mama. After updating her family, Nick and a few close friends, Dani changed her voice mail message. "Big Mama is doing well," it said. "If you're interested in visiting, contact the nurses' station first to get the okay." Then she switched off her phone.

While her mother napped, she and Jewel sat quietly in matching orange vinyl chairs, Jewel working on the cardigan she was knitting for Big Mama, and Dani attempting to read a romance novel that had been in her to-be-read pile forever. Although the book was excellent, Dani was acutely tuned into her mother's every move and sound, and had trouble focusing on the story.

Big Mama woke up and within moments was glaring at Dani. "Quit hovering over me. You did it while I slept and you're doing it now."

To be that bossy, she must be feeling pretty good. Dani exchanged a glance with Jewel, who raised her eyebrows and smiled.

"How can she hover when she's sitting in a chair?" Jewel asked.

"She just is, and stay out of this, Jewel. You're hovering, too. You should go down to the cafeteria and get yourself something to eat, and Dani should be at the restaurant, making sure everything is running smoothly."

Under normal circumstances, Dani would have agreed. But with her mother in the hospital, she couldn't leave. "I trust Sadie and Mike," she said.

"Up to a point. Fridays can be busy, and they need someone to answer to. If it can't be me, it ought to be you."

Dani crossed her arms. "I'm not leaving you."

"Baloney. Sitting around here making small talk is no way to spend a morning. I'm so bored that I'm ready for another nap. Go on, get out of here. Both of you."

"The drill sergeant has spoken," Jewel quipped. "I'm making decent progress on your sweater, Trudy, and I can just as well do it here as at home. But I'm hungry so I'll take your suggestion and go down to the cafeteria and get myself some breakfast."

"Could you sneak me up a muffin?" Big Mama asked, with a hopeful expression. "Chocolate chip, if they have it."

Dani shook her finger. "No more of that for you. From now on, you're following the diet the nutritionist is preparing for you."

"Now who's the drill sergeant," Big Mama said, but she didn't argue further.

Jewel stood. "I'll be back in a little while, Trudy. Dani, I'll touch base with you later."

As soon as she left, Big Mama crooked her finger and beckoned Dani closer. "What is it?" Dani asked.

"Jewel told me that Nick was with you when she called at eleven the other night. She also said he had his hands all over you while I was in surgery." She gave Dani a sly smile.

Dani was going to kill Jewel. "He did not! We're best friends. His arm was around me because I needed him. As for the other night, we both happened to be at Sly and Lana's for March Madness."

No point in enlightening her mother that Nick had actually been at her place when Jewel's call had come in.

"When you get so huffy about it, I can't help but wonder whether you and Nick are more than friends."

Her mother's words surprised her. How had she guessed?

"Well, stop wondering," Dani said. "We're the same as we always have been."

Big Mama ignored her. "I've always secretly hoped the two of you would realize that you were made for each other. What a fine couple you'd make."

She was wrong about that. They would never be a couple. Nick didn't want the same things Dani wanted. "That's never going to happen," she said. "Now please, drop it."

"All right," Big Mama replied, but her eyes held an unconvinced gleam. "I'm tired again. Leave." She closed her eyes.

"Maybe I should stay."

Her mother cracked one eye open. "What part of 'leave' don't you understand?" She made a "shoo" gesture. "Get out of here and go to work."

It was clear that she wanted Dani gone, and maybe that was for the best. Big Mama would be unable to work for at least six weeks. This was Dani's chance to prove that she could run the restaurant for an extended period of time. She may as well start today.

"All right, I'm going." She stood and kissed her mother's cheek. "I'll be back after we close and I catch up on the paperwork."

Chapter 12

To Dani's surprise, Big Mama's Café was packed that Friday morning—busier than it had been in ages. As she walked toward Shelby, a hush settled over the room.

"Thank heavens you're here," Shelby said in a low voice. "It's been crazy, like the old days. Sadie, Colleen and Melanie are running themselves ragged."

Dani barely had a moment to wonder at this before Jackson Martin, a retired cattle auctioneer and breakfast regular, called out. "How's your mother, Dani?"

Other diners echoed versions of the same question.

They were here because they cared about Big Mama. Overwhelmed, Dani placed her hand over her heart. "I appreciate your concern, and so will my mother. She'll be in the hospital for a few more days, but she's going to be okay."

A collective sigh of relief filled the room.

"Will she be coming back to work, or is she going to retire?" asked Carol Cook, who did Big Mama's hair at the beauty salon down the block.

"I doubt she's ready to retire just yet," Dani said.

"Show her the card," someone else said.

Shelby pulled a giant card from behind the hostess desk that had to be three feet tall. "It's from all of us," she said. "We're inviting everyone who comes in today to sign it."

For a moment, Dani was speechless. When she recovered herself, she said, "Thank you all so much. Big Mama's going to love this."

After lunch the crowd thinned considerably and Dani sent Melanie and Colleen home. By the time she locked the door at two o'clock, Big Mama's Café was empty.

Leaving Sadie to finish readying the restaurant for the next day, Dani grabbed the two-day stack of mail and headed for the office.

She sat down at her mother's desk and, as usual, sorted everything into piles—catalogues, bills, miscellaneous. An envelope from the bank caught her eye. The monthly statement wasn't due for a week or so, and this didn't look like an ad. Curious, she opened it.

The single sheet of paper was a notification that the restaurant's checking account was overdrawn and listed the hefty fee charged for covering a business overdraft. Dani frowned. Big Mama had always been meticulous about balancing the checking account. She would never let it go into the red. Surely the bank had made a mistake.

Her mother kept the drawer containing the checkbook and ledger locked, but Dani knew where she hid the key. Within moments, she was studying the ledger.

The balance in the restaurant's checking account actually *had* dipped below zero.

What the heck? Dani unlocked the filing cabinet and pulled out the bank statements for the past year. To her shock, almost every month, the account had incurred overdraft charges.

Abruptly, Dani sat back. She felt sick to her stomach, and not just because the restaurant was in such a shaky financial condition. It was bad enough that her mother didn't trust her to run the restaurant. That was wrapped in her control issues. But this... Hiding something so serious from her own daughter was far worse.

Dani couldn't help but to view it as a betrayal, one with which she was all-too familiar. The kind that happened when someone she loved and trusted completely broke that trust.

This latest betrayal, like an old, unwanted companion, hollowed out her heart with a pain worse than any breakup she'd ever experienced.

The resulting empty feeling took Dani straight back to that first breach of trust. She'd been four years old, and devastated by her mother's death from cancer. Underneath the loneliness and anguish, an unspoken question smoldered.

How could her mother, who she loved and leaned on completely and without question, leave her?

Of course, her mother hadn't wanted to die, but to Dani's four-year-old mind that was a betrayal.

Two years later, her father had followed her mother into the grave—another betrayal. Then the uncle who took in Sly and Seth had rejected her.

Betrayal after betrayal. From the time Dani had entered the foster care system, she'd worked with a social worker. Thanks to years of therapy, she'd come to understand that most of what had happened in her life was simple bad luck, and had nothing to do with her. She'd accepted this and believed she'd put it all behind her.

Now she realized she hadn't.

As she fought to shake off the pain and anger, the office phone rang, jerking her into the here and now. She actually jumped in her chair, banging her funny bone hard.

"Ouch!" she cried.

What a mess she was.

In no mood to talk to anyone, she considered ignoring the phone. But this was the restaurant line. Rubbing her elbow, she picked up. "Big Mama's Café, Dani speaking."

"You don't sound so good."

Nick's voice was a balm to her heart. At least he hadn't let her down. The hurt receded a little. "I just hit my funny bone," she said. "And it's been kind of a bad day."

"That sucks. I tried your cell phone, but it went straight to voice mail."

"I was getting so many calls about Big Mama this morning that I switched it off at the hospital. You just reminded me that I forgot to turn it back on. How did you know where to find me?"

"I just got home from visiting your mom."

For some reason, the thought of Nick sitting with her mother caused the pain to bloom again. "Oh?" Dani said.

"Yep. She looks much better than when I saw her a few days ago. She says she might get to go home soon."

"We hope it will be next week, but that's up to the medical staff."

This was great news, but Dani realized that it created another problem. Big Mama would need someone to take care of her for a few weeks. With the restaurant to run, Dani couldn't volunteer. She would have to hire someone to come in, even though Big Mama staunchly refused to admit that was necessary. Before Dani had opened the bank notice, she'd assumed her mother would be able to pay for whatever Medicare didn't cover. Now with her money problems, the whole thing was up in the air. But Dani would have to worry about that later.

"When I visited her this morning, she was well enough to boss me around," she said. "She ordered me to come to the restaurant."

"That's a positive sign. She bossed me around, too. I brought her flowers, and she said I shouldn't have wasted the money."

"Huh."

"That was supposed to make you laugh."

As raw as she felt just now, how could she possibly laugh?

At least now she understood why her mother was against making any changes to the restaurant. Changes cost money, and there was none.

"Dani? You still there?"

In an effort to avert a looming headache, she massaged her temples. "I'm here."

"Something's bothering you," Nick said. He knew her too well. "Look, if this is about us and what happened the other night…"

The very mention of those kisses and caresses warmed her. She smiled. "I wanted it, Nick."

"Me, too. I enjoyed what we did."

"So did I."

The silence that fell between them was thick with unspoken feeling. "I want to be with you tonight," he said.

"Come over."

His low growl of approval shot a bolt of heat through her. Grateful for the hunger that drowned out her pain, she closed her eyes.

Then and there, she decided to fill Nick in on Big Mama's money troubles. She needed his input. Needed him, period.

Although the door was closed and no one could hear, Dani lowered her voice. "You asked why I'm upset. Well, I just found out about something..." At a loss how to describe what she'd uncovered, she paused. "Something interesting."

"Yeah?"

"I can't talk about it on the phone, though. I'll explain when we're together."

"You've got me really curious. Text when you leave the hospital tonight, and I'll come right over."

As upset as Dani was with her mother, she was in no mood to face her later. Delivering the big get-well card could wait. She would call and plead work, fatigue and a headache—all very real.

"There's a lot to do here," she said. "So I won't be making another trip to the hospital tonight. Come over anytime after dinner."

Curious about Dani's "something interesting" and looking forward to the rest of their evening together, Nick rang her to buzz him in shortly after seven.

A few minutes later, she opened her door to him.

"The rain is really coming down out there," he said, closing it behind him. "Did you hear the thunder?"

Dani nodded. "There's lightning, too. I've been watching out the window. I heard a weather alert that it will continue for a couple of days. I wish it would clear up."

"Yeah. That cat of yours is probably hiding someplace."

Her usual *let's indulge Fluff* grin was absent. "He's under the couch."

Shadows filled her eyes, and her features were drawn and tense. She was in bad shape, as shaken as she'd been the night Jewel had called and broken the news that Big Mama was in the hospital.

Nick's heart contracted in his chest. "Something happened to your mom."

The statement elicited a bitter smile. "She's doing just fine, getting better every day. But you know that."

"Well, something's got you rattled."

"Understatement of the year." Dani flopped onto the couch.

As soon as Nick tossed his jacket aside, he joined her.

She tugged on the cuff of her pullover sweater. "I'm not sure what to do about her. I could sure use some advice."

He was used to this. Dani often sought his advice on her relationship troubles. Not that she ever took it. "Fire away."

"You know that Big Mama refuses to let me pay the bills for the restaurant or so much as let me peek at the checkbook." She fiddled with her sleeve again.

So that's what had her so worked up. "This is the right time to ask her to add you to the account as a co-owner, and also to grant you power of attorney in case something happens to her. That way if you need to, you'll be able to access the funds for payroll and bills. Don't let her put it off. Remind her what happened after my father's heart attack—no one could get into his bank account. It was a big mess."

"Those are good ideas, Nick, but not why I'm upset. Hey, do you want a beer or a pop?" she asked, as if just now realizing she'd forgotten to ask.

"Nah, I'm fine."

She nodded.

"If you're not careful, you'll wear out that sleeve. Spit it out, Dani. What's wrong?"

With a sigh she placed her hands in her lap. "Just before you called this afternoon, I opened a letter from the bank. The business checking account is overdrawn. Of course, after I made today's deposit that's no longer the case. But we were charged a hefty overdraft fee. In the past, Big Mama always kept the checkbook balanced."

"Now and then, everyone overdraws their bank account. I've been there once or twice myself. It sucks, but it's not worth tying yourself in knots."

She gave him a frustrated look. "This isn't some one-time fluke, Nick. I checked the bank statements going back a full year. It's been happening once or twice, almost every month."

"Big Mama always makes payroll, though, right?"

"Since no one has complained about getting a bounced paycheck, she must be. I assume the rest of the bills are also current. Otherwise we wouldn't have electricity or be able to order the food and supplies we need."

"That's a relief. Yeah, the bank balance is a worry—

but it isn't really a surprise. You'd be the first to admit that business *has* been falling off."

"That isn't the point! I'm Big Mama's daughter, Nick. Her only family. Yet she doesn't trust me enough to share this with me? If the notice from the bank had arrived on a day when she was at the restaurant, I would never have known."

It was strange, all right, and not good. "You definitely ought to talk with her about this."

"No, *she* should bring it up with *me,* but she never will. What am I supposed to say—that I'm furious with her for not trusting me enough to let me in on how bad things are?" Dani glared at him, and he understood that she was picturing her mother. "She's healing from heart surgery. She's supposed to stay calm."

"I doubt this has anything to do with her trusting you, Dani."

"Oh, no?" Her face contorted in pain, and he realized he'd hit a nerve. "Then why would she keep something so important from me? I can't believe she did that."

Nick had no answers, but he hated seeing Dani hurt. "She probably didn't want to upset you."

Her laugh lacked any humor. "Well, that sure worked."

"I hear you, Dani, but you're making this bigger than it is."

"It's big to me. Huge."

At a loss what to say, Nick tucked her hair behind her ears. "You're her daughter. She loves you."

Her gaze skittered away from his. "She has a funny way of showing it."

This kind of talk was new to him. It was almost as if she doubted Big Mama's love. "You two really need to have a conversation about this," Nick repeated.

"I can't."

"You can. I've seen you do it a hundred times."

"This is different."

Nick frowned. "How so?"

"When two people trust each other, it's easy to disagree or argue because you know that no matter what, you're there for each other."

"Like us." He nodded. "It's the same with you and your mom."

"I used to believe that, but now I'm not so sure. If she doesn't trust me enough to confide in me about the financial situation of the business I've been a part of for years, a business that's supposed to be mine someday, then she doesn't trust me, period."

"I'm not following."

Dani was quiet a moment, thinking. "It's like this," she said. "I've always trusted her completely. Sure there are certain things I don't tell her because some things are private." Her eyes met his, and Nick knew she was remembering what they'd started the other night.

"But she's in on the really important stuff," Dani continued. "That's what families do—talk about the things that matter. Finding out that she's keeping our restaurant's financial problems from me only proves that my trust is one-sided. It feels like a betrayal, Nick. And I can't help but wonder what else she's hiding from me."

Dani chafed her arms as if she were cold. Seconds ticked by before she spoke again. "Say something, Nick."

"What do you mean, 'betrayal?'" he asked.

"If I tell you, you'll think I'm crazy."

"We're best friends, Dani. Nothing you say will change that."

She let out a strangled laugh. "But I'm such a basket case."

"I've always appreciated your basket case moments," he teased.

Biting her lip, she searched his face. Whatever she found there seemed to reassure her. She nodded and exhaled heavily.

"When I found out about the bank account? The hurt I felt reminded me of when I was little and my mom died. And then my dad." She hugged her waist. "Most of the people I really care about have left me."

Her pain was obvious. Nick squeezed her shoulder in sympathy, and thought about his own childhood. "In a way, I can relate," he said. "I was older than you when I lost my parents, although they didn't die. But they were so caught up in their own crap that they more or less withdrew from my life. I could've run away and I'm not sure they'd have noticed. After they divorced it was even worse. Why do you think I ate dinner with you and Big Mama so often?"

Dani's brow wrinkled, and she gave him a sideways look. "You've never mentioned this before."

"You never said you felt betrayed when your parents died. I guess there are still some things we don't know about each other."

Amazed at that, he played idly with a lock of her silky hair, letting it fall through his fingers. "You're lucky, Dani. Big Mama wanted you so much that she adopted you. You're her daughter and she really does love you."

She let out a sigh. "I suppose I should talk to her.

But right now I'm so upset that I'm not sure I can face her by myself." She hesitated and studied her nails for a moment, before meeting his eyes. "Will you be there with me?"

She'd always been so proud of her independence. Sure, now and then she asked him for advice, but she'd never allowed him to get involved in her relationship with Big Mama.

"I don't want you to say anything," she added. "Just be in the room when I talk to her."

"I can do that. When?"

"Definitely while she's in the hospital. That way she won't be able to make too much of a scene. She's supposed to be going home Monday, so it'll have to be either tomorrow or Sunday. How about late tomorrow afternoon, after the restaurant closes and your day winds down?"

Nick nodded. "Works for me."

"We can meet at the hospital. I'll text you when I'm on my way."

"Sounds like a plan."

"Thanks, Nick. Sometimes... I don't know what I'd do without you."

"Back at ya."

But Dani's soft, loving expression worried him. He hoped she wasn't falling for him.

"This is what friends are for," he said to remind her that the physical attraction between them could never make their relationship any deeper than it already was.

"And you are a dear friend." She smiled at him. "The best."

That was better. Relieved, Nick grinned back.

Their gazes locked. And bam, everything shifted.

The color of her eyes changed from silvery-blue to burnished silver. The color of her desire. Her lips parted slightly, a silent supplication for his kiss.

Hunger for her steamrollered through him. Needing to touch her, to give her the kiss she wanted and a whole lot more, he tipped up her chin. "Dani—"

"Shh." She laid her finger against his lips. "We've done enough talking for now."

She reached for him.

Chapter 13

With a sigh, Dani gave herself over to Nick. No matter what, he would always be there for her. She loved him for that.

Loved him, period.

No, she didn't. *Did not.* Down that road lay certain heartache and loneliness.

He pulled away to press his sexy mouth on the sensitive place just below her ear and she forgot about everything but being with him, here and now.

"I'm going to make love to you tonight," he murmured against the crook of her shoulder.

Each movement of his lips sent delicious sensations through her.

"I'm so ready." Her bedroom was too far away so she tried to pull him down right where they were.

"Not on the couch. In your bed. Come on." He clasped her hand and pulled her to her feet.

On the short walk down the hall, they stopped to share searing kisses that left her breathless, hungry for more and damp between her legs. She lost her sweater and Nick shed his shirt. By the time they reached the bedroom, she was about to go up in flames.

The rain beat furiously against the bedroom windows. Nick flipped on the bedside reading lamp, while Dani pulled the curtains. Facing each other, they slowly finished undressing. Shoes and socks, jeans, until they stood in their underwear. Dani wasn't wearing plain beige this time. She hoped Nick liked her favorite lavender lace bra and matching bikini panties.

But at the moment, she was too busy looking her fill at the man she wasn't supposed to fall in love with to worry about her underwear. Long, lean and muscled, he wore gray boxers. And he was aroused. Because of her.

But it was the tender expression in his eyes that melted her heart. He might not love her, but he cared a lot for her. He trusted her as no one else did. And she trusted him. He would never let her down.

Who was she kidding? She was *head over heels, consequences be damned* in love with Nick.

If he found out, he would cut and run. If she were smart, so would she. But she was too far gone to stop what had been set in motion with that first sizzling kiss all those weeks ago. She needed to make love with him the way she needed her next breath.

Her only salvation was to keep her feelings a secret. Then everything would be fine.

Nick made a slow, heavy-lidded perusal down and

up her body. "As much as I like that pretty underwear, it has to go."

With her gaze fastened on his, Dani unhooked the front clasp of her bra and let it slip from her body. His dark chocolate eyes glittered with desire.

As she stepped out of her bikini underwear, he removed his boxers. He was well-endowed and gloriously erect. Dani wanted him so badly. She swallowed.

The corners of his mouth lifted in a smile—he was well aware of his effect on a woman. But the smile faded as his heated gaze returned to her.

"You're perfect," he said in a voice husky with emotion.

Dani knew she wasn't. "No, I'm not. I'm at least fifteen pounds overweight."

"Dani, Dani, Dani, what am I going to do with you? Look in the mirror and see yourself through my eyes."

He pivoted her around so that they faced the full-length mirror that hung on her bedroom door. Stepping behind her, he wrapped his arms around her waist.

Even in the cool spring weather he was sun-bronzed, and his arms were dark next to her pale skin.

She wanted to turn away from her reflection, but he held her where she was. His big, warm palm splayed across her stomach. She considered sucking it in, but changed her mind. She would do as Nick asked, and study herself.

He met her gaze in the mirror. "What do you see, Dani?"

"I see…" The man who owned her heart, holding her tenderly. "I see a handsome cowboy."

"Holding a goddess. Big, round breasts."

With his forefinger, he traced her areola. Pleasure

rolled through her, settling in her lower belly. She wanted to close her eyes, but instead stared at her own nipple as it contracted and stiffened. It happened again on the other breast. Watching herself and Nick together in the mirror was the most erotic thing Dani had ever seen.

He clasped her hips. "Curvy hips," he went on, his voice velvety and rich. "Great legs. And the sweetest behind in Montana." He pulled her hard against his erection and nipped the crook of her neck.

Dani moaned. "You're right, Nick, I am beautiful. And so are you."

Wanting him as she'd never wanted a man before, she angled her head up to kiss him. This time he allowed her to pivot around. Wrapping her arms around his neck, she pulled him down for a deep, passionate kiss.

When it ended, they were both breathing hard. "What do you like, Nick?" she whispered. "Tell me how to please you."

"Tonight isn't about pleasing me, Dani. It's about you and what you want."

Not one of her previous lovers had ever asked or offered to put her first. Her melting heart expanded, until she was lit up from the inside. "I want you to make love with me, Nick."

"That would be my greatest pleasure." Still kissing her, he walked her toward the bed.

In anticipation of tonight, she'd already removed the spread and turned down the covers.

She wanted to lie down, but Nick kept her upright. "Now what, Dani?"

"Kiss me."

"Where?"

"My mouth."

She lost herself in a long, deep kiss that she never wanted to end.

All too soon, Nick broke away. "Now where?"

"My breasts—the nipples."

He took forever getting there, stopping to plant kisses on her neck and shoulders along the way. But then... The first flick of his tongue across her nipple sent heat spiraling through her. Her bones seemed to dissolve, and she was glad to be on the bed.

Later, when she was restless with need and arching up, he raised his head. "Where else?"

She could barely form words. "Everywhere, Nick."

He complied. Each touch and lick was heaven—and torture. The problem was, he was taking too long. Impatient, she grabbed hold of his ears until he was forced to glance at her.

"Lower," she said.

"Here?" His tongue dipped into her navel.

"That's nice, but even lower."

He continued to tease her until finally he put his mouth where she most wanted him. Seconds later, Dani climaxed.

When she floated back to earth, Nick was grinning. "That was amazing to watch."

"Oh, yeah? Your turn. On your back, Mr. Kelly." As big and strong as he was, he allowed her to push him down. "I hope you brought condoms."

"One or two." He gave her a wicked grin. "Hang on, and I'll get them."

He started to roll to his side, but she stopped him. "Just tell me where they are."

"Yes, ma'am, Miz Pettit. Right hip pocket of my jeans."

"Don't move a muscle."

Dani found several foil packets. She tossed all but one onto the bedside table.

Following her instructions, Nick hadn't moved. Feeling wicked and wild, she straddled him. She opened the packet, extracted the condom and started to roll it on. Nick gritted his teeth.

Dani hesitated. "Am I doing it wrong?"

"You're doing it so right that I'm about to go over the edge. I'm not letting that happen without you." He removed her hand and sheathed himself.

Then he pulled her down on top of him. As sated as she'd been moments ago, she wanted him again.

A moment later, poised above him, she lowered herself slowly down, until she was exactly where she wanted to be—intimately joined with Nick.

He groaned.

"Do you like that, Mr. Kelly?"

"I do."

She began to move. Slowly at first, then faster, until heat and need took control of every cell in her body. She was on the verge of letting go when Nick moved his hand between them and thumbed her most sensitive place.

For the second time, Dani shattered. He swiftly followed.

Later, when her heart had slowed from warp speed to normal, she found herself cuddled against his chest.

He kissed the top of her head. "How are you doing?"

Dani ached to confess that she loved him, but that would ruin everything. She propped herself up on her elbow and gave him a bright smile. "Good. *Really* good. I really enjoyed focusing on my pleasure. You?"

Nick's grin was pure male satisfaction. Outside, thunder rumbled so hard, it shook the windows. Despite the curtains, the lightning that followed was clearly visible.

"I enjoyed pleasing you," he said. "And you—you blew me away." He reached over and flipped out the light.

His easy reaction reassured her that he had no idea that he owned her heart, lock stock and barrel. Drowsy, content and secure that her secret was safe, she closed her eyes.

Her last thought was that she should put herself first more often.

Lying on his back beside Dani, his head propped on his arms, Nick stared into the darkness. She lay curled against his side, sleeping as only a thoroughly sated woman can. The sex had been fantastic, the best he'd ever experienced, and he should've been asleep, too.

Or waking her for more.

His body approved of that idea and began to stir. But instead of allowing his hunger to lead him, Nick hesitated. Tonight had been unforgettable, and not just because of the sex. Dani had been through a lot. Revealing the deep, childhood wounds she still carried took courage and trust.

As raw and vulnerable as she'd been, making love with her probably hadn't been the smartest move. He should have stopped while he still could. But Dani had wanted to make love as bad as him, and she'd been impossible to resist.

In the throes of passion, she was something special—

her skin flushed and her head thrown back. Pleasuring her had been a real turn-on.

But after... The pure joy shining in her sweet smile, the soft, trusting glow in her eyes... Nick had realized exactly what she felt for him.

Love.

Dani had fallen for him.

She'd promised she wouldn't, but he knew how it was with her, had figured she wouldn't be able to keep this particular promise.

And yet he'd gone ahead and let his desire drown out his common sense.

Calling himself every bad name in the book, he silently swore and wished to God that he could travel back in time, to the night he'd first kissed her, and undo it. Then he wouldn't be in this mess.

Too late now.

The ceaseless rain pummeled the window, and a burst of thunder shook the air, as if Mother Nature herself was angry with him. Lightning flashed, so bright it lit up the room despite the curtains. Too close for comfort.

Murmuring something unintelligible, Dani burrowed closer. Feeling fiercely protective of her, Nick pulled the covers up over her shoulders and brushed her hair out of her face. Tenderness washed over him, and his chest expanded with emotions he didn't understand.

They scared him.

Dani had been hurt too often—she'd reminded him of that earlier tonight. He didn't want his name added to the list of people who'd let her down. That was the source of his fear, he assured himself.

Because no matter how badly he wanted to avoid

hurting her, and he wanted that more than anything, he would not be like his father, wouldn't let Dani or any other woman sidetrack him from his goals of making the ranch profitable. He would never fall in love.

Dread for the morning ahead filled him. Waking up beside Dani, bearing the full light of those love-filled eyes...

Nick itched to get up and leave *now,* but he wasn't about to walk out on her while she was sleeping. He might be a dog, but he wasn't that low.

There had to be a way out of this while still keeping the friendship intact. But for the life of him, he didn't know what it was.

"Wake up, Dani. It's almost four-thirty."

Groggy, Dani opened her eyes. Light from the hall-way spilled into the room. "Did the alarm go off al-ready?" she mumbled. "I didn't hear it."

"I turned it off when I got up." Instead of lying next to her, Nick was standing by the bed. Fully dressed.

"You can't leave without breakfast," she said, pull-ing the covers with her as she sat up.

"I have to. Everyone but Blake and Wally has the day off, and there's a lot to do."

"None of the coffee places are open yet. At least let me make you a cup. You can take one of my thermoses." She flipped on the reading lamp, blinking in the sud-den brightness.

"I don't have time to wait."

Dani was too groggy to argue. "Did you get any sleep last night?"

"Some, but the rain kept me up. It didn't stop until

a little while ago. I need to get home and check on my animals."

As plausible as that sounded, something felt off. Nick seemed tense.

Did he regret making love with her last night? Or even worse, had he somehow guessed that she loved him?

Swallowing back her anxiety, she managed a calm tone. "Are we okay, Nick?"

"Of course we are. We're still friends, and we always will be."

His smile reassured her that her secret was still safe, and that he had no clue that he owned her heart. Dani relaxed. "I'll text you this afternoon and let you know what time to meet me at the hospital," she reminded him.

"Great. I'll let myself out."

He dropped a quick kiss on the top of her head, the way he used to. Like a friend.

Then he was gone.

Determined to get Dani and what they'd shared out of his head, Nick attacked the morning chores with a vengeance. As yet, the spring grass wasn't hearty enough to nourish the cattle, so he helped Blake and Wally load the flatbed with hay for them. It was hard work, and by the time the truck was loaded, he'd worked up quite a sweat. While they delivered the hay, he stayed in the barn.

The rain had stopped, but Nick's desire raged on. Even knowing he couldn't give Dani the love she deserved, he still wanted her. More than ever. Eager to forget his hunger, he approached his bay gelding, Benny.

The horse's ears pricked forward in curiosity. "Morning," Nick said. "Hope you slept better than me. What do you say we take a ride?"

The animal neighed and Nick saddled him up. Moments later, they were trotting across the ranch. At some point, Nick sighted a calf, headed for a slippery ravine. Swearing softly, he dismounted, tethered Benny to a tree and on foot, chased the calf away from the precipice, slipping in the mud in the process.

Wet and filthy, he rode Benny back to the barn. After brushing down his horse, he stabled him. He changed clothes, then spent an hour or so tinkering with a tractor engine that kept stalling out. Inside the house again, he sat in the small room he used as an office and worked on creating a spreadsheet for next month's cattle market and paying bills.

And yet as busy as he was, for the first time ever, he couldn't shut off his thoughts or his feelings. If this had happened with any other woman Nick would have cut and run. He couldn't do that with Dani. He couldn't hurt her.

But he could put a stop to the physical side of their relationship. There would be no more incredible sex with her. He would explain tonight, after she had that talk with Big Mama.

He was eating lunch and damn it, fantasizing about Dani, when the rain began again, with a vengeance. Lightning streaked across the sky, swiftly followed by ominous thunder. A loud *crack* shook the air.

Nick jumped up and raced through the back door, onto the porch. He didn't notice anything unusual, but he smelled smoke. It was coming from the south, in the direction of the barn.

The barn had been struck by lightning.

He pulled on his boots, shrugged into his jacket and headed outside. As he raced toward the barn, he slid his cell phone from his pocket and called Blake.

"That lightning you just heard hit the barn," he said as he ran. "Call the fire department, then get Wally and meet me there."

Both men arrived shortly after Nick. Smoke was pouring from the roof now, and they all heard the panicky squeals of the five terrified horses stabled inside.

Fearing the worst, Nick shouted out orders. "Blake, help me get these horses out of here. Wally, grab the fire extinguisher and do what you can."

Smoke filled the barn, and the air was hazy and thick with it. No wonder the horses were spooked. Leading them to safety wouldn't be easy.

Nick covered his mouth with a bandanna. Speaking in a low, calm voice, he approached Benny. "Easy, boy." The bay's eyes were wide with fear, but he allowed Nick to quickly bridle him and lead him out.

Blake led two other horses toward the door, the animals following Benny's lead. By the time all five were safely out of harm's way, the fire department had arrived.

Between putting out the fire, contacting the vet and meeting with the insurance adjustor, the hours flew by.

When Nick finally trudged toward the house, it was dark and he was tired, dirty, hungry and discouraged.

Nearly half the barn had been destroyed, the rest ruined by smoke damage. The new roof, only a month old, was too damaged to save, and the hay Nick had expected to last another week or so was ruined.

And just when he was getting closer to his goal.

The ranch insurance wouldn't cover much and he didn't have enough money to pay for this unexpected expense, meaning he'd have to borrow the rest. If, please God, all went well at the cattle market and his cattle fetched a decent price, he could pay off the debt and replenish his bank account. If not, he'd have to figure out another way to bring in some money.

Nick scrubbed a weary hand over his face. For every two steps the ranch progressed, it seemed to fall back one. He'd be damned if he'd fall into the same trap his father had, piling on the debt. Yet at times like this, he could understand why it had happened all those years ago. Unfortunately, his love for Nick's mother had only exacerbated the situation.

Nick tried to count his blessings. At least the fire had been contained quickly. It could have been a lot worse. When he got through this, and he would, he would open an account for emergencies, and make sure to add to it regularly.

He didn't check his cell phone until he'd showered and changed and grabbed something to eat. He noticed that Dani had texted him that she was on her way to the hospital and would see him soon. The message had been sent over an hour ago.

Nick swore. He'd promised to be there for her, and could only guess what she must be thinking. He wanted to call her, but by now she was probably talking to Big Mama. He sent a text instead.

Chapter 14

Standing in the waiting room, Dani checked her cell phone for the dozenth time. She'd texted Nick over an hour ago to meet her at the hospital. When he hadn't replied, she'd left a voice message. She hadn't heard from him, nor had he shown up at the hospital.

Where was he? He knew how important this was, and how much she wanted him here today. She hoped everything was all right at the ranch. Deeper down, she wondered if the problem had to do with last night. This morning he'd assured her that things were fine between them. Maybe over the course of the day he'd changed his mind.

Dani didn't think she could bear that. But Nick wouldn't just pull away like that. Would he?

Her cell phone beeped, signaling a text message. It

was from Nick. *Finally*. She blew out a relieved breath and read the screen.

Trouble at the ranch. Sorry I couldn't make it 2night. Call me when you're finished.

Her spirits sagged, and so did her courage. How was she going to do this without Nick?

You can do this, Dani. The mini pep talk she'd heard from him too often to count popped into her mind and gave her the boost she needed. It was time for the dreaded heart-to-heart.

She hefted the get-well card from the restaurant and marched into her mother's room.

Wearing the robe Dani had brought her from home over her hospital gown, Big Mama was propped up in bed, reading a paperback. Her color was good. She looked like her normal self at bedtime, not an invalid recovering from surgery.

As soon as Dani entered, she set the book aside. "You're rarely late, but you are tonight. I was beginning to wonder. You must have been busy today."

"As if you didn't know. You only called four times to check on me."

"My, you're testy. I thought Nick was coming with you."

"He was supposed to meet me here, but something came up at the ranch."

"What's that you're carrying?"

"It's a card from our employees and customers."

Dani delivered it to her mother. The huge thing dwarfed her lap.

"Well, isn't this nice." Over her bifocals, she smiled at Dani. "Come over here, honey, while I read this."

Dani stood at her shoulder and read along with her.

Big Mama exclaimed over the messages. When she finished, she handed the card to Dani. "Put that on the windowsill so I can look at it." While Dani did that, her mother went on. "Thank them for me, will you?"

Dani nodded. Enough with the chit-chat. She pulled a chair to the side of the bed and squared her shoulders. "You and I need to talk."

"Should I be worried about the determined gleam in your eyes?" Big Mama said. "Because if you're going to hound me about making changes to the restaurant, I've already said—"

"We'll discuss that later. This is about something else."

"Let me guess—you ran into some problems today at the restaurant that you didn't mention when I called." Big Mama shook her head. "I knew I should've talked Dr. Adelson and the nurses into letting me go home sooner so I could get back to work. What happened, Dani?"

Big Mama was really skilled at baiting her, but tonight Dani couldn't afford to let that bother her. "You haven't worked weekends for years, so you wouldn't have come in today, regardless. I handled any issues that came up as well as you would. And FYI, you're not going back to work until the doctor gives his okay, and even then only part-time." She spoke calmly and firmly.

"Part-time? No. I can't do that."

"You can, and you will." Big Mama's stubborn expression gave Dani pause, but at least she didn't argue.

"On the way home from the hospital Monday, we're

stopping at the bank so that you can add me as co-owner on the business account," she went on. "You should probably also add me to your personal account. That way, if anything happens, I'll be able to pay the bills. I also want to set up a power of attorney, just in case."

Her mother looked taken aback. "You talk as if I'll be dead and buried tomorrow."

Dani agreed—that sounded extreme, and it made her feel terrible. She thought about dropping the subject and talking about something unemotional like the nasty weather, but she'd come too far to stop now.

Nick's words came back to her. *You can do this.*

After sucking in a fortifying breath, she went on. "I hope you live to be a hundred. But what I'm suggesting is the smart thing to do. You remember what happened when Nick's dad had his heart attack. No one could access his bank account, and it caused a lot of problems."

"I remember." Her mother sniffed, as if she was seriously put-out. "All right, I'll add you to both the accounts. But there's no need for you to be involved with either one right now. I'm perfectly capable of handling the money and bills myself."

Here goes. Dani cleared her throat. "According to the notice from the bank, you're not handling the restaurant's money so well."

Big Mama's jaw dropped in surprise. She could've won an acting award. "I have no idea what you're talking about."

"Don't play coy with me," Dani said. "I opened the mail yesterday. I read the overdraft notice."

Up went her mother's chin. "An overdraft isn't a crime."

"No, but it's expensive. Those bank fees add up, especially when you overdraw once or twice a month."

"You snooped through the bank statements?" Big Mama gave an indignant huff.

"That's right. Big Mama's Café is barely making it, and you didn't…" Dani stopped just short of accusing her mother of not trusting her. That wouldn't get her anywhere. "Why didn't you tell me?"

Uncharacteristically quiet, her mother fiddled with the sash of her robe.

"Is it…" Fear made Dani's throat go dry. Swallowing didn't work. She had to force the words out. "I don't understand why you don't trust me," she said, struggling to unclench her clasped hands.

"You're mumbling, Dani. What did you say?"

"I said—" Dani cleared her throat again. "I don't understand why you don't trust me. I'm your daughter."

There, the words were out. Hardly realizing what she was doing, she caught her breath and braced for the worst.

"Oh, honey, I do trust you." Her mother hung her head. Now she was the one speaking softly, and Dani barely made out the words. "I didn't say anything because I'm ashamed."

"Ashamed," Dani repeated. Of all the possible explanations she'd considered, she'd never imagined that her confident, independent mother would ever feel shame.

Big Mama gave a sheepish nod. "You've always looked up to me, and I've always stressed the importance of balancing your bank account. I couldn't bear for you to think less of me for my financial difficulties."

As proud as Big Mama was, Dani could only imagine

how difficult it must be for her to admit this. "You're my mom," she said. "I'll always look up to you."

"Even when I make bad mistakes?"

"Who hasn't?"

"The restaurant would be all right if our business hadn't fallen off and I hadn't made some foolish investments a few years ago. Last year those investments went sour, and I haven't been able to catch up."

"I wish you'd just come out and told me right away." It would have saved Dani hours of anxiety and frustration. "Is that why you refuse to consider any of the changes to the restaurant that I've suggested?"

Her mother nodded. "We can't afford to make any."

"And yet if we don't, Big Mama's Café will never be what it used to be. Don't worry, we'll figure this out together. You really do trust me?" Dani asked, not quite believing it.

"Completely. I love you, honey."

Dani's relief was so great, she wanted to sob. "You, too."

"Are those tears I see?"

They were. Dani quickly swiped them away. "I'm just happy, Mom. Talking honestly with you feels good."

Nick had been right. Wait until he heard about this.

Something else occurred to her. "Is this why you're against hiring a health aide to take care of you when you get home? Because of the money?"

"I don't want anyone's help." Her mother compressed her lips. A moment later, she sighed. "But you're right, I also don't have the money to pay for an aide."

"Medicare will cover some of the cost," Dani said. "And I have enough money in my savings account to cover the rest."

"I can't ask you to use your hard-earned savings on me, Dani. That's for a rainy day."

"This *is* my rainy day," she said. "I'm your daughter, and I want to help." She'd use any money left over to upgrade the restaurant. "I'll make some calls right away and line up someone before Monday."

"I see by the look on your face that you won't take 'no' for an answer." Big Mama shook her head. "Why am I not surprised? All right, go ahead, but I will pay you back. Make sure you get a woman—I don't want a man prowling around the house."

"Okay. If we're lucky, she'll be able to come over Monday to meet you. And the best way to repay me? Trust me to manage the restaurant."

"I do, but—"

Dani held up her hand, palm up, until her mother closed her mouth. "If you *really* trust me, here's how to prove it." She used her fingers, ticking off each item on her list. "First, no more calling me during work hours unless it's a medical emergency. Second, we share the bill-paying responsibilities for the restaurant. And third, if I come up with low-cost ways to modernize the restaurant, I get a chance to test them. Do we have a deal?"

"Do I have a choice?" her mother countered.

Dani shook her head.

"Then, I guess we have a deal."

Dani's fears and worries slipped away, and suddenly she felt worlds lighter, as well as empowered and heard. "Excellent."

"I guess I should thank you for talking to me about these things, Dani."

"This conversation was long overdue. Next time you have a problem, share it with me."

"As long as you do the same. Now come give your Big Mama a hug. Then go home, and let me get some sleep."

Dani was smiling as she left her mother's room. She wished Nick had been with her tonight. He'd be so proud of her.

He was waiting to hear from her, and she was eager to talk to him. She was also curious about what had happened at the ranch. It must have been pretty bad to keep him away.

As soon as she slid into the driver's seat of her car, she speed-dialed him.

Nick was sprawled in the recliner, mindlessly stuffing popcorn into his mouth, channel-surfing and wondering about Dani and her mom, when she called at last.

"Hey, Dani." He turned off the tube.

"I was so worried earlier," she said. "Are you okay? What happened at the ranch?"

"We had an emergency this afternoon and I lost track of the time. That's why I texted you back so late, and why I couldn't make it to the hospital." He felt bad about that. "You were counting on me to be there when you talked to your mom, and I'm awful sorry I wasn't there. How did it go?"

"First I want to hear what happened at the ranch. You said there was trouble?"

"I'll explain in a minute. Tell me about Big Mama."

"I did it, Nick—I talked to her." She sounded pleased with herself. "And it went better than I expected."

For the first time in hours, he smiled. "Yeah?"

"Uh-huh. You'll never guess why she never mentioned those overdrafts. She was ashamed. She thought I'd think less of her."

"Seriously? You're right, I would never have guessed."

"Me, either. I took your advice and reminded her what a mess you and your family were stuck with when your father died and you couldn't get into his account. She agreed to add me as a co-owner of both the business and personal accounts. We're going to stop at the bank on the way home from the hospital."

"Wow. I'm impressed."

"I can hardly believe it myself. Oh, I also laid down the law. She agreed not to call me on her days off unless it's a medical emergency. We're going to share the bill-paying responsibilities, *and* she's going to let me make some changes to the restaurant. Is that cool, or what?"

Dani sounded so happy, that Nick's own spirits lifted. "I'd say you hit the jackpot tonight. I'm proud of you, Dani."

"Thanks. I'm sorry you missed all the fun. So what happened to you?"

He'd have preferred to forget about that for a little while, but he wanted to tell her. "You know how bad the lightning has been. This afternoon, one 'lucky' strike hit the barn."

She made a horrified sound. "Oh, no, Nick. Please tell me that your crew and the horses are okay."

"When it happened, only Wally, Blake and I were here. Palmer, Clip and Jerome didn't come back until later. We got the horses safely out. They were pretty spooked, and they inhaled some smoke, but the vet examined them and said they seemed all right."

Dani let out a loud breath. "That's a relief."

"Don't I know it. Still, to be on the safe side, Clip's

going to bunk with the horses tonight and keep an eye on them."

"Not in the barn, though, huh?"

"In one of the sheds." An old but solid structure that had housed supplies and various spare machine parts. "The crew put up five makeshift stalls. The horses settled right in."

"How damaged is the barn?" Dani asked.

Just thinking about that made Nick feel weary clear to his bones. He closed his eyes and massaged the place between his eyebrows. "It's bad. The fire department did their best, but what the fire didn't destroy, smoke damage did. The whole thing is pretty much totaled. We were able to salvage the saddles and horse tackle, but the feed and hay are gone."

"Oh, no," Dani said. "I'm so sorry. And after all the time, work and money you put into building the new roof."

"It's a bummer, all right." Absently Nick rubbed his shoulder, which he'd somehow strained during all the chaos. "The foundation is fine, but I'm going to have to rebuild the rest."

"Not by yourself, I hope. I remember what happened when you tried to make a doghouse in high school shop class."

"You remember that lopsided disaster?" Nick chuckled at the memory, and was surprised that she'd managed to coax a laugh out of him. "I'll help with the barn, but a contractor I know is coming out tomorrow to give me an estimate."

"Good luck. Hey, it's early yet, and after my talk with Big Mama, I'm too keyed up to sleep. I could come over tonight," Dani said, sounding slightly breathless at the idea. "I'll bring something to help you feel better. What would you like—cookies? Ice cream? Me? Or all three."

Nick seriously considered the tempting offer. But she was in love with him, and for that reason, he had to keep his distance.

"Neither of us slept much last night, and I'm dead on my feet," he said. That was true. "Plus, we both have to get up at the crack of dawn and work tomorrow."

"As usual, you're right. Sleep well, Nick."

"I will. You, too."

"No 'sweet dreams, Dani?'" she asked.

"Sweet dreams, Dani," he echoed, hoping her dreams weren't about him.

Chapter 15

"Denise seems wonderful," Dani commented after the home health aide left Big Mama's house on Monday afternoon. They'd barely gotten home from the bank when the woman had arrived. In her fifties and seemingly friendly and competent, she'd stayed about an hour, asking questions and jotting down notes while she talked with Dani and Big Mama.

Even better, she was available to start tomorrow morning. She wasn't going to stay all day—Big Mama didn't need that kind of care—but knowing somone would be with her lifted a huge burden off Dani's shoulders.

"She claims she can make the blandest diet taste great," Dani went on. "It'll be nice to have her cook your meals, bring in the mail, clean house and drive you to your doctor's appointments."

"I suppose," Big Mama grumbled.

"I thought you liked her."

"What does that have to do with anything? I like most people." Her mother all but rolled her eyes. "But I hate not being able to drive or care for myself."

"It's only for a few weeks. Besides, it's not as if you're an invalid. You can shower, feed and dress yourself. You can also take walks. And just imagine all the books you'll finally have a chance to read. Maybe you'll even watch a few episodes of *Restaurant: Impossible*. That might help you get some low-cost ideas for the restaurant."

"Those things will hardly fill up the day. I don't know how I'm supposed to sit around here when I'm used to working. I'd rather be at the restaurant to put out fires and keep it running smoothly."

"Uh-uh-uh." Dani waggled her finger at her mother. "You're going to trust me to do those things, remember?"

"I remember." Suddenly looking very tired, Big Mama yawned.

"It's been a really busy day," Dani said. "Why don't you lie down for a while, and I'll run out and pick up groceries for the week. What should we have for dinner?"

"You're staying for dinner?"

Not about to leave her mother alone on her first night home, Dani nodded. "I'll leave when you're in bed tonight and ready to go to sleep."

"Just cook something you want."

"All right, I'll pick up some fish to broil." Broiled fish wasn't at the top of Dani's favorite foods list, but it was supposed to be good for her mother's heart.

Her mother wrinkled her nose. "Couldn't you fry it instead?"

"You're not supposed to have fried foods."

"Does Nick know that I've been discharged from the hospital?"

Dani nodded.

Big Mama brightened. "Let's invite him over for dinner, to celebrate that I'm home and on the mend. After working on that barn mess and all the other ranch responsibilities the poor man is dealing with, he's bound to appreciate the invitation for a home-cooked meal. The three of us at my dinner table—it'll be like the old days."

Not the same at all. A great deal had happened since those days. Dani and Nick had made love. Now he owned her heart. The challenge was to keep him from finding out.

"And you can cook something he likes—meatloaf or pot roast," Big Mama added. "Neither are fried."

Laughing, Dani shook her head. "You're incorrigible. You know you're supposed to cut way down on red meat. Tonight, we're eating broiled fish. But inviting Nick is a great idea. I'll give him a call."

"Do that," her mother said. "Now I'm going to lie down."

Dani headed for her car. On this last day of March, the sky was a brilliant blue and the air was warm enough for only a sweater. Enjoying the sun on her face, she sat down on the bottom porch step and dialed Nick.

"Hi," she said.

"Hey. Hold on a sec." He covered the phone, but she heard him say, "It's Dani. I'll be just a minute."

"I hear pounding in the background," she said.

"The contractor will be here first thing tomorrow, and Blake, Wally and I are busting up the last of the barn to get ready for him. We're tossing what we can't reuse into a flatbed. They'll haul it to the burn pile."

"Sounds as if you're making progress. We have, too. We met Big Mama's home health aide. She's great, and she also starts tomorrow. Big Mama's at home now, and ta-da—I'm officially the co-owner of both the business checking and her personal accounts."

"Way to go. I'll bet she's *real* happy to have someone come in and fuss over her."

Dani smiled at his teasing tone. "She's complaining about it, all right. But as I reminded her, it's only for a few weeks. Right now, she's taking a nap and I'm about to pick up some groceries for the week. We'd love for you to join us for dinner tonight."

Nick hesitated just long enough for Dani to wonder why.

"I would, but there's so much to do around here," he said. "You should see the mess. It has to be cleaned up today."

"We aren't planning to eat until after sunset. Surely you won't be working in the dark."

"There's too much to do," he repeated. "I can't make it."

Now she felt downright uncomfortable. "I know you have a lot on your plate," she said. "But something's weird."

"How so?"

Dani had to mull that over for a moment. "You're… You seem distant. Is it because we made love the other night?"

Nick's second, longer hesitation all but gave her the answer to her question and filled her with dread.

"This isn't a conversation I want to have right now," he said.

Ominous words. Her heart stuttered in her chest.

She was such a dunce. Nick couldn't have realized she loved him or he would have done more than pull away, but he was still wary. So what was his problem?

Dani gave her forehead a mental smack. "I'm not like the other women you've slept with, Nick. I'm not chasing after you."

"Did I say I thought you were?"

"I know how your mind works. FYI, inviting you to dinner tonight was Big Mama's idea, not mine. It's just a meal."

"I get that."

"Could've fooled me." She was getting angry. "What's the deal, Nick?"

"Come on, Dani. Now isn't the time or the place."

He wanted her to drop it, but something inside her wouldn't let her. "The time or place for what? I have no idea what you're talking about. But then, that's your M.O."

"What the hell does that mean?"

"It means that whenever you're involved with a woman and things start to get too deep, you walk away and never look back. Not that this is remotely like a breakup. It can't be—I'm not your girlfriend."

She almost choked on her words. Because this definitely *was* a breakup. Her heart ached as if it had been ripped into pieces. "I can guess what comes next— you're going to say that you need your space."

He didn't refute her words. "Maybe we should talk about this in person," he said.

Let him see her cry over him? Never. "You know what? Forget about dinner. I could use some space, too, so if you have anything else to say, you'd best say it now."

"Dani," he said, sounding sad and weary. "I don't want to hurt you."

"Too late. Goodbye, Nick." She disconnected.

Next door, Gumbo woofed and trotted to the chain-link fence for a pat. "Not now," she said as the tears began to flow.

Sitting in the car with the windows rolled up, shaking and bawling, she wanted to drive straight to Lannigan's for a gallon of rocky road, then go home and distract herself with a three-hanky movie.

But her mother needed her. There was nothing to do but hold herself together.

Dani blew her nose, sat up straighter and reminded herself that at least Nick hadn't figured out she loved him. That was something to be grateful for.

As she headed for the grocery, she found an oldies station on the radio. "Garden Party," the Rick Nelson oldie, was playing. *"You can't please everyone, so you've got to please yourself."*

Dani was too downcast to sing along, but as she listened to the words, a new resolve hatched in her chest. She agreed wholeheartedly with Rick Nelson.

She was through trying to please other people. Specifically men. Ironic that Nick had been encouraging her to do just that for ages, and that during their lovemaking, he'd shown her the joys of putting her own pleasure first.

From now on she was going to do just that—please herself.

* * *

Friday evening, Dani sat at Big Mama's kitchen table, picking at her meal. Her mother seemed to be feeling better. Just tonight, she'd become more talkative and less irritable. While Dani was the opposite.

"Denise's cooking is growing on me," Big Mama commented. "This low-fat casserole is surprisingly tasty."

She said something else, but Dani tuned her out. It had been four days, but she hadn't told her mother or anyone else about Nick yet. The end of their friendship was too new and she was still too raw.

"Dani!"

Dani jerked to attention. "Did you want something?"

"I said, I don't think you care for this casserole."

She'd sampled a few bites, but in her opinion, the stuff was tasteless. But lately, everything tasted blah. "It's not bad," she said.

Her mother eyed her. "I'm recuperating from surgery, but you seem to be the one who's sick. I know you've been working extra hard at the restaurant, but still. You haven't been acting like your usual self for days now. I hope you're not coming down with something."

"If I were, I wouldn't be here. I'd never expose you to anything."

"Well, you certainly are worried about something. You don't have to protect me. I'm not that frail. Is the bank account overdrawn again?"

Dani shook her head. "Everything's fine at the restaurant."

Now that she had her mother's okay to make some changes at Big Mama's Café, she'd begun to look seriously at low-cost options, searching for sales and high-quality discount stores. Finally having the freedom to do what she knew in her bones was the right thing for the restaurant was exciting. At least it should have been. As downhearted as she was right now, it wasn't easy to muster up much enthusiasm.

"I'm trying to be cheerful so that I'll heal faster, but your mood is depressing me." Her mother gave her the pointed, no-nonsense look that meant she expected an explanation.

Should she share her troubles or not? Dani tried to gauge whether she was strong enough to tell her mother about Nick without breaking down. For the past four nights, she'd cried herself to sleep, often feeling as if she'd never stop. She didn't want to get that emotional now.

Her debate lasted all of a few seconds before she came to a decision. She *needed* to talk about this. Why not with her mother? For that matter, why not tell Lana, and Christy, Becca, Janelle and everyone else? Sooner or later they were all bound to find out. The story may as well come from her own lips.

"You're right, I am in bad mood," she said. "Nick and I…" Getting the words out wasn't easy. A huge lump formed in her throat, and tears gathered behind her eyes. "We broke up."

Her mother seemed puzzled. "How can you break up when you've never been boyfriend and girlfriend?"

"That's a very good question." Dani smoothed her napkin over her lap and pulled herself together. "The thing is, my feelings for Nick have moved beyond friendship. Unfortunately, his for me haven't," she summarized. Right now, that was the best she could manage.

"But you're perfect for each other. I've always said so."

"Please don't, Mom."

"Oh, honey. That must hurt."

"It does." Big Mama had no idea, and her sympathetic expression only made things worse. Dani bit her lip against a rush of pain and heartache. "We decided not to see each other anymore."

"Not ever?"

They hadn't discussed how much space they both needed, but Dani knew the answer. This time, the tears behind her eyes leaked out. "Never."

Big Mama's eyes filled, too. "Whose decision was that?" she asked, sniffling.

Dani doubted she could handle a cry-fest with her mother. Making a monumental effort, she sucked in a calming breath and brushed her tears away. "It was mutual."

"But he's been in your life for so many years. Are you sure this is what you want?"

Dani couldn't lie. "No, it isn't."

"What's the matter with Nick, agreeing to something like that? I'm going to call that boy and give him a piece of my mind."

"Please don't. He's always been honest with me. It's not his fault I fell in love with him." Her own reasonable tone amazed her. She sounded calm and rational, when inside she was a tangled up mass of pain.

By her mother's widened eyes, she was similarly surprised. "You're not upset with Nick?"

Dani shook her head. "At the moment life seems pretty awful, but eventually I'll be okay."

"Of course you will. Still, I hate that you're hurting."

"I've been hurt before, and I always manage to bounce back. I'm a survivor."

Her mother gave her a watery smile. "That you are, from the time you were a little scrapper and I first took you in. Some kids take days or weeks to adjust, but you? It was obvious that you were scared, but you were so brave. You came in and made yourself at home. Then and there, I decided that I wanted you for my own daughter."

For some reason, the words bolstered Dani's morale. "Do you remember about a month ago, when you and I had cinnamon rolls together, right here at this table?" she asked. It seemed eons ago. Dani waited for her mother's nod. "You said then that I don't need a man to be happy. At the time, I blew it off, but lately I've been thinking a lot about it. Now don't go into shock, but I've decided you're right."

Her mother pantomimed exactly that, widening her eyes and dropping her jaw. Dani almost smiled.

"I can definitely be happy without a man," she said. "From now on, I'm going to put myself first and do what pleases me. You'll see."

Her mother absorbed this in silence before she spoke again. "That sounds very wise, Dani. And I'm certain that Nick will come to his senses. He's going to miss you and your friendship terribly."

"I'm not so sure that he will." Dani was tired of talking about her broken heart. "Can we change the subject now? I want to run something by you. It's about the restaurant."

"So you have more ideas about the changes you're going to make. I can't wait to hear them."

Her mother's one-eighty attitude adjustment was

amazing, but since Dani had agreed to stick to a low-cost budget, paid for with funds from her own savings, her mother had actually grown excited about the restaurant facelift. That was something to be grateful for. Though with Dani also paying part of the cost of the home health aide, she didn't have as much money to spend as she would have liked. By necessity, she'd pared down the renovations she wanted to make.

"This isn't about a change, exactly, but it is related," Dani said. "I keep remembering how everyone signed that get-well card for you. They care about both you and the restaurant, and I'm sure they want it to be here for many years to come. Why not announce that we're going to make updates to boost business, and ask them for their ideas?"

Her mother sniffed. "Airing our private problems with customers or anyone else doesn't sit well with me. Neither does asking for help."

Dani understood and normally she would have agreed. But she was into pleasing herself now, and ensuring a long, profitable future for Big Mama's Café definitely pleased her. Wasn't that more important than hiding the restaurant's problems and letting the business slide even further into the red?

"When I had that trouble with Charlie and then when you were in the hospital, I learned just how much our customers and employees care about us," she said. "I say we swallow our pride, admit that we're in trouble and see where it takes us."

"I vote no, but it's your savings account and your future. Besides, it's obvious from the expression on your face that you've already made up your mind."

This was her mother's way of showing that she

trusted Dani to do what was right for them both and for Big Mama's Café. Dani was happy about that. At least this part of her life was on track. It helped to salve the gaping hole in her heart.

The following morning, Dani arrived at Big Mama's Café with the hand-lettered poster she'd made the night before. It had taken a while for her to come up with just the right wording, but focusing on the sign had beat moping around, crying over Nick.

Before propping the poster on an easel beside the hostess desk, she turned it around backward and set it aside. Last night she'd asked the entire Saturday staff— Naomi, the forty-four year old weekend hostess, Sadie, Colleen, Mike, Jeff—who also cooked—and the bus-boys, Carl and Gene, to come in thirty minutes early, for a meeting. She'd also invited Shelby and Melanie. It was still dark out, and everyone yawned sleepily, but Sadie had made coffee.

"You're all aware that business has been steadily falling off for a while now," Dani said after they filled their mugs. "We're in trouble."

The staff exchanged worried looks.

"Are we going to lose our jobs?" Sadie asked, clutching her hands together at the waist. She was suddenly wide-awake.

"Not if we make some changes that bring in new customers. This restaurant needs a facelift and a re-vised menu, and for that, we're going to require help."

"What kind of help?" Mike asked. "Are you talking about money?"

Admitting she needed help was one thing, but solic-iting money? At the very idea, Dani's stomach balled into a knot of unease. "We are on a strict budget, but I'm leaning more toward finding experts who are willing to work for a discount," she said. "Some of our regulars are carpenters and electricians. I'm hoping to work a trade of sorts—free meals in exchange for a lower fee."

"That's a great idea," Shelby said. "But I don't know why we shouldn't ask for money, too."

"We could host a fund-raiser!" Colleen brightened up. "We did that at Serena's—" her daughter's "—school. People who donated wrote their names on slips of paper and put them in a box. At the end of the fund-raiser we drew some of the names for prizes. It was a big success."

"What kinds of prizes?" Sadie asked. "Dani probably doesn't have much money for that."

Mike stroked his chin. "How about a free breakfast or lunch, or we could name a new dish after the person whose slip we draw." He glanced at Dani.

She barely had a chance to mull that over before Colleen added her two cents.

"We could have two containers—one for the donations, and the other for the names of each donor. We'll draw several and offer the winners the choice of the free meal or having a dish named after them."

The whole staff was getting excited now, and so was Dani. The idea of giving out prizes in exchange for donations wasn't half bad, and the knots in her stomach loosened. "I'll consider it," she said.

As if she hadn't commented, they went right on planning.

"I just tossed an empty coffee can into the kitchen trash," Mike said. "I'll pull it out."

"I'll cut a slit for the money in the plastic lid," Jeff volunteered.

"I'll wash it," Carl offered.

Colleen nodded enthusiastically. "I just emptied a box of sugar packets. We can use it for names. I also happen to have a bag full of art scraps in the car, left over from an art project at Serena's school. I'll pick something from there to decorate the box and the can."

Sadie smiled. "I'll cut strips of paper for people who donate to write their names on."

"Can employees donate?" Gene asked. "I'll put in five bucks."

"Me, too," Melanie said.

"I'll make flyers and bring them in on Monday," Shelby offered.

"We can tack them up all over town," Mike said.

They were all so gung-ho that Dani decided to swallow her pride whole hog. "All right," she said. "Let's do it."

Sadie nodded at the poster. "Show us the sign."

Dani propped it on the easel.

Help us save Big Mama's Café! Ask us what you can do.

The waitress clapped her hands. "It's perfect!"

"Thanks, Sadie. Thank you all." Dani smiled and checked her watch. "We open in less than thirty minutes. Let's get busy."

By the end of the day, she'd lined up a printer who'd agreed to do the new menus in exchange for a few months' worth of free brunches. An interior designer who was new in the business had offered to provide free consulting services, just to get the experience. And the restaurant had collected almost a hundred dollars.

Not bad for one day. Dani had to pinch herself to make sure it was real. She high-fived her staff and let out several hi-pitched *squees*. They were off to a great start.

Chapter 16

On a late Friday afternoon in mid-April, Nick stood in line at Carson Building Supply to pay for some building supplies for the barn.

"How's that new barn coming along?" asked Marty Sloan, a short, round clerk who'd been handling the cash register since Nick had first come into the store as a kid with his dad. Marty was a big gossip, and over the years Nick had learned to choose his words with care.

"Not bad," he said. "If all goes well, I'll able to stable the horses in there next week, a few days ahead of schedule."

As great news as that was, Nick couldn't summon up much enthusiasm. Nearly a month after his split with Dani, he was still messed up, and his dark mood colored everything—his work, his sleep—his *life*.

Which was pretty damn ironic, considering that their

"breakup" was supposed to have kept his focus on the ranch instead of her.

She'd given him what he wanted—plenty of space. They knew a lot of the same people and frequented many of the same places, but both to his relief and his disappointment, he hadn't seen or spoken with her since the day she'd called to invite him to her mom's for dinner. The day their relationship had imploded.

He was still kicking himself for the way that had gone down. A couple of times over the past few weeks, he'd reached for the phone, just to hear her voice and check on her. He'd always stopped himself. Contacting her would only make things worse.

"Going to the cattle market next weekend?" Marty asked.

"Wouldn't miss it." Thanks to a diet of lush spring grass, Nick's livestock had gained weight steadily, which would help him get a good price for them.

"Ranchers come away from that market flush with cash," Marty said. "Sure is great for our business."

Tired of making small talk, Nick frowned. "I should get going. Is there a problem?"

Marty banged on his cash register. "Darned computer's awful slow today. It'll come back up in a minute. You look tired, Nick, even for this time of year. Putting in extra long hours?"

"Yep."

Yet as long and hard as Nick worked each day—and most days he pushed himself until he was ready to keel over, trying to banish Dani from his thoughts—she was always with him. Even in his dreams.

Penance for screwing things up with her, for doing the one thing he'd sworn never to do. Hurting her.

Which made him the number one ass of the year.

He'd heard that she was getting ready to make some of the changes at Big Mama's Café that she'd talked about. Apparently she'd held some kind of fund-raiser, which surprised him. She wasn't one to ask for that kind of help. Wanting to donate, but not about to set foot in the restaurant, he'd made an anonymous cash donation through the mail. It didn't make up for what he'd done—nothing could—but at least it was something.

Marty gave him a shrewd look. "It's all over town that you and Dani broke up. Funny, huh, when you two have never been together."

Forgetting to watch himself around the clerk, Nick scowled. "Who the hell told you that?"

"It's just something I heard. I see from your reaction that you and Dani *were* involved." The computer beeped, and Marty tapped a few keys on the keyboard. "Ah, we're up again. All these years, I assumed you two were just friends."

Nick narrowed his eyes. "How much do I owe you, Marty?"

The clerk hastily totaled the amount. "As always, your order will be waiting for you at the delivery dock."

Moments later, Nick slid into the truck. He drove it to the pickup area and loaded the supplies.

On the drive to the ranch he found a jazz station and cranked up the radio, hoping the beat and the loud music would silence his mind.

No such luck. He missed Dani more than he'd ever imagined.

But even if he did feel like crap, steering clear of her was for the best, he assured himself. She needed time to get over him.

Then maybe he could fill the hole in his chest and he could start enjoying his life again.

Sewing machines and fabric littered Janelle's dining room table. Dani glanced approvingly at the stack of curtains she, Janelle, Becca and Christy had sewn in just a few hours.

"I never could have made all these myself," she said. "What a lucky break that you were all free and willing to give up your Saturday afternoon for this."

Since she'd broken off with Nick almost a month ago, her friends had spent a fair amount of time with her.

The past few weeks had been especially busy. Asking for help had yielded results Dani could never have imagined. The restaurant regulars were almost as vested as she was in turning business around at Big Mama's Café, and had jumped at the idea of helping.

Boy, had they. The fund-raising can had quickly filled—numerous times. She'd even received an anonymous cash donation. Combined with the money from her savings and the discounts from the carpenter and electrician—who'd agreed to lower their rates in exchange for free meals—there was enough to do almost everything Dani envisioned.

Awarding free meals and naming menu items after donors seemed small prices to pay for revitalizing Big Mama's Café.

After weeks of hard work, everything was coming together. Exactly one week from tomorrow, Big Mama's Café would close so that Dani's dreams for the restaurant could at last become a reality. She could hardly wait.

She smiled at her friends. "Have I told you lately that you're the best?"

"Only a couple times." Christy laughed.

"I'm glad I could make it today," Becca said. "Sewing with you guys has been fun—almost as much fun as that silk painting class we took. If you leave out Christy's meltdown that day."

"Come on, ladies," Christy said. "Everyone suffers pre-wedding jitters."

She and Per had compromised over the wedding. It was still going to be held at the Falls, but had been scaled down to a less costly event.

"Pre-pre-pre wedding jitters," Janelle teased. "I don't care that much about sewing, but I'll do anything for chocolate." She helped herself to the last chocolate meltaway in the hefty bag of goodies Dani had brought over. "Chocolate *and* dinner on Dani tonight? Who needs a date when I've got my three amigos to party with?"

"And just think, we're contributing to the new and improved Big Mama's Café." Becca blew on her nails and polished them on her blouse. "The restaurant is going to look so cool with our curtains hanging in the windows. This is such great fabric. The artsy cartoon sketches of people eating makes me smile, and the colors are so bright and fun."

Dani agreed. "Which is exactly the mood I'm going for. Would you believe I got it on sale?"

"Who knew you were such a talented bargain shopper?" Christy said. "I should hire you to help with my wedding."

As pleased as Dani was for her friend, all that joy was painful to witness. She shook her head. "No way. I already have my hands full with the restaurant."

Between running the business, streamlining her plans and visiting and consulting with Big Mama, she barely had a moment to think. Which was good. It saved her from continually dissolving into tears.

She'd assured Big Mama that she could be happy without a man, and she was determined to prove it to herself. She wasn't there by a long shot, but she was confident that eventually she would be.

"I can't believe that in just seven days, you'll be closing Big Mama's doors for a whole week," Becca lamented. "Where will I go for Sunday brunch?"

"We won't be closed any Sunday, not even next week—if you come before noon," Dani said. "That's when we're locking the doors so that we can start the remodel. Monday doesn't count, because we're always closed Mondays. So really, we're only closed four days, Tuesday through Friday. Two weeks from today, on Saturday, we re-open."

Dani and everyone she'd hired would need every second of that time to complete the remodel.

"How about a sneak peek?" Christy said. "Do you have any sketches to show us? Or if you don't have those with you, at least give us an idea of what Big Mama's will look like."

Dani shook her head. "No way—it's a surprise. Come to the grand reopening and you'll find out."

"But we're your BFFs," Janelle pushed. "You have to give us preferential treatment."

They were supportive and wonderful friends, and Dani loved them dearly. But she doubted she'd ever feel as close to them as she had to Nick. Theirs had been a rare friendship that could never be duplicated.

"No can do." She smiled. "But I will tell you that Sly will be installing some amazing new light fixtures."

"Sly on a ladder—there's a sight I'd pay to see. Lana's so lucky." Janelle let out an admiring sigh. "Speaking of your brother, does he still want to deck Nick?"

"Probably, but I've warned him that I'll kill him if he tries."

Like everyone else, Sly knew that her friendship with Nick had crashed and burned. His protective, big-brother gene had kicked in, but Dani had stated in no uncertain terms that what had happened was none of Sly's business—or anyone else's, for that matter—and had ordered him to mind his own business.

"What about Big Mama?" Christy asked. "Is she still upset about Nick?"

Her mother had been reasonably understanding, but she also continued to bug Dani to make up with him.

She hadn't heard from him in weeks, which told her everything she needed to know about that. There wasn't going to be any making up.

"The past few days, she finally stopped bringing up his name," she said. "Now, with so much about to happen at the restaurant, she's been distracted—thank You, God."

"So your mom's cool with closing the restaurant for a few days?" Christy asked.

"She's pretty excited. She can hardly wait for the grand reopening."

"Will she be well enough to attend?" Janelle asked.

Dani nodded. "It's been almost six weeks since the surgery. She's just about back to normal, and her cardiologist has already given her the okay—as long as she promises not to stay too long. He says that if all goes well, she'll be able to return to work soon. But only for a few hours a day, a couple days a week."

Becca snorted. "As if she'll settle for that."

"She will, or I'll send her straight home," Dani said.

"Listen to you, all take-charge." Janelle shook her head. "Things have really turned around between you. I never imagined you'd get there."

"Your new 'please myself' plan is really working for you, Dani." Christy gave a thumbs-up.

Dani agreed. "I wish I'd figured it out ages ago." If she had, she'd probably have saved herself a lot of headaches and heartache—especially the biggest heartache.

As things stood, she was definitely not going to attend Nick's mother's wedding. Instead of contacting Nick, she'd phoned his mother directly. The woman hadn't heard that their friendship had ended, and had been shocked.

As was Dani—still. Even now, accepting what had happened was difficult. Nick had been her best friend for over half her life, and she missed him terribly. It was as if a part of her had died. She was trying hard not to think about him, a Herculean task that was all but impossible.

And certainly leeched the joy out of the rest of her life.

Not that she wasn't grateful for everything that was happening at the restaurant. It was just that sometimes she felt as if she would never be happy again.

She was ready to give up on the dream of finding her Mr. Right. In a way, she'd become a lot like Nick. A twist he'd probably appreciate. Only he would never know.

Here she was, all sad again, and her friends were openly scrutinizing her. If they guessed how miserable she still felt, the entire evening would become a giant "poor Dani" party. She smiled brightly. "Help me lay these curtains in the trunk of my car, and then let's go eat!"

They gave her sympathetic looks. So much for fooling them.

"Are you sure you're up to going out tonight?" Christy asked.

"Definitely. Lately Big Mama and the restaurant have taken up all my waking hours. Tonight, I could use some fun."

"All right, then." Becca squared her shoulders, the picture of a determined woman. "Where do you want to go?"

"Someplace with tasty food and a live band. How about the—"

"Bitter & Sweet!" Becca, Janelle and Christy chimed in unison.

Everyone laughed, Dani included.

"It's been a while since I danced," she said. Since before she and Jeter had broken up. A lifetime ago.

"Let's take separate cars," Christy said. "That way when I'm ready to go home to my sweetie, you three can stay out and keep partying…"

"Great idea," Dani said. "We'll meet there."

The Bitter & Sweet was packed, as it always was on a Saturday night. Despite the palpable energy in the room, the fabulous food and frequent bouts of laughter, Dani was drained by the time she finished her dessert and was ready to leave. A few minutes before the band was due to come on stage, she signaled for the check.

"I changed my mind about dancing," she told her friends in her new please-myself mode. "You know how busy the restaurant is on Sunday mornings. Plus, I still have a lot to do before the remodel. I'm going home."

It was obvious that they were disappointed. The old Dani would have put on a happy face and stayed to please them. The new Dani was unapologetic. "Quit worrying about me and enjoy yourselves," she told them. "I'll see you all in a couple of weeks, at the grand reopening of Big Mama's Café."

Chapter 17

"Happy, boss?" Palmer asked as he and Nick sat in a tavern after the close of the Saturday cattle market.

Nick's livestock had sold for record prices. Once again, he was in the black—and then some. A big relief. He'd pay off his loan and padded the account he'd earmarked for emergencies.

He patted the fat check in his pocket. "I'm doin' okay."

"It's been a decent year, not counting what happened to the barn. And even that turned out okay in the end. The new one will last for decades." Resting his forearms on the table, Palmer shook his head. "I've watched this ranch almost fail under the people who owned it before you, but now that you're in charge… You're focused, you have smarts and plenty of can-do attitude. That's a potent combination, and I have a strong hunch you'll make this ranch fly."

High praise from the seasoned foreman. Nick dipped his head. "Appreciate that."

"Let's toast Kelly Ranch and your good fortune." Palmer raised his mug.

When Nick joined in half-heartedly, Palmer studied him. "I thought for sure that big check would ease the load off your shoulders. But you're as down as a newborn calf without its mother. You've been in a crappy mood for weeks, and I'm sick of it. I'm not the only, either."

In no mood for a lecture, Nick narrowed his eyes. "Save the pep talk for someone who needs it."

"That would be you. If you miss Dani, talk to her."

It seemed everyone had heard about him and Dani. The looks and whispers only made it harder to forget what had happened. "You can go to hell," Nick growled, setting his mug down none too gently. "I'm outta here."

His foreman muttered something about the stick up Nick's butt as he followed Nick to the truck, but after that he kept his big mouth shut. Smart man, Palmer.

Traffic was light. The sun had dropped low in the sky, and vivid pink streaks accented the horizon. It was the kind of evening Dani would say was made for romance.

In a worse mood than ever, Nick scowled at nothing at all.

They weren't far from the ranch when his damned foreman started up again. "Next Saturday, Big Mama's Café is having their grand reopening. I'm taking Pam over there for breakfast. You going?"

"Probably not," Nick said. "My mom's getting married next weekend."

Palmer made an *are you kidding me?* face. "She's getting married on Friday. Look, I realize you and Dani aren't getting along, but she'll have your hide if you're not there."

"She doesn't want to see me."

Nick missed her more every day. His chest felt like there was a gaping hole in it. Everything seemed colorless and dull, even the brilliant sunset.

"How can you be so sure she doesn't want to see you?" Palmer asked.

Because it would take her a while to get over him. Nick shrugged. "I just do."

"You two have always been like *this*." Palmer pressed two fingers together and held them up. "In the two years that I've known you both, you've never had anything close to a fight. You must've done something really bad."

Wasn't that the truth. Nick had hurt her, and in the process he'd also hurt himself. Forgetting he'd yelled at Palmer to back off moments ago, he blew out a heavy breath. "I really screwed up."

"What exactly did you do?"

He glanced away from the road to glare at his foreman. "Don't push it, Palmer."

Unperturbed, the foreman calmly met his gaze. "Whatever you did, fix it. Or I swear, I'll smack you upside the head."

"You would, too," Nick grumbled. "Maybe I can't fix it."

"Have you tried?"

Nick debated how to reply. "Dani needs space," he summarized. "So do I."

Palmer snorted. "Yeah, I can see that."

When Nick let loose with a string of oaths, the foreman shook his head. "From time to time every man needs his space, but come on, enough is enough. I doubt Dani's any happier about whatever's keeping you apart than you are. You're too important to each other. Have you tried to contact her?"

"Nope."

The foreman's responding chuckle lacked any humor. "With all the women you've dated, I figured for sure you understood them."

Nick's lips twisted in a poor parody of a smile. "What man has ever truly understood a woman?"

Palmer thumped his chest with his thumb. "You're looking at one. Why do you think my marriage has lasted twenty years and counting? If you miss Dani, do something about it."

She wouldn't want to see him. "She probably won't talk to me."

The foreman gaped at him as if his brain had fallen out of his head. "When someone is that important to you, you don't take no for an answer."

Dani *was* important to Nick, but he didn't want to make things even worse for her.

She was better off without him.

Besides, he needed to stay focused on moving the ranch further into the black.

He spent Sunday by himself, doing just that—checking through price lists for new cattle to replace those he'd sold, making a new budget that accommodated the money he'd made, washing the truck. And keeping his mind off Dani.

It was best that way. So why was he miserable?

Friday at three o'clock, Nick entered the courthouse to witness his mother's third wedding. As she'd promised, the affair was small and simple, with the entire ceremony lasting roughly a quarter of an hour. Afterward, the happy couple treated Nick, Jamie and Hank to an early dinner at a restaurant near the courthouse. It was a beautiful afternoon, warm and sunny, with a light breeze.

Nick's mother looked radiant. Dave seemed pretty darned happy, too. They'd been together long enough to know each other's quirks and habits. And totally out of character, his mother had agreed to a small, inexpensive wedding instead of a big, costly one. Maybe this marriage would actually stick.

To help celebrate the joyous occasion, the restaurant sat them at a table festooned with flowers and gave them a free bottle of champagne. A few glasses of bubbly, and the joyous mood rose to new heights.

For everyone except Nick.

When Dave cracked a joke and Nick glared rather than laugh, his sister elbowed him hard.

"Ow!" He trained his glare on her. "What'd you do that for?"

"This marriage is a wonderful thing for both Mom and Dave. At least pretend you're happy for them," she chided.

"I *am* happy for them."

"If this is your definition of happy, I'd hate to see you miserable."

Nick excused himself to get some air and use the facilities. When he exited the men's room, his mother was waiting for him.

She took his arm and steered him to a bench under a loft tree outside. "Son, are you all right?"

"Yeah." He wanted to punch something, but he couldn't have said why. Instead, he shoved his hands in his pants pockets.

"Well, you look terrible. That chip on your shoulder doesn't suit you at all. It's this trouble with Dani, isn't it?"

Having nothing to say about that, he frowned at a flower, bowing in the soft wind.

"She's the best thing to ever happen to you, and yet you let her walk out of your life?" His mother made a disgusted sound. "You can be awfully thick-headed."

"I'm so glad I came today," he muttered.

His mother scrutinized him. "I swear, there are times you remind me so much of your father."

"What's that supposed to mean?"

"You don't smile, you don't make conversation. You're spoiling for a fight. That black cloud over your head won't do you or anyone else any good."

"What black cloud? And you and I both know that Dad had a solid reason to be bitter."

"I hurt him, and I'm sorry for that and for what I did." His mother bit her lip and appeared contrite. "And I'm grateful that at the end, he forgave me. But the breakup of our marriage wasn't all my fault."

Nick snickered. "The hell it wasn't."

She opened her mouth, seemed to hesitate, then sighed. "It's time you knew the full story."

Her excuses for cheating were the last thing Nick

wanted to hear, but she really wanted to talk. He shrugged. "I can't wait to hear this."

"Thank you." Looking relieved, she went on. "Your father and I never talked much about our feelings, but before we got married, I made sure he understood that I was independent and that I needed more than just the ranch and kids to be happy. I wanted close female friends and a career. He led me to believe that he supported me in that, but I quickly found out that he didn't. He wanted to be my everything, so that I wouldn't want other people in my life or a career. When he realized that he couldn't possibly do that, he tried to buy my happiness with things."

Nick opened his mouth to remind her that she'd sure never complained about the jewelry and fancy clothes he lavished on her, but she wouldn't let him speak.

"It's true that I love beautiful things, Nick, but what your father did wasn't love. It was control. It was his need to control my life that destroyed our marriage and cost us the ranch."

With her words, some of the puzzling things Nick had never understood fell into place. His father, despondent and brooding for days on end for no seeming reason, the arguments between his parents that had started long before they'd sold the ranch. His mother's unhappiness despite the expensive gifts from his father. None of it had ever quite added up.

Now it did. He'd always blamed his mother for the loss of the ranch and the divorce, but he realized now that a fair portion of the blame lay with his father.

"Why did you let me believe everything that happened was your fault?" he asked.

"Guilt. I started up with another man while I was

still married to your father, and that was wrong. But this isn't about what I did or your father's control issues. It isn't about his bitterness, either—it's about your own. Don't be like him. Don't let it eat you alive."

Startled at the words, Nick frowned. "I'm not bitter."

"Oh, no? The next time you glance in the mirror, take a good look at yourself."

The rest of the day and into the night, he chewed over his mother's advice. He didn't want to be like his father, had always prided himself on being upbeat and content with his life.

Sure, he was out of sorts right now and maybe a little angry, but he wasn't bitter.

Was he?

He thought back on his behavior over the past several weeks. Sometime in the wee hours, he realized that his mother was dead on. Without Dani in his life, he'd become hostile, unfriendly and negative—just as his father had been the last eighteen years of his life. Yes, he'd managed to save the ranch, but he wasn't any happier than his father had been.

Mad at himself for slipping into such a dark place, Nick flipped on the reading lamp. Blinking in the harsh light, he sat up. "What the hell am I going to do?" he wondered out loud.

He didn't have to think long before the answer came to him. For starters, he was going to kick his bitterness on its ass and right out of his life.

Yeah, that felt pretty good.

Next he considered his father's need to control his mother. That disgusted him, and caused him to look at both his parents from a different perspective. Neither of them was more responsible than the other for their financial problems or their failed marriage. That was a real eye-opener. If only they'd talked to each other about their feelings...but they hadn't.

Nick was thankful that he didn't share the urge to control other people. He was grateful, too, that he and Dani had always been able to talk to each other about anything and everything.

Great.

So now what?

In the silence, Palmer's words echoed in his mind. *When someone is that important to you, you don't take no for an answer.*

Dani was more than important. She was everything.

In a flash, everything came clear. He was in love with her.

Nick swallowed hard, but there was no use denying it. He loved Dani.

Admitting that scared the hell out of him, but living the rest of his life without her scared him more.

Loving her wouldn't distract him from focusing on making the ranch profitable, it would help. She wanted marriage and kids. Shock of all shocks, Nick realized that he did, too. He hadn't wanted to repeat his parents' patterns, but he realized now that he never would.

Suddenly he knew exactly what to do.

Shortly after Big Mama's Café unlocked its doors for the grand reopening Saturday morning, Nick entered the restaurant. The place was packed with people, some of whom he recognized. Lots of new faces, too, which was a definite positive.

Dani was sure to be busy, but this couldn't wait.

Naomi was showing someone to a table, leaving the hostess station empty. Beside it, Big Mama sat on a high chair. Nick hadn't seen or spoken with her since his split with Dani. She stared coolly at him without so much as a twitch of her lips. That stung, but he deserved it for being a jackass.

Determined to make amends, he greeted her. "You're looking like your regular self again, Big Mama, but shouldn't you be at home, recuperating?" he asked over the noise.

Some of the stiffness eased from her posture. "The doctor cleared me for a few hours. It's nice to see you, Nick. You look good yourself. Maybe a little tired. I don't believe you've been this dressed up since you and Dani double-dated to your senior prom."

He was wearing a sports coat and dress pants because what he wanted to say to Dani was important.

"Dani's done a wonderful job with the remodel, hasn't she? The skylight and our pretty wheat-colored walls make the restaurant so bright and cheerful, and our beautiful ceramic light fixtures really add to the ambiance."

Nick glanced up, then around, past the sea of people and nodded absently. "Where is she?"

Big Mama gave him an astute once-over, and at last smiled. "It's crazy today. I haven't seen her since we unlocked the doors, but she's around here somewhere."

"Thanks. Talk to you later."

He turned around and ran smack into Sly, Lana and their cute little girl. Sly about scowled him to death.

Nick ignored the other man's dirty glare. "Can you point me in Dani's direction?" he asked.

"She's busy."

"I need to find her."

"What for? You broke her heart."

"Hush, Sly," Lana said, placing her hand on the big rancher's forearm.

He let out a painstaking sigh. "What do you want with her?"

"That's private," Nick said. "But it's all good."

Provided he could convince Dani to forgive him for being such a lunkhead.

A long look passed between him and Sly before Sly nodded. "When I last saw her, she was headed for the kitchen."

Nick was on his way there when the door swung open and Dani headed through it. Her hair was tied back, and she was dressed in a short, bright spring dress. It was obvious she loved the excitement—her face was flushed and her eyes sparkled. She'd never looked so beautiful.

Warmth filled Nick's chest. "Hey," he said, moving toward her.

"Nick." Her eyes widened and her eyebrows jumped in surprise. "I— You— Um, you're here."

"That's right. The place looks great. I want to talk to you."

"Now? Have you noticed the size of this crowd? We're swamped, and even with Sadie, Colleen and Melanie waitressing, I need to pitch in and help. I don't have time."

"Make time. People will understand."

He grabbed her hand and pulled her forward. Dani dug in her heels. "You haven't called me in over a month," she said. "You can't just waltz in here and expect me to go blindly off with you to talk."

Nick couldn't believe he'd waited so long. He wanted

badly to make up for the lost weeks. "I have important things to say to you."

"They'll have to wait," she said firmly.

This was a side of Dani he didn't recognize. "There's something different about you."

"I put myself first now and do what I want to do," she said. "At the moment, I want to make sure all these customers are happy so that they come back often. Excuse me."

Nick put two fingers in his mouth and whistled. Instantly the room quieted.

"Dani, I have something to say to you," he announced. "If this is the only way you'll listen, so be it."

Regulars and new faces were all staring avidly at them. Nick spotted Palmer and his wife across the way. The foreman gave him a thumbs-up and a grin.

Dani rolled her eyes. "Go on and talk then, so I can get to work again."

At a nearby table, Janelle, Becca, Christy and Per watched wide-eyed, making Nick feel like a specimen in a glass fish bowl.

Damn. He'd meant this to be private. He cleared his throat. "This past few months, I've— Hell, I can't do this here. Dani's taking a short break." He grabbed hold of her elbow.

"I can't leave right now," she repeated, again digging in her heels.

"We'll be fine," someone assured her.

"You two go on and patch things up." That was Jewel, and she was smiling like somebody's doting grandma.

Nick steered Dani through the doors that led to the office.

As soon as they stepped into the room, he closed and locked the door, shutting out the noise.

"About what I was saying," he continued. "Remember when your mom was in the hospital and we talked about my father's heart attack? We both wanted our parents to make appointments their doctors, but neither of them listened to us. I realized then that I can't make anyone do what they don't want to do. That's a long way of saying that I can't make you forgive me for hurting you, but I'm sure as hell going to try."

The skeptical lift of her eyebrows wasn't exactly encouraging, but Nick wasn't about to let that stop him.

"This past month, I've missed you," he said.

"Could've fooled me."

Her arms were crossed now, and she still wore that doubtful expression. She wasn't making this easy.

"I was trying to give us both space," he explained.

"Right." She compressed her lips.

"It's true."

"I really don't want to hear about—"

"Will you please just listen."

Dani glanced at the ceiling and sighed, but she kept her mouth closed.

"I realize that I don't want space. And I've learned something that I think you'll want to hear. Without you, my life is empty. *I'm* empty."

He had her attention now. She angled her chin a fraction. "Go on."

Nick took that as a positive sign. This next part almost stuck in his throat, but he needed to say it. "I've been a stubborn fool. Dani Pettit, I love you. I think I always have, but I've been too pig-headed and scared to admit it." Later he would tell her what he'd learned from his mother and how the new insights had changed him. "That's why no other woman has ever held my interest for long."

"You loved Ashley."

"The woman I met in college?" Nick scoffed. "At the time I assumed I did, but compared to my feelings for you, she was just a crush. I love how independent you are. I love your big heart and your enthusiasm and your mac and cheese casserole. You're not afraid to stand up to me, either, and I love that. I don't care much for those chick flicks you make me watch, but they make you happy, and that's what matters." He shut his mouth.

Dani just stood there, staring at him. He couldn't read her expression. "Say something," he urged.

"I'm dumbfounded."

Not what he'd hoped to hear. With a sinking feeling, Nick realized he'd waited too long to talk to her. Still, he had to try. "Just tell me the truth," he said. "Have I lost my chance with you?"

For a long moment she let the question dangle in the air.

He was about to go crazy when she shook her head.

"You think I'm that fickle? Well, think again. Because I love you, too."

Relief almost bowled him over. "Come here, you."

He pulled her into his arms and kissed her soundly. Holding her again was like coming home. When they were both breathing hard, he broke away and rested his forehead against hers. "What's your stance on getting married?"

"You already know the answer to that—someday I definitely will."

"I mean to me. Now."

She pushed him away and made a face. "Marriage isn't for you—you've always said so."

"Hey, a guy can change his mind. I've let go of the past and it doesn't scare me anymore. I love you, Dani, and I never want you out of my life again. How about it?"

She re-crossed her arms. "I want kids."

Nick pictured a couple of little Danis, running around the ranch. "You drive a hard bargain, woman. Lucky for you, so do I."

He went down on one knee and clasped her hands. "Dani, I love you, and I promise to do everything in my power to make you happy now and forever. Put me out of my misery and marry me. The sooner, the better."

Her eyes filled. "Yes, Nick, I'll marry you."

Outside the door, people cheered.

Nosy so and so's, but Nick was too busy kissing the woman he loved to care.

* * * * *

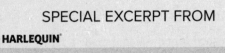
Mackenzie Wallace is back and wants excitement with her old crush. She hopes there's still some bad boy lurking beneath the single father's upright exterior. Dan Adams isn't the boy he was—but secrets from his past might still manage to keep them apart.

Read on for a sneak preview of the next book in the Gallant Lake Stories series, Her Homecoming Wish, *by Jo McNally.*

"There's an open bottle of very expensive scotch on the counter, just waiting for someone to enjoy it." She laughed again, softly this time. "And I'd *really* like to hear the story of how Danger Dan turned into a lawman."

Dan grimaced. He hated that stupid nickname Ryan had made up, even if he *had* earned it back then. Especially coming from Mack.

"Is your husband waiting upstairs?" Dan wasn't sure where that question came from, but, to be fair, all Mack had ever talked about was leaving Gallant Lake, having a big wedding and a bigger house. The girl had goals, and from what he'd heard, she'd reached every one of them.

"I don't have a husband anymore." She brushed past him and headed toward the counter. "So are you joining me or not?"

Dan glanced at his watch, not sure how to digest that information. "I'm off duty in fifteen minutes."

Her long hair swung back and forth as she walked ahead of him. So did her hips. *Damn.*

"And you're all about following the rules now? You really have changed, haven't you? Pity. I guess I'm drinking my first glass alone. You'll just have to catch up."

He frowned. Mackenzie had been strong-willed, but never sassy. Never the type to sneak into her father's store alone for an after-hours drink. Not the type to taunt him. Not the type to break the rules.

Looked like he wasn't the only one who'd changed since high school.

Don't miss
Her Homecoming Wish *by Jo McNally,*
available February 2020 wherever
Harlequin® *Special Edition books and ebooks are sold.*

Harlequin.com

WE HOPE YOU ENJOYED
THIS BOOK FROM

HARLEQUIN
SPECIAL
EDITION

Believe in love. Overcome obstacles. Find happiness.

Relate to finding comfort and strength in the
support of loved ones and enjoy the journey
no matter what life throws your way.

6 NEW BOOKS AVAILABLE EVERY MONTH!

SPECIAL EXCERPT FROM

H HARLEQUIN
SPECIAL EDITION

*When Jed Dalloway started over, ranching a
mountain plot for his recluse boss is what saved him.
So when hometown girl April Reed offers a deal
to develop the land, Jed tells her no sale.
But his heart doesn't get the message…*

*Read on for a sneak preview of
the next book in* New York Times *bestselling author
Allison Leigh's Return to the Double C miniseries,*
A Promise to Keep.

"Don't look at me like that, April."

She raised her gaze to his. "Like what?"

His fingers tightened in her hair and her mouth ran dry.
She swallowed. Moistened her lips.

She wasn't sure if she moved first. Or if it was him.

But then his mouth was on hers and like everything
else about him, she felt engulfed by an inferno. Or maybe
the burning was coming from inside her.

There was no way to know.

No reason to care.

Her hands slid up the granite chest, behind his neck,
where his skin felt even hotter beneath her fingertips, and
slipped through his thick hair, which was not hot, but
instead felt cool and unexpectedly silky.

His arm around her tightened, his hand pressing her
closer while his kiss deepened. Consuming. Exhilarating.

Her head was whirling, sounds roaring.

It was only a kiss.

But she was melting.

She was flying.

And then she realized the sounds weren't just inside her head.

Someone was laying on a horn.

She jerked back, her gaze skittering over Jed's as they both turned to peer through the curtain of white light shining over them.

"Mind getting at least one of these vehicles out of the way?" The shout was male and obviously amused.

"Oh for cryin'—" She exhaled. "That's my uncle Matthew," she told Jed, pushing him away. "And I'm sorry to say, but we are probably never going to live this down."

**IF YOU ENJOYED THIS BOOK
WE THINK YOU WILL ALSO LOVE**

LOVE INSPIRED
INSPIRATIONAL ROMANCE

Uplifting stories of faith, forgiveness and hope.

Fall in love with stories where faith helps
guide you through life's challenges, and discover
the promise of a new beginning.

6 NEW BOOKS AVAILABLE EVERY MONTH!

Love Harlequin romance?

DISCOVER.

Be the first to find out about promotions,
news and exclusive content!

Facebook.com/HarlequinBooks

Twitter.com/HarlequinBooks

Instagram.com/HarlequinBooks

Pinterest.com/HarlequinBooks

ReaderService.com

EXPLORE.

Sign up for the Harlequin e-newsletter and
download a free book from any series at
TryHarlequin.com

CONNECT.

Join our Harlequin community to
share your thoughts and connect
with other romance readers!
Facebook.com/groups/HarlequinConnection

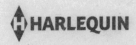

HSOCIAL2020